After
That
Night

ALSO BY KARIN SLAUGHTER

The Silent Wife

False Witness

Girl, Forgotten

eBook Originals

Snatched

Cold, Cold Heart

Busted

Blonde Hair, Blue Eyes

Last Breath

Cleaning the Gold (with Lee Child)

Novellas and Stories

Like a Charm (Editor)

Martin Misunderstood

After That Night

A Will Trent Thriller

Karin Slaughter

HARPER LARGE PRINT

An Imprint of HarperCollinsPublishers

FIRST HARPER LARGE PRINT EDITION

ISBN: 978-0-06-332292-9

Library of Congress Cataloging-in-Publication Data is available upon request.

23 24 25 26 27 LBC 5 4 3 2 1

For Liz

Remember to speak from the scar, not the wound.

Anonymous

Good morning Dani I really enjoyed the other night . . .
not often I get to be with someone who's smart as well as
beautiful . . . rare combination.

                                                        ·   ???

I've got the contact info for the Stanhope campaign if you're
still interested in volunteering?

                                            Who is this?

Funny! I know they are looking for canvassers are you still
interested in helping?
I could pick you up on my way to campaign HQ if you want?

                        I'm sorry I think you have the wrong person

You're on Juniper in the Beauxarts bldg right?

                                    No I moved in with my boyfriend

I love your sense of humor, Dani
Really want to spend more time with you
I know you love taking in the view of the park
from your corner bedroom
Maybe you can introduce me to Lord Pantaloons

                                How do you know about my cat?

I know everything about you.

Srsly did Jen put you up to this?
Yr creeping me out

I keep thinking about that mole on your leg and how I want to kiss it
. . . again . . .

Who the fuck is this?

Do you really want to know?

This isn't funny. Tell me who the fuck you are.

There's a pen and paper
In the drawer beside your bed
Make a list of everything that terrifies you
That's me

Prologue

Sara Linton held the phone to her ear as she watched an intern assess a patient with an open gash on the back of his right arm. The newly minted Dr. Eldin Franklin was not having his best day. He was two hours into his emergency department shift and he'd already had his life threatened by a drug-altered MMA fighter and performed a rectal exam on a homeless woman that had gone very, very wrong.

"Can you believe he said that to me?" Tessa's outrage crackled through the phone, but Sara knew her sister didn't require encouragement to complain about her new husband.

Instead, she kept her eye on Eldin, wincing as he pulled Lidocaine into a syringe like he was Jonas Salk testing the first polio vaccine. He was paying more attention to the vial than he was to his patient.

"I mean," Tessa continued. "He's unbelievable."

Sara made conciliatory noises as she switched the phone to her other ear. She found her tablet and pulled up the chart for Eldin's patient. The gash was a secondary concern. The triage nurse had noted the thirty-one-year-old man was tachycardic with a temperature of 101, and experiencing severe, acute agitation, confusion, and insomnia.

She looked up from her tablet. The patient kept scratching his chest and neck as if something was crawling on his skin. His left foot was shaking so hard that the bed shook along with it. To say that the man was in full-on alcohol withdrawal was to say that the sun was going to rise in the east.

Eldin was picking up on none of the signs—which was not completely unexpected. Medical school was by design a system that didn't prepare you for the real world. You spent your first year learning how the systems of the body work. Year two was devoted to understanding how those systems could go wrong. By year three, you were allowed to see patients, but only under strict and often needlessly sadistic supervision. Your fourth year brought about the matching system, which was like the worst beauty pageant ever, where you waited to see if your residency was going to be served at a prestigious, major institution or the equivalent of a veterinary clinic in rural East Jesus.

Eldin had managed to match at Grady Memorial Hospital, Atlanta's only public hospital and one of the busiest Level I trauma centers in the country. He was called an intern because he was still in the first year of his residency. Unfortunately, that didn't stop him from believing that he had seen it all. Sara could tell his brain had already checked out as he leaned over the patient's arm and began numbing the area. Eldin was likely thinking about dinner or a girl he was going to call or maybe compounding the interest on his many student loans, which roughly equaled the cost of a house.

Sara caught the head nurse's eye. Johna was watching Eldin, too, but like every nurse ever, she was going to let the baby doctor learn the hard way. It didn't take long.

The patient pitched forward and opened his mouth.

"Eldin!" Sara called, but she was too late.

Vomit blasted like a fireman's hose down the back of Eldin's shirt.

He staggered, experiencing a moment of shock before starting to dry heave.

Sara stayed in her chair behind the nurses' station as the patient fell back against the bed, a momentary sense of relief washing over his face. Johna pulled Eldin to the side and began to lecture him as if he were a toddler. His mortified expression was familiar. Sara had interned at Grady. She had been on the receiving end of similar lectures. No one warned you in medical school that this was how you learned how to be a real doctor—humiliation and vomit.

"Sara?" Tessa said. "Are you even listening to me?"

"Yes. Sorry." Sara tried to turn her focus back to her sister. "What were you saying?"

"I was saying how hard is it for him to see the fucking trash can is full?" Tessa barely paused for a breath. "I work all day, too, but I'm the one who has to come home and clean the house *and* fold the laundry *and* cook dinner *and* take out the trash?"

Sara kept her mouth shut. None of Tessa's complaints were new or unpredictable. Lemuel Ward was one of the most self-involved assholes Sara had ever met, which was saying a lot considering she had spent her adult life working in medicine.

"It's like I got secretly signed up for *The Hand-maid's Tale.*"

"Was that from the show or the book?" Sara worked to keep the bite out of her tone. "I don't remember a taking-out-the-trash scene."

"You can't tell me that's not how it started."

"Dr. Linton?" Kiki, one of the porters, rapped her fingers on the counter. "Curtain three is being brought back up from X-ray."

Sara mouthed a thank-you as she checked her tablet for the films. The patient from curtain three was a thirty-nine-year-old schizophrenic who had signed himself in as Deacon Sledgehammer and presented with a golf-ball-sized welt on his neck, a temperature of 102 and uncontrollable chills. He'd freely admitted to a nearly lifelong heroin addiction. Subsequent to the veins in his legs, arms, feet, chest and belly collapsing, he'd resorted to injecting subcutaneously, or what was called "skin-popping." Then he'd started injecting directly into his jugular and carotid arteries. X-rays confirmed what Sara had suspected, but she took no pleasure in being right.

"My time is just as valuable as his," Tessa said. "It's fucking ridiculous."

Sara agreed, but she said nothing as she walked through the emergency department. Usually, this time of night they were covered up in gunshot wounds, stabbings, car accidents, overdoses and a fair share of heart attacks. Maybe it was the rain or the Braves playing Tampa Bay, but the department was blissfully calm. Most of the beds were empty, the whirs and beeps of machines punctuating occasional conversation. Sara was technically the attending pediatrician, but she'd offered to cover for another doctor so that he could attend his daughter's science fair. Eight hours into a twelve-hour shift, the worst thing that Sara had seen was Eldin getting splattered.

And to be honest, that had been kind of hilarious.

"Obviously, Mom was no help," Tessa continued. "All she said was, 'A bad marriage is still a marriage.' What does that even mean?"

Sara ignored the question as she punched the button to open the doors. "Tessie, you've been married for six months. If you're not happy with him now—"

"I didn't say I'm not happy," Tessa insisted, though every word out of her mouth indicated otherwise. "I'm just frustrated."

"Welcome to marriage." Sara walked toward the bank of elevators. "You'll spend ten minutes arguing that you already told him something instead of just telling him again."

"That's your advice?"

"I've been really careful not to offer any," Sara pointed out. "Look, this sounds like a shitty thing to say, but you either find a way to work it out or you don't."

"You found a way to work it out with Jeffrey."

Reflexively, Sara pressed her hand to her heart, but

time had eased the sharp pain that usually accompanied any reminder of her widowhood. "Are you forgetting I divorced him?"

"Are you forgetting I was there when it happened?" Tessa paused for a quick breath. "You worked it out. You married him again. You were happy."

"I was," Sara agreed, but Tessa's problem wasn't an affair or even an overflowing trash can. It was being married to a man who did not respect her. "I'm not holding out on you. There's not a universal solution. Every relationship is different."

"Sure, but—"

Tessa's voice fell away as the elevator doors slid open. The distant beeps and whirs of machinery faded. Sara felt an electric current in the air.

Special Agent Will Trent was standing at the back of the elevator. He was looking down at his phone, which allowed Sara the luxury of silently drinking him in. Tall and lean. Broad shoulders. Will's charcoal three-piece suit couldn't hide his runner's body. His sandy-blond hair was wet from the rain. A scar zig-zagged into his left eyebrow. Another scar traced up from his mouth. Sara let her mind ponder the exquisite question of what the scar would feel like if it was pressed against her own lips.

Will looked up. He smiled at Sara.

She smiled back.

"Hello?" Tessa said. "Did you hear what—"

Sara ended the call and tucked the phone into her pocket.

As Will stepped off the elevator, she silently cataloged all the ways she could've made more of an effort to look presentable for this chance meeting, starting with not twisting her long hair into a granny bun on the top of her head and ending with doing a better job of wiping off the ketchup that had dribbled down the front of her scrubs at dinner.

Will's eyes zeroed in on the stain. "Looks like you've got some—"

"Blood," Sara said. "It's blood."

"Sure it's not ketchup?"

She shook her head. "I'm a doctor, so . . ."

"And I'm a detective, so . . ."

They were both grinning by the time Sara noticed that Faith Mitchell, Will's partner, had not only been on the elevator with him but was standing two feet away.

Faith gave a heavy sigh before telling Will, "I'll go start the thing with the thing."

Will's hands went into his pockets as Faith walked toward the patient rooms. He glanced at the floor, then back at Sara, then down the hallway. The silence dragged out to an uncomfortable level, which was Will's particular gift. He was incredibly awkward. It didn't help matters that Sara found herself uncharacteristically tongue-tied around him.

She made herself speak. "It's been a while."

"Two months."

Sara was ridiculously delighted that he knew how much time had passed. She waited for him to say more, but of course he didn't.

She asked, "What brings you here? Are you working on a case?"

"Yes." He seemed relieved to be on familiar ground. "Guy chopped off his neighbor's fingers over a lawnmower dispute. Cops rolled up. He jumped into his car and drove straight into a telephone pole."

"A real criminal mastermind."

There was something about his sudden burst of laughter that made Sara's heart do a weird flip. She tried to keep him talking. "That sounds like an Atlanta police problem, not a case for the Georgia Bureau of Investigation."

"The finger-chopper works for a drug dealer we've been trying to take down. We're hoping we can persuade him to talk."

"You can *chop* down his sentence in return for his testimony."

There was no thrill of his laughter this time. The joke fell so flat that it could've been a piece of sandpaper.

Will shrugged. "That's the plan."

Sara felt a blush working its way up her neck. She desperately tried to find safer ground. "I was waiting for a patient to come up from X-ray. I don't usually hang around elevators."

He nodded, but that was all he offered before the awkwardness roared back in. He rubbed his jaw with his fingers, worrying the faint scar that ran along his sharp jawline and down into the collar of his shirt. The glint of his wedding ring flashed like a warning light. Will noticed her noticing the ring. His hand went back into his pocket.

"Anyway." Sara had to end this before her cheeks burst into flames. "I'm sure Faith is waiting for you. It's good seeing you again, Agent Trent."

"Dr. Linton." Will gave her a slight nod before walking away.

To keep herself from staring longingly after him, Sara took out her phone and texted an apology to her sister for hanging up so abruptly.

Two months.

Will knew how to get in touch with her, but he hadn't gotten in touch.

Then again, Sara knew how to get in touch with Will, but she hadn't either.

She silently went back over their brief exchange, skipping the *chop* joke so that her face didn't start glowing red again. She couldn't tell if Will was flirting or if he was being polite or if she was being stupid and desperation had set in. What she did know was that Will Trent was married to a former Atlanta police detective with a reputation for being a raging bitch and a regular habit of disappearing for long stretches of time. And that despite this, he was still wearing his wedding ring.

As Sara's mother would say, *A bad marriage is still a marriage.*

Fortunately, the elevator doors opened before Sara could spiral any farther down that rabbit hole.

"Hey, doc." Deacon Sledgehammer was slumped in his wheelchair, but he made an effort to straighten up for Sara's benefit. He was wearing a hospital gown and black wool socks. The left side of his neck looked painfully red and swollen. Round scars dotted his arms, legs and forehead from years of skin-popping. "Didja find out what's wrong with me?"

"I did." Sara took over from the orderly, pushing Deacon down the hall, fighting the urge to turn back toward Will like Lot's wife. "You've got twelve needles broken off in your neck. Several of them have abscessed. That's why your neck is swollen and you're having such a hard time swallowing. You've got a very serious infection."

"Damn." Deacon let out a raspy breath. "That sounds like it could kill me."

"It could." Sara wasn't going to lie to him. "You're going to need surgery to remove the needles, then you'll need to stay here at least a week for IV antibiotics. Your withdrawal will have to be managed, but none of it's going to be easy."

"Shit," he mumbled. "Will you come visit me?"

"Absolutely. I'm off tomorrow, but I'm here all day Sunday." Sara scanned her badge to open the doors. She finally allowed herself to look back at Will. He was at the far end of the hall. She watched until he turned the corner.

"He gave me his socks."

Sara turned back to Deacon.

"Last week when I was over by the capitol." Deacon pointed down to the pair of thick socks he was wearing. "It was cold as hell. Dude took off his socks and gave 'em to me."

Sara's heart did the weird little flip again. "That was kind."

"Fuckin' cop probably bugged 'em." Deacon pressed his finger to his lips to shush her. "Be careful what you say."

"Understood." Sara wasn't going to argue with a schizophrenic suffering from a life-threatening infection. The fact that she had auburn hair and was left-handed had already led to a lengthy discussion.

She angled the chair toward curtain three, then helped transfer Deacon into bed. His arms were skeletal, almost like kindling. He was malnourished. Grime and dirt were clumped into his hair. He was missing several teeth. He was nearly forty, but he looked sixty and moved like he was eighty. She wasn't sure he would make it through another winter. Either the heroin or the elements or another raging infection would get him.

"I know what you're thinking." Deacon leaned back in the bed with an old man's groan. "You wanna call my family."

"Do you want me to call your family?"

"No. And don't be callin' no social services neither." Deacon scratched his arm, his fingernails digging into a round scar. "Listen, I'm a piece of shit, okay?"

"That hasn't been my experience."

"Yeah, well, you got me on a good day." His voice caught on the last word. It was sinking in that he might not see tomorrow. "My mental health being what it is, and my addiction. I mean fuck, I love dope, but I don't make it easy for people."

"You were dealt a bad hand." Sara kept her tone measured. "That doesn't make you a bad person."

"Sure, but what I put my family through—they disowned me ten years ago this June, and I don't blame 'em. I gave 'em plenty of reasons. Lying, stealing, cheating, beating. I told you—a real piece of shit."

Sara leaned her elbows on the bed railing. "What can I do for you?"

"If I don't make it, will you call my mom and let her know? Not so she feels bad or nothin'. Being honest, I think it'll be a relief."

Sara took a pen and pad out of her pocket. "Write down her name and number."

"Tell her I wasn't scared." He pressed the pen so hard into the paper that Sara could hear the scratch. Tears seeped from his eyes. "Tell her that I didn't blame her. And that—tell her that I loved her."

"I hope it doesn't come to that, but I promise I'll call her if it does."

"But not before, okay? Cause she don't need to know I'm alive. Just if I'm . . ." His voice trailed off. His hands shook as he returned the pad and pen. "You know what I'm saying."

"I do." Sara briefly rested her hand on his shoulder. "Let me call up to surgery. We'll get a central line started so I can give you something to help make you comfortable."

"Thanks, doc."

Sara closed the curtain behind her. She picked up the phone behind the nurses' station and paged surgical for a consult, then tapped in the orders for the central line.

"Hey." Eldin had showered and changed into a fresh pair of scrubs. "I front-loaded my drunk with IV diazepam. He's waiting for a bed."

"Add multivitamins and 500 milligrams thiamine IV to prevent—"

"Wernicke's encephalopathy," Eldin said. "Good idea."

Sara thought he sounded a little too confident for someone who'd just been sprayed with projectile vomit. As his supervisor—even if it was only for the night—it was her job to set him straight so that it didn't happen again.

She said, "Eldin, it's not an idea, it's a treatment protocol to prevent seizures and to calm the patient. Detox is hell on earth. Your patient is clearly suffering. He's not a drunk. He's a thirty-one-year-old man who's struggling with alcohol addiction."

Eldin had the decency to look embarrassed. "Okay. You're right."

Sara wasn't finished. "Did you read the nurse's notes? She took a detailed social history. He self-reported four to five beers a day. Is there a rule of thumb they taught you last year?"

"Always double the number of drinks a patient reports."

"Correct," she said. "Your patient also reported that he was trying to quit. He stopped cold turkey three days ago. It's right there in his chart."

Eldin's expression turned from embarrassed to outraged. "Why didn't Johna tell me?"

"Why didn't you read her notes? Why didn't you notice your patient had acute onset super-flu, and was scratching at phantom ants crawling on his skin?" Sara watched the shame return, which was to his credit. He recognized that he was the one to blame. "Learn from this, Eldin. Serve your patient better the next time."

"You're right. I'm sorry." Eldin took a deep breath and hushed it out. "Jesus, am I ever going to get the hang of this?"

Sara couldn't leave him lying in the dirt. "I'll tell you what my attending told me: I believe you're either a damn good doctor, or you're a psychopath who's managed to fool the smartest person who's ever supervised you."

Eldin laughed. "Can I ask you a question?"

"Sure."

"You did your residency here, right?" He waited for Sara to nod. "I heard you were locked in for a fellowship with Nygaard. Pediatric cardiothoracic surgery. That's hella impressive. Why did you leave?"

Sara was trying to formulate an answer when she felt another change in the air. This wasn't the electric current she'd felt when she'd seen Will Trent standing at the back of the elevator. This was years of her doctor's intuition telling her that the rest of the night was about to go sideways.

The doors to the ambulance bay burst open. Johna was running down the hall. "Sara, MVA happened right outside. Mercedes versus ambulance. They're pulling the victim from the car right now."

Sara jogged toward the trauma bay with Eldin close behind. She could feel his anxiety ramping up, so she kept her voice calm, telling him, "Do exactly as I say. Don't get in the way."

She was slipping on a sterile gown when EMTs rushed in with the patient strapped to a gurney. They were all soaking wet from the rain. One of them called out the details. "Dani Cooper, nineteen-year-old female,

MVA with LOC, chest pain, shortness of breath. She was going about thirty when she hit the ambulance straight-on. Abdominal wound looks superficial. BP is 80 over 40, heart rate's 108. Breath sounds are shallow on the left, clear on the right. She's alert and oriented. IV in the right hand with normal saline."

Suddenly, the trauma bay was crowded with people in a well-choreographed, disarrayed ballet. Nurses, respiratory therapist, radiographer, transcriber. Every person had a purpose: running lines, drawing blood gas, cross and typing, cutting off clothes, wrapping the blood pressure cuff, pulse ox, leads, oxygen, and someone to track every step that was taken and by whom.

Sara called out, "I need a chem twelve with differential, chest and abdomen X-rays, and a second large-bore IV for blood in case we need it. Start a foley and get routine urine and drug screen. I need a CT of her neck and head. Page CV surgery to be on standby."

The EMTs transferred the patient onto the bed. The young woman's face was white. Her teeth were chattering, eyes wild.

"Dani," Sara said. "I'm Dr. Linton. I'm going to take care of you. Can you tell me what happened?"

"C-c-car . . ." Dani could barely manage a whisper. "I w-woke up in the . . ."

Her teeth were chattering too hard for her to finish.

"That's okay. Where does it hurt? Can you show me?"

Sara watched Dani reach toward her upper left abdomen. The EMTs had already placed a piece of gauze over the superficial laceration just below her left chest. There was more than that, though. Dani's torso was slashed dark red where something, possibly the steering wheel, had hit her with force. Sara used her stethoscope, pressing it to the belly, then listening to both lungs.

She called out, "Bowel sounds are good. Dani, can you take a deep breath for me?"

There was a wheezing of labored air.

Sara told the room, "Pneumothorax on the left. Prep for a chest tube. I need a thoracostomy tray."

Dani's eyes tried to follow the flurry of movement. Cabinets were opened, trays were loaded up—drapes, tubing, Betadine, sterile gloves, scalpel, Lidocaine.

"Dani, it's all right." Sara leaned down, trying to pull the woman's attention away from the chaos. "Look at me. Your lung is collapsed. We're going to put in a tube to—"

"I d-didn't . . ." Dani labored for breath. Her voice was barely audible over the din of noise. "I had to get away . . ."

"Okay." Sara brushed back her hair, checking for signs of head trauma. There was a reason Dani had lost consciousness at the scene. "Does your head hurt?"

"Yes . . . it . . . I keep hearing ringing and . . ."

"All right." Sara checked her pupils. The woman was clearly concussed. "Dani, can you tell me where it hurts the most?"

"H-he hurt me," Dani said. "I think . . . I think he raped me."

Sara felt a jolt of shock. The sounds in the room faded so that all she could hear was Dani's strained voice.

"He drugged my drink . . ." Dani coughed as she tried to swallow. "I woke up and he . . . he was on top of me . . . then I was in the car, but I don't remember how . . . and . . ."

"Who?" Sara asked. "Who raped you?"

The woman's eyelids started to flutter.

"Dani? Stay with me." Sara cupped her hand to the woman's face. Her lips were losing color. "I need that chest tube now."

"Stop him . . ." Dani said. "Please . . . stop him."

"Stop who?" Sara asked. "Dani? Dani?"

Dani's eyes locked onto Sara's, silently begging her to understand.

"Dani?"

Her eyelids started to flutter again. Then they stilled. Her head fell to the side.

"Dani?" Sara pressed her stethoscope to Dani's chest. Nothing. The nineteen-year-old's life was slipping away. Sara put her panic in another place, telling the room, "We've lost the heartbeat. Starting CPR."

The respiratory therapist grabbed the Ambu bag and mask to start forcing air into the lungs. Sara interlaced her fingers and placed her palms over Dani's heart. CPR was a stop-gap measure intended to manually push blood into the heart and up to the brain until they could hopefully shock the heart back into a regular rhythm. Sara pressed down into Dani's chest with her full weight. There was a sickening crack as the ribs gave way.

"Shit!" Sara felt her emotions threaten to take over. She reined herself back in. "She has a flail chest. CPR is no good. We need to shock her."

Johna had already brought over the crash cart. Sara could hear the defibrillator reaching full charge as the paddles were pressed to Dani's limp body.

Sara held up her hands, keeping them away from the metal bed.

"Clear!" Johna pressed the buttons on the paddles.

Dani's body lurched from three thousand volts of

electricity aimed directly into her chest. The monitor blipped. They all waited the interminable few seconds to see if the heart restarted, but the line on the monitor flattened as the alarm wailed.

"Again," Sara said.

Johna waited for the charge. Another shock. Another blip. Another flat line.

Sara ran through the options. No CPR. No shocking her. No cracking open her chest because there was nothing to crack. A flail chest was described as two or more contiguous ribs broken in two or more places, resulting in a destabilization in the chest wall that altered the mechanics of breathing.

From what Sara could tell, Dani Cooper's second, third and fifth ribs had sustained multiple fractures from blunt force trauma. The sharp bones were free-floating inside her chest, capable of slicing into her heart and lungs. The nineteen-year-old's chance of survival had dropped into the single digits.

All the noises that Sara had blocked out as she worked on Dani suddenly filled her brain. The useless hiss of oxygen. The grinding groan of the blood pressure cuff. The crinkling of PPE as they all silently played the diminished odds.

Someone turned off the alarm.

"Okay." Sara spoke the word to herself and no one

else. She had a plan. She peeled off the gauze covering the laceration on Dani's left side. She poured Betadine into the wound, letting it spill over like a fountain. "Eldin, tell me about the costal margin."

"Uh—" Eldin watched Sara's hands work as she slipped on a fresh pair of sterile gloves. "The costal margin is composed of the costal cartilage anteriorly around and up to the sternum. The eleventh and twelfth ribs float."

"In general, they terminate about the mid-axillary line and within the muscular of the lateral wall. Right?"

"Right."

Sara picked up a scalpel from the tray. She cut into the laceration, carefully incising the fatty layer down to the abdominal muscle. Then she cut through to the diaphragm to make a hole about the size of her fist.

She looked at Johna. The nurse's lips were parted in surprise, but she nodded. If Dani had any chance of survival, this was it.

Sara reached her hand into the hole. The diaphragm muscle sucked around her wrist. Rib bones traced along the back of her knuckles like the keys of a xylophone. The lung had flattened to an airless balloon. The stomach and spleen were slick and supple. Sara closed her eyes, concentrating on the anatomy as she reached into Dani's chest. The tips of her fingers brushed against the blood-filled sac of the heart. Carefully, Sara wrapped her hand around the organ. She looked at the monitor and squeezed.

The flatline jumped.

She squeezed again.

Another jump.

Sara kept pumping blood through the heart, flexing her fingers and thumb, forcing the rhythm into the normal cadence of life. Her eyes closed again as she listened for a beep from the monitor. She could feel the roadmap of arteries like a topographical drawing. Right coronary artery. Posterior descending artery. Right marginal artery. Left anterior descending artery. Circumflex artery.

Of all the organs in the body, the heart was the one that inspired the most emotion. Your heart could be broken or filled with love or joy, or it could do a weird little flip when you saw your favorite crush in the elevator. You covered your heart to pledge allegiance. You patted your hand over your heart to convey fealty or honesty or respect. Someone who was cruel might be called heartless. In the South, you said *bless your heart* to someone who was not particularly bright. An act of kindness *does your heart good*. When Sara and Tessa were little, Tessa had often crossed her heart. She would steal Sara's clothes or a CD or a book and swear that she didn't do it—*cross my heart, hope to die.*

Sara wasn't sure whether or not Dani Cooper would die, but she made a promise on the woman's heart that she would do everything she could to stop the man who'd raped her.

Three Years Later

1

"Dr. Linton." Maritza Aguilar, the attorney for Dani Cooper's family, walked toward the witness stand. "Can you tell us what happened next?"

Sara took a breath before saying, "I rode on the gurney up to the operating room so that I could continue manually pumping Dani's heart. I was scrubbed in to the procedure, then the surgeons took over."

"And after that?"

"I watched the surgery." Sara blinked, and even three years later, she could still see Dani lying on the operating table. Eyes taped closed, tube coming out of her mouth, chest splayed open, white shards of ribs scattered inside the cavity like confetti. "The surgeons did everything they could, but Dani was too far gone. She was pronounced dead at approximately two forty-five that morning."

"Thank you." Maritza went back to her notes at the table. She started flipping through the pages. Her associate leaned over to whisper something. "Judge, if I could have a moment?"

"Quickly," Judge Elaina Tedeschi said.

The courtroom went quiet but for jurors shifting in their chairs and the occasional cough or sneeze from the half-filled gallery. Sara took another deep breath. She'd already been on the witness stand for three hours. They'd just come back from the lunch break, and everyone was tired. Still, she kept her back straight, her head facing forward, eyes on the clock at the back of the room.

There was a reporter in the gallery typing on her phone, but Sara was doing her best to ignore the woman. She could not look at Dani's parents because their grief was almost as crushing as their hope that something, anything, could give them a sense of closure. Nor could she look at the jury. Sara didn't want to make eye contact with one of them and convey the wrong thing. The courtroom was hot and stuffy. Trials never moved as quickly or were as interesting as they appeared on TV. The medical facts could be dense and confusing. Sara needed the jury to focus and listen, not wonder why she had looked at them the wrong way.

This lawsuit wasn't about Sara. It was about keeping

the promise she had made to Dani Cooper. The man who had hurt her had to be stopped.

She let her gaze glance over Thomas Michael Mc-Allister, IV. The twenty-two-year-old was sitting between his high-priced lawyers at the defense table. His parents, Mac and Britt McAllister, were directly behind him in the gallery. Per Judge Tedeschi's instructions, Tommy was being referred to as *the respondent* rather than *the defendant* so that the jury was clear that this was a civil case and not a criminal trial. The stakes were not prison versus freedom but rather millions of dollars for the wrongful death of Daniella Cooper. Mac and Britt could well afford to pay, but there was something else at risk that even their enormous wealth couldn't guarantee: their son's good reputation.

So far, they'd done everything they could to make sure Tommy was protected, from hiring a publicist to shape the media narrative to retaining Douglas Fanning, a lawyer who was known as The Shark for his ability to eviscerate witnesses on the stand.

The trial was only two days in, and Fanning had already managed to keep out some of what he termed Tommy's "youthful indiscretions," as if every youth had been arrested at eleven years old for torturing a neighbor's dog, accused of rape their junior year of high school, and caught with a party-sized supply of MDMA in his backpack an hour before graduation. That's what $2,500 an hour bought you: a predator turned into a choirboy.

Tommy was certainly dressed for the part, trading in the bespoke suit he'd been sporting in an *About Town* gossip column last year for an off-the-rack black suit with a muted, light-blue tie and a not-too-crisp white Oxford shirt—all likely selected by a jury consultant who for months had focus-grouped the most advantageous keywords and strategies, then worked closely with Douglas Fanning to select the best jurors, and was now running a shadow jury somewhere close to the courthouse that was presented with the same evidence to help the defense shape their approach.

Even with all that, there was still no hiding the arrogant tilt to Tommy McAllister's chin. He had spent a lifetime in Atlanta's most cloistered spaces. His great-grandfather, a surgeon, had not only pioneered early joint replacement techniques but had helped start what had become one of Atlanta's major orthopedic hospitals. Tommy's grandfather, a retired four-star general, had overseen infectious disease research at the Centers for Disease Control. Mac was one of the most respected cardiologists in the country. Britt had trained as an obstetrician. It was no surprise that Tommy was continuing the family business. He was about to enter his first year of medical school at Emory University.

He was also the man who had drugged and raped Dani Cooper.

At least that was Sara's belief.

Tommy had known Dani Cooper most of his life. They had both come up in the same private schools, been members at the same country club, hung out in the same social circles, and at the time of Dani's death, they were both enrolled in pre-med courses at the same university. The night that Dani had died, Tommy was seen arguing with her at a frat party. The discussion had been heated. He'd grabbed Dani by the arm. She'd wrenched away from him. No one could say what happened next, but it was Tommy's $150,000 Mercedes Roadster that Dani was driving when she crashed into a parked ambulance outside the hospital. It was his sperm that was found inside her during the autopsy. It was Tommy McAllister who couldn't provide an alibi for the hours between when Dani left the party and when she'd arrived at Grady. It was also Tommy Mc-Allister who knew the intimate details that were included in the threatening texts that Dani had received the week before she'd died.

Unfortunately, the Fulton County prosecutor could only act on evidence, not belief. A criminal trial was decided on guilt beyond a reasonable doubt. Sara would freely admit that there was doubt in this case. The frat party had been filled with other young men who were close to Dani. No one could contradict Tommy's claim that the argument had been resolved. No one could contradict Tommy's claim that Dani had asked to borrow his Mercedes. No one could contradict his claim that his sperm was inside of Dani because they'd had consensual sex two nights before she'd died. No one could definitively say that Tommy left the party with Dani that night. Lots of people at the party had known the intimate details of Dani's life. More importantly, no one could locate the burner phone that had sent the threatening texts.

Fortunately, a civil trial was decided on a preponderance of evidence rather than reasonable doubt. The Coopers had a lot of circumstantial evidence on their side. The wrongful death suit they had filed against Tommy McAllister asked for damages in the amount of $20 million. It was a hell of a lot of money, but they were not in it for the cash. Unlike Mac and Britt, getting the case to trial had cost them their life savings. The Coopers had refused all settlement offers because what they wanted, what they needed in order to make sense of their daughter's tragic death, was for someone to be held publicly accountable.

Sara had warned them that they weren't likely to win. Maritza had told them the same thing. They both knew how the system worked, and it rarely favored the people who didn't have money. More importantly, the entire case hinged on whether or not the jury found Sara to be a credible witness. The trauma bay had been chaotic the night that Dani Cooper had died. Sara was the only one who'd heard the young woman say that she had been drugged and raped. Because of the nature of the case, that meant Sara's personal life would be put under a microscope. To break her testimony, they had to break her character. Everything that she had ever done, everything that had ever happened to her, was going to be dissected, analyzed and—most distressingly for Sara—criticized.

She wasn't sure what terrified her most: having the darkest parts of her life exposed in an open courtroom or breaking her promise to Dani.

"Dr. Linton." Maritza was finally ready to proceed. She walked back to the stand, holding a sheet of paper between her hands. She didn't offer it to Sara. She kept it close to her chest, trying to build suspense.

The trick worked.

Sara could feel the jury's attention coming into focus when Maritza said, "I'd like to take a step back for a second, if you don't mind? Review something from earlier today?"

Sara nodded, then, for the court reporter's benefit, said, "Okay."

"Thank you." Maritza turned, walking past the jury box. Five women, four men, a typical Fulton County mixture of white, Black, Asian, and Hispanic. Sara could see their eyes following the lawyer, some studying her face, some trying to scrutinize the sheet of paper.

Maritza took her yellow legal pad off the table and placed it on the podium. She had her pen in her hand. She slipped on her glasses and looked down at her notes.

She wasn't Douglas Fanning, but she was damn good at her job. Maritza didn't need a jury consultant to tell her how to dress any more than Sara did. They were both women who'd come up in male-dominated fields and had both figured out that, for better or worse, their appearance mattered more to a jury than what came out of their mouths. Hair pulled back to show they were no-nonsense. Light make-up to show they were still making an effort. Glasses on to show intelligence. Modest skirt and matching blazer to show they were still feminine. Heels no more than two inches high to show they weren't trying too hard.

Show, show, show.

Maritza looked up at Sara, saying, "Before the lunchbreak, you walked us through your education and credentials, but to remind the jury, you're both a board-certified pediatrician and a board-certified medical examiner, correct?"

"Yes."

"And the night Dani Cooper was brought into the emergency department, you were employed by the Grady Healthcare System as the attending pediatrician, but currently, today, you are employed by the Georgia Bureau of Investigation as a coroner, correct?"

"Technically, my title is medical examiner." Sara allowed herself to look at the jury. They were the only people in the courtroom whose opinions mattered. "In all but four of Georgia's counties, the office of coroner is an elected position that doesn't require a medical license. If foul play is suspected, the county coroner will generally refer the death investigation to the GBI's Medical Examiner's Office. That's where my colleagues and I come in."

"Thank you for the explanation," Maritza said. "So, when you initially examined Dani Cooper in the emergency department, would you say that you were calling on both fields of your extensive expertise?"

Sara considered the best way to frame her response.

"I would say that I evaluated Dani first as a doctor, then later as a medical examiner."

"Have you reviewed the autopsy report on Dani Cooper, already marked as Exhibit 113-A?"

"I have."

"What, if any, were the toxicology findings on controlled substances?"

"The blood and urine screens were determined to be inconclusive."

"Did that surprise you?"

"No," Sara said. "At the hospital, Dani was given multiple therapeutics, including Versed, or midazolam, which was used as a pre-surgical muscle relaxer. In a toxicology screening, the drug can chemically mimic Rohypnol."

"Previously, you explained to us that Rohypnol is a so-called date-rape drug, correct?"

"Yes."

"As a doctor, or someone working in a medical facility, how easy would it be for you to steal a vial of Rohypnol, if you were so inclined?"

"Rohypnol wouldn't be at a hospital. The drug is not approved by the FDA for use in the United States. And trying to steal a vial of Versed would be incredibly risky. There are multiple internal controls in place to prevent theft and abuse," Sara said. "On the other hand, Rohypnol is readily available on the streets, so hypothetically, I would find a drug dealer and buy it from them."

"Can you tell us if any DNA evidence was found during Dani Cooper's autopsy?"

"Sperm was swabbed from Dani's anterior vagina and cervix. The sample was sent to the GBI lab for processing. The lab was able to generate a DNA profile for comparison."

"Can you tell us the lab's conclusion?"

"The DNA was identified within a scientific certainty as matching the sample collected from Tommy McAllister."

Maritza paused again, pretending to review her notes as she gave the jury time to catch up. Sara let her eyes travel toward Douglas Fanning. The Shark kept his head down as he scribbled on his legal pad, for all intents and purposes behaving as if nothing Sara said could possibly matter. He'd done the same thing during her deposition six months ago. At the time, she'd recognized it as a ploy to throw her off.

Now she was annoyed to realize that it was working.

Maritza cleared her throat before continuing, "Dr. Linton, can you tell me anything else you observed that night that seemed out of the ordinary?"

"I was told Dani was driving the car, but the laceration to her torso was here, on her left side, just below her ribs." Sara indicated the area on her own body. "When you're driving, the seat belt goes from your left shoulder to your right hip. If the laceration had been caused by a seat belt, it would have been on Dani's right side, not her left."

Maritza didn't push for a conclusion, instead moving on to the next piece of the puzzle. "You've viewed Exhibit 108-A through F, the security footage from outside the hospital that night. It captured the respondent's Mercedes driving straight into the ambulance, correct? What would be called a head-on collision?"

"Yes."

"What other impressions did you form while watching the security footage?" Maritza saw Fanning begin to stir for an objection, and added, "Your impressions as someone who has been involved in motor vehicle accident investigations?"

Fanning settled.

Sara answered, "It appeared to me that the car was being driven toward the emergency department parking lot, then at the last moment, the wheels straightened, the speed decreased, and the car hit one of the ambulances parked in the bays."

"Okay, on the footage, you cannot see the driver through the windshield, correct?"

"Correct."

"Also on the footage, you can see that Dani was pulled from the driver's side of the Mercedes, correct?"

"Yes."

"You stated earlier that you read the accident investigation report prepared by Sergeant Shanda London. Do you recall how fast the car was going when it ran into the ambulance?"

"The ECM showed the car was going twenty-three miles per hour at the moment of impact."

"We heard about the ECM from Sergeant London yesterday morning, but can you give us a quick refresher?"

"The Electronic Control Module records all data in the seconds around a collision. The easiest way to think of it is like a black box on an airplane, but for your car."

"And did anything else you read in the ECM data strike you as interesting?"

"Two things: it confirmed the deceleration I had noted on the security footage; the Mercedes went from thirty-four to twenty-three miles per hour. And it also revealed that the car did not brake before impact."

"Your Honor?" Maritza approached the judge with the sheet of paper. "If I can refer to exhibit 129-A?"

Judge Tedeschi nodded, "Go ahead."

Fanning finally deigned to look up. He slid his reading glasses down the bridge of his nose. The lenses were smudged. If Tommy McAllister was programmed to look like a young but struggling professional, Douglas Fanning was counterprogrammed to look like anything but the slick defense attorney to the mega-wealthy that he actually was. His long gray hair was pulled back into a braided ponytail. His suit was wrinkled, his tie stained. He affected a southern drawl that Sara hadn't heard since her grandmother was alive. He often pretended to fumble for information in order to play down his Duke law degree. Where Sara and Maritza had made every effort to appear competent and professional, Fanning would be afforded both of those qualities without appearing to give an actual shit.

"Dr. Linton." Maritza finally placed the sheet of paper on the overhead projector. "Do you recognize this exhibit, marked 129-A?"

Sara had turned toward the monitor on the wall along with everyone else. "That is a copy of the body diagram I downloaded from the internet so I could make proper anatomical notations of my findings. That's my signature at the bottom of the page along with the date and time."

"You downloaded the form from the internet," Maritza repeated. "Wouldn't it have been easier to take photographs?"

"As a healthcare professional, any data I collect is subject to HIPAA, which is a federal law governing the storage and dissemination of sensitive healthcare information. My Grady-issued phone didn't have a camera, and I couldn't guarantee the security of my personal phone."

"All right, thank you." Maritza pointed at the screen. "Those Xs across the ribs, what do those represent?"

"The bone fractures that contributed to what is called a flail chest."

"You explained that term to us this morning, so I'll ask: in Dani's case, could the seat belt be responsible for the flail chest?"

"Not in my opinion. The car wasn't going fast enough to cause that damage."

"What caused that damage?"

Fanning stirred again. He was making it clear that Sara had his attention now. His pen had made a slash mark on the pad. He made noises like he was about to object, but Maritza beat him to it.

"I'll rephrase." She kept her eyes on Sara. "In your experience as a medical examiner, Dr. Linton, what sorts of traumas can cause a flail chest?"

"I had a case where the decedent fell from the roof of a two-story office building. Another was driving a truck that impacted a concrete highway divider at approximately ninety miles an hour. Another was a child who'd been beaten to death by a caretaker."

The courtroom collectively flinched.

Maritza continued, "So, we're not talking going twenty-three miles per hour and smacking into the side of a parked ambulance?"

"Not in my opinion."

Fanning made another slash.

"A previous expert witness told us that the airbag inside of the Mercedes was placed under recall six months prior to the accident. It deployed, but we have no idea of knowing whether it deployed properly. Does that change your evaluation?"

"No. In my opinion—" Sara saw Fanning make yet another mark on his legal pad. "Even if there had been no airbag, Dani's chest impacting the steering wheel at that rate of speed would not have caused the severity of those injuries."

"In Dani's case, was there a lot of bleeding from the flail chest?"

"Yes, but internally—inside the body. Externally, the only visible blood came from the superficial laceration."

"Dani had a collapsed lung. Did that make it difficult for her to talk?"

"Yes, her air supply was restricted. She could only speak in a whisper."

"As a doctor, given Dani's dire medical situation, do you attach more significance to her telling you that she had been drugged and raped?"

"Yes," Sara said. "Generally, when I have a patient in significant distress, their focus is on getting out of that distress. Dani's focus was on telling me what had happened to her."

Maritza returned to the body diagram on the screen. "What's that X mark on the back of Dani's head?"

"It indicates blunt force head trauma."

"Can you explain to the jury what you mean by 'blunt force head trauma'?"

Sara started to answer, but she was suddenly gripped by anxiety. Fanning was openly staring at her, his dark, beady eyes taking in every detail as he clutched the pen in his hand. She dreaded his cross-examination almost as much as he clearly relished the thought of it.

Maritza gave her a barely perceptible nod. They both knew what was at stake here. This was for Dani. This was about Sara keeping her promise.

She made her voice steady as she told the jury, "A blunt force head trauma refers to a blow to the head that doesn't penetrate the skull, and results in either a concussion injury, a contusion, or both."

Maritza asked, "What did Dani Cooper have?"

"A grade three concussion."

"How did you come to this conclusion?"

"Among other things, I found an edema at the back of her head post-mortem."

"What's an edema?"

"A collection of fluid in the tissue or cavities of the body." Sara told the jury, "It's basically swelling. You injure yourself—like you bump your knee on your desk. The body sends fluid as a way of saying, 'Hey, be careful with your knee while I try to repair it.'"

"Grade three." Maritza was clearly trying to help Sara get her footing back. "Explain that, please."

"There are five grades of concussion, escalating in severity. Grade three is characterized by loss of consciousness for less than one minute. There are also other factors such as pupillary reaction, pulse, blood pressure, respiration, speech patterns and response to questioning, and of course the edema."

"Could the headrest in the driver's seat be the cause of Dani's grade three concussion?"

"Not in my opinion." Sara saw Fanning's pen slash again as she turned back toward the jury. "We think about the headrest as something to make us comfortable when we drive, but it's actually designed for our safety. If you're involved in a front- or rear-end collision, your head jerks forward and back. The head restraint keeps you from experiencing severe whiplash, or damage to your spine, or even death. Given the rate of speed at which the Mercedes was traveling, the protective structures inside the head restraint would not have caused that trauma."

"Did you have occasion to look inside the Mercedes before it was towed away?"

"Yes."

"What was your first impression?"

"There was no blood on the airbag."

"Why is that significant?"

"As we've discussed, Dani had a superficial laceration on her left side that bled through her shirt. If the injury had occurred during the accident, I would expect to see blood on the airbag."

Maritza paused before moving to the next piece of the puzzle. The jury was engaged now. Most had started writing in their spiral notebooks. "Let's focus on that word, 'laceration.' It has a specific medical meaning, doesn't it, Dr. Linton?"

Fanning sat back in his chair. His reading glasses came off, but he kept his pen at the ready. He knew that he had shaken Sara before. He was trying to do it again.

Sara tried to concentrate on the jury, explaining, "We classify a wound as a laceration when the muscle, tissue or skin is cut open or torn. From a forensic standpoint, they are classified as split, stretched, compressed, torn, or chopped."

"What type was Dani Cooper's laceration?"

"Split, so basically enough blunt force was used to break apart the skin."

"And 'superficial' means?"

"To be obvious, superficial means that it's not deep," Sara answered. "So, bleeding, but not requiring sutures. The blood would eventually coagulate and the wound would heal on its own."

"Was there anything inside the Mercedes that could've caused the laceration?"

"Not that I could find."

"You searched the vehicle?"

"I did," Sara answered. "Dani's injuries didn't make sense to me. I wanted an explanation."

"How much time did you spend looking at the car?"

"I had around ten minutes before the tow truck arrived."

"Twelve minutes, according to the security footage," Maritza provided. "In your experience, as both a doctor and medical examiner, what have you seen that can cause a superficial laceration in that same spot during an automobile accident?"

"Broken glass, though the Mercedes' windows were all intact. The seat belt, but again, Dani's injury was on the left when a driver would have an injury on the right." Sara had to pause before continuing. Her mouth had gone dry. They were getting to the end of Maritza's questions. "There are also projectiles that could be inside the vehicle at impact. I've seen laptops, plastic toys, iPads, phones—anything with a hard edge can cause that type of laceration if it's moving at speed on impact."

"Did you find anything of that nature in the car?"

"No. From what I could see, the only item in the car was a shoe, a black slide sandal that was jammed under the front seat. The rest of the interior was completely clean."

"We heard earlier that the car was moved off to the curb so the ambulance bay would be clear. Do you know how long the car sat unattended?"

"I don't know the exact time, but Dani was in surgery for roughly three hours."

"All right, let's go back to your drawing." Maritza pointed toward the screen again. "These round red marks you indicated here on Dani's backside. Can you explain their significance?"

"In my opinion—" Sara saw Fanning make another tick on his notepad. "Those appear to be marks left by fingers digging into the skin. You can see the pattern suggests someone gripped the back of her left leg and buttock."

"Did you witness anyone in the trauma bay or operating room grabbing her in these areas?"

"I did not."

"What about the ambulance crew when they took her out of the car?" Maritza clarified, "I know you weren't present outside when Dani was removed, but could they have caused those marks?"

"The marks I saw on Dani's body were not recent. I would say by their color that they were several hours old."

"What are you using to base this timeframe on?"

"A bruise occurs when an injury causes blood to leak into the skin or the tissue behind the skin. Over time, the leaked blood loses oxygen and starts to change color. This process can take a few hours or a few days. That's when you see the blue, purple, or even black color. Dani's bruises were red in color. In my opinion—" Sara caught Fanning's pen moving yet again. "—the color indicates the bruises were at least an hour old. Possibly more."

"You base this on your experience as a doctor?"

"As a pediatrician," Sara said. "Children routinely find ways to give themselves lots of bumps and bruises.

They're often not the most reliable narrators of their mishaps."

One of the jurors gave a knowing nod. She was early thirties, probably a mother with a toddler at home. Sara had noticed the woman from the outset. She'd thought of her as "The Note-Taker" because, of all the jurors, the woman had been taking the most notes.

"Dr. Linton." Maritza clasped her hands together as she leaned against the podium. "Let me get the sequence of events straight, if you don't mind. You were told that Dani Cooper was driving the car?"

"Yes."

"But the laceration on her side could not have resulted from the impact of the car hitting the ambulance?"

"Not in my opinion."

Fanning ticked another mark.

"And the flail chest, in your opinion, was not caused by the car hitting the ambulance?"

"Not in my opinion, no."

Tick.

"And the blunt force trauma to the back of her head was not caused by the car hitting the ambulance?"

"Not in my opinion."

Tick.

"And the fingerprint marks on Dani Cooper's left

thigh and buttock, in your opinion, were not caused either by the accident or how she was handled inside the hospital?"

"Not in my opinion."

Tick.

"So, as a medical examiner who has seen victims from hundreds of vehicle collisions, and a doctor who has treated hundreds of patients who've been involved in vehicle collisions, and as the physician who both treated Dani Cooper and saw the video footage that recorded the car accident, how do you square all of these contradictory findings?"

"They can't be squared," Sara said. "The damage to Dani Cooper's body was not caused by the car accident."

Maritza gave the jury another long moment to let that sink in. "Dr. Linton, are you saying that someone hurt Dani Cooper before she got behind the wheel of that car?"

"In my professional opinion, Dani was severely beaten with a blunt object. Somehow, she managed to get into the Mercedes. She drove to the hospital, but lost consciousness as the car rounded toward the emergency department parking lot. Her body went lax. Her hands dropped from the steering wheel. Her foot released the pedal. The car coasted into the ambulance."

Sara looked directly at the jurors. "Dani knew that her injuries were life-threatening. She begged me with her last breath to stop the man who'd hurt her."

There was total silence in the courtroom.

The jurors stared back at Sara. The Note-Taker rested her chin in her hand, clearly mulling over the information.

There was only a faint *click* as the clock on the wall marked the passing of another hour.

The silence was broken by Douglas Fanning giving a heavy sigh. He picked up his reading glasses, then noisily flipped through the pages of his legal pad. There had been ample opportunity for him to object during Sara's testimony, but he'd kept his mouth closed. Sara wasn't delusional enough to think he'd been silenced by her mastery of the subject matter. Fanning was confident that his cross-examination would be so brutal that the jury would start to doubt every word that had come out of Sara's mouth.

"Thank you, Dr. Linton." Maritza looked at the judge, "Your Honor, no further questions at this time."

Tedeschi looked at the clock. Sara was torn between wanting to get the next part over with and dragging it out another day, but the judge's hand did not reach for the gavel.

"Mr. Fanning," Tedeschi said. "We've got about an

hour left on the schedule. Would you like to break for the day and resume tomorrow morning?"

Douglas Fanning stood, smoothing down his tie over his round belly. "No thank you, Your Honor. This won't take long."

Sara slowly exhaled as Fanning gathered his things. Her heart was pounding inside her chest. Her hands had turned sweaty. As a doctor, she had learned to compartmentalize her feelings. You couldn't help a patient when you were swallowed up by panic or grief. Now, facing down a man whose only job was to humiliate and embarrass her, she had to work to strengthen her resolve.

Fanning drew out the moment. He took a long drink from a glass of water. He was trying to unnerve Sara again. She was a very good witness, the crux of the Coopers' case. Tommy's jury consultant, the media person, particularly his parents, would've all discussed during strategy sessions that Fanning's main objective was to blow Sara's credibility into a thousand pieces.

Britt McAllister in particular would've been able to provide ample ammunition.

"Dr. Linton." Fanning gripped the sides of the podium with visible exuberance. "Do you know how many times in the last five minutes you uttered the phrase '*in my opinion*'?"

Sara nodded, because she'd kept track of his ticks. "I believe it was twelve times."

Fanning pressed his tongue into the side of his cheek, but she could see the flash in his eyes. He wasn't irritated. He was delighted. Blood in the water.

He said, "That's right. Twelve times, you said the phrase '*in my opinion*.' That's because what you just told us—all this conjecture about Dani being beaten then getting in the car—that's all just your opinion, right?"

Sara knew better than to equivocate. "Yes."

"We're all here in this courtroom because of your opinion, right?"

She clasped her hands in her lap. "I can only speak for myself. I'm here because I was asked to testify."

"The circumstances surrounding Dani's tragic death—you said they just didn't look right, based on your opinion." He looked at her over his glasses. "Yes?"

"Yes."

"You persuaded the Fulton County Medical Examiner to perform an autopsy on Dani Cooper, right?"

"You would have to ask Dr. Malawaki about his thought processes."

"But you gave him your opinion, right?"

"Yes."

"And Sergeant Shanda London, the motor vehicle ac-

cident investigator for the Atlanta Police Department—
you gave her your opinion, right?"

"Yes."

Fanning returned to his legal pad. He traced his
finger down the side as if he wanted to make sure he hit
all the important facts, but this was all just preamble.
"At what point did you find out that the Mercedes belonged to Tommy McAllister?"

"Sergeant London told me."

"Sergeant London testified that you responded, and
I quote, 'Shit, I went to school with his father.' Is that
right?"

"Yes." Sara let her lips part for a tiny breath of air,
steeling herself against what was to come. "Mac and I
were at Emory medical school together, then we both
interned and served our residencies at Grady Hospital."

"During that time, Tommy's mother, Dr. Britt Mc-
Allister, was also at Grady, right?"

"Yes." Sara felt the knot of tension draw tight. "Britt
is older. I believe she was five or six years ahead of us."

Sara caught Britt stiffening in her seat. Britt had
always been sensitive about the age difference. And the
fact that she'd locked down Mac during his undergrad
by getting pregnant with Tommy.

"Are y'all close?" Fanning asked. "You and the Mc-
Allisters? Do you socialize with them?"

"I haven't seen either of them in fifteen years."

"Because you left Grady after your residency?"

"Yes." Sara had to stop to swallow. He was circling closer to the target. "I moved home to be with my family."

"We'll get back to that." Fanning studied her carefully to see how she responded to the warning. "Don't you worry."

Sara kept her expression passive. She waited for him to ask a question.

"In medical terms, what is a fellowship?"

"After you fulfill your residency, you can choose to either start practicing general medicine or continue your education in a specialty field. For the latter, you enter into what's called a fellowship where you receive hands-on advanced training in a particular sub-specialty."

"A specialty being something like pediatric cardio-thoracic surgery?"

"Yes."

He said, "Tommy's father, Mac—he was your fiercest competitor during your residency, right?"

"Residents are constantly evaluated against each other. We were all each other's fiercest competitors."

"Be that as it may, it was you and Mac who were

both in contention for a very prestigious fellowship in pediatric cardiothoracic surgery, right? The Nygaard Fellowship?"

She fought the urge to clear her throat. "You would have to ask Dr. Nygaard who she was considering."

"But Mac got the fellowship and you—as you said—went home, right? Back to South Georgia, where you worked in a pediatrician's office. Right?"

Sara swallowed down the part of her ego that wanted to tell him that she had eventually bought the practice. "Yes, that's right."

"As a doctor—as a medical examiner—*in your opinion*, which is more prestigious, being a pediatric cardiothoracic surgeon in Atlanta or working for someone else in a South Georgia pediatric clinic?"

He wanted her to sound defensive. Sara wouldn't give that to him. "In the medical hierarchy, Mac is definitely above me. He's one of the top surgeons in Atlanta."

Fanning's eyebrow went up. It wasn't just Atlanta. Mac was consistently in the top five of every national ranking. "Nevertheless, that must feel like quite a comedown. One minute you're at the height of your profession, the next minute you're dealing with earaches and runny noses."

The judge stirred, clearly expecting an objection, but Maritza had told Sara she wouldn't object unless Sara looked to her for help.

Sara kept her eyes on Fanning. He was gripping the podium again, preparing to go in for the kill. All she could do was wait for it to come.

"Dr. Linton," he said. "You have a personal stake in all of this, don't you?"

Her stomach clenched. "A nineteen-year-old woman died. I take that very personally."

"But there's more to it than that, isn't there?"

Sara wasn't going to make it easy on him. "Every doctor cares about their patients, but when you lose one, you carry them in your heart for the rest of your life. I made a promise to Dani that I would see this through."

"*See this through.*" He repeated the phrase with a preacher's zeal. "My daughters tell me there's a phrase—hashtag believe women. Do you support that, Dr. Linton? Do you believe women?"

Sara tasted bile in her mouth. He was seconds away from the strike. "In general, or do you mean specifically?"

"Well, when you're investigating a crime involving sexual assault, do you always go into it believing that the woman is telling the truth?"

"If I'm investigating, that means the victim is deceased, so no, I don't approach the case assuming the victim lied about being murdered."

One of the jurors laughed.

The sound was loud and sharp in the cavernous room.

It had come from the Note-Taker, the probable mom of a toddler, the woman who'd been paying close attention all along, the person Tommy's jury consultant probably believed would be elected forewoman when the jury convened to discuss their verdict.

The woman was clearly mortified by her outburst. Her hand covered her mouth. She gave the judge an apologetic look. Then she shook her head at Sara in apology, too.

Sara didn't respond, but she let out a long, slow breath. The laugh had changed things. The knot of tension had gone slack. She could feel it in every part of her body.

So could Fanning. He looked down at his notes. He ran his tongue along his top teeth. He said, "Your Honor, may I have a moment, please?"

"Quickly," Tedeschi said.

Fanning went back to the table to confer with his colleague. Sara couldn't hear them, but she knew what they were saying. Did the laugh mean that the

Note-Taker was on Sara's side? If Fanning went after Sara, would that turn the potential forewoman against Tommy? Would the woman sway the jury to do the same? Was their carefully prepared trial strategy really going to fall apart because a thirty-something-year-old mother had laughed?

There was nothing Sara could do but wait.

She looked down at her hands. She saw the glimmer of her engagement ring. The stone was cheap green glass, scratched on the side. She'd had to replace the original silver band with white gold because it had tarnished on her finger. The only thing that Sara loved more than the ring was the man who had given it to her.

"Dr. Linton?" Douglas Fanning returned to the podium.

Sara looked directly into his beady little eyes. She let go of the anxiety and dread. There was literally nothing she could do right now that would influence the next words that came out of his mouth. The only thing Sara could control was her reaction. The relief that came from acceptance made the corner of her mouth tug up in a smile.

She said, "Yes?"

"The, uh—" Fanning had lost his place. He nervously looked back at his colleague. Then he flipped through the pages of his notes. "Experts are moving away from the old grading system for concussions, correct?"

"It depends on the hospital, but at the time of Dani's death, that was the protocol."

"All right." He paused to clear his throat. "Grade three concussions—do those come with memory loss? Amnesia?"

Her mouth opened. She was able to take her first full breath. "Sometimes, but it's generally temporary."

"What about speech difficulties?"

Sara took another breath. Fanning was the one who was flustered now. She was fine. "Sometimes, but again, they're—"

"Temporary." The fact that he'd finished the sentence for Sara was a clear sign of his retreat. He wanted to get this over with. He stuck to the script on his legal pad. "What about hallucinations? Do those come with grade three concussions?"

"Rarely," Sara worked to keep the triumph out of her tone. "But it can happen."

"Your colleagues, Dr. Eldin Franklin and the head trauma nurse, Johna Blackmon, both testified that they did not hear Dani say anything that night. Are you surprised by that?"

"No. As I said earlier, Dani was suffering from a collapsed lung." Sara took another full, cleansing breath.

"Also, in the trauma bay, everyone has a clearly defined role. I was in charge, so it was my job to communicate with the patient. Eldin and Johna had their own tasks."

Fanning glanced down at his notepad. "Did Dani mention the anonymous text messages on her phone?"

"No."

Another glance. "Drugging someone, assaulting them, those are serious crimes, correct?"

"Yes."

Another glance. "Did you report to your colleagues what Dani had said to you?"

"No," Sara said. "There wasn't time."

"How about up in surgery? Did you tell any of the surgeons or the nurses?"

"No." Sara felt like she was on autopilot. "There wasn't time."

"The first person you told was over five hours later, right? You told Sergeant London about Dani's claims, but only after the sergeant had told you that the car belonged to the son of your old rival, Dr. Mac McAllister. Right?"

"Sergeant London was the first person I told, yes."

"Tell me." Fanning turned the page to continue down the list of questions. "After consensual sex, how long can sperm stay in the vaginal area?"

"Whether the sex is consensual or not, ejaculated

sperm can be found in the female reproductive tract anywhere from five to seven days later."

"Do you have any proof of the date or time that the sperm was deposited?"

"No."

"Do you have proof—such as a weapon you can show us—that something was used to hurt Dani that night?"

"No."

"Do you have proof of what caused the bruises to her left thigh and buttock?"

"No."

"Do you have proof that Dani didn't freely take recreational drugs that night?"

"No."

"Do you have proof that she left the party with Tommy McAllister?"

"No."

"Do you have proof as to how she came to be driving his Mercedes?"

"No."

"Do you have proof that she passed out behind the wheel before hitting the ambulance?"

"No."

"Do you have corroborating proof that Dani told you she was drugged and raped that night?"

"No."

"So there's really no actual, verifiable proof of all this stuff that you're alleging. Is there, Dr. Linton?" Fanning grabbed the legal pad off the podium. "It's all just your opinion."

Sara watched him walk back toward the table. She waited as he sat in his chair. Placed his pad on the table. His pen. Smoothed down his tie. Straightened his suit jacket. Looked up at the judge. Sara was holding her breath again as Fanning's mouth opened.

He told the judge, "I'm finished with this witness, Your Honor."

And it was over.

Three years of heartache. Six months of dread. Nearly four hours of testimony.

It was finally over.

Sara expected to feel elation, but what she felt instead was a dulling of her senses. She heard the judge dismiss her as a witness, but the sound traveled slowly. Sara could have been moving through water as she stood up, found her purse, and stepped down from the stand. Only then did she look at Maritza, who gave her an approving nod. Dani's mother and father offered pained smiles of encouragement. Sara could feel the newspaper reporter staring at her, madly typing into her phone. Britt was staring, too, but not out of curiosity. She was clutching Mac's arm. Their animosity was like a malevolent presence in the courtroom. The heat of their hatred followed Sara until the doors closed behind her.

The hallway was almost empty. It was late in the day. There was a crowd waiting at the elevators. Sara couldn't face being around people right now. She walked in the opposite direction, finding the bathroom. She bypassed the sinks and went into the last stall. She sat on the toilet, put her head in her hands, and let herself cry.

For Dani. For her parents.

And finally, out of the glare of the courtroom, away from the reporter and Douglas Fanning and the jury and Britt-fucking-McAllister, Sara cried for herself. She had survived. She had done everything possible to keep her promise to Dani. All the anxiety and fear that had haunted Sara every time she thought about testifying was slowly ebbing away. She looked down at the ring on her finger, reminding herself that life always found a way to get better.

The bathroom door slammed open.

The sound was like a shotgun going off.

Sara warily raised her head. She saw a pair of navy

Manolo Blahniks stab their way across the tiled floor. They stopped in front of the sinks. The faucet was turned on full blast. There was a moment of nothing but the loud rush of water circling down the drain before the woman let out a low, mournful moan.

"Oh, God," she whispered. "Oh-God-oh-God-oh-God."

The woman's knees buckled. She sank to the floor. Her ten-thousand dollar Hermès Kelly bag dropped alongside her, the contents skittering across the tiles. Make-up, keys, wallet, tampons, chewing gum. Sara had pulled back her feet as a pair of Cartier sunglasses shot under the stall door and smacked against the base of the toilet. She recognized the glasses. They had been hanging from the pocket of the purse that matched the shoes that matched the Versace suit that was being worn by Britt McAllister.

"God!" Britt cried. She doubled over, her head nearly touching the bathroom floor.

Sara kept her feet lifted out of the way. There were countless reasons for her to dislike Britt McAllister, but she could not take pleasure in seeing another woman literally bent over by grief. The moment was too raw, too personal. Sara wanted nothing more than to disappear. Then she looked down at the sunglasses and the earlier wariness came rolling back in. She waited through almost a full minute of Britt's tears, hoping, praying, that Britt would abandon the glasses and leave.

Britt did not.

She sniffed as she sat up, trying to collect herself. She sniffed again. Regardless of the glasses, she would want a tissue to dry her eyes. The lock on the stall door rattled when Britt tried to push it open.

Sara felt physically ill.

"He—" Britt's voice caught. "Hello?"

Sara didn't know what to do but pick up the sunglasses. She stood from the toilet. She opened the door.

Britt was still on her knees. She looked up at Sara. The surprise registered a beat too late. Britt was clearly under the influence of something. She was swaying. Her pupils were pinpricks. Her eyes had a tell-tale glassiness. Sara noticed a silver pill case had fallen open under the sink basin. The tiny blue pills had a distinctive V-shape missing from the centers that identified each as 10mg of Valium. There were over a dozen, which was a hell of a lot to keep in your purse.

Sara turned off the faucet. She placed the sunglasses by the sink. Every single molecule in her body wanted to leave. Britt had never been an easy woman to get along with. She was petty and conniving and often vicious, but she was also a mother whose son was on trial. No matter Tommy's guilt, he was still her child.

Sara rolled out some toilet paper. She handed it to Britt, asking, "Do you want me to get Mac for you?"

"No, I—" Britt's hand went to her mouth as she tried to hold back her emotions. "Please, Sara. Please tell me it's not too late."

Sara heard the raw desperation behind the request, but it had the opposite effect. Was this woman literally on her knees begging Sara to go back into the courtroom and lie? "My testimony is over. I told the truth about what happened."

"Don't you think I know that?" Britt yelled, her hands clenching in the air. "I know you told the truth! I know what he did to that girl!"

Sara was too stunned to respond.

"I know who he is." Britt's hands dropped into her lap. She looked away from Sara, staring at the floor. "I've lived with the fear for twenty years. I know exactly who he is."

Sara couldn't move. She couldn't think. She couldn't breathe.

I know what he did to that girl.

"He'll stop now," Britt whispered. "Tommy's scared. I know he'll stop. There's still time for him to become a good man."

Sara could feel her heart pounding inside her chest. Her mind was racing. She knew that Tommy had been accused of raping another girl two years before Dani had died.

I know who he is.

Slowly, Sara knelt in front of Britt. She didn't know what she was going to say until the words came out of her mouth. "How do you know what he did to Dani?"

"I heard them."

"You heard them?" Sara tried to keep the anguish out of her voice. Dani could've been saved. "You heard Dani being—"

"It's not Tommy's fault. He still has time to change." Britt started shaking her head. "He'll learn from this. He's not like Mac."

Sara felt overwhelmed by what she was hearing. She could barely process the information. "Was Mac involved, too?"

"Mac is always involved." Britt's tone was flat, matter-of-fact. "I can't stop the rest of them, but I can save my boy."

"The rest of them?" Sara repeated. "Britt, what do you mean?"

Britt did not answer. Instead, she wiped her eyes with her hands. Mascara smeared across the tips of her fingers, down her face. She seemed to notice her scattered belongings for the first time. Wallet. Lipstick. Keys. Her eyeshadow palette had broken apart, dusting the tile with earthy hues. Britt started circling her finger into the powder. Sara watched, almost transfixed, as Britt's words ricocheted around her brain.

I know who he is. I've lived with the fear for twenty years.

Twenty years ago, Tommy was only two years old. No mother lived in fear of her two-year-old becoming a monster. Was she talking about Mac? What had Mac done?

Mac is always involved.

"Britt." Sara worked to keep her voice from trembling. "Please talk to me. I don't understand. Did Tommy go to Mac for help the night that Dani died?"

Britt didn't answer.

"Who is *them?*" Sara could hear herself pleading, but she didn't care. "You said you couldn't stop the rest of them. Who is *them?*"

Britt finally looked up at Sara. She narrowed her eyes, trying to focus. "What are you doing?"

Sara noted the change in Britt's demeanor. Reason had started to cut through the fog of Valium. Still, she tried, "Please talk to me. Tell me what happened to Dani."

"How would I—" Britt's hand went to her face. She looked around the bathroom as if she had just realized where she was. "Were you hiding in the stall? Waiting on me?"

"No," Sara said. "Britt, you just told me—"

"I didn't tell you a damn thing." Britt picked up her keys, the lipstick. She started throwing stuff back into her purse. She snatched the sunglasses off the counter as she struggled to stand. "Given your tragic past, I'd think you'd avoid the handicap stall."

Sara felt as if she'd been slapped in the face. This was the Britt McAllister she remembered: angry, nasty, filled with spite.

Britt said, "Whatever you think you heard—"

"I know what I heard." Sara stood, going back into the stall. She grabbed her purse off the back of the toilet and turned to leave.

Britt blocked the way. "I'm not going to let you destroy my child."

"Dani Cooper was somebody's child, too."

"What do you know about being a mother?"

Sara felt every ounce of cruelty in the question. Britt of all people knew why she wasn't a mother. Sara was finished holding herself back. "You've done a great job with Tommy. Is this the second or third time he's been accused of rape?"

"You haven't changed a bit, have you?" Britt rested

her hand on the wall, making it clear that Sara wasn't going anywhere. "Saint Sara the plumber's daughter with your cheap costume jewelry and your kitten heels, holding forth on high like you know every-fucking-thing."

Sara wanted to shove her back to the ground. "What I know is that I will move you myself if you don't get the fuck out of my way."

"What do you make at the GBI, a hundred grand a year?" Britt gave a derisive snort. "Mac's already cleared two mil this quarter."

"Wow!" Sara filled the word with sarcasm. "Send him my congratulations for profiting off my misfortune."

"You think what happened to you fifteen years ago was misfortune?" Britt laughed. "Just a spot of bad luck?"

"Fuck your bad luck." Sara clenched her fists. This was bullshit. Britt was playing one of her psychotic games. "Move out of my way."

"Poor Saint Sara. So brilliant. Such a tragic loss. Fifteen long years of not knowing, of suffering, because you couldn't see what was right in front of you."

Sara blocked out her words. She had to get out of here before she lost it. "I told you to—"

"Sara!" Britt hissed out her name like a snake.

"You're not listening to me. What happened to you. What happened to Dani. It's all connected."

Sara felt her mouth moving, trying to form a response, but nothing would come out.

"Don't you remember the mixer?"

Sara had lost her voice, her senses, her reasoning.

Britt laughed again. "You stupid cunt. You don't know anything at all."

2

Faith Mitchell sat at her kitchen table scrolling through her phone. "Jesus, this idiot."

"Which idiot?" Aiden Van Zandt looked up from making dinner.

"Spork Face." Faith had names for all the annoying mothers at her daughter's preschool. "She just bragged on Facebook about doing coke at her high school reunion."

Aiden laughed as he grabbed two plates from the cabinet. "You gonna arrest her?"

"Fuck no. I'd have to take over her snack days." Faith copied a link to the Georgia statute on possession of a controlled substance and posted it without additional comment. Then she slid her phone across the table so that Aiden could see. "That'll learn 'er."

He grinned, but said, "Don't be so hard on her. The

thing about doing coke is it makes you want to tell everybody you're doing coke."

Aiden was an FBI agent, but he worked in counterterrorism, not narcotics. "Have you ever done coke?"

"Are you kidding?" His eyes had gone wide behind his glasses. "Not after Regina Morrow died the first time she tried it."

"You read the Sweet Valley High books?"

"I was thirteen. My sister told me there was sex in them." He placed dinner on the table. "I told you she was mean."

Faith looked at the plump ravioli, which he'd made from scratch with groceries he'd paid for himself and brought to her house. The smell was unbelievable. The sauce looked like it had come from real vegetables instead of a chemical-squirting machine.

Aiden said, "Forgive me for noticing, but I see that you're freaking out."

"I'm not freaking out," Faith said, freaking out. She didn't like men who wore glasses. She didn't date men who paid for groceries and cooked fresh pasta and had stable jobs with 401(k) retirement plan and who knew without being told that you were supposed to drink water. She dated cheaters and liars and assholes and rednecks who never had cash to pick up the check and wasted a thousand dollars on Georgia tickets even though they were six months behind on their child support.

He said, "It's okay to lean on other people sometimes."

"All right, Dr. Phil." Faith picked up her fork, but Aiden kept staring at her as if he expected something more. "I don't know what you've heard, but I'm fine."

"You're fine holding down your desk?"

"I'm on desk duty because my partner is on a top-secret undercover assignment." Faith shrugged. "I'm not even allowed to know where he is."

Aiden cleaned his glasses with the tail of his shirt. "You know I was raised by a single mother who worked as a cop. I saw how hard it is."

"Really?" she asked. "Because my son was raised by a single mother who works as a cop, and he still thinks a magical laundry fairy bleaches the streaks out of his undershorts."

"I'm a little older than Jeremy is."

"Not by much." Faith watched him laugh, but it was true. She had given birth to Jeremy when she was fifteen. Then three years ago, despite using nearly every form of birth control, she had given her college-aged son an adorable baby sister. "I'm not even forty yet and I've spent twenty-two years of my life being a single mother."

"I find your exhaustion intoxicating."

Faith felt her eyes roll so hard she could see her entire ass. Then she took a bite of pasta and her eyes rolled for a different reason. "My God, who taught you how to make this?"

"My father. All the men in my family cook."

Faith concentrated on chewing. Aiden's father had died when he was young. He had started dropping hints lately that he was open to talking about it, but Faith never picked them up because they weren't in a relationship and she wasn't supposed to feel like her heart was breaking when she thought about him as a bespectacled little boy standing by his father's casket.

He said, "Would it be so terrible to have somebody you can call on? Maybe if you needed help with something? A favor, even?"

"Aiden, I'm a very private person. Remember when I yelled at you for talking to my Google clock?" Faith knew he knew what she was really saying. "This is a hook-up, okay? A booty call."

"Six months is a lotta booty." Aiden finished his beer. "Who eats the bad pancake?"

"Is that sex stuff? You know how I feel about hygiene."

"It's life," Aiden said. "When you cook pancakes, there's always a bad pancake. You can't throw food away. You need somebody around who will eat it."

Faith didn't want to, but she started smiling. "My dad used to eat the bad pancake."

"See?"

Faith was saved further introspection when her phone pinged. She dropped her fork. "You've got to go."

"What?"

"Out the back." Faith was already dragging him up by his arm. "Jeremy's almost here."

"How do you—"

"Hurry." Faith yanked open the sliding door. "I don't want my son catching my fuckbuddy in his child-hood home."

"I prefer booty call."

"I prefer your ass out the door." Faith grabbed his jacket off the back of the chair and threw it at him. "Your car is on the street, right?"

"Yes." Aiden stood in the open doorway. "Do I get a kiss?"

"Go!" She pushed him out and jerked the slider closed. She raked the curtains across the rod. The headlights from Jeremy's car splashed the front of the house as he pulled up the driveway.

"Fuck!"

Faith shoved her phone into her back pocket. The dirty pots and pans got jammed into the cabinets. She sponged down the counters, randomly threw dirty utensils into the dishwasher. She tossed Aiden's beer bottle into the trash, then stashed his plate of pasta in the fridge. She heard Jeremy's key scrape in the lock of the front door. Faith barely had time to check her reflection in the small mirror by the sink. She patted down her hair, praying she didn't look like she'd spent her evening like a queen being fucked and eating pasta.

"Mom?" Jeremy shut the door with a loud bang. His feet were heavy as he walked down the hallway. "Did you wash my hoodie?"

Faith crossed her arms as she leaned against the counter. "Be more specific, bub. You have ten thousand hoodies."

"The white one." He looked at the table, her nearly finished meal. "Did you go to Olive Garden?"

"Uh-huh."

"Why is it on a plate?" His suspicions were not unwarranted. "Did you get breadsticks?"

She summoned her Mother Voice. "Jeremy, I'm diabetic. You know I have to be careful with carbs."

He opened the fridge and stuck his head in. "Why did you order two servings?"

Jesus, she'd raised a nosy kid. "I thought you might drop by."

"Are you tracking me?" His phone came out of his pocket. "Did you mess with my Snap settings?"

"I can't believe you asked me that. Of course not." Faith would never touch his phone. She had hidden the tracker inside the trunk of his car. "Maybe you left your hoodie in your room?"

"Maybe." Jeremy was still looking at his phone as he walked back into the hall. "Did you see the picture Grandma posted from Las Vegas?"

Faith had blocked her mother for using too many emojis. "She's having a blast."

"Yeah." Jeremy started up the stairs, his eyes stuck on the screen. "I FaceTimed Emma this morning. She wanted to show me the Boo Bucket that Victor got her."

Faith grinned as she followed him up. She loved that her ex had spent two thousand dollars to take their child and his new girlfriend on a fall break vacation and all Emma cared about was the cheap plastic bucket from her Happy Meal.

"Mom." Jeremy had stopped at the top of the stairs. He looked down at Faith. She could tell something was bothering him before he opened his mouth. "Victor's girlfriend's been posting videos of Emma on Insta. Are you down with that?"

"You mean am I okay with a woman I've never met posting videos of my child that strangers who might be perverts can look at? And am I cool that my child's father doesn't have the balls to tell her to take them down because we have an agreement about not ever posting photos or videos of our child on social media that perverts can look at?" Faith jerked up her shoulder in a violent shrug. "Sure."

Jeremy's face took on a bashful expression. "I kind of cracked her password."

"What?"

"The new girlfriend. Her name is Delilah? And she's got a labradoodle named Doodle. So I kind of played around with some combinations and got into her account." Jeremy nervously glanced at Faith. "I deleted all her videos of Emma."

Faith had never been so proud of him in her life. "Jeremy, that's illegal."

"Yeah, well." He loped toward his bedroom. "That's my baby sister."

Faith felt like her heart was going to burst with love. Instead of following him into his room, she opened the doors to the hall laundry. Nothing was really lost until your mother couldn't find it. The dirty clothes basket had spilled onto the top of the dryer. She guessed by the smell of sweat and Tom Ford cologne that it was mostly Jeremy's things.

"Nice." Jeremy reached past her and dug out the

hoodie from the bottom of the pile. He sniffed it, then put it on as he made his way back toward the stairs. "I'll see you later."

"Bub, hold on a second." Faith trailed after him, trying not to sound clingy. "You've got that dinner with the guys from 3M this weekend, right?"

"Uh—" His attention was firmly back on his phone. "Yeah. Friday."

"That's a big deal, right?" Faith had learned to frame everything as a question. "You're going to graduate from Georgia Tech and go straight into a cushy job, right?"

"Sure." He opened the front door. "See ya."

Faith was pathetically grateful when he turned back around and kissed her cheek. She stood in the open doorway as he walked toward his Kia. The porch light was off. Night had come quickly. Her boy was nothing more than a suggestion of Ombré Leather and perspiration as he climbed into his car. The engine cranked. The headlights flickered on. He reversed out into the street so fast that he nearly clipped the mailbox.

"Faith?"

"Fuck!" She jumped back, her hand reaching for the Glock that wasn't there.

"Sorry." Sara was lurking in the shadows. All that Faith could see was the wild curls in her hair. "I meant to call on my way, but I forgot my phone."

Faith tried to swallow her heart out of her throat. "Where's your car?"

"I walked here."

"From your house?" Faith knew the route, which was filled with junkies and homeless people. "Are you crazy?"

"Possibly." Sara turned toward the street where a neighbor was walking his dog. "Somebody offered me twenty bucks for a blowjob. That's low, right? I've got all my teeth."

"Teeth aren't necessarily a positive."

Faith switched on the porch light. She was stunned by what she saw. Sara's auburn hair was a mess. Her clothes were wrinkled. Faith knew she had testified at the Dani Cooper trial today. Obviously, Sara had traded out her heels for sneakers and slogged the two miles to Faith's house. Her eyes were bloodshot. She'd clearly been crying. And probably had a few drinks, judging by the fact that she'd risked hepatitis rather than getting behind the wheel of her BMW.

Faith waved her in. "Come inside. It's cold."

"Do you have alcohol?"

"No, but my mom's in Vegas and there's a full bar at her house."

"Deal me in."

Evelyn's place was only three streets over. Faith

grabbed her keys off the hook and locked the door. She shivered from the chilly night air as she walked down the concrete stairs. She didn't bother to go back for her jacket. There was something bracing about the cold.

Sara was waiting for her on the sidewalk. She'd clearly come here to talk, but she kept silent as they walked down the road. Faith tilted back her head and looked up at the night sky. No stars. The moon was a fingernail sliver. The streetlights were so far apart that they could only occasionally see each other. Not that it mattered. Sara's expression was unreadable.

Faith decided to let her take the lead, both figuratively and literally. Sara was half a foot taller. Faith had to practically skip to keep up. They passed the man walking his dog. Because of Emma, Faith only knew her neighbors by their pets. The man was Rosco's dad. The people who lived in the yellow house were Tiger's mommies. The ancient asshole who never brought in his trashcan from the curb was Duffer's grandpa.

Sara didn't speak until they'd rounded the corner. "Have you talked to Will?"

"No," Faith said. "Do you know where he is?"

"West of Biloxi. He told me he'd be home around one tomorrow morning."

Faith looked at her watch. That was another six hours.

Sara sniffed. She pulled a tissue from her skirt pocket and wiped her nose.

Faith could count on one hand the number of times she'd seen Sara cry. "I guess the Dani Cooper trial's not going well?"

"I don't know. The verdict, I mean—I don't know which way it will go. Maybe if the jury feels sorry for Dani's parents. But then the McAllisters will appeal, which means more money, more waiting." Sara didn't sound hopeful. "I don't know."

"I'm sorry." Faith felt the need to apologize, though there was nothing more she could've done. Sara had asked her to review Dani Cooper's file. For once, Faith had agreed with a prosecutor who didn't want to indict. The evidence was thin. The GPS on Tommy's Mercedes had not been activated, so there was no way to track the car. The McAllisters' Buckhead mansion had security cameras, but weirdly, the recorders had been malfunctioning on the night in question. Likewise, the city's street cameras were out of service, but that was down to lack of funding rather than design. The only reason Dani's parents had a chance in hell of winning the judgment was because Sara was such a compelling witness. She was the only person who had heard Dani's dying words. The entire case hung on her credibility. To Faith's thinking, those were pretty damn good odds.

"What about you?" Sara rubbed her arms to fight the chill. "How's desk duty going?"

"Oh, you know," Faith said, but Sara couldn't possibly know. She had never been sidelined in her life. "Amanda's buried me in so much paperwork I can't even remember what the sun feels like."

"Was it worth pissing her off?"

"Absolutely."

Instead of laughing, Sara let the silence return. She hugged her arms to her waist and looked down at the road. Their feet made steady progress. A dog barked in the distance.

Faith took a deep, cleansing breath of cold air. She tried to let go of some of the stress in her body. No one knew where Faith was right now. No one was asking her to talk about their relationship or flooding her inbox with smiley emojis or wailing at her because their Totoro blankie was in the washer, or casually confessing that they had violated section 1030 of the federal criminal code, aka the 1986 Computer Fraud and Abuse Act.

They turned another corner at the house where Pappi's mommy and daddy lived. Up ahead, Faith could see the soft glow of her mother's porch light. Evelyn stocked a very good bar. Faith could use a drink right now. She would have to check her insulin pump. Fortunately, she had a doctor two feet away from her. She was about to ask Sara what to do, but she didn't have time to get the question out of her mouth.

Sara said, "I was raped."

Faith stumbled, catching herself at the last minute. She felt as if she had been punched in the face. "What?"

Sara didn't repeat herself. She was watching Faith closely, gauging her reaction. "I'm sorry."

"I—" Faith could feel tears in her eyes. Sara was one of her closest friends. Next month, Faith was going to be Will's best man at their wedding. This felt like a physical blow. She desperately searched for the right response, but could only come up with, "When?"

"Fifteen years ago. At Grady. I'm sorry I never told you."

"It's-it's okay." Faith tried to control her tears. The worst thing she could do right now was make Sara feel like she had to comfort her. "Does Will know?"

"It was one of the first things I told him. We weren't even dating yet. I just blurted it out." Sara started walking again, but slower this time. "It tore apart my first marriage, keeping it a secret. Jeffrey saw me a certain way. He thought I was so strong. I didn't want him to see me as a victim. Please don't see me as a victim."

"I won't. I don't." Faith wiped her nose with the back of her sleeve. She couldn't think of what to say other than, "I'm sorry."

"Don't be," Sara said. "I despise having that asterisk by my name. Not Sara the doctor or the medical examiner or the daughter or the sister or the friend or the colleague. Sara the rape victim."

Faith understood the anger in her voice. This was about the trial, Sara's testimony. Defense attorneys were not known for their discretion. Faith could only imagine how gleefully Douglas Fanning had torn into her. No wonder she needed a drink.

Sara said, "I don't want to be defined by one of the worst things that ever happened to me, you know?"

Faith could feel Sara staring at her again. She was so wary of how Faith might or might not respond. Faith decided to own it. "I'm not sure what to say other than I'm sorry and telling you I'm sorry is so fucking useless."

Sara gave a dry laugh. "Most people want to know if he was caught."

Faith took it as a sign of her own shock that she hadn't. "Was he?"

"Yes. He was the head janitor in the emergency department. There was a trial. You can find the transcript on PACER. It would be easier for me if you read it instead of me telling you the gory details."

"I don't have to—"

"You can, though," Sara insisted. "I don't mind because it's you. He was sentenced to eight years. He got out and raped two more women. I wasn't allowed to testify at their trial. The judge said it would be prejudicial. Still, he got five more years. He's out now, but he's on parole for some other violations."

Faith was glad the asshole was being monitored, but she couldn't help but read between the lines. The man wouldn't have been working at Grady if he'd had an arrest record. Eight years was a hell of a long sentence for a first offense. Usually, they pleaded down to a lesser charge and got parole. Which meant that what had happened to Sara must have been particularly bad.

"I'm not ashamed of it," Sara said. "It wasn't my fault."

Faith knew how useless it would be to tell her she was right.

"The thing is, it's so fraught, you know? No one blames you if your car is broken into or you get robbed or your grandfather was shot by a burglar, but with rape, there's a way that people expect you to act, or talk about it or—I don't know." Sara shook her head, like it was a mystery she had spent the last fifteen years trying to solve. "Should I sound outraged, or matter-of-fact, or emotional, or devoid of emotion?"

Faith didn't have an answer.

"People always have an idea of how a rape survivor should and shouldn't exist in the world. They judge you based on how they think *they* would act if it happened to them, or how they think *you* should act, and there's no possible way to satisfy all of them. So, you just say to yourself—why? Why am I having to convince someone, usually a stranger, that I didn't deserve this traumatic, life-altering assault that happened to me? Or worse, why do I have to convince them that I'm not making it up for—for what? For attention? Or, oh, God, if they feel sorry for you and elevate you to some kind of sainthood, like you're a better person because you suffered? And should I call myself a victim or a survivor? Because sometimes, even fifteen years later, I feel like a victim. And other times I feel like, fuck yes, I'm a survivor. I'm still here, aren't I? But the words are so politicized, and it stops being about how you feel, and it becomes about how everyone else feels. And at the end of the day, it's easier to just shut up about it and try to live your life and hope—pray like hell—that it doesn't come up, so you don't have to deal with it again and again and again."

She was rambling, but Faith understood every word that had come out of her mouth. Faith had seen it happen as a cop. She had seen it happen as a woman who lived in the world. She felt it in her soul right now because what she really felt was so fucking useless. She wanted to *do* something—which wouldn't help Sara a damn bit.

She asked, "How do you feel about it?"

"Back then, I was completely broken. I couldn't concentrate at work. I stopped taking care of myself. The guy I was living with couldn't handle it. And fair enough. He didn't sign up for that." Sara hugged her arms to her waist again, but this time it seemed more for protection. "My parents eventually drove up to Atlanta and took me home. That's when it got really bad. I would panic if my mother left the room. My sister came home from college to help take care of me. My father slept on the floor with a shotgun because that was the only way I could sleep. God, it was such a horrific time for them. I still feel so guilty for putting them through it."

Faith had no doubt that she would gladly wield a shotgun against anyone who threatened her family. "How do you feel about it now?"

"I try not to think about it," Sara said. "Because if I do, what I feel is angry. So. Fucking. Angry."

They were under a streetlight. Faith could see the emotion on her face.

"I got pregnant from it."

Faith's heart felt as if it had been pierced. She had always wondered why Sara had never had kids.

"I was seven weeks. It was an ectopic pregnancy, and I knew the signs, of course I knew the signs, but I ignored the pain, and I let it get worse. Maybe part of me felt like I deserved it."

Faith watched Sara take out the tissue again and blow her nose.

"My tube ruptured before my aunt could get me to the hospital. Uterine atony led to uncontrolled bleeding and—and that's why I can't have children. They had to remove my uterus."

Sara shrugged as if it was nothing, but Faith had seen how much she adored children. It was everything.

"The fact that I was raped—I was resigned to that getting out during my testimony at Dani's trial. It's part of the public record. It's bound to come out eventually. But the pregnancy, and what I lost because of it, that's my private stuff. It wasn't brought up in the original trial against the man who assaulted me. I refused to testify against him unless it was kept out. But I've come to terms with the loss. I had to. And it's a tragedy, but I don't want people to think that I'm some kind of tragic figure. That's not who I am."

She was looking at Faith, almost daring her to argue.

Faith asked, "How would Douglas Fanning be able to legally access your medical information? Even if it was fifteen years ago, there are laws about—"

"Britt McAllister," Sara spat out the name. "She was friends with the attending who was on call when I was brought into Emory Hospital. He told her. Britt told everyone else."

"But, legally, a doctor can't . . ." Faith let her voice trail off, because at the end of the day, it didn't really matter.

"I've been living under this crushing dread for the last six months. Talking about it in open court—laying out my life for everyone to pick apart—I kept going over it in my head. How should I act? What should I say? How do I even describe it? As a woman? As a doctor?" Sara's voice was filled with anguish. "Most people don't understand what an ectopic pregnancy even is. The egg is literally outside of the uterus. There's no chance for it to become viable, but the treatment falls under abortion, which means that Douglas Fanning could tell the jury that I had an abortion. It doesn't matter that I was going to die without it. All Fanning needed was one juror taking against me and everything Dani's parents have been through—losing their daughter, losing their marriage, their life's savings—would have been for nothing."

Faith's jaw clenched. She often hated the world, but not with this intensity.

"I told the Coopers what might happen. I didn't want them to be blindsided, but they still wanted me to testify. They needed me to testify." Sara bit her lip, fighting back her grief. "I'm the only person who heard Dani. It was entirely on me to tell her story. And Fanning, the fucking Shark, all he had to do was make me seem like a bitter, barren, hysterical, baby killer who screams rape everywhere she goes."

Faith had never met a defense attorney who didn't go for the jugular. She silently cursed herself for not taking time off work to be at the trial today. "How did he bring it up?"

"He didn't." Sara's tone was filled with surprise, like she still couldn't believe it. "Six months of fighting off panic attacks, and he didn't mention it."

Faith felt her eyebrows knit. "Why?"

"Maybe the focus groups and jury consultants got into his head. I'm an articulate, college-educated, straight white woman with a medical degree on her wall and an engagement ring on her finger. That probably counted for way more than it should."

Faith had seen how Sara's intelligence and confidence could intimidate lesser men. She knew there was more to the story. "That's good, right? The jury liked you, so they'll believe you're being honest about what Dani told you."

"Maybe," Sara allowed. "Fanning still drew some blood. He made it seem like I'm holding a grudge against Mac McAllister for winning the fellowship. I was offered it. Did you know that?"

Faith shook her head. She had no idea what fellowship Sara was talking about.

"The day before I was attacked, Dr. Nygaard called me. She was going to make the official announcement the next morning. I went to the monthly mixer to celebrate. All the residents would hang out at a bar near Grady the last Friday of every month. Before that night, I had always begged off. I very rarely went to parties. I graduated high school a year early. I finished my undergrad in three years. I was always so focused on becoming the best doctor I could be, but not that night. I went out. I had one drink. Then two hours later, I clocked into Grady for my shift, and then—"

Faith watched Sara give an open-armed shrug.

"I was drugged. I don't know when, but about twenty minutes into my shift, I was talking to a patient, and I started to feel sick. I'd had a Coke in the doctors' lounge earlier. Maybe he spiked it. I poured it from a bottle in the fridge that had my name on it." Sara turned to Faith. "He was the head janitor. He'd just cleaned the lounge. He also had all the keys. The staff bathroom was locked, so I had to use the patient restrooms. Clever, right? Like closing off a maze so the mouse goes in the right direction?"

Faith said nothing as Sara looked down at the ground. She clearly needed a moment to collect herself.

"There was caution tape over the regular stall, so I had to go into the handicap one," Sara said. "He was so fast. He'd thought it through. My mouth was taped shut before I could think to scream. I tried to fight back, but he handcuffed me to the rails."

Faith's cop brain stirred. Unlawful restraint.

"He stabbed me. He used a hunting knife."

Serious bodily harm.

"The serrated blade went in here." She put her hand to her left side. "The same place Dani had a superficial laceration. Almost exact."

Faith knew the spot. She had seen the photos from Dani Cooper's autopsy.

"The day before it happened, someone keyed the word *cunt* into the side of my car."

Faith flinched at the disgusting word.

"I thought it was Britt. She despised any woman who worked with Mac. She thought we were all trying to steal her husband. I wouldn't put it past her to trash my car."

Faith had met that kind of woman at every stage of her life. But that wasn't the point of what Sara was telling her. "You see a pattern."

"I see a *connection*." Sara put a weird emphasis on the word. "Dani was sent threatening messages. I was sent a threatening message. Dani was at a party. I was at a party. Dani was drugged. I was drugged. Dani was raped. I was raped. Dani was wounded on her left side. I was wounded on my left side. Dani died at Grady. I nearly died at Grady."

Faith silently repeated each detail back in her head. She could see what Sara was talking about, but as a cop, she could also see the cold, hard truth.

"Sara, I'm not taking away from anything you're saying, but a lot of women are drugged and raped. Tens of thousands, maybe hundreds of thousands, of women every year." They were away from the streetlights. Faith couldn't evaluate her reaction. "The detail about the wound on her side, yeah, that's a weird coincidence."

"But?"

"What's the statistic? Every two minutes in America another woman is raped?" Faith had looked up the harrowing figure when she'd found out she was carrying a girl. "The thing about these guys is that for the most part, they're all so fucking predictable. They all go by the same playbook: stalk, harass, threaten, rape. What happened to you is—I don't even have words for it, and I don't want to diminish your experience. But it happens a lot. Every day. Every two minutes."

"No connection, then?" Sara asked. "It's just bad luck?"

"The worst luck."

"That's what I thought, too." Sara stopped walking. She turned to look at Faith. "Until Britt McAllister told me it wasn't."

Hi Leighann! Checking that you found that book on the
Protestant Reformation?

Lol wut?

Luther and Cajetan at the Imperial Diet, Augsburg, 1519?
You were asking about it at the library last week?

Who dis?
Librarian?

Love your sense of humor!
I knew I had a copy at home.
I could drop it by your place if you want?

Wrong # sry

You don't care about the Reformation anymore?
Gonna be hard making a 95 on your thesis.

v funny is this Jake?
U asshole
Fking had me bro

Not Jake. Remember he was going hiking this weekend?
Broke up with Kendra before they could pack the car.
Went on his own.
We can laugh about it when I bring the book.
You're still in the Windsong Apartments, right?
#403-B?

Uhhhh no rly who is this?
That's not where I live
Moved last month
Staying w/parents

That's funny, Leighann.
Like I didn't see you walking around your bedroom
last night . . .
in your thin white T-shirt and silky pink panties . . .

Who the fuck is this?
My dad is a cop.
I am calling him now.

Wow that's really cool!
Does Coca-Cola know their IT director is working two jobs?

No kidding STOP this shit isn't funny

Wish I could STOP thinking about that tight T-shirt.
The way it shows off your breasts.
How I want to kiss them and bite your nipples with my teeth
. . . again . . .

Who the fuck are you?

You'll need a hand-held mirror.
There's one in the drawer where you keep your make-up.
Look for the small black circle on the back of your left knee.
The one that looks like someone drew it with a Sharpie.
That's me.

3

Will Trent sat at the back of the packed GBI training room trying not to fall asleep. The lights were off. Heat was blasting through the air vents. The monitor at the front of the room was flickering. The screen on Faith's laptop kept up a steady glow as she perused 3M's corporate website.

They were supposed to be learning how to use the GBI's updated software, but the guy leading the tutorial had the kind of voice that was indistinguishable from the grind of the compressor on an old air conditioner. Worse, he kept waving his hands in the air, wielding his laser pointer like a methed-out Darth Vader. Will had already developed a fantasy about the laser temporarily blinding him so that he had a valid excuse to crash on the couch in his office and sleep.

"Now," the Compressor said. "If you look at section G, you'll notice it's very similar to the earlier version marked D. But don't be fooled."

Will couldn't fight it anymore. He closed his eyes. His chin dipped down to his chest. His undercover assignment had required him to work for twenty-four hours a day over fourteen consecutive days. He'd spent most of last night and part of the early morning driving nearly six hours straight down unlit, Podunk highways. He'd come home to a woman who had vigorously distracted him from rest and three dogs who had gotten used to sleeping on his side of the bed.

His body ached. His skull felt like it was in a vise. He was punch-drunk from exhaustion.

Faith elbowed him before his head gonged into the desk.

Will squinted at the screen as a new slide came up. He felt a sharp stinging at the corner of his eye. He'd turned into the wrong side of a fist and lost some skin in the process. He'd suffered far more dire but less aggravating wounds. It was like the worst paper cut ever, but on his face.

"Then there's this new area in blue," the Compressor said. "The keen-eyed among you might think this looks familiar. I'll say it again. Don't be fooled."

Faith let out a long, audible sigh.

Will glanced down at her laptop. She'd been tapping on the keyboard from the start, but as far as Will could tell, she'd spent the entire time texting with her mother, price-matching a tricycle, bidding on a glass windchime, clicking links to 3M's global research laboratories, and occasionally checking an interactive map that seemed to be connected to a live GPS tracker.

He looked ahead. Tried to read the slide. The words jumbled together, letters bouncing around like fleas. His eyelids felt heavy again.

Without warning, the overhead lights came on.

Will squinted against the stabbing pain in his retinas. Then against the paper cut in the corner of his eye.

The Compressor made a hacking noise that was probably meant to be a laugh. "I'll see you guys after the break."

"Oh, God," Faith mumbled. "There's more?"

Will had to ask, "The last hour was about form 503 being replaced with 1632, right?"

"Yes."

"And the stuff we usually put in the green box goes in the blue box now?"

"Right."

"That's it?"

"That's it," she said. "The rest was a recap of the same shit we've been doing since I got here."

Will looked at his watch. The break was only fifteen minutes. "Did you talk to Sara this morning?"

"Yep."

Will carefully studied the side of Faith's face, because she had stopped looking at him and was suddenly very interested in her eBay auction.

He asked, "How's she doing?"

"Sara?" Faith slowly scrolled through the description she had read half an hour ago. "Great. She looks really beautiful today."

Sara looked really beautiful every day, but that wasn't the issue. Will had been partnered with Faith Mitchell for nearly five years. During that time, he had known her to be both a prolific and accomplished liar.

Until now.

Before he could press her for details, Will heard a sharp snapping sound, like someone was making some very angry popcorn.

"You two," Deputy Chief Amanda Wagner called from the doorway. She was wearing one of her dark red power suits with a pair of black stilettos. Her salt-and-pepper hair had been freshly helmeted. She glanced at her watch, clearly annoyed that snapping her fingers hadn't made them jump to attention.

She said, "Let's go. I don't have all day."

Will groaned as he stood. The desk was not built for

a 6' 3" man who was trying to sleep. He was limping by the time he reached the door.

Amanda gave him a suspicious look, like he had broken himself on purpose. "What's wrong with you?"

Will declined to answer.

Faith said, "Please tell me someone's been brutally murdered so we don't have to sit through the second part of this class."

Amanda leveled her with a look. "You're working murder cases from your desk now?"

Faith also declined to answer.

"My office." Amanda started up the hallway at a brisk pace, her pointy heels sinking into the industrial carpet like vampire teeth. She had her phone in her hand because she couldn't take more than a few steps without alerting the rest of her coven.

Will let Faith go ahead of him because Amanda got annoyed when he cast her in shadow. They all matched Amanda's quick steps to the end of the hall, then went single file down the flight of stairs. He watched the tops of their heads bob in front of him, one salty, one blond.

He should've been at least curious about why Amanda was taking them to her office, but Will was gripped by the sudden need to talk to Sara. Something had felt off last night. And this morning. She was gone by the time he'd gotten out of the shower. No kiss. No note. Definitely not like her. Will had chalked it up to re-entry pains after being apart for two weeks. Now, Faith's uncharacteristic lack of believable duplicity had him concerned.

Amanda had stopped at the door. Will reached forward and held it open, then he followed them down the next hallway.

Last night, Sara had told him that the trial had gone as well as could be expected. Douglas Fanning had gotten in some hits, but her private life and the intimate details of her loss had not been opened up for dissection. Now that Will silently rewound the conversation, he realized that Sara hadn't sounded relieved. She hadn't acted relieved, either. Which was odd. Sara had worried about the trial for months. She had lost sleep, was up at weird times reading or going for a run or staring out the window. Sometimes, she'd needed distractions, other times, she'd asked to be alone.

Will hadn't begrudged her any of it. He knew her dread, had lived it most of his life. There were details about his childhood that he didn't want people picking apart, either. A guy who had grown up in an orphanage wasn't generally the type of guy who liked to talk about why he'd grown up in an orphanage.

"Faith." Amanda was still typing on her phone as

she walked into her office. "When will those reports be completed?"

Faith gave Will an eye roll. "I've made my way through half of—"

"Email them all to me by the end of the day." Amanda dropped her phone on the desk. She crossed her arms. "Bernice's daughter had her baby."

Faith made the soft noises women make when they hear about babies.

Will waited for the noises to turn into a curse. Bernice Hodges was in charge of the GBI's anti-fraud unit. They worked in concert with the federal government to prosecute able-bodied people who were illegally collecting disability payments. Someone would need to cover for Bernice while she helped take care of her daughter.

"Fuck." Faith had finally gamed out the baby news. "You want us to sneak around with a camera trying to catch some criming jackass doing CrossFit?"

"That's exactly what I want you to do," Amanda said. "Do you have a problem with that?"

"Hell yes I have a—" Faith put her fist to her mouth to physically shut herself up. She took a breath before continuing, "Ma'am, don't you feel like our skills would be better suited working more pressing cases?"

"The GBI's anti-fraud unit helped save the state of Georgia ninety million dollars last year. I'd call that very pressing." Amanda's desk phone started ringing. She took off her gold hoop earring and lifted the receiver. She listened for a second, then told Will and Faith, "Step out into the hall."

Faith dragged her feet all the way out the door.

She looked up at Will. "It's not just me, right? This is bullshit."

Will didn't disagree, but there were more important things on his mind. "Did you talk to Sara while I was gone?"

Faith was suddenly very interested in her phone. "Yeah, why?"

"Did she say anything to you about the trial?"

"Just that she was glad it was over." Faith kept looking at her phone. She had opened an email, but she didn't seem to be reading it. Or typing a response. Or commenting on how stupid it was.

Will heard Amanda slam the phone back into the cradle.

"Faith," she called. "Bernice is waiting for you downstairs. Go do the handover. Will, come back in and close the door."

Faith closed the door before he could, and not too gently. The photos on Amanda's walls shook.

Amanda ignored the slight, sitting behind her desk. She stared at Will like an anaconda. "What happened to your eye?"

"Pinky ring."

"And the owner of the ring?"

"Won't be using that hand for a while."

"Stop hovering." She pointed for Will to sit. "I don't have time to read your report. Bulletpoint it for me."

Will burned through a full three seconds trying to switch his brain into the right gear. He'd spent the last two weeks hanging around the periphery of a Mississippi militia as part of a fact-finding mission for the FBI's domestic terrorism team. The work was as grueling as it was tedious. Or maybe Will was getting to a point in his life where not regularly showering, eating or sleeping had lost its appeal.

He said, "White supremacists. Heavily armed. Poorly trained. Hate the government. Love tequila, but not where it comes from. Some military role-play, but none of them served. That's where the pinky ring came in. Guy was stoned out of his mind. Tried to coldcock me. Paid the price. Mostly they drink too much and smoke too much and whine about how much they hate their wives and wanna strangle their girlfriends."

"It's funny how you never meet a white supremacist

who's also a feminist." Amanda steepled together her fingers on her desk. "How's Faith?"

He feigned ignorance. "She seems fine to me."

"Really?" Amanda didn't buy it, but she had to know Will wasn't going to rat out his partner. Faith assumed that she had been put on desk duty because she'd mouthed off one too many times to Amanda. The truth was that the last case they'd worked had gotten to her in a bad way. If Will was being honest, it had gotten to him, too. He wasn't completely unhappy about pointing a camera out of a van window for a couple of weeks.

Amanda ordered, "You're going to tell me if Evelyn needs to come home."

Evelyn was Faith's mother. She was also Amanda's former partner and best friend, which made Faith's life as difficult as you'd think.

He nodded, but said, "She'll be fine."

"Do you know how to dance?"

Will was used to Amanda's sudden changes in subject, but this time it was like she had made up a new language.

She said, "For your wedding. Next month."

Will rubbed his jaw with his fingers. They were having a small get-together at Sara's condo, nothing fancy. No more than thirty people.

"Wilbur." Amanda walked around her desk and

sat down beside him. He often forgot how tiny she was. Sitting on the edge of the chair, she looked small enough to fit in his pocket, if he was the type of man who would put a live scorpion in his pocket.

She said, "I know your first marriage was a sham, but at real weddings, the bride and the groom have to dance together."

"Technically, it wasn't a sham. It was a double-dog dare."

Amanda gave him a sharp look, like he was the only one making a joke. "Sara's family is very traditional, so she'll probably start the dance with her father, then he'll hand her off to you."

Will shook his head. He had no idea where Amanda was going with this.

Then she placed her hand on his arm. "You need to start practicing now. Don't worry about the music. Every slow song has the same beat. Find some videos on YouTube."

"I—" He fought the need to stutter. She was actually being serious. "What?"

"Practice, Wilbur." She patted his arm, then stood up and walked back around her desk. "Everyone will be watching. Sara's family, her aunts and uncles, her cousins, their spouses."

Will had a vague recollection of Sara explaining that

this person was her great-uncle on her dad's side and that person was a second cousin of her mother's and then the Hawks had started a twelve-point comeback and his attention had turned away from what he now realized was a very important conversation.

Amanda said, "You could always take lessons."

Will was not going to say *what* again. "Lessons?"

"Give a man a parachute, he flies one time. Push a man out of an airplane, he flies for the rest of his life." She picked up her desk phone. Started punching numbers. "Why are you still here?"

Will stood up. He left her office. He pulled the door closed behind him. He walked to the end of the hall. He went into the stairwell, but he was denied a moment to ponder what the hell had just happened because Faith was waiting for him at the top of the landing.

She asked, "What did Amanda say to you?"

"The—" Will had to take another second to reset. "She asked me to run down my undercover."

"And?"

"And then she said I should take dance lessons before the wedding."

"That's not a bad idea. FYI, your best man will be dancing with every dude under eighty while her grown son sulks in the corner." Faith clearly thought that settled it. She started walking down the stairs. "This fraud assignment is Amanda's way of shoveling another load of shit down my throat. I know I shouldn't have yelled at her, but come on. The last time you pissed her off, you got airport duty for one week. This is going on a month."

Will circled back to more important things. "You and I were talking about Sara before."

"Were we?" Faith rounded the next landing, but not before he caught the panicked look on her face. "What I'm worried about is my boss not letting me do my job."

Will hadn't brought worry into the conversation, but now he was wondering if he should be worried about Sara.

"Do you know how heartless fraud investigations can be?" Faith demanded. "I mean sure, some of them are thieving, lazy assholes, but then some of them are just getting by. So what if they have a good day and they can garden outside with their grandkids? I'm gonna jump out of a bush with a camera and take away their disability?"

Will had realized a long time ago that Faith had a weirdly sympathetic streak for people who screwed over the federal government. It was the one characteristic she shared with the Mississippi militiamen.

He tried, "Maybe it's good to ease back into the job. Good for me, I mean."

"Good for you?" She had been reaching for the door, but she spun around to glare at him. "What the hell does that mean?"

Will realized he had walked into a trap. This was the thing about Faith lately: she had always been easily annoyed, but after working their last case, she was easily enraged. Which was why she'd been on desk duty and why they were taking over for Bernice when the anti-fraud team was perfectly capable of covering for her.

Faith was still waiting for an answer. "Why is a bull-shit assignment good for you, Will?"

"You know what it's like to go undercover." She had never worked undercover. "I've been living in the woods for two weeks. I need some time to bring my detective skills back online."

"Seriously?" Her voice had turned hard. "I don't need my hand held. Especially by you. I'm fine. I can do my fucking job."

Will knew that if she was really fine, she wouldn't be this angry. "Let's take a beat."

"You're telling me to take a beat? I don't need a fuck-ing beat. I need to be doing my job like I was trained to do." She was practically yelling at him. "I didn't waltz into my badge like you did, Will. I came up working the streets. I pulled over drug dealers for speeding in the middle of the night who could've shot me in the face, and then I went home and took care of my kid and I was fine. Do you hear me? I was fucking fine then, and I'm fucking fine now."

"You're right." He wasn't going to give her the fight she clearly wanted. "I know."

"You know? You know?" She couldn't stop scratching for blood. "You know who doesn't need your condescending bullshit right now? Here's a clue, detective: her fucking name rhymes with Maith."

Will held up his hands in surrender.

"Fuck you." She jerked open the door and stormed into the hall.

He let the door close behind her. He watched Faith through the glass. She stopped outside Bernice's office and forced her fists to unclench before going inside.

The first time Faith had gone off on him like this, Will had been concerned. Now he knew to let it go. One good thing about growing up in state care was that it taught you people had to figure out their own shit. You couldn't do it for them.

Will's office was one floor up, but he headed down to the ground floor instead. Will shouldered open the emergency exit door, then shielded his eyes from the sudden glare of sunlight. The wind sliced through the open space between the main building and the recently expanded morgue facilities. Will looked down at the ground as he followed the path. There were two vans parked outside the new part of the building. He skirted through an open bay door.

The first thing that hit him was the smell, which wasn't from the dead bodies but from the chemicals they used to clean them. Two weeks away wasn't long, but it was an odor anybody would be eager to forget. He felt his eyes sting from the pungent, vinegary floor wax as he headed down the long hallway toward the back office. One side of the walls was covered with photographs of crime scenes and highly detailed pieces of evidence. The other side had glass windows over-looking the autopsy suite. A junior medical examiner was suiting up beside a body. Male. Gunshot wound to the head. The skull had split open.

Will heard Sara's voice before he saw her. She was clearly on the phone. Her office was inside the main building, but she usually transcribed her autopsy notes inside a former storage closet. A desk and office chair had been wedged against the wall. A folding chair was crammed into the corner beside it.

He stood in the doorway, but Sara had no idea that he was there. Her GBI phone was peeking out beneath scattered pages of notes. He counted at least three pens, probably because she had a habit of misplacing them.

Her personal phone was stuck between her shoulder and ear while she typed on her laptop.

"Correct, but the picture you sent me looks like she's using a quadrupod grasp." Sara ran her finger down her handwritten notes, double-checking herself against the form on her laptop. "No, I wouldn't worry. It's less efficient, but she's basically a genius, so who cares?"

Will assumed that Sara was talking to her sister. Tessa and her daughter had moved into Sara's building last month, but they still spoke on the phone at least once, sometimes twice a day, often about their mother, who Sara usually talked to every other day, and Will had been told that all of this was perfectly normal.

He knocked on the open door.

Sara turned, smiling when she saw him. She reached out to hold his hand. "Tessie, I have to go."

Will waited for her to end the call before he leaned down and kissed her cheek. She smelled a hell of a lot better than the rest of the building.

Sara pointed to her laptop. "Can you give me a second?"

Will sat in the chair beside her desk while she finished. He turned so that he could take in the view. Faith had been sort of truthful about one thing, at least. Sara didn't just look beautiful today. She looked fucking hot.

Her hair was down around her shoulders. Her make-up was darker than usual. Instead of her usual scrubs, she was wearing a nicely fitted green dress that showed off her legs and a pair of shoes that had cost more than two of Will's monthly paychecks, which he only knew because he'd accidentally seen the receipt and felt like an electric cattle prod was pressed against his testicles.

"Okay." Sara closed the laptop and turned to Will. "That was Tessa on the phone. She's worried about the way Isabelle is gripping her pencil."

Tessa's daughter was a little older than Faith's. "Is that a thing?"

"Yes, but also no. Tessa's deflecting. Lem's being an asshole about the divorce." She took off her glasses. "Aren't you supposed to be in software training right now?"

Will was exactly where he was supposed to be. "Are we going to dance together at our wedding?"

Sara's face lit up with a smile. "Don't you want to?"

He guessed that he did now. "What rhymes with Maith?"

Sara's brow furrowed. "Context?"

"Something Faith said to me. 'Her name rhymes with Maith.'"

"Faith rhymes with Maith. Your dyslexia doesn't like that kind of wordplay." Sara was smiling again, but she started twisting her engagement ring around her finger. "Orthographic processing allows you to visualize letter symbols in your mind's eye, which helps you decipher that particular type of rhyme. Your brain uses a different area for language processing."

Will figured he should use his brain to process what was going on right in front of him. Something was clearly wrong with Sara. She was fidgeting. She never fidgeted. "Did you tell Tessa about Dani's trial yet?"

The smile faltered. Sara shook her head. She hadn't told her family anything about Dani Cooper, which was very unlike her and, in retrospect, had been a giant red flag that Will had missed.

She said, "Maybe it will help you better contextualize a rhyme if I show you how your brain processes the information."

Tessa was good at deflecting, but Sara was a master.

He watched her flip over a sheet of paper and start drawing what he guessed was supposed to be his brain. Her engagement ring stood in sharp contrast to her pricey clothes. One of the few items that Will had left of his mother was her collection of costume jewelry. She'd been a teenager when she'd died, working as a prostitute on the Atlanta streets. Her tastes had not been sophisticated. For some reason, Will had thought it was a good idea to propose to Sara with one of his mother's rings. He'd chosen the green glass because it matched her eyes.

Sara treated it like it was a diamond.

"This area"—she tapped the drawing with her pen—"that's where a typical brain—"

Will covered her hand with his.

He used his foot to ease the door closed. "Tell me about last night."

"What about it?"

"Things got a little rough."

"Isn't that what I asked for?"

She had raised her eyebrow. A challenge, but also another deflection. Sara was fiercely intelligent, sometimes to her own detriment. Will remembered the abject terror that had kept him from asking her out the first time they'd met. And the second time. And the fifth and sixth time. He'd kept retreating into his familiar place, what Sara called his awkward silence.

Now he used the silence strategically.

Sara didn't last long.

"Are you saying you didn't enjoy it?" Her smile had lost its tease. "All I have to do is sneeze really hard to prove you wrong."

Will smiled, too, but he kept pressing. "What happened at the trial yesterday?"

"I told you." Sara slipped away her hand. She sat

back in her chair. Suddenly, there was a lot of space between them. "I nailed my testimony. Douglas Fanning lost his nerve. Court is in recess tomorrow. The judge wants the lawyers to talk about a settlement, which won't happen because the Coopers don't want money. They want the world to know that Tommy McAllister is the reason that she died."

Will studied her expression. There was no crack in her armor. She was putting on that side of herself that was completely in control.

He said, "I was thinking about the last case we worked together."

Sara pressed together her lips. The last case was the same case that was causing Faith to show every symptom of post-traumatic stress disorder.

Will said, "One of the victims, she told you that after it happened, after she was raped, that she couldn't be with a man unless he was hurting her. Do you remember?"

Sara's lips parted for air, but she didn't look away.

"The woman asked you if you ever felt that way, too," Will said. "You told her that you did."

"Sometimes," Sara corrected. "I told her I felt that way *sometimes*."

"Was last night one of those times?"

"You would never hurt me."

"Did you want me to?"

Sara took another shallow breath. She looked up at the ceiling. She shook her head, but not to disagree with him. He had seen her do this before. She was hardening her defenses, forcing down her feelings. Which was a great trick in a lot of situations, but not this one.

He said, "This Superwoman version of Sara that you're showing right now—you can do that for yourself, but you don't ever have to do it for me."

Sara finally broke, but not by much. Tears welled in her eyes. She used the tips of her fingers to try to hold them back. "I didn't tell you last night because I was afraid that you would make me do the right thing."

Will shook his head, but not only because he would never try to make Sara do anything she didn't want to do. In the years that he had known her, she had always been driven to do the right thing.

"I don't want to do it, Will. I don't want to sacrifice my—my sanity. My sense of self. I don't want to go back to that dark place. I don't want to put my family through it. To put you through it." She leaned forward, her hands clasped between her knees. "I'm not sure I'll survive it."

Will felt her anxiety like a metal strap tightening around his chest. "What happened?"

Sara placed her hand over her heart as if she needed

to protect it. "I had this—I don't know what to call it—altercation? With Britt yesterday. We were in the bathroom. I'd just finished testifying. She came in and—"

Sara tried to wipe her eyes again. There was no holding back her tears now. Will reached into his pocket and offered his handkerchief. Sara held on to his fingers for a moment. Then she took a deep breath like she was about to dive to the bottom of the ocean.

"Britt admitted that she knows Tommy is responsible for Dani Cooper's death."

Will's surprise was only momentary. He understood the implications. Sara had been devastated when the criminal case against Tommy McAllister had fallen apart. Britt had handed Sara the prosecution on a silver platter. "Is she willing to go on the record? How does she know?"

"No, she won't go on the record. She was stoned out of her mind when she told me. And then she realized she'd said too much and turned into an absolute bitch again."

Will kept Sara's original fear at the front of his mind. She was worried that he would make her do the right thing. So far, there was nothing wrong that she had done. "What else did Britt say?"

"That she hoped the trial would stop Tommy. That there was still a chance for him to be a good man."

Will doubted that. He knew from the private investigator's report that Tommy had been accused of rape before. He also knew that rape was seldom a one-off crime.

He asked, "What else?"

Sara folded the handkerchief, finding a fresh section to dab under her eyes. Will waited for her to continue. He had learned the hard way that Sara had almost perfect recall. She had probably spent every second since the altercation reciting the exchange in her head.

"She—" Sara's voice caught. "She said that what happened to me fifteen years ago—when I was raped— that it wasn't because of bad luck."

"What else could it be?"

"I don't know." Sara gave up on drying her tears. She placed his handkerchief on the desk. "The obvious interpretation would be that it wasn't luck, it was by design, right? But how is that possible?"

Will didn't know the answer, but he had met women like Britt McAllister before. They weaponized their bitterness against everyone else. His ex-wife had been exactly the same way.

He asked, "Is there any chance that she was just fucking with you?"

"Possibly?" Sara shrugged, but more out of hope. "She connected them, Will. She told me that what happened to me and what happened to Dani, that they were both connected. That's the word she used—connected."

Sara was looking at him with such intense need that he knew this was the important part. Everything else had been leading to this moment. This was the intersection between right and wrong.

He asked, "Did she tell you how they're connected?"

"No. She laughed in my face and walked out, but—" Sara had to stop to catch her breath again. "Dani was stalked. She was threatened. She was at a party. She was drugged. She was raped. She was cut here, on her left side."

Will watched Sara touch her fingers just beneath her ribs. He had seen the scar from the hunting knife at least a thousand times. His mouth knew the jagged shape by heart.

"Britt said it's not a coincidence. You see it, too, right?"

Will silently replayed what Sara had told him about the bathroom altercation, trying to put it all together in his mind. Then he added another piece of information that had fallen to the wayside. "You told Faith all of this last night?"

A look of remorse flashed in her eyes. "I'm so sorry. I should've come to you first."

"I don't care about that." He reached for her hands, trying to allay her guilt. "What did Faith think?"

Sara didn't answer immediately. She looked down at their intertwined fingers. Her thumb stroked the back of his hand. "That the way Britt broke down over it, the way she was practically praying in the bathroom that the trial would stop Tommy—that means that there are probably other victims we don't know about. And if there are previous victims, there will be potential new victims. Britt was hoping the fear of prosecution would stop him, but it won't stop him."

Will knew Faith had told Sara more than that. "Faith sees the connection, too, right? Britt's lived in fear of Tommy turning into Mac. Tommy is a rapist. You were raped fifteen years ago. Mac was someone you worked with. So, was Mac involved in what happened to you?"

"That's the brick wall Faith and I kept hitting our heads against. I knew the man who raped me. I saw his face while it was happening. His identity was never in doubt. He went on to rape again. Mac has never had anything like that in his past. He was an arrogant prick, but his reputation was spotless."

"Did Mac know—"

"They didn't know each other." Sara would never say her rapist's name, nor did she ever want to hear it. "Mac's the kind of asshole who snaps his fingers at waiters. There's no way he would be friends with a hospital janitor. And even if they were, you're talking about a level of collusion that would require a tremendous amount of trust. The man who raped me served eight years hard time. His lawyer was a public defender. He's still on parole."

"Say the crazy part out loud," Will told her. "What are the chances that Mac bribed the janitor to rape you so that he would get that fellowship you were both up for? Or maybe Britt bribed him herself?"

"He's a serial rapist. He doesn't need cash to compel him."

"I said it's crazy," Will reminded her. "What are the chances?"

"Where's the money?" Sara asked, and it was a good question. "Britt and Mac are multimillionaires. The janitor still lives in poverty. His parole officer told me he's living in a halfway house off Lawrenceville Highway. If he did it for money before, it's impossible to think that he wouldn't blackmail Mac or Britt for more money now. They could give him enough cash to leave the country. He might be a sadistic rapist, but he's not stupid."

Will knew what she was saying was true. He was also a cop. He could only see one path forward—the path that Faith would've seen last night, the path that

Sara clearly wanted to avoid. "When two things are connected, you investigate both things. So, in order to look at what Tommy's been up to, we'd have to look into what happened to you. And if we're good at our jobs and find the connection that Britt is talking about, that means there's a criminal prosecution, and if there's a criminal prosecution—"

"I would have to testify in open court about everything that happened to me fifteen years ago."

Sara's tears were falling in earnest now. She looked afraid, which was the hardest part for Will to see. She had spent more than a decade trying to work through what had happened to her at Grady. She still carried the scars from that day. He had seen them on display as recently as last night. Sometimes, the world could make you feel so numb that the only emotion that could cut through was pain.

He got down on his knees in front of her. He cupped her face between his hands. He looked her in the eye. "There's no right or wrong here. There's only what you can live with. All you have to know is that I've got you either way."

"I know you do." She took another deep, bottom-of-the-ocean breath. She had made her decision. "I promised Dani I would do everything I could to stop Tommy. If that means exposing my life to strangers, then that's what I'll have to do. I couldn't live with myself if I let her down."

Will's heart broke a little, because for the last six months he had watched Sara living with the abject terror of that very thing happening. He stroked back her hair, tried to smooth some of the worry out of her brow. "We can keep this informal, all right? Nothing has to be official yet. We'll meet with Faith tonight and figure out the best way to go forward. Okay?"

"Okay."

Sara slid into his arms. Will could feel her body tremble as she held onto him. Even with that, he knew that some of her torment had lifted now that the choice had been made.

He asked, "Is there anything else?"

"I need to tell you about the Friday mixer."

Fifteen Years Ago

"Mixer?" Cathy Linton's voice sounded perplexed across the long-distance line. "I don't believe I understand how you're using that word."

Sara put her head in her hand. She had called her mother to tell her about being awarded the Nygaard Fellowship and now she was having to explain university Greek life. "It's a closed party between one fraternity and one sorority, usually at a frat house."

"But none of you are students anymore." Her mother was still perplexed. "And it's at a bar, so why are they calling it a mixer instead of a party?"

"Because they've spent their entire lives obsessing about who's in and out of their special little club."

"Be that as it may," Cathy allowed. "You've got the fellowship, Sara. If anyone deserves to go to this *mixer* to celebrate, it's you."

"I don't know." Sara looked at the stack of journals she needed to catch up on. Her fluffy white cat had fallen asleep on top of the pile. Apgar's head dangled off the side like a second tail. "I'm on the graveyard shift for another week."

"Then why did you bring it up?"

Sara wasn't sure anymore, but she felt like it had something to do with persuading her parents not to drive up to Atlanta to celebrate.

"You can't live like a monk," Cathy said. "You will never succeed as a doctor if you don't succeed as a human being."

Sara felt blindsided. "You think I'm failing as a human being?"

"What I am saying," Cathy began, her voice stern. "Is that I'm so happy for you right now, but you will eventually reach a point where that tight control you have over every single aspect of your life is going to fail spectacularly. Something is bound to happen. And it might be good, or it might be bad, but you'll learn something from it. And that is a profound opportunity. Change tells you who you really are."

"You're right," Sara said, though she vehemently disagreed.

If anything, now was the time to exert even more control. Sara was going to be the best surgeon that

Dr. Nygaard had ever trained. She was going to receive competitive offers from all the top hospital systems. She was going to establish a thriving practice. She was going to get married and have two children before she turned thirty-five. Hopefully, they would both be girls. Tessa would have at least three of her own by then. They would raise their kids together and live close by and everything would be perfect.

That was the plan. Nothing was going to change it.

"Sweetheart," Cathy said. "You should know by now that agreeing with me will not shut me up."

"Wouldn't that be a profound change?"

Cathy laughed. "Yes, but we have strayed from my original objective, which is to get you out of your head and into the world. You've got the fellowship. Take this one night to go out to a bar and let your hair down. Your sister does it all the time."

Her sister was currently being treated for chlamydia. "Mom, every person I work with was born to this. They had the kind of advantages that I never even knew existed."

"Is that so bad?"

"No, I'm grateful that I had to work for it, but I'm also mindful of what my family sacrificed to get me here."

"It was no sacrifice," Cathy insisted, though both of her parents had worked their asses off so that Sara's career choices were not limited by debilitating student loan debt. She would've never tried for the fellowship, let alone gotten it, without their support.

Still, her mother insisted, "If you want to pay us back, pay us with your happiness."

"I *am* happy." Sara was aware that she did not sound happy. She absently stroked the cat's head. Apgar rolled over, almost falling onto the floor. "I'm sorry, Mama. I've got a dozen articles I have to read before tomorrow. I'll go to the party next month. Mixer. Whatever they call it. All right?"

"No, it's not all right, but I've made my wishes clear. As have you. Discussing it further would be a waste of our time." Cathy's tone said that was the end of it. "Hold on. Daddy's out of the shower. He wants to congratulate you."

Sara picked up Apgar and held him in her arms. She could hear the phone cord being stretched from the kitchen into the living room. She could picture her father getting settled in his chair, strapping a heating pad on his back and ice around his knee because he'd spent his life shimmying through tight crawl spaces and fixing clogged toilets so that his oldest daughter could become a pediatric cardiothoracic fellow and his youngest daughter could become a regular patient at the Bryn Mawr free clinic.

"Sweetpea!" Eddie boomed. "I was singing in the shower and got some soap in my mouth, so it turned into a real soap opera."

Sara rolled her eyes, but she also laughed. "Daddy, that's awful."

"I can come up with a better one," he warned, but spared her the attempt. "You got the fellowship, huh?"

Sara felt a stupid grin on her face. "Yeah, Dad. I got it."

"I never doubted it for a minute," he said. "Did you?"

"Never," Sara lied. Mac McAllister had been in close contention. He had the skills, but more importantly, he had the confidence. Sara had been so stressed out about meeting Dr. Nygaard that she'd thrown up before the interview.

"Baby, I'm so damn proud of you," Eddie said. "I know how hard you've been working, but I want you to do a little something for me. Okay?"

"Okay."

"Listen to your mother and go to that fucking party."

The phone crackled again as the cord moved. He'd handed the receiver back to Cathy. Sara knew what was coming, but she waited for it anyway. Her parents often disagreed but they were always aligned.

They had both hung up on her.

Sara put the phone back on the hook. She carried Apgar around her tiny one-bedroom apartment, which she could only afford because it was over her aunt Bella's garage. Her eyes found the kitchen clock. She had five hours before her shift started. The window was closing fast if she wanted to go to the mixer. A glass of wine would take around three hours to metabolize. She felt the journals calling to her like Sirens pulling her toward the rocks. Dr. Nygaard didn't sleep. She was notorious for asking about studies that were so new the print had barely dried. Sara had already bookmarked an article on minimally invasive cardiac surgery using minithoracotomy with peripheral cannulation. Dr. Nygaard's team was actively enrolling patients into the national study. She would expect Sara to have a more than passing understanding of the procedure.

Sara was pulled out of her thoughts by the sound of a car door slamming. Apgar asked to be put down. She was filling the cat's bowl with kibble when the door opened.

Mason James asked, "Did you cut the grass?"

"I did." Sara was constantly looking for ways to thank her aunt Bella. "Two days ago."

"You remarkable creature." He held her by the arms and kissed her. "I couldn't find the damn button to turn on a lawn mower if you put a gun to my head."

Sara laughed at the thought of him even walking into the shed.

"Good evening, young man." Mason leaned down to pet Apgar. "What are your plans before your shift begins?"

Sara took a moment to realize he wasn't asking the cat. "My mother told me to go to the mixer, but—"

"Your sainted mother is right. I'd be delighted to have my gal on my arm." He kissed her again. "Let me grab a quick shower. The gang will be shocked to see you finally turn up. And in something other than scrubs."

Sara watched him go into the bedroom. The shower turned on.

The gang.

He pronounced the phrase like a character from *Gatsby.* Which he sort of was. There was a reason her sister referred to him as Sara's fancy man.

Mason James was New England born and bred. His WASPy mother exuded the warmth of dry ice. His emotionally unavailable father had started a chain of urgent care centers, then run off with his mistress. Not that Mason had spent that much time with his parents.

He'd attended a boarding school in Connecticut and done his undergrad at NYU. He'd chosen Emory medical school because he'd heard the winters were easier in Atlanta.

In fact, everything about Mason's life seemed to be in the pursuit of ease. He was exactly who Sara was talking about when she'd told her mother that the people around her were born to it. He was a good doctor—Sara couldn't be with him otherwise—but he was the very definition of a front runner. Mason was never going to work any harder than it took to stay at the front of the pack. Which was the sort of man Sara needed right now. He didn't pout if she did better than him or get jealous if she was singled out. He was very easy to be around. The sex was good. He was never going to make any demands on her and she was never going to marry him.

Sara could never give her heart to a man who didn't know how to crank a lawn mower.

She went to the closet and raked through her clothes. There wasn't much to choose from. Mason was right about the scrubs. Sara wasn't going to waste money on dresses when she could spend it on books and cat food. Fortunately, the gang tended to dress down. She settled on black leggings and a soft blue sweater from Mason's side of the closet.

Sara stood in front of the mirror. The sweater was nice, but the collar was frayed. She could see a small hole in the elbow of one of the sleeves. She would blend in perfectly with the gang. One thing she had learned about shittifyingly rich people was that they could live in squalor and walk around with holes in their clothes because all that mattered was that they were shittifyingly rich.

Mason walked into the room. Naked. Hair still damp. He gave Sara an admiring once-over. "I would like to propose an alteration to the evening's schedule."

Sara took the time to admire his body, too. She'd been working overnight shifts. He'd lucked into a long series of day shifts. They hadn't had sex in nearly three weeks. "What did you have in mind?"

"Beautiful lovemaking, then the mixer, then more beautiful lovemaking, then you go to work and Apgar and I enjoy a boy's night of single malt and *The Mentalist*."

That didn't sound like a lot of time for beautiful lovemaking, and Sara was too distracted for a quick fuck to get her over the line. "My shift starts at eleven. If I'm going to have a drink tonight, it needs to be within the next hour."

"I'll tell Apgar to set the DVR." He pulled random

clothes from the closet and started to dress. "Nygaard's announcing her decision tomorrow. That have anything to do with your first foray into the Friday mixer?"

Sara pressed together her lips.

"Unless you've already heard something?" He'd been in the middle of buttoning his jeans, but he stopped. "Have you?"

This was another reason Mason was not a long-term prospect. She didn't trust him to keep a secret. Losing the fellowship was not news that Mac McAllister deserved to hear shouted at him across a noisy bar.

She asked, "Do you think I would keep it a secret?"

"I do indeed." He seemed untroubled by the fact. He threw on a ratty old button-down shirt over his jeans and ran his fingers through his hair. "How do I look? Presentable?"

Sara thought he looked good enough to reconsider the schedule. But her mother was right about getting out more. And her father had told her to go. And it might be nice to have a drink surrounded by adults instead of sitting at the table with her head bent over the *American Journal of Neonatal and Pediatric Cardiology*.

The phone rang.

Mason was closest to the bedside table. He answered, "Yes?"

Sara watched him pump his fist in the air. A huge grin spread across his face.

"Excellent, old chum, we're heading out the door." He dropped the phone back into the cradle. He looked very excited. "You'll never guess who's coming tonight."

4

Will could hear the strain in Sara's voice as she told them about the phone call. "Mason said that Sloan Bauer was going to be at the mixer."

"Bauer." Faith looked up from writing in her spiral notebook. "Could you spell that?"

Sara started to spell the name.

Will put his hands in his pockets as he leaned against the counter. They were in Faith's kitchen. The metal windchimes off her back porch were giving a low moan. It was cold and dark outside. The sliding glass doors reflected the two women sitting at the table. Faith was doing the questioning. Will was letting her take the lead because this was how they did interviews. His job was to observe and evaluate. With Sara, his only observation was that she was back in Super Woman mode.

Her only tell was the way she kept absently twisting her engagement ring around her finger.

Faith asked, "Why was it a big deal for Mason that Sloan was going to be there?"

"He liked her a lot. They were both from the same part of the country. They knew the same people. They talked the same language." Sara shrugged. "She was more his friend than mine, but I liked her, too."

"She wasn't living in Atlanta?"

"No, Sloan matched at Columbia after she graduated med school. She was only in town for a week, I think?" Sara shook her head, almost apologetic. "It's hard to remember all the details. After what happened to me, the mixer disappeared from my mind."

"But something happened at the mixer," Faith said. "That's what Britt told you—'don't you remember the mixer?'"

She wasn't asking a question. Within seconds of leaving the courthouse, Sara had transcribed every word that had come out of Britt McAllister's mouth. She'd filled an index card front to back. Faith had it beside her spiral notebook on the table.

Will knew there were only a few details on the card that mattered.

He said, "There are two avenues of investigation.

One is Tommy McAllister. The other is Sara. What clues did Britt give for each?"

"This is getting complicated." Faith looked at her fridge, then at her kitchen cabinets, then said, "We should do one of those crazy string walls like they do on TV."

She didn't wait for consensus. She got up and started searching drawers. Every single one was filled with kid stuff and kitchen crap. She found a pair of scissors, magic markers, Hello Kitty adhesive tape, construction paper, magnets with cartoon characters on them.

Will's hand was too big for the scissors. He used the edge of the counter to tear some of the construction paper into strips, then separated them by color. Sara started clearing the fridge of photos and Emma's crayon drawings.

Faith uncapped a marker. "Sara?"

Sara looked reluctant, but she picked up the index card. Will could see her eyes scan back and forth as she searched for the relevant information.

She read aloud, "The first one is, 'I know what he did to that girl. I know who he is.'"

Faith started writing in big block letters on a red strip of paper. "She obviously meant Tommy. Put it on the left side. Mac can be on the right. Let me do some headers so we can keep this straight."

They waited for Faith to finish writing. She passed the strips to Sara. Will could see a slight tremble in Sara's hands as she started to put them on the fridge.

He took over, placing the magnets on the strips when Sara held them up to the correct side. Will knew the longer name had to be Tommy. He put Britt's first clue underneath it.

"Next one." Sara held the card between her hands. She read, "'I've lived with the fear for twenty years.'"

Faith said, "Timing-wise, that feels like it should go on the Mac side."

Will waited for her to finish writing, then put the strip under Mac's name.

Sara read, "'I know he'll stop after this.'"

Will pinned the statement on the Tommy side.

"'I heard them.'"

Will asked, "Tommy?"

"For now." Sara kept going, "Two more: 'Mac is always involved.' Then, 'I can't stop the rest of them, but I can save my boy.'"

Faith asked, "Is that the same *them*? I heard *them*. I can't stop the rest of *them*."

Sara shrugged again. "Either way could tie back to Mac."

Will put the last two strips on the Mac side. He waited for Sara to read the next one.

She said, "That's it for Tommy and Mac. The rest was about me."

Will told Faith, "We need another column. Call it the Connection."

"Tape it on the cabinet." Faith chose pink paper, then wrote out the header. She passed it to Will. He used the Hello Kitty adhesive tape to affix it to the painted metal cabinet beside the fridge.

Then he looked at Sara.

She took a quick breath before reading, "'Fifteen years of not knowing, of suffering, because you couldn't see what was right in front of you.'"

"Definitely part of the connection," Faith said, handing Will the paper. "This has to point back to the mixer, right?"

"Yes," Sara agreed.

Will got to work with the tape as Sara read the next line.

"'What happened to you. What happened to Dani. It's all connected.'"

Will waited for Faith to record the sentences. Of all the things that Britt had said, this part was the most important. He framed the strip of paper with pink tape, making it stand out from the rest of the pieces.

Sara continued, "There's only one more clue. Before

she walked out the door, Britt said, 'Don't you remember the mixer?'"

Faith and Will did their parts while Sara stood back, her gaze taking in the various pieces of information. Will could see her out of the corner of his eye. The Superwoman facade was dropping. The tremble had not left her hands.

Faith was more interested in the crazy wall. Her passion was synthesizing data. "If Sara's ID on the janitor was shaky, I would say the wrong man got convicted."

"It's not shaky," Sara said. "I saw his face. I knew him. There's no question."

"The mixer," Will said. "Everything definitely points to that. According to Britt, something happened that night that's directly connected to your assault, and your assault is connected to Dani Cooper's."

Faith asked, "So what are we saying? Mac told Tommy what happened to Sara and Tommy got off on it and did the same thing to Dani?"

Sara was shaking her head. "I can't imagine that's the kind of thing they talked about at the family dinner table. Once I was gone, I doubt they ever gave me another thought."

"Britt did," Faith reminded her. "She had a lot to say in the bathroom. She knows what you went through. Why you can't have—"

Faith had the sense to stop herself, but Sara didn't need to hear the words. She was pretending to study the crazy wall. Will could see the overhead light catching tears in her eyes.

He said, "We could silo these as two different cases. Tommy is the current threat. He's raped once, maybe twice before. Britt's wrong about the trial stopping him. He got away with it. All that's left is his parents writing a check. Tommy could already be looking for new victims. He should be our focus."

Faith pivoted along with Will, telling Sara, "Refresh my memory about Tommy's previous accuser in high school. I read the report from the Coopers' private investigator, but why did it turn into a dead end?"

"Mac and Britt paid for it to go away," Sara answered. "The police report listed the victim as Jane Doe. The school records are inaccessible. The girl signed an NDA as part of the settlement. The detective could barely remember the case. He didn't even get a chance to interview the victim. The family stopped cooperating. We only know there was a settlement because it appeared on the docket. Everything is sealed."

"Great," Faith mumbled. "Your justice system at work."

Sara crossed her arms. She was looking at the column of pink construction paper. "I can't believe I let Britt walk out of the bathroom. If I'd had the presence of mind . . ."

"It was a lot," Will said. "You did what you could do."

"The crazy string wall isn't making anything clearer," Faith said. "We could talk to Britt. That's the obvious solution."

"She won't talk again." Sara was studying the notes, trying to see the solution. She pointed to the Mac side of the fridge, saying, "Who is *them*?'"

Faith suggested, "Two people? A group of people?"

"I was attacked by one person," Sara said. "None of the autopsy findings on Dani Cooper indicated that she was gang-raped."

Will knew they had hit this same brick wall last night. They needed more information. He told Sara, "Talk about the mixer. What do you remember?"

Sara closed her eyes like she was trying to imagine the scene. "It was Friday, so the bar was packed. Our group was around fifteen or twenty people. There was a core gang of regulars who attended the mixer every single month. That's what they were called—the gang. The rest were called the *hangers-on*. And then there was me. I'd never been to the mixer before, but Mason talked about how wild things would get. Sometimes, he would straggle in at four in the morning. They would close the place down, then go to another bar afterward. He was much more social than I was."

"Wait a minute," Faith said. "Tommy was how old when his parents were hanging out at a bar until four in the morning?"

"Around six or seven," Sara answered. "They hired a sitter."

"That's a choice," Faith said. "I didn't let myself take night-time cold medicine until Jeremy was in college."

Will asked, "How did you know the gang? Was it from work or school?"

"Both," Sara said. "But Mason and I went to dinner parties with them. We would spend some weekends on the tennis courts at Piedmont. There was a softball league. I wasn't a complete wallflower, but the mixer was on Friday nights, and if I had a Friday open, I didn't want to spend it at a bar where people were getting drunk and obnoxious."

Will asked, "Who was obnoxious?"

She shrugged. "It was just a general sort of obnoxious that comes from drinking too much. No one person stood out. They all liked to drink. It's very boring when you're the only one who's not shitfaced."

Will had an intimate understanding of that situation. "What time did you get to the bar?"

"Around six thirty. I stayed for about an hour. That would've put me at the hospital around eight at the latest. My shift started at ten."

Faith recorded the times in her spiral notebook. She gathered the purple strips of paper, uncapped the marker again. "Let's get some names written down. Who was in the gang? Sloan, Britt, Mac, you, Mason— who else?"

Sara took a quick, short breath before saying, "Chaz Penley. Blythe Creedy. Royce Ellison. Bing Forster. Prudence Stanley. Rosaline Stone. Cam Carmichael. And Richie—I don't remember Richie's last name."

"Was it Rich?" Faith asked as she kept writing. "Because half of these names sound like cartoon characters and the other half sound like every asshole jock in a John Hughes movie."

Sara allowed a smile, but said, "I know it seems that way, but they weren't all stereotypes. Rosaline volunteered at Planned Parenthood. Chaz and I worked some of our off days at the homeless shelter. Royce gave up his summers for Doctors Without Borders. Blythe mentored with a 'girls in STEM' program at Atlanta City Schools."

Will wasn't interested in their good deeds. He started taping up the names on the other side of the Connection. Right now, everything looked like it was separate, but he felt in his gut that they were going in the right direction.

He told Sara, "Stay on that night at the bar. What was Britt doing?"

Sara shook her head, but answered, "She was draped over Mac the whole time I was there. That's what she did. If anyone talked to him—especially a woman—she would insert herself into the conversation."

"Was she jealous?"

"That's part of it, but Britt's one of those women who defines herself by her husband's success. Her whole identity was tied up in him. Which was strange, because she was already an accomplished, practicing doctor. She managed having a baby in med school, then she was the top OB attending. Mac was still an intern, but Britt would always defer to him, even if he was wrong. Especially if he was wrong. She would rip into anybody who said otherwise."

"What a lovely couple." Faith tapped her pen on the counter. "What were you doing that night? Sitting at a table? Standing at the bar?"

"I stood around for part of the time talking to different people. Then I sat at a booth in the back and got trapped across from Mac and Britt. That's one of the reasons I decided to leave early." Sara gripped her hands together. "It wasn't just Britt. I felt uncomfortable around Mac because I knew he'd lost the fellowship. Dr. Nygaard was going to tell him the next day before she posted the announcement."

"Tell us about Mac," Faith said. "How was he acting that night?"

"Dismissive, arrogant. The usual. He talked to me, but it was more like talking down to me. He never really saw me as competition."

Will said, "But you were both up for the fellowship."

"We were," Sara agreed. "But Mac is exactly like Tommy. He's always gotten everything he wanted. I'm sure he assumed the fellowship was already his."

Faith asked, "Do you remember what you had to drink that night?"

"One glass of white wine." Sara looked down at her hands again. "I was watching the clock. I couldn't finish it in time to be clear for my shift, so I left it on the table."

"Who got the drink for you?"

"Mason. He also got some appetizers. We all shared them."

"At any point when you were drinking," Faith said, "did you go to the bathroom or—"

"My drink wasn't spiked," Sara interrupted. "GHB, Rohypnol, Ketamine—they all take anywhere from fifteen to thirty minutes to reach full effect. I never felt any of the symptoms. Not until after I had started my shift, and that was four hours later."

Faith tapped her pen as she studied the crazy string wall.

Will tried to check in with Sara. Her eyes were back on her engagement ring. Her thumb was worrying the scratch in the glass. She was going to break it before he had a chance to slip the matching wedding band on her finger.

Faith asked, "How did you get from the bar to the hospital?"

Sara looked up. "I walked. They're only a few blocks apart. I felt like I needed to clear my head."

"Clear your head of what?"

"I was feeling a little low after getting the fellowship. When you work really hard to reach a goal, it's almost depressing when you achieve it, because what now? What's the next goal?"

"That makes sense," Faith said, though Will could tell she didn't think it made sense. "So, you didn't tell Mac McAllister you got the fellowship?"

"No."

"And Britt McAllister didn't know?"

"No."

"What about Mason?"

"No."

"And these other guys, Richie Rich and the gang"—
Faith indicated the list—"none of them knew?"

"Not from me."

"Did any of them seem off that night?"

"Not that I noticed."

"What about now? Where are they? What are they
doing?"

"I—"

"Hey." Will kept his voice soft, but he shot Faith a
look that told her to slow down. This was not an interrogation. It was Sara's life. "Maybe we should take a
break."

"I'm okay." Sara pointed to the purple strips on the
cabinet, going down the list. "Mason is in plastics.
He opened his own practice in Buckhead. Sloan is a
pediatric hematologist at Children's Hospital in Connecticut. You know about Mac. Britt left medicine.
Chaz is a hospitalist; he's at Atlanta Health. I don't
know anything about Bing except that he was very
annoying."

Faith asked, "Creepy annoying?"

"Nerdy annoying, but well-intentioned." Sara
shrugged it off as she continued. "Blythe and Royce
are both ENTs, both in Peachtree Corners. They got
married after I left Atlanta. She cheated on him a few
years later with Mason. Mason cheated on her with

someone whose name I can't remember, but that was two wives ago. Ros does OB/GYN in Huntsville. Pru is a breast specialist at MD Anderson in Houston. Cam was at Bellevue in Manhattan. He died eight years ago. He took his own life."

"Cameron?" Faith waited for her to nod, then wrote something on her spiral pad. "What kind of doctor was he?"

"Trauma surgeon, but Bellevue is a Level I trauma center, so nothing was easy."

"Were you surprised that he killed himself?"

"It's sad, but it's not unusual. Doctors have the highest suicide rates of any profession. It's difficult to get help. Depending on the state, we're required to renew our license to practice every two or three years. All but a few require you to disclose whether or not you've sought therapy or psychiatric help. If you lie, you can lose your license. If you say you've gotten help, you could lose your license."

Faith said, "That doesn't make sense."

"If I'm not in the right frame of mind, I could end up killing a patient. Or I could self-prescribe anything from Prozac to Fentanyl. But you're right, there should be a balance."

Faith stared at the list. "Richie Rich. Do you remember anything about him?"

"He didn't go to Emory. He matched at Grady from out of state. He wore bow ties. He talked too much. He dressed too well."

Faith looked confused. "How can you dress too well?"

"It's a class thing. You can spend a lot of money on clothes, but they have to be the right type of clothes. Your car has to be the right kind of car. Same with where you live, down to the section of the street. And where your kids go to school and what organizations you support and the club you go to and—" Sara shrugged. "They're the gatekeepers of what's cool and what's trying too hard. It's an ever-changing ideal."

"Oh," Faith said. "They're all just a bunch of mean girls."

"Exactly."

Will felt like they were moving in the wrong direction. "You walked from the bar to the hospital. Could you have been followed?"

"By whom?" Sara asked. "The janitor? Even if he did, so what? I know now that he was stalking me."

Will could hear the edge in her voice, but he had to keep pressing. "You could've seen him do something at the bar. Pick out another victim. Drug a victim, even. It doesn't matter if you saw it. What matters is maybe he thought you saw it."

Sara shook her head, but he couldn't tell if she was saying that she didn't know or that she couldn't bring herself to talk it through.

Faith asked, "What about Mason? Would it be worth looking him up?"

"No," Sara said. "I can't ask him to relive that night. And I'm not sure he would. Mason doesn't like when things get messy."

Will's bad opinion of Mason James got worse.

"Talk to me about Britt," Faith said. "What kind of bitch is she? What's her MO?"

"Exactly what happened in the bathroom," Sara said. "Brutal, vicious honesty. She'd announce that Pru had been humiliated during rounds or Blythe had fucked up a surgery or that Cam had lost a patient."

"How did she hurt you back then?"

"By constantly reminding everyone that I grew up poor."

Will caught Faith's stunned reaction.

So did Sara. Her face turned crimson. "I'm sorry, I should've said poor by their standards. Obviously, not poor by any reasonable stretch. My parents provided a very good life for me and Tess. We were—are—incredibly lucky."

Will intervened. "Stay on that night. You said that you walked from the bar to the hospital?"

"Yes."

"It was late." Will had a theory about why Mason was okay with her walking through downtown Atlanta alone in the dark, but now wasn't the time to share it. "Did you see anybody in the street?"

"Nothing remarkable. And when I got to the hospital, I don't remember seeing anyone or hearing anything unusual. I got on the elevator. I went down to level two. There's a lounge with beds and a television. No one was there. I read some journals, then got some sleep before my shift."

"We need a map for the wall." Faith opened her laptop. "The area around Grady has changed in the last fifteen years. Is the bar still in the same spot?"

"They knocked it down a while ago. The whole block is upscale apartments with a high-end market on the ground floor." Sara sat down across from Faith. "The bar was owned by a Morehouse grad. I can't remember the name, but he was a hepatologist, that's liver, gallbladder, pancreas, bile ducts. Anyway, everybody called it De-Liver's."

For some reason, Faith gave a surprised laugh.

Sara looked at Will.

She smiled at him.

He smiled back.

"All right, I think I've got it." Faith turned her laptop

around so they could all see the map. She pointed to the intersection of two streets. "There's a fancy market on the corner of Arendelle and Loudermilk. Does that sound right?"

Sara nodded. "De-Liver's was in the center of Arendelle. I think a shoe store was on one side. Sneakers and athletic wear. That kind of thing."

Faith again looked up at the crazy string wall. Her arms were crossed. She was clearly trying to come up with a plan.

Finally, she said, "This is how I would do the investigation. Start with a reverse property search. Get the name of the bar, locate the owner, go through his payroll info to locate the former wait staff, talk to them, see if there were any suspicious characters they remember from that night or any of the previous mixers. Then I would do a general crime report search in that area—were there any other assaults on or around that night? Did anyone see anything suspicious? Were there attempted robberies that could've been failed assaults? Then I would run deep background checks on Richie Rich and the gang to see what dirty secrets are in their closets. Then I would start knocking on their doors and asking questions."

Sara was nodding. She looked hopeful, which was the worst part.

Will wasn't going to make Faith be the one to disappoint her.

He said, "We can't do any of that. The GBI has to be asked or assigned to work an investigation. Atlanta usually plays fair with us, but we don't have enough probable cause to approach APD. They'd never open a case based off what we have."

"You're not opening a case." Sara looked up at Will. "I thought we could do this informally."

He said, "This was the informal part."

Faith told Sara, "That case number you use on your autopsy reports, we're the ones who generate those. We have to plug them in each time we take a witness statement or talk to a suspect or file a report or log into the GBI portal. Otherwise, everything I described can be considered illegal, abuse of power, police harassment or—I'm sure I'm leaving something out."

Will provided, "Unauthorized use of law enforcement resources."

They were all silent, all trying to see a way around this.

Will said, "I can piggy-back off one of my existing case numbers. We'll have at least a week, maybe more, before somebody flags it."

"No." Sara was adamant. "Absolutely not."

Will didn't see how she was going to stop him.

"Hold on," Faith said. "Britt isn't the only source for what happened that night. We don't need probable cause to talk to a parolee. We can interrogate Jack Allen Wright."

Sara had physically recoiled at the name of the man who had raped her.

"Oh, fuck." Faith knew what she had done. "Sara, I—"

Sara stood up so fast that the chair raked across the floor. She left the room. Will heard the front door close behind her.

He walked into the hallway, but not to go after her. He needed a minute to collect himself so that he did not completely destroy the woman who had been his partner for five years.

"I'm sorry." Faith stood behind him. Her remorse was palpable. "I'll go apologize."

"Wait until she comes back."

"I should check on her," Faith said. "Or you should. One of us."

"Did you want me to check on you this morning?"

She didn't answer.

Will turned around.

Faith had walked back into the kitchen. She slumped down into the chair. She peeled open her laptop. She started typing.

He was still furious with her, but he wasn't going to let Faith risk losing her badge and pension for performing an illegal search.

He said, "Use my log-in."

"I'm not using your log-in. I'm using Google." She looked up at him. "The gang, they're all doctors working at hospitals. We can at least confirm where they are. Give me one from the list."

Will didn't need to look at the cabinets. He recited from memory. "Dr. Sloan Bauer, pediatric hematologist, Children's Hospital, Connecticut."

Faith typed in the search.

The hospital page loaded quickly. Sloan was whippet-thin with long blonde hair, a sharp nose, and lips that looked unnaturally full. Her gold-rimmed glasses were too large for her face, but he guessed that was part of her look.

Faith said, "Mason was screwing Sloan Bauer behind Sara's back, right?"

"Yep." You didn't walk your girlfriend to work late at night when your out-of-town girlfriend was still at the bar. "Chaz Penley. Hospitalist. Atlanta Health."

Will looked over Faith's shoulder as she typed. Chaz Penley was at the top of the page, so obviously their main guy. Blond hair. Blue eyes. He probably hadn't lacked for company fifteen years ago, but those days were clearly over.

Faith said, "I guess we know what happened to Rolf after he ratted out the Von Trapps."

"Print out the photos." Will watched her go through the previous pages and hit print. "Blythe Creedy is next. ENT. Peachtree Corners."

Faith opened another tab. Then another. They went through the rest of the gang, printing out photos of each one. Royce Ellison. Bing Forster. Prudence Stanley. Rosaline Stone. Mac McAllister. Professional headshots accompanied long lists of accomplishments and specialties on hospital websites and slick-looking private practice *about* pages. Every single doctor looked like the kids who'd sat at the geek table in middle school.

Not that Will had spent much time in the cafeteria. He was usually in the principal's office.

"Let's do Britt," Faith said. "I bet she looks like every other Buckhead Betty."

Finding Britt wasn't as easy as the others. She wasn't listed on a hospital page or private practice because she wasn't working as a doctor anymore. Instagram, TikTok, and Facebook were all a bust, but they found her on Twitter.

Britt's profile photo showed Mac with his arm

around Tommy, who was wearing a cap and gown. The background banner was the sun setting over a lake with mountains in the distance.

Faith said, "Add a couple of bathtubs and it could be an ad for erectile dysfunction."

She scrolled too quickly for Will to make anything out, but she provided, "She retweets a lot of medical stuff—articles, advisories, other doctors, mom shit. She doesn't do much original content."

"Probably had her account professionally scrubbed before Tommy's trial."

"Probably." Faith skipped past an ad that tried to autoplay. "Day one of the trial, Britt tweeted, 'So proud of my Tommy for being strong. I can't wait to get back to our regular lives. He will be an amazing doctor one day just like DH.'"

"Who?"

"DH, it's mommyblog code for 'my idiot husband.'" Faith kept reading. "Day two: 'I can't believe how stoic my Tommy is. These so-called experts have no idea what they're talking about. Wait until we get our turn!'"

"What about yesterday when Sara testified?"

"'A lot of lies are being told today. Perjury is illegal the last time I checked. My Tommy should not even be here, but we will fight this as a family.' Hold on, a new one just came through." Faith clicked to see Britt's most recent tweet. "'Court in recess tomorrow, then we get our turn. Bliss! Going to hit some balls in the AM then cook dinner for my two amazing guys.'"

"You hit balls on a tennis court," Will said. "Try the Atlanta Women's Racquet Association."

"Damn, you're right. She's gotta be in AWRA." Faith was already pulling up the website. "All those former power moms are hypercompetitive. Tennis is the only thing that keeps them from driving their Range Rovers off a cliff."

Will recognized the bright green logo with a pink tennis racket in the center. Atlanta was a tennis town. The badge was ubiquitous around the city. Faith navigated to a map of the metro area and chose the Buckhead team. There were a ton of group photos—women on the court, women holding ribbons and trophies, women drinking wine—but no captions to put names to the Botoxed faces.

Will said, "There has to be a charity or an event that they sponsor."

"Charity?" Faith sounded dubious, but she kept scrolling.

"There." Will pointed to a colorful turkey surrounded by canned goods. "Thanksgiving food drive."

"How do you know so much about these people?"

"I'm observant."

"No shit." She clicked the turkey, which took her to another page with another bunch of photos, but these were all of individuals. Faith clicked on one. She laughed out a sound of triumph, saying, "Dr. Britt McAllister, volunteer coordinator."

Britt was wearing a bright pink tennis dress. She had a tennis racket in one hand and a glass of wine in the other. Her forehead was unnaturally stiff. The skin around her eyes was tight. The smile on her face looked like it was causing her physical pain.

Faith said, "All the plastic surgery in the world can't erase that kind of evil."

Will thought that was a good way to describe it. Britt McAllister was a hard-looking woman. Her bones were too sharp, her features too prominent. She looked too thin. Too brittle. Too a lot of things. He leaned in for a closer look, but not at her face. He wanted to see the background. Britt was standing on a clay tennis court. Atlanta's public courts were all concrete. There was a blurred sign on the building behind her.

He pointed at the gold and blue medallion, telling Faith, "She's a member of the Piedmont Hills Town and Country Club."

Faith gave a low whistle. Piedmont Hills ran along the Chattahoochee River and was surrounded by estates that started north of ten million. "How did you figure that out?"

"I'm—"

"Observant. Right. Let's put these assholes up on the wall." Faith printed out the picture of Britt. Will went into her pantry where her color printer was hidden behind art supplies, canned vegetables, too many tote bags, and several crinkled rolls of wrapping paper.

Faith said, "I'm sorry to you, too. For what I said. I know Sara's not the only person it hit wrong."

Will nodded his appreciation as he laid out the photos on the table. "We're missing two people."

"Mason James is in plastics in Buckhead." Faith opened another search on her laptop. She gasped when the photo loaded. "Fuck me."

Will rubbed his jaw with his fingers.

Mason was leaning against a sportscar with his jacket thrown over his shoulder like he was modeling for a Hugo Boss ad. His hair was so perfect he'd probably sprayed it in place. The stubbly five o'clock shadow was too neat to be natural. The worst part was the car, a Maserati MC20 coupe in *Rosso Vincente*, which was how you said red when you had half a million bucks to spend on a car.

"My God." Faith mumbled. "Sorry, man, but holy shit this dude could put me through puberty again."

Will reached down and hit the keys to print the page. "What about Cam Carmichael?"

"Cameron." She had the decency to overwrite the tab with Mason's photo. The new search brought up a news article from a tabloid website.

Will easily recognized some of the words in the giant headline because they came up a lot in his line of work. He said, "How did an emergency department doctor get a Glock in New York City?"

Faith turned to look up at him. "You read that?"

"I'm not a moron," he said. "Just print out the damn article."

"What article?" Sara walked up behind him. She rested her hand on Will's shoulder.

"Sara," Faith stood up. "I'm really sorry for being so careless. I shouldn't have—"

"It's fine." Sara interrupted, which made it clear that it wasn't fine, but she wanted to drop it. "I don't want him contacted, all right? Or his parole officer called, or anything like that. Understood?"

"Understood," Faith said.

Sara squeezed Will's shoulder again, then picked up the laptop.

Without being asked, she started reading the article out loud.

"'The body of thirty-four-year-old Dr. Cameron

Davis Carmichael, a trauma surgeon at Bellevue Hospital, was found this morning after the victim's sister requested NYPD perform a wellness check at his Chelsea apartment. Dr. Jeanene Carmichael-Brown of Princeton, New Jersey, became worried when she had not heard from her brother for more than a week. A Bellevue colleague who wishes to remain anonymous claimed that Carmichael had become despondent after losing a patient, and had not shown up at work for several days. According to the medical examiner's office, the victim died from a self-inflicted gunshot wound. A Glock 19 that had previously been reported stolen in Fairfax, Virginia, was confirmed to be the weapon used. NYPD has reported an increase in gun violence in the Kips Bay precincts. Detective Danny DuFonzo, who was at the scene, reported that police believe Carmichael purchased the illegal gun from a hospital patient. Anyone wishing to provide an anonymous lead can contact Crime Stoppers.'"

"He lost a patient," Faith said. "He was depressed."

Sara placed the laptop back on the table. She rested her hand on Will's shoulder again. She wasn't telling him she was okay. She was holding onto him.

Will asked her, "What's the plan?"

"There's no plan." Sara had clearly made up her mind. "We don't have probable cause to open a case.

We don't know the name of Tommy's first victim. We don't have a way to approach Britt that won't get you fired at worst and at the top of Amanda's shit list at least. I appreciate you guys looking into this, but the brick wall hasn't moved. If anything, it's become even more impenetrable."

Faith looked confused. "Are you telling us to drop it?"

"Yes," Sara answered. "What other choice is there?"

Faith said, "We can knock and talk the gang. There's no harm in that. We can go online right now with a credit card and do background checks."

"To what end?" Sara asked. "Knowing how Cam killed himself, or even finding out whether Chaz has a gambling problem or Pru was sued for malpractice— what does that give us?"

"Leverage," Faith said. "People will do anything to hide their secrets, whether it's a gambling problem or a lawsuit or whatever. They'll talk to us because they'll be worried that we'll start talking about them."

"No." Sara didn't just sound frustrated. She sounded angry. "I feel like I shouldn't have to repeat this, Faith. I said let it go. There's nothing any of us can do."

"Of course there is." Faith's tone matched Sara's. "We can't let Britt get away with this. She knows something. She told you there's a connection between your rape and Dani's death. I get why you'd want to drop it for personal reasons, but don't you care about Dani?"

"Are you fucking serious?" Sara exploded. She held out her arm to keep Will from intervening. "Tell me how to help her! Tell me what to do! There's nothing!"

"There are ways—"

"What ways?" Sara demanded. "I'm not going to put you and Will at risk. Faith, you have a toddler at home! You need your job, your benefits, your pension. Enough people have already been hurt because of me. I'm not going to let anyone else suffer."

"You know who needs to suffer?" Faith shot back. "Britt McAllister. We can start with her."

"How?" Sara was really asking for an answer. "Tell me how you can speak to Britt without destroying your life."

"We have a legitimate reason to follow up on what she said to you in the bathroom."

"Okay, let's accept that at face value. But no one has to talk to the police if they don't want to. Britt's richer than God and surrounded by lawyers. You won't make it past the front gate to her house. She'll tell the maid not to buzz you in."

"We can follow her. Ambush her. Throw her off guard."

"At the courthouse? The spa? The yoga studio? Do

you know how ridiculous that sounds? She'll laugh in your face and walk away."

"Her country club. She's a member at Piedmont Hills."

"Faith—"

"No." Faith pointed her finger at Sara. "You said yourself that Britt is obsessed with class. She won't lose her shit in front of her own people. She'll be embarrassed. We can work with that."

"Do you know how exclusive that club is? It's filled with judges and politicians. They don't let cops stroll in and harass members."

"I'll ask for a tour."

"They don't give tours to people off the street!" Sara yelled. "It's one of the top ten clubs in the country. They run your name. They screen you for high net worth and connections and access. Do you have any of those things?"

Faith wasn't giving up. "There has to be another way to get in."

"You have to be a member or know a member. That's the only way in. Do you know a member, Faith? Do you know someone who shelled out $250,000 to join and pays two grand a month in dues?"

Will had to end this.

He said, "I do."

5

Sara stared at Will's hazy reflection in the back of the elevator doors. He was being infuriatingly silent as they rode up to her condo. Her throat was sore from keeping her voice raised for almost the entire two-mile drive from Faith's house. Sara hated being the kind of woman who raised her voice. She hated that Faith was willing to risk her job, that Will was ready to risk his peace of mind, all because of some stupid, bullshit remarks that Britt McAllister had made in a fucking toilet. This was the fallout that Sara had dreaded most over the last six months. Opening up about her assault had only ever opened up fresh wounds in the people around her.

"My love." She tried to keep her tone even. "You told me that you would support whatever decision I made. This is my decision. I'm not going to let you do this."

The *let* earned her a cutting look before he stared back at the doors.

Sara wanted to grab him. To shake him. To beg him not to do this. They would find another way to get to Britt McAllister.

She was not going to let him ask his aunt Eliza for help.

Will had not grown up in state care because there were no other options. At the time of his mother's death, she'd had one living relative, a brother who'd inherited generations of unimaginable wealth. The man could've easily arranged for Will's private adoption, or hired nannies, or paid boarding school fees, without ever even seeing his face, but instead he and his wife Eliza had left Will to rot in state care.

As far as Sara was concerned, the only decent thing Will's uncle had ever done was die of a massive stroke three years ago. The obituary stated he was on the third hole at Piedmont Hills Town and Country Club, where he and his wife were longtime members. If there was any justice in the world, Eliza would soon be joining him. They could both burn in hell atop their piles of blood money.

The elevator had arrived at the top floor. The doors slid open. Will stepped back so that Sara could go first. Instead of getting off, she turned, looking at him.

"Will, please. It's not worth the trouble. Britt isn't going to magically open up again. The only reason she did the first time was because she was stoned and upset and—"

The doors started to close. Will reached out to stop them so that Sara wouldn't take the hit. But he still didn't speak. She knew he would stand there for the rest of the night if she didn't move. He was so damn intractable.

Sara had no choice but to walk down the hallway toward her condo. She expected to hear the dogs on the other side of the door, but when her key slid into the lock, there was only silence.

"Hey, y'all." Tessa was standing at the sink washing dishes. She had the baby monitor on the counter in case her daughter woke up. "I was going to walk the dogs, but—"

Will grabbed the leashes off the hook. Billy and Bob, Sara's two greyhounds started to amble over. They waited patiently for the leashes to be clipped to their collars. Will pulled the trash bag out of the can, cinched the top.

He finally spoke, but not to Sara. "Betty."

The small dog stayed perched on her satin pillow. Will had to walk to the couch to pick her up. Betty cuddled into his chest and licked his neck, which somewhat diminished his stoic silence. He gave Sara a rueful look as he grabbed the bag of trash. The chihuahua was a stray he hadn't had the heart to leave at the pound.

Tessa waited for the door to close behind him. "That was frosty."

Sara wasn't going to pull her sister into this mess. "What are you doing? We have a dishwasher."

"It's better to do them by hand."

Sara didn't know who it was better for, but she reached for a towel to help dry.

"I've got it," Tessa said. "Keep me company."

Sara reluctantly sat down. Since Tessa had moved into the building, they had fallen back into a familiar pattern of Tessa doing more than she should. When you were on the road to becoming a highly successful man, your wife ran the essential domestic parts of your life. When you were a woman on the road to success, you either lived in squalor or relied on your family.

Sara tried again, "Tess, you don't have to clean up after me."

"You're helping me with rent."

"For selfish reasons." Sara picked up the baby monitor. She could hear soft breathing. "How's my little niece?"

"Your precious Isabelle stuck a piece of bread up her nose because she said she wanted to see how it tasted."

Sara smiled. "She's right. The epiglottis—"

"I don't consent to an anatomy lesson."

Sara put down the monitor. She saw her engagement ring and felt all the anxiety well back up into her chest. The hardest part, the part that Sara did not want to admit, was that she wanted Faith and Will to get in Britt's face. She wanted the woman to feel cornered. To be scared and helpless, the same way that Sara had felt in the bathroom. But exploiting Will to make that happen, forcing him to establish a connection with a woman who had discarded him like trash, felt like the height of selfishness.

Sara couldn't do it.

"What's going on?" Tessa asked. "You've been very mysterious lately."

"Just tired." Sara changed the subject. "What about you? Why are you up here washing my dishes in the dark of night?"

Tessa easily relented. "Lem called."

"Oh?" Sara didn't have to issue a formal invitation. Tessa launched into a detailed report on the most recent conversation with her ex. None of the information was new or unexpected. Sara sat back on the bar stool and tried to listen, but her thoughts kept getting pulled into the past.

Fifteen years ago, once the news had gotten out that

Sara had been raped, her colleagues at the hospital had scattered, some quitting, others asking to be moved to different departments. Mason had reverted to his baser instincts. Sara's aunt Bella had started sleeping with a loaded revolver beside her bed. Her other aunts and uncles and cousins had all turned either clingy or distant or too inquisitive or not inquisitive at all. Her father had never looked at her the same way again. Her mother was hypervigilant to this day. Tessa had never fully recovered. She had been different after watching Sara struggle to find herself again. Tessa had always thought of her big sister as invincible, the person who would protect her no matter what. Everyone had felt more vulnerable and raw because of their connection to Sara.

That was why she hadn't told her family about Dani Cooper.

That was why she would not give Eliza the opportunity to hurt Will.

"So I told Daddy about it," Tessa was saying. "And he said if I decided to murder Lem, I should do it with a Tupperware lid because no one can ever find the tops."

Sara forced a smile. "Talk to me before you do anything. I'm good with murder."

"Absolutely." Tessa drained the sink. "Okay, now

you can tell me about the tension between you and Will. Is it cold feet?"

Sara shook her head, because that was the one thing she didn't have to worry about.

"For what it's worth, I think he's good for you," Tessa said. "He's different."

Immediately, Sara felt defensive. "He's not that different."

"I'm not talking about his weirdness. I'm talking about comparing him to all the other guys you've been with."

"All the other guys?" Sara repeated, because, barring a few bad one-night stands, they both knew that Sara was serially monogamous. "That's a short list."

"Exactly my point." Tessa started folding the kitchen towel. "Steve was boring as hell."

"Every boy in high school is boring."

"Not the boys I knew. Or the girls." Tessa dropped the towel on the counter. "Mason was louche and flashy. Your life would've been the same with or without him."

Sara silently agreed. Mason was the equivalent of mayonnaise; except she would miss mayonnaise if it wasn't around. "Can you skip ahead to your point?"

"Will knows who you are. You're more yourself with him than any other man I've seen you with."

Sara's eyelids were already chapped from so much crying. She looked over Tessa's shoulder at the photos on the fridge. "He's a good man."

"He's a mighty good man," Tessa said. "I mean, shit, this is what Salt-N-Pepa were talking about. He takes out the trash without being asked. He listens to you."

Sara laughed, because he sure as hell wasn't listening to her right now.

"I should go." Tessa walked around the counter. "You'll tell me what's really been bothering you when you're ready."

Sara nodded. "Okay."

Tessa clipped the baby monitor on her jeans. When she opened the door to leave, Will was reaching for the doorknob. They did a quick dance as Tessa navigated around the greyhounds. Sara heard them speak softly to one another. Will shut the door. He gently placed Betty back on her pillow. She watched him walk across the room. His jaw wasn't as tight. The time outside had done him good. But she knew he hadn't changed his mind.

Will placed his phone on the counter in front of her.

The screen lit up. The wallpaper showed a photo of Sara on his couch with all three dogs stretched out around her. She remembered the day the picture had been taken. The Falcons were on TV. They'd eaten way too much for lunch. They'd had the kind of slow, sensual day that makes you realize that what you're really doing is falling in love.

Sara tried a different approach. "Why do you have Eliza's number?"

He paused before answering. "Amanda made me put it in my contacts. She said I might have questions one day."

"Have you ever had questions?"

"You don't ask a liar for the truth." He obviously wouldn't be distracted. "Britt McAllister is our only viable lead. Unless she was lying on Twitter, she'll be at the country club tomorrow morning. Eliza is our best shot at getting in."

Sara had to find a better strategy. She had tried yelling. She had tried begging. Now she was going to logic the hell out of him. "Take me through it. You persuade Eliza to put you and Faith on her guest list. You go to the club. Tell me how you'll make Britt talk."

"Faith and I will get her alone, then—"

"That kind of club has separate spaces for men and women. You'll stick out."

"I'm used to sticking out."

"Not like that," Sara said. "And I love Faith, but she'll stick out, too. She has a giant chip on her shoulder about those kinds of people and those types of places. Which is fair, but she won't have the home field advantage. Britt will. And she'll use it."

"Then I'll have your name put on the guest list instead," Will told her. "You know Britt better than either of us. You know which buttons to push. And you know how to fit in."

Sara was nearly without words. "I'm not a detective. And you're forgetting I completely folded in the bathroom yesterday. I let her run all over me."

"She had the element of surprise. This time, you'll have it."

Sara started shaking her head, though part of her relished the thought of a rematch. "There's still a fundamental problem. I'm not doing anything if it means you have to ask Eliza for a favor. She'll expect something in return. Nothing is worth that to me. Not even being able to confront Britt."

"But if there was another way, you would do it."

He was so fucking clever. He had gotten Sara to admit that she wanted to do it.

He said, "I told you I would support you. This is what you want. I'm supporting you."

"My love, please." Sara couldn't battle him anymore. "We're going around in circles. I know you're tired. I'm tired. Let's get ready for bed. We can sleep on it."

He didn't even pretend to consider the suggestion. "Tell me about Mac. You said he's like Tommy. How?"

Sara didn't know where the question was coming from, but if talking about the McAllister men bought her some time, she was going to take it. "I only know Tommy from the trial, and he comes off like an arrogant prick, exactly like his father. Even the way he tilts up his chin. It's so fucking condescending."

"What about when you worked with Mac? What was he like?"

"Are you interviewing me?"

"I'm just asking questions."

He was interviewing her.

She said, "Mac was brilliant, one of the finest surgeons I've ever seen."

"That's his job. What's his personality?"

"One informs the other. The heart is an intimate organ. When it's inside a child or an infant or a fetus, it's as if you're touching life itself. You have to be confident, patient, careful, focused."

"Like you were with Dani."

"What I did to Dani couldn't have happened with an infant. They're much smaller, more vulnerable. Think about how small Betty's heart is."

"That's tiny, like a plum," Will said. "How do you fix it?"

"With your hands."

He stared at her until she relented.

"It's the closest thing I've ever come to witnessing a miracle." Sara felt ashamed for sounding glib about something so extraordinary. "My first time, I was assisting Dr. Nygaard on a two-month-old with VSD—a ventricular septal defect. There's a hole in the wall between the two lower chambers of the heart, and it's more complicated than I'm making it sound, but when you crack the sternum, you get to the actual heart, and it's so shocking the way it sits in the chest. It's on bypass, so it's com-pletely still. You can tell how amazing it is, like a sculpture. And then Dr. Nygaard let me take over the repair, and the easiest way to describe it is that it's a combination of patching dry wall and darning a sock."

Will looked puzzled, probably because he'd done both of those things.

"There's a woven patch you use to seal the hole, and once it's sewn into place, that's it. You take the heart off bypass. Sometimes you have to give it a little squeeze to coax it into rhythm again. Almost like a pinch of encouragement. And that's it. You've given that child the rest of their life."

Will offered her his handkerchief.

For once, Sara didn't care that she was crying. There was no greater gift than a child's life. "After the heart heals, they can run and play and have fun and grow up and get married and maybe have children of their own. But that's *you* inside of their heart. You're the one who made that possible. It gives you an unbelievably intimate connection to another person's life."

"So," Will said. "What you're saying is that Mac is careful, and pays attention to detail, and—what else is he?"

"An arrogant control freak." Sara laughed as she wiped her eyes. "All surgeons are arrogant control freaks. You need that to do the job. But you can be a good surgeon and a bad human being. Mac could never admit when he was wrong. He blamed other people when a case went sideways. His temper was off the charts. His biggest problem was patients' parents. He couldn't talk to them. He'd get too technical and lose sight of the fact that after a while, they don't care about the ejection fraction and T-waves. They are literally placing their child's heart in your hands."

"They want you to be compassionate."

"Yes, but they also want you to be realistic about what to expect. Mac refused to be honest with parents. Sometimes, you can't fix everything. You can only try to make it better. Mac couldn't handle those conversations, especially if the prognosis was poor. Parents are so vulnerable when their child is sick. They break down, they cling to you, they argue or scream or want to pray."

"Mac didn't like that?"

"He hated it. He called it *parent drama*," Sara said. "I watched Dr. Nygaard tear him apart over it during an M&M—that's the Morbidity and Mortality conference. Every time a resident has an adverse event like a death, they have to present the case to a roomful of doctors. They question you and pick apart your decisions and try to figure out if you could've done something better."

"That sounds humbling."

"It can be excruciating, but it can also be a safe space to learn. Unless you're Mac McAllister. He didn't think he had anything to learn. He turned livid whenever anyone questioned him. So did Britt, for that matter. She had a pathological need to believe in him, and Mac had a pathological need to be worshipped."

"Is that why you got the fellowship instead of him?"

Sara would only say this to Will. "Dr. Nygaard offered me the fellowship because I was the better surgeon."

He grinned. "You're better at most things."

Sara didn't feel particularly good at anything right now. She reached up to Will's face and gently touched the scar that zigzagged through his eyebrow. The thin scar tracing up from his lips was bright pink against his skin. She thought about the first time she had kissed him. Her knees had literally gone weak. She'd felt dizzy from his taste. She'd only learned afterward that the scars on his face, the scars on his body, were because his aunt and uncle had lacked the basic decency to shelter a defenseless child.

"You're trying to protect me," Will said. "Stop it."

"You're trying to protect me," Sara said. "What's the difference?"

"Tommy McAllister," he answered. "All those things you told me about Mac—that he's arrogant and selfish and a liar and blame-shifter and he doesn't care who gets hurt in the process. Tommy is exactly like his father. He got away with hurting a girl in high school, and two years later, Dani ended up dead. He's gonna skate on hurting Dani, too. Even if he loses the lawsuit, Tommy won't be writing the check. Do you think Britt was right? Do you think the kid will learn his lesson? Or do you think he'll do it again?"

Sara let her hands drop into her lap. Deep down,

Britt knew the truth. So did Sara. Tommy would do it again. Another girl would be hurt, maybe end up dead. Another family could be shattered. Friends, lovers, colleagues, classmates, teachers—all of them would be caught up in the horror of a single, violent act.

"Okay," Sara relented. "Get me into the club."

The Downlow

The pop-up dance club was so loud that Leighann could barely hear herself think. The bass boomed inside her ribcage. She kept getting jostled around. People had their hands in the air, their faces turned up, as the music machine-gunned around the cavernous space.

"Let's go!" Jake screamed into her ear. When she didn't move, he dragged Leighann into the pulsing mob that had overtaken the dance floor.

The Downlow popped up once a month in various warehouses around the city. No one knew when or where until a text came on their phone. The news of tonight's party had spread around campus faster than syphilis. The warehouse was packed tight with sweaty, grabby strangers, but Leighann wasn't going to let fear stop her from having fun.

Four days had passed since she'd gotten any sinister texts from the dude she was calling the Creeper. Leighann was sick of sleeping on Jake's couch. She couldn't hide away for the rest of her life. She wasn't going to let the Creeper win.

"This way!" Jake danced like a baby chimp, his arms hanging in the air, his knees bouncing, a goofy grin on his face. Leighann mirrored him, pushing off from the floor like she was on a trampoline. She looked up at the lights. There was a disco ball throwing off color. The music was so loud that she could almost see the air pulsing. She needed something to take her higher. She reached for the Molly in Jake's pocket. Her fingertips brushed against the edge of the small plastic bag just as he pivoted away.

"Jake!" she yelled, but he was already chimping on a girl who was way out of his league. Leighann started laughing as he made his move. His jeans were so baggy that she could see the actual crack of his flat white ass.

She dug her phone out of her purse to take a picture.

Leighann froze.

There was a notification on the screen.

The Creeper had texted her again.

The music dulled. Everything did. She had to blink to pull herself out of the trance.

She looked for Jake. He'd moved on to another girl. There were dozens of people between them. Leighann stared back at her phone. The timestamp said the text had been sent six minutes ago.

Her fingers were sweaty when she swiped the screen.

Hi, Leighann! Are you getting down at the Downlow?

Leighann scanned the crowd, looked up to the balcony, to the bar that was four deep with sweaty students. No one looked back. No one was paying attention. She searched for Jake again. He had moved even farther away. All she could see was the top of his curly hair as he jumped to the beat.

Her phone vibrated. A new text.

Why aren't you dancing?

Leighann's arm jerked up. Someone had bumped into her. She'd nearly dropped the phone. Another person jostled her. She pushed her way out of the crowd. Stood with her back to the wall. She felt like she couldn't catch her breath. The phone vibrated again. Another text had come through.

You look beautiful tonight.

Her eyes were on the screen when a fourth text popped up.

As always!

The sweat on her body turned cold. She could feel her actual heart beating. She was too drunk to deal with this right now, but her brain threw out a memory anyway. The hand-held mirror from her make-up drawer in the bathroom. After the first creepy texts, she had closed all the blinds in her apartment, got on the bed, and contorted herself around to look at the back of her knee.

Just like the Creeper had said, there had been a circle drawn in the exact center of the fold in her left knee.

Her phone buzzed again.

Don't you want to dance?

Leighann started to cry. She needed to find Jake. He would tell her that the circle on her knee was a joke. That she'd gotten drunk at a pool party, that she'd found a marker and made the circle herself, that she'd fallen asleep and someone else had drawn it, or that she'd been sitting on the bleachers during track and one of her teammates had thought it would be funny to tag her.

But Jake wasn't there to tell her these excuses, and she knew that her teammates weren't that twisted, and that no one would draw a stupid circle on her body as a joke, and that even with the mirror, there was no way in hell Leighann could've drawn that perfectly round, perfectly centered circle on the back of her left knee because all the beer and Molly in the world couldn't change the fact that it would be physically impossible for her to do it because she was fucking left-handed.

Another text popped up on the screen.

I love what you've done with your hair tonight.

She closed her eyes, pressed the edge of the phone to her forehead. She could picture the Creeper lurking in a corner. Or maybe he was on the balcony looking down, watching her, getting off on seeing how terrified she was, relishing every second of the control he had over her very existence.

Every girl Leighann had ever met had been subjected to this level of freakiness at least ten times in her life. Beckey had walked out of the smoothie place to find that some cocksucker had slashed her tires. Frieda's ex-boyfriend slut-shamed her with a bunch of nudes she'd sent him while they were dating. When Denishia was little, her brother's best friend had tried to cop a feel while she was asleep and her brother had gotten mad at her for telling their parents.

And that wasn't counting online, where the rape threats, sexist insults, and unsolicited dick pics flooded every site Leighann visited. This was why you checked socials on dudes before you went out with them. Why you texted your friends before and after a date. Why you kept your location services on and your mace in your purse and slept on a friend's sweaty, fapped-out couch because it was fucking terrifying to have a vagina in this world.

Leighann was not going to let the Creeper win.

She lifted her chin in defiance as her gaze angrily darted around the packed club, daring anybody to look back at her. Nobody had the balls. She felt her phone vibrate from another text, but she was finished with that shit. Everybody knew that the best way to deal with stalkers was to ignore them. You couldn't *be* a victim if you didn't *act* like a victim.

Leighann unlocked her phone. She blocked the number and deleted the texts. Her phone went back into her purse. She opened her mouth and yelled loud and long. No words, just sound, as she spun herself into the throng of revelers, looking for a stranger to dance with.

She didn't have to look for long. Less than a minute had passed before a straight-up hottie caught her eye. He had been dancing with another girl, but Leighann easily coaxed him away. He was a good dancer. His body moved in perfect time to the beat. Not too tall, but fit and muscular. He got closer and closer. Soon, Leighann was practically undulating against him, clutching his strong arms to hold on. He was older, his face unshaven, his baseball cap twisted to the side. She felt his stubble brush her cheek when he leaned down and whispered in her ear.

"Let's get out of here."

Leighann laughed off the suggestion. He was too good-looking to be this thirsty. She let her hands travel along his back. His shirt was damp from sweat. Gyrating bodies were packed around them. They both kept getting crashed into, which made them move closer, until there was no more space between them. Despite the driving bass, they started slow dancing, swaying together. He looked down at Leighann, his eyelids heavy because he was either stoned or filled with lust or both.

He tried again. "You want a drink?"

She shook her head. She was already halfway drunk and, besides, she wasn't going to be one of those stupid bitches who got roofied. The Creeper was still out there. She had promised Jake that he was the only man she was going home with tonight.

"Come on," he said. "Are you teasing me or what?"

Leighann was fine with teasing him. She licked her lips to draw attention to her mouth. He got the hint. He started kissing her. Sweetly at first, but then he got down to business. His hands were on her hips. She could feel her body responding to his tongue. The club started to disappear. They were surrounded by people but completely alone. The kiss got deeper. She went up on tiptoe as he gripped her ass and started grinding against her.

Fuck, he was making her hot.

He slipped his hand up the back of her shirt. Leighann knew he was testing her. Sure enough, his hand moved and his thumb started stroking the side of her breast. Which felt really good. Then his hand slipped around to the front of her bra. She was about to tell him to slow his roll when she felt a sharp pinch.

Her mouth broke away from his.

Leighann's first thought was that the button on his sleeve had accidentally scraped the bottom of her ribs, but the pain was too intense, too familiar.

An insect bite? A bee sting?

A needle.

Leighann looked down. She saw the syringe in his hand. He flipped back the plastic cover on the needle, tucked the syringe into his pocket, and it was like it had never been there.

Except for the memory of the pain just below her ribs. Except for the liquid heat that was rushing through her body. The feeling in her soul that something bad had happened, that something far worse was on the horizon.

The room started spinning. She tried to look at him, memorize his face. Their eyes locked. He was smiling as the drug took effect. She had mistaken predatory fascination for lust. He wrapped his arm around her waist. His other hand was pressed between her shoulder blades. He wasn't holding her. He was waiting to catch her when she passed out. All the things Leighann had been taught, all the things that she absolutely knew she would do if this ever happened, rushed through her mind—

Scream! Run! Hit him! Scratch him! Bite him! Claw his eyes out! Kick him in the nuts! Wave your hands! Act crazy! Try to get attention! Memorize his face! Make sure his DNA is under your fingernails! Throw up! Piss yourself! Shit yourself! Drop to the floor!

None of that was going to happen.

Every single one of Leighann's muscles stopped

working at the same time. Her head flopped back. Her eyes went wild, desperately searching for Jake. She couldn't control her movements. Her skull was too heavy. Her vision started to blur. Her eyelids fluttered. The music changed. The new beat pounded inside her chest. She saw hands reaching up toward the ceiling. Lights flashing. Mirrored disco ball spinning, spinning, spinning.

Then everything went black.

6

Will stood in the reception area of the Piedmont Hills Town and Country Club. Before walking through the massive front doors, he had blocked out all the noise in his head from the night before. The only way he was able to work undercover was to remove his actual self from the narrative. Real Life Will, the man who was worried about his fiancée, who was concerned that Sara was close to breaking, was buried in the back of his brain. For now, in this place and at this time, he was the douchey-looking spoiled nephew of a woman who took a perverse pleasure in hurting other people.

He glanced around the room, projecting a sense of bored entitlement. The place managed to look both opulent and cheap at the same time. The carpet pads under the rugs were thick enough to suck at the soles of his boots, but the rugs themselves were worn at the edges. The silk upholstery on the chairs and couches had lost its sheen. Gold chains and crystals dripped from the ornate lighting, but several of the bulbs were burned out. The ceiling was painted in pastoral scenes with plump sheep and lots of milkmaids who couldn't keep their shirts from falling off their shoulders, but cobwebs were in the corners. Hand-carved mahogany paneling covered every visible wall. Gashes had not been repaired. Inlaid mirrors offset some of the more damaged sections.

Everywhere Will looked, he caught his reflection. Which was a good reminder of who he was supposed to be. No three-piece suit. His hair was gelled in place. He hadn't shaved this morning. He was wearing a long-sleeved cashmere polo that Sara had given him last Christmas and a pair of tight Ferragamo jeans that still had the tag tucked into the back because he was going to return them by the end of the day. The Diesel boots he might keep, but only because they'd been half off.

The only item that connected him to Real Life Will was the watch on his wrist. The Timex was old school, nothing fancy, with a leather strap that was peeling because Will had sweated out every liquid in his body alongside the Mississippi militia. He looked at the

time. Eliza had told him to meet her here at exactly
ten o'clock.

She was ten minutes late.

"Mr. Trethewey?" A slim blonde approached Will
with her hand out. She was carrying a thick leather
folder. "I'm Ava Godfrey, the membership director for
the club. I'm sorry you had to wait."

Will shook her hand. He had no idea why she was
calling him Trethewey. He'd told the guy at the gate
that he was Eliza's nephew, but he hadn't offered his
name.

"Your aunt is in the lounge." Ava pulled a brochure
from the folder. "I've brought you a map of the club.
I hope you and your family will enjoy using the facilities while you're in town. I'd be happy to provide you
membership information when the time comes."

Will pretended to study the color-coded drawing,
but he'd already memorized the plan by the front door.
Sara had been right about the separation. The women's
locker room was all the way over by the tennis courts,
in the basement of what was labeled the Racquet Pavilion. The men's facilities were in the main clubhouse,
close to the three restaurants and two bars. Then there
was the men's private lounge on the top floor. As if the
name wasn't enough of a warning, they'd added a tiny

line of text along the bottom about how ladies were not allowed.

"If you'll follow me?" Ava didn't wait for his response. She passed by the Men's Lounge sign and started up the stairs sideways to accommodate her very high heels.

Will followed her at a distance, squinting at the burst of sunlight streaming through the second-story windows. The lounge offered a spectacular view of the course. Bright blue sky, rolling hills, the Chattahoochee River snaking by, golfers idling in carts as they waited for their tee times.

Early on in their relationship, Sara had tried to show him how to play golf. At the time, Will would've played Tiddlywinks if it meant being alone with her. Now, he supposed it was an okay game if you were the type of man who could waste five hours riding around in a toy car whacking a small white ball with a stick.

He turned his back to the windows. Despite the unrelenting sunlight, the room felt dark and depressing. Worse, it was filled with the odors of his miserable childhood: stale cigars, burning cigarettes and spilled alcohol. The stench permeated every surface, from the long bar on the side of the room to the leather couches and chairs. Even the ceiling, which had been painted dark brown to hide the tobacco stains, seemed to hold onto a fug of smoke.

There was only one occupant in the room.

Eliza had taken center stage in a large, semicircular booth at the back. She had changed since the last time Will had seen her. She had always been slim but now she looked desiccated. As she tapped her cigarette into an ashtray, Will could see the skin hanging from her bony wrist like a piece of wet linen. And yet, her face looked like it belonged on a different body. Will didn't know much about plastic surgery, but whoever had sliced and rearranged Eliza's features had done a damn good job.

Her face looked younger than Will's.

Ava started walking toward the booth. Along the way, she offered a rambling description of the club, but Will tuned her out, struggling to keep his undercover persona in place because every muscle in his body fought to turn him back around.

"Good morning, ma'am." Ava stopped in front of the semicircular booth. "I've brought your nephew and the paperwork."

Eliza had tracked their progress across the lounge, but she'd looked down at the last minute, rolling her cigarette in the already full ashtray. A gold Zippo was on the table in front of her. A glass of amber liquid. A gold engraved cigarette case.

Ava placed the leather folder on the table. The club's emblem was embossed in gold. Eliza still didn't look up, even when Ava said, "When you're ready, ma'am."

Will watched the younger woman take the hint and scurry toward the stairs. When he turned back around, Eliza was still looking at the ashtray, seemingly content to roll her cigarette around the glass edge until the end of time.

She told Will, "They banned smoking in the general areas back in the nineties, but I told them I'd joined as a smoker and I would continue to smoke."

Will stared at the top of her head. She was wearing a wig. He could see the holes in her fake scalp.

"This was the compromise. I get the place until ten thirty." She waved her hand, indicating the room. "I've always gotten along better with men anyway. Women can be so tedious with their petty games."

Will knew she was playing a petty game right now.

He slid into the booth, keeping his distance. The temperature in the corner had dropped several degrees. He could hear the wind rattling the large windows. Cigarette smoke fogged the air around them. Judging by the ashtray, she had been here a lot longer than the ten minutes he'd wasted downstairs.

He asked, "Trethewey?"

"I assumed you'd want to be incognito. Your first name is John. Do you like it?" She didn't just look up at Will. She took in every detail. "Is that cashmere?"

Will jerked away his arm when she reached out to touch his sleeve.

"Steady now. I charge extra to bite." The cigarette went back to her mouth. She watched him through the curl of smoke. "Is it Will or Wilbur?"

Will didn't answer. He wasn't going to be here long enough for her to use his name.

She breathed out smoke from her nostrils. "Well, nephew, you're a police officer. I imagine you want me to add another police officer to my guest list. Who are you investigating at the club?"

He said nothing.

"There are so many criminals to choose from," she said. "Congressmen and senators and judges, oh my. They collude like gangsters. You can spot them by their colors. Louis Vuitton, Zegna, Prada. The Birken Bitches run quite a racket during the holidays trying to see who can raise enough money to feed the poor. It's a shame they don't simply pay their fair share of taxes and let the poor feed themselves."

Will hadn't come here for an eat-the-rich diatribe. He reached for the leather folder.

"Not yet." Eliza waited for him to take his hand from the folder. "You told me you need a favor. I need a favor, too."

Will had expected her to make this difficult. What he hadn't expected was to feel physically ill every time he looked at her. "What do you want?"

"Your silence."

Will routinely gave his silence for free. "If you're worried I'll tell people how you knew my mother—"

"No, I don't care about that. Every other woman in this place is a prostitute. At least I got paid for it." She carefully stubbed out the cigarette. "I need to tell you something."

"I'm not your priest."

"Good thing," Eliza said. "Every time I walk into church, the altar catches on fire."

She was waiting for him to laugh.

Will didn't laugh.

"I want you to listen to me for thirty seconds, uninterrupted. Then I'll do what you asked."

He stared out the window. He pretended to think about it, as if listening to her would be some kind of hardship because she actually thought Will gave a shit about what she had to say.

She prompted, "So?"

He took off his Timex. He placed it flat on the table. He waited for the second hand to come round to twelve, then said, "Go."

"I've already done you a tremendous favor."

Will watched the secondhand tick toward the one. She was burning through time, drawing it out as she smoked her cigarette.

"I kept you away from your uncle because I owed that much to your mother. You would not be the man you are today if you had lived in your uncle's house."

He watched the hand stutter past the three, then the four. Eliza was either deluding herself or toying with him. Will had been around damaged people all his life. Some of them never came back from it. Some of them saw their pain as a license to damage everybody else. Survival of the shittiest. His ex-wife excelled at it. Eliza was the queen.

She said, "Your mother ran away from home for very specific reasons. There was no safety there. No peace. That's how she ended up on the streets. That's how she ended up dead."

Her thirty seconds were up. Will sat back in the booth. He looked out the window at the stark blue sky. "She ended up on the streets because she was tricked out by a psychopath."

"Not all psychopaths lurk on street corners." Eliza snapped open the cigarette case. "I have one more thing to tell you."

Will heard men laughing at the bar. A handful of golfers had started to trickle in. They were dressed in loud pants and shirts. Some of them were lighting cigars.

"I'm dying." Eliza watched his face, looking for a response that he would never give. "You've made it clear you don't want my money."

"Did it buy you happiness?"

"No, but it gave me fewer things to be unhappy about." She had an unsettling smile on her face. "I suppose I'll leave it all to Antifa and Black Lives Matter now."

Will was the wrong audience for her jokes.

"See that fella?" Eliza nodded toward one of the men at the bar. "Former congressman. Got caught dipping his stubby fingers into the wrong panties. Now he's a lobbyist for a tech company. Makes millions a year."

Will had a vague recollection of the story from the news, but he had no idea why she had pointed out the man.

"That fat cocksucker beside him," Eliza said. "Tenured law professor who said the N-word. Still collects his salary while he plays golf all day."

Will's only surprise was that Eliza hadn't said the actual N-word.

"And the other one, the twit in the bow tie," she continued. "Former medical school professor. Practicing doctor. Got caught with his dick out around a patient. They gave him a golden parachute. He makes a fortune as a consultant."

Will turned his back to the bar. "Why do you think I care about any of these people?"

"You're investigating someone here," Eliza said. "I'm letting you know the odds are stacked against you. They've got too much money, too much power, too much reach. None of them ever face the consequences of their actions. Look at your uncle. He got away scot-free."

His uncle had keeled over a few hundred yards from where they were sitting. "They'll lose eventually."

"Nephew, you know the rules of this game. Even when they lose, they still win."

Will reached for the leather folder.

"Take Tommy McAllister." Again, Eliza waited for his hand to move away from the folder. "There's constant talk of lawsuits in this place, but Tommy's wrongful death suit is *the* hot topic. Not that anyone speaks to me. I'm the miserable old bitch in the corner. But I hear things."

He waited for her to tell him the things.

"Poor Britt and Mac. Poor Tommy. That girl's parents are just looking for a payout. If they win, it's only because the jury wants to punish the one percent. Tommy is the real victim. Those greedy fuckers are trying to ruin his life."

Will slid the folder in her direction. "We made a deal."

Eliza pushed it back. "Do you think men like Mac and Tommy McAllister actually pay a price for anything? Not the way your mother paid. Not the way we paid."

Will ran his tongue along the inside of his teeth.

"Mac is a god in the medical community. Impeccable reputation. Inherited a disgusting sum from dear old pappy, who was an absolute poonhound, by the way. I could tell you some stories about what really happens in this room. Enough to make Caligula blush." The unlit cigarette bobbed in her mouth. "Meanwhile, Britt is the one I feel sorry for."

Will couldn't stop the look on his face.

"Nephew, let me tell you something." She took the cigarette from her mouth. "Girls are born with these gaping holes in their hearts. They need love and security. They need to feel valued. Protected. Cherished."

Will figured everybody needed those things. Especially children.

"That's where pimps come in," Eliza said. "They make you feel special. They sweep you off your feet. They buy you things. They make sure you've got food and clothes and a roof over your head and before you know it, you've got nothing and they control everything. That's when they tell you to get on your knees. And you do it, because they have all the power."

He watched her flip open the lighter and touch the flame to her cigarette. She blew the smoke out of the corner of her mouth, away from Will.

"They call it *tricking* for a reason," she said. "Pimps trick you into giving up everything so that you're completely powerless. All he has to do is give you this *look*. You know he's going to beat you down later. That he could take away everything. Kick you out into the street. Leave you with nothing. Break your heart. It's terrifying to live under that kind of constant fear."

Will didn't need the details. He had spent the first eighteen years of his life living with that fear.

She said, "Look over at the bar. Don't be fooled by the hideous clothes. Most of them are harmless, but a few are straight-up pimps. You can see how the other men respond to them. One look, and they're like dogs heeling to their master. All hail the great man."

Will glanced over at what appeared to him to be a bunch of overweight, middle-aged day-drinkers who were just as likely as his uncle to have a massive stroke on the golf course.

"They control their wives, abuse them, humiliate them, cheat on them, treat them like shit. And the wives put up with it. They tell themselves that they love their husbands, or that a divorce would hurt the kids, but the truth is that they're terrified. They don't want to be poor. They sure as hell don't know how to be alone. At least I knew I was bought and paid for. Britt still thinks she's got a choice."

"What's the angle here?" Will asked. "Britt's son raped and beat a nineteen-year-old girl who died from her injuries, but I'm supposed to let that go because her husband is mean to her?"

"I'm just telling you the odds, nephew." She started turning the ashtray with her fingers. "Your mother had very strong opinions about right and wrong. It was a bizarre trait to see in a whore, but she really felt that the world should make sense. Is that how you feel?"

Will started to put his watch back on.

"She loved music. Did you know that?"

Will had seen some of her posters. Aerosmith. The Cure. Bowie.

"She loved reading, too," Eliza said. "Pulp, mostly. Love stories. She was a sucker for a bodice ripper. She always had her nose in a book. When it wasn't in a man's crotch."

He glared at her.

"I wish that I could've saved her. I wish that I could've done more for you."

Will pulled the band tight on his watch. "Are you looking for redemption?"

"Me?" She sounded offended. "Redemption is for pussies."

He nodded toward the folder. All he needed was for her to fill out the form. "I gave you more than thirty seconds."

Eliza's bony fingers crept out like a spider's legs as she opened the leather folder. A gold pen was clipped inside. She twisted the barrel. "What's the name of this friend you want me to put on my list?"

Will took a piece of paper out of his pocket. He'd typed out Sara's name ahead of time.

Eliza glanced at the name. "That won't do. Ava's a nosy little bitch. She'll look her up on the computer. Let's call your friend Lucy Trethewey. Does that work for you?"

Will didn't answer the question. "Won't she have to show her ID?"

"No one cares about IDs here. It's not like you're trying to vote Democrat." Eliza signed the bottom of the form with a flourish. "My membership number is thirteen-twenty-nine. Feel free to charge whatever you like at the bar."

Will watched her slide around the other side of the booth. Her frailty was more evident as she moved. She was clearly in pain. Standing took visible effort. When she reached back for her cigarettes and lighter, her face contorted, and Will got a look at the old woman under the unnaturally tight skin.

He handed her the leather folder so she didn't have to reach again.

Eliza held it to her chest, but she didn't leave yet. "Your mother's dying wish was for you to live. You might be the only man who never disappointed her."

Will didn't watch Eliza go. She had left the slip of paper with Sara's name by the ashtray. He folded it in two, then folded it again. Then he put it in his pocket because he didn't want anyone finding it by mistake.

He hated the thought of Sara being in this place.

He hated even more that Eliza had figured out what he was up to.

The men at the bar had broken into groups. The handsy congressman-turned-lobbyist was toasting the racist law professor. The former medical school professor who'd flashed a patient was fiddling with the bow tie around his thick neck. He was dressed differently from the other men. It was hard to pin down, but his clothes were almost too nice. Unlike the man he was speaking to. His companion was taller, a bit jowly, and had the arrogant bearing of a pediatric cardiothoracic surgeon.

Mac McAllister looked exactly like his photograph.

Will stood up. He tried to take a breath that wasn't clogged with Eliza's venom and cigarette smoke as he worked to push Real Life Will out of his brain. His undercover skills had kept him alive on more than one dicey occasion. A sex offender and an asshole in plaid golf pants were hardly a challenge. Will slipped back into the douchey nephew persona as he walked toward the bar.

"Richie?" he called to the man in the bow tie. "Jesus, is that you? I can't believe it! What are the odds?"

Richie turned, clearly not recognizing Will. His mouth opened, but Will wasn't going to let him talk just yet.

"When's the last time I saw you?" Will smelled alcohol on the man's breath as he shook Richie's hand and gave him a firm slap on the back. Not even eleven in the morning and the guy was already a few drinks in. "Was it at Royce and Blythe's party? That was right before he found out about Mason, right? Jesus, that guy will slip it into anything."

"Uh—" Richie's eyes went to Mac, but even pervy assholes were bound by the social graces. He grinned at Will, saying, "Must've been. How long ago was that?"

"Not long enough for Royce." Will laughed, then put a surprised look on his face. "Mac McAllister. Are you guys getting the gang back together without me? When's the mixer?"

Mac's smile was tight, like a crocodile's. He wasn't as loose as Richie. In fact, everything about him was wound very tight. He was clearly about to ask Will who the hell he was.

Will robbed him of the chance. "Speaking of which, have you guys been by the old place lately? What did we call it? Liver something?"

"Delivery." Mac was watching Will as he took a drink.

Will shook his head. "That doesn't sound right."

"It was De-Liver's," Richie volunteered. "Andalusia's been our spot for a while. It's off Pharr. The gang's still together, but we've lost some of the hangers-on.

We're doing a father–son thing this Friday. Do you have—"

"What was the real name?" Mac interrupted. "De-Liver's. What was it really called?"

"The Tenth," Richie provided, though the question was clearly meant for Will.

Mac did an okay job of hiding his irritation. He placed his glass on the counter, squaring it to the edge. He shot Richie a look of warning.

Richie was oblivious. "They tore down De-Liver's yonks ago. Pity to see it gone."

Will said, "Probably the only way to get the floors clean."

They all laughed, but Mac was still guarded. He tried again to pin down Will. "Haven't seen you at the club in a while."

"I should've never moved away. Richie, don't panic, but I think I can see the bottom of your glass." Will stuck his hand in the air for the bartender. He asked Richie, "Are you still teaching?"

Richie exchanged a quick look with Mac. "You didn't hear?"

"You really have been away." Mac was more comfortable talking now that it was at another man's expense. "Poor sod got MeToo'd."

"Damn, I know your pain." Will lowered his voice. "That's actually why I'm moving back to Atlanta. I'll spare you the salacious details. Let's just say that the wife insisted on a fresh start."

"Lucky you. Mine ran off with half my money." Richie had let the bartender fill his glass. He swallowed half of it down before he spoke again. "I barely managed to land on my feet."

"Bourbon, neat," Will told the bartender. He watched the man automatically pour a double. "Mac, I heard about your kid. Terrible thing to have to deal with. How are you and Britt holding up?"

Mac ratcheted down even tighter, but said, "You do what you have to do."

"Everybody's looking for a handout, am'aright?" Will picked up his glass. The smell of alcohol was noxious. "If that happened to my boy, I'd go to the mat the same way you are."

Mac took the bait. He wanted clues to Will's identity. "How old is your son now?"

"Eddie's twenty-two." Will mashed together Sara's father's name with details about Faith's kid. "He's graduating Tech in a few months. 3M is recruiting the hell out of him. Tommy's in medical school?"

Mac's shoulders relaxed a little, but not by much. "If he makes it through the trial intact."

"He's his father's son," Will said. "He'll come out stronger."

"Fucking Sara Linton," Richie slurred. "You'd think that bitch would know to shut her mouth by now."

"Linton? What's she up to?" Will put the glass of bourbon to his mouth and pretended to drink so that he didn't punch Richie's teeth into the back of his skull.

Mac said, "It's nothing. An irritation."

"As per her usual." Richie jabbed his thumb at Mac. "She's always been jealous of his skills."

Mac shook the ice cubes in his glass. "She certainly played the long game."

"You look at what happened to Cam," Richie said. "Why him and not her?"

"Rich," Mac warned, glancing at Will.

Will held up his hand like he was playing the peacemaker. "It's okay."

"It's not okay," Richie said. "Saint Sara gets all the pity while Cam rots in his grave? I don't think so."

Mac gently returned his glass to the bar. He didn't speak, but there was something about him that sucked up all the oxygen in the room. Eliza was right to compare him to a pimp. Mac had given Richie the *look*, and Richie had been quickly brought to heel.

"I'm sorry." Richie nervously adjusted his bow tie.

"I've had a bit too much to drink. I can't even remember your name."

Mac was tensed, like the wire on a hunting bow. He was waiting for the answer.

Will forced out a boisterous laugh. He slapped Richie on the back. "You're hilarious, man. Don't ever change."

7

Sara drove through the winding entrance of Piedmont Hills Town and Country Club. The guard at the gate had barely glanced up from his tablet when she'd provided the fake name. She supposed she looked the part. Her BMW X5 probably blended in with all the other cars that came through. So would Will's 1979 Porsche 911, though he hadn't written a check for the classic sportscar. He had restored it from the ground up with nothing more than his brain and his two hands.

She made the curve around the main building, which looked like a French country manor. The golf course followed the rushing waters of the Chattahoochee River. The place felt busy for a weekday. The weather was magnificent, only slightly chilly with the sun piercing a cloudless sky. She had to slow for a few golf carts to pass. One of the men tipped his hat at Sara.

The tennis courts were a good distance from the main building. The cars thinned out the farther she got from the first tee. Sara swallowed down her nervousness as she turned toward the Racquet Pavilion. Her hands were slick on the steering wheel. She reminded herself why she was here.

What happened to you. What happened to Dani. It's all connected.

Sara was not going to give Britt a moment of peace until she had an explanation.

She heard the muted *thunks* of rackets hitting balls as she got closer to the courts. Will's Porsche was tucked into a space on a slight rise in the parking lot. He'd chosen an area off to the side that gave him a view of the eight clay tennis courts and the Racquet Pavilion, which had the women's locker room in the basement. The perch gave him a clear line of sight to all the comings and goings, like a hawk watching for prey.

As of five minutes ago, he had not seen Britt McAllister.

Sara pulled into a space behind him and to the left. Will got out of his car. She bit her lip, because she absolutely hated the way he looked. The cashmere polo was nice—she had picked it out for him last year—but the fitted jeans and gelled hair belonged to an entirely different kind of man. Worse, he hadn't shaved this morning, so his face looked rough and stubbly.

The door opened. He said, "Still no sign of her."

Sara's stomach clenched as Will climbed into the BMW. The man who'd raped Sara had worn a shaggy beard. The memory of the coarse hair scratching her face could still make her physically ill. Instead of offering her cheek for Will to kiss, Sara held onto his hand.

He said, "Faith just checked in from fraud patrol. She put in a call to APD. She wants to talk to the detective who took the complaint of the rape charge against Tommy in high school. Maybe she can persuade him to give up the girl's name."

Sara was more interested in how Will was doing. On the phone, he hadn't said anything about the meeting with Eliza. She looked down at their hands. He was still holding onto her. That was probably as close as he was ever going to come to admitting how hard it had been to be in the same room with his aunt.

She said, "The name you told me to give at the gate. Who's Lucy Trethewey?"

"One of my mother's aliases. Eliza had me down as John Trethewey. Get it—John?" Will kept his gaze on the building, but she could feel a fractious energy coming off him. "Speaking of names, Richie's last name is Dougal."

Sara felt a click in her head. Now she remembered the bow-tied hospitalist. "How did you find out?"

"I got it off the bartender after Mac and Richie left the Men's Lounge."

Sara felt her lips part in surprise. "You saw them?"

"I didn't just see them. I talked to them."

Sara didn't know what to say.

"Eliza set it all up. That's why she told me to meet her at the club at exactly ten. She knew I was looking into Tommy McAllister."

Sara couldn't make sense of the deceit. "You weren't looking into him until last night. How the hell did she even know?"

He finally turned toward her. Will would talk about the puzzle before he talked about his feelings. "It's no secret that I'm engaged to you. You testified at Tommy's trial yesterday. Everybody at the club knows about the lawsuit. Then I showed up out of nowhere asking Eliza to get a friend into the club. She knows I'm an investigator. It's not a difficult connection to make if you're paying attention."

Sara did not ask the obvious question—why was Eliza paying attention?

"What's that list called," he said. "The one where you sign up to play golf?"

"The tee sheet." Sara knew that the information was

posted for any club member to see. That's how you found out who was playing and which slots were open. "Why?"

"Eliza must've looked at the tee sheet. Saw what time Mac was going to be here. Those guys have a routine, I guess. Hit the bar. Hit the course. She played me like a fiddle. Even made me wait ten minutes to give them time to dawdle."

Sara watched his face turn away. He was looking for Britt again. She hadn't heard any emotion in his voice, but she still felt last night's guilt welling back up inside her. This was her fault. Will had only stepped into Eliza's line of fire because of Sara.

She tightened her grip on his hand. "You said that you spoke to Mac and Richie?"

"Briefly," he said. "Mac's exactly like you described. Like Eliza described. He's an arrogant control freak. You were right about the way he tilts his head. If that guy had been at my school, he would've been punched in the face every day of his life."

From the sound of his voice, Will seemed ready to punch him now. "Did he say anything about my testimony at Tommy's trial?"

"Richie did. Said you've always been jealous of Mac. Asked why Cam was dead while you were still alive. Called you Saint Sara."

She'd always hated the nickname. Anyone would be a saint by comparison to the gang. "Why would he bring up Cam's suicide in relation to me? Was he saying it like it was an either/or? Either Cam kills himself or I do?"

"No idea, but it was strange." Will looked back at Sara again. "Richie could've been posturing. He knows how Mac feels about you testifying."

"What else did he say?"

"Something like, why is Cam rotting in his grave while Sara gets all the pity?"

Sara mulled the information over in her head. Another either/or statement. But Will could be right about the posturing. What little she remembered of Richie Dougal was that he could be a bit of a sycophant. Which was probably why he was still in Mac's life. There was a reason Mac was still married to a woman who worshipped him.

She told Will, "It's hard to feel insulted when I couldn't even remember Richie's last name."

"That's a good way to look at it." Will turned away, back on duty. "He was drunk anyway. I got a little bit more out of him before Mac shut him down. The bar they used to go to, the real name was the Tenth. The gang is still doing the mixer at a new place called Andalusia. They bring their sons occasionally. Passing on the torch, I guess."

Sara felt an inexplicable betrayal to hear that the mixer was still going on. For some reason, she had assumed that what had happened to her that night at Grady had altered the gang in a meaningful way.

He said, "None of them were wearing wedding bands."

Sara thought it was an odd detail for him to pick up on. "A lot of men don't."

"Not this man." Will turned his wrist to look at his watch. "Do you think Britt changed her plans?"

"Maybe."

Sara stared at the tennis courts, which were filled with fiercely competitive, well-toned women. Every single one was driving the ball across the net like Steffi Graf taking on Martina Navratilova. Britt would easily fit in with the players. If she deigned to make an appearance.

Sara took in a deep breath as she thought about confronting Britt.

Back when Sara was training as a surgeon, she would spend the night before a big operation visualizing the procedure. Sometimes, she would even move her hands in the correct positions, trying to train into her fingers the small, almost imperceptible movements of repair. There were always surprises but mapping out a strategy ahead of time was the best way to be prepared.

Now Sara mapped out her plan to confront Britt. She was by no means looking for a catfight. She wanted to be direct and honest and try to get the same from Britt. Only one of them would be worried about the other women overhearing. Sara would have the element of surprise, but not for long. She had winnowed down all of her questions to just three: How was Sara's fifteen-year-old assault connected to Dani's? Where did Mac and Tommy fit in? Who were the *them* that Britt couldn't stop?

Will said, "You told me that Britt's purse spilled onto the bathroom floor. Did you see her key-fob? Did it have a logo?"

Sara closed her eyes, summoning the memory. She hadn't recognized the logo. "A silver circle with blue? Maybe a cross? A squiggle?"

"Was it on a keyring?"

"Not exactly," Sara said. "You'd expect Cartier or something expensive, but it was a cheap-looking blue plastic ring with a white center. It attached to the key-fob with a blue nylon cord."

Will let go of her hand so he could retrieve his phone

from his pants pocket. He said, "Hey, Siri. Show me an Apple AirTag."

Sara instantly recognized the image of the small tracking device. "That's it."

"Britt McAllister sounds too uptight to lose her keys that much." Will slipped his phone back into his pocket. He held onto Sara's hand again. "My guess is she's driving an Alfa Romeo Stelvio Quadrifoglio in Misano blue."

"That's very specific."

"The squiggle you saw on the keyfob is a serpent, the Biscione. The cross is George's Cross. Both date back to the crusades. They've been on Alfa Romeo's badge since the early 1900s. Two-thirds of the cars in this lot are SUVs. Alfa Romeo's SUV is the Stelvio. The more expensive model is the Quadrifoglio. I'm guessing the color based on the plastic tag."

"Nice work, Sherlock." Sara had watched him pore over car magazines the way she pored over the *American Journal of Forensic Medicine*. "What would you guess I drove if my purse spilled on the floor?"

"A garbage truck." He was smiling when he resumed his surveillance. Sara was not the tidy one in the relationship. That he didn't murder her every time he walked into their bathroom was a small miracle.

She heard a sharp burst of conversation as a group of women walked out of the locker room and headed toward their cars. Some of the sets on the court had started to change over. Sara looked at Will's watch. Barely three minutes had passed. "Is this what you and Faith do all day? Sit in a car and wait for people?"

"She usually brings snacks." He stroked her hand with his thumb. "You're better company."

Sara smiled as she sat back in the seat. A lone woman was pacing in front of the entrance to the locker room as she talked on her phone. She kept throwing her hand in the air. She was clearly arguing with someone.

Will said, "Husband's trying to explain how he accidentally adopted a chihuahua."

Sara laughed. She loved that Will had accidentally adopted a chihuahua. "More like she just found out he's been cheating."

"You could call Mason."

The suggestion was so out of the blue that Sara didn't quite know how to respond. Was he worried about her cheating with Mason, or was he thinking through contingencies in case Britt didn't show up?

She settled on a neutral question. "Where did that come from?"

"Mason was at the mixer. He knows everybody in the gang. He might've seen something that night. Or he remembers something. He's a doctor, too. He'll have a good memory. And he was close to you at the time, so even a stray detail might've stuck in his head."

"Would it bother you if I talked to him?"

"Should it?"

She waited for him to look at her. "No."

He nodded. "I don't know how to say this, but I think Sloan Bauer—"

"Was screwing Mason while we were living together?" Sara had finally found a way to surprise him. "I kind of knew, but I kind of didn't care. He never made me crazy. I never felt like I was going to explode if we were in the same room and I wasn't touching him."

Will looked down at their clasped hands. He was smiling when he turned back to the Pavilion.

Sara was about to say something mushy that would embarrass the shit out of him when she caught a flash of metallic blue in the distance.

An SUV was turning into the Pavilion parking lot. The front side panel of the Alfa Romeo Stelvio had a small white triangle with a green four-leaf clover, or *quadrifoglio*, in the center. Britt McAllister was behind the wheel. She was driving slowly, looking for a parking space close to the courts.

Sara felt the acid in her stomach start to roil. She had told herself she was prepared for this, but suddenly, she felt very unprepared. She couldn't lose her courage now. Not after what Will had put himself through. Not when she thought about Tommy McAllister stalking his next victim. Sara's palm still held the memory of Dani Cooper's heart, like an invisible tattoo that would stay with her for the rest of her life. If Sara couldn't do this for herself, she could do it for Dani.

"You good?" Will asked.

"Yep." They had practiced some of the scenarios last night. Sara had to find a way to make Britt feel trapped. That wouldn't happen in the parking lot beside her car, or on the courts surrounded by her friends. The best place was the same place as before: the women's room.

Britt got out of the SUV holding her phone in one hand and a yellow Yeti water bottle in the other. Her yellow tennis outfit was in two pieces with a loose-fitting, long-sleeved top and a flowing skirt that fell a few inches above her knees. She opened the SUV's back door and took out a bright yellow leather backpack that matched her outfit. Then she put on a hat that was so close in hue to the other yellows that Sara wondered if she'd had it custom dyed.

Will asked, "That's a nice backpack. Who makes it?"

Sara gave him a curious look. He was never interested in brands. "Hermès. She dropped at least 5K on it."

"The cheap plastic holder on the AirTag bothers me." He was rubbing his jaw again. "Those high-end designers make holders. Look at how she's dressed. She's not buying accessories at the dollar store."

Sara had missed the detail, but now it was bothering her, too.

He said, "Eliza's membership number is thirteen-twenty-nine if you want to charge anything."

"I'll die from dehydration before I spend a dime of her money."

Will didn't laugh. He was studying Sara in that careful way of his. "It's not too late. You can always back out. We can leave right now. Go get some coffee."

Will didn't drink coffee.

Sara squeezed his hand one last time before she got out of the car.

The wind caught her skirt as she closed the door. She could see Britt making her way to the locker room as she walked toward the Pavilion. Sara checked out her own reflection in a car window. Her hair was loosely braided down the back. Her make-up was light. She'd put more thought into her outfit this morning than she had since her first date with Will. She'd finally decided on a deep purple, long-sleeved Lululemon tennis dress. The fit was tighter across the stomach than the style Britt was wearing, but as Britt had pointed out,

Sara was not a mother. She wasn't twenty-two years out from giving birth and still sporting a post-partum roll of redundant skin around her mid-section that no amount of plastic surgery could hide.

Sara passed by the woman who was pacing and arguing on her phone. She looked up at Sara, rolling her eyes, which meant that she was definitely talking to her husband. Sara absently twisted her engagement ring. She tried to steel herself, but she realized it was unnecessary. She felt an odd sense of peace as she got closer to the locker room entrance.

As far as Sara knew, Britt had never had close friends. Even without the hatefulness, Britt could be off-putting and slightly annoying. Pop culture eluded her. She didn't read or follow the news. She had been a very good doctor, but she hadn't practiced in years. Tennis offered a unique opportunity to smooth out Britt's hard edges. All that mattered on the court was how well you played. If you were on a team, then the women on that team were your friends. The club gave Britt entrée into a life that she would not otherwise have. She would feel safe here.

Sara was about to destroy that.

Warm air wafted around her as she walked into the building. There was a small lounge with a few tables, a snack station, and a machine that dispensed wine if you put in your membership number. Four women were playing bridge at the largest table. Older, skin the color of tobacco from decades of exposure to the sun. None of them were looking at the giant TV on the wall. Sara caught the words scrolling across the bottom of the local news.

Student missing from dance club since last night . . . police asking for information . . .

Another day. Another missing girl.

Sara went through a set of double doors to the main locker room. Photos of women sporting tennis outfits dated back to the middle of the last century. Sara had to think some of the leather-skinned card-players were among the black-and-white photos of women raising trophies and rackets over their heads. There was a leaderboard near the toilet stalls.

Britt McAllister was listed as the nineteenth-best women's tennis player at the club.

Not bad for her age.

Sara stood at an angle so that she could see the row of sinks. No Britt. All the toilet stall doors were ajar. She doubted Britt was taking a shower or relaxing in the hot tub, steam room or sauna, so she bypassed the door to the wet room. That left the actual locker room.

She counted twelve horseshoe-shaped sections, each with a bench running down the center. The lockers were generous, floor-to-ceiling, which unfortunately meant that Sara couldn't see over the tops. Everything felt rich, yet slightly scuffed. Dark wood paneling, gold trim, name plaques embossed in blue to match the club colors. Miffy Buchanan. Peony Riley. Mrs. Gordon Guthrie. Faith would be having a field day.

"I said leave me the fuck alone!"

Sara easily recognized Britt McAllister's voice.

A younger woman in a blue tennis dress rushed out of the last horseshoe section. Her head was down. She looked chastened. She passed by Sara without a glance.

Sara's stomach roiled again. The anxiety was back. Her knees felt stiff as she forced herself to keep walking. She was not going to go back to her car and tell Will that she had failed.

She found Britt sitting on a bench. Her head was down as she stared at her phone. The locker in front of her was open, but her bag and water bottle were at her feet.

She must've sensed Sara's presence, but she didn't look up. "Ainsley, I'm sorry I yelled at you. Please, I need a minute alone."

Sara caught a hint of despair in her tone. Of all the scenarios she had prepared for—a defiant Britt, an angry Britt, even a violent Britt, this one was the least expected.

The woman looked broken.

Sara wasn't going to be suckered into comforting her again. She took a quick breath before saying, "Britt."

Britt's head swung up. She gasped at the sight of Sara. She was too caught off guard to form a biting insult.

Sara crossed her arms over her chest. "What's the connection, Britt? How is my fifteen-year-old—"

Britt stood up so fast that she nearly tripped backward over the bench. She shoved her belongings into the locker. She kicked the door closed. She turned to Sara. Her mouth opened, but instead of speaking, she walked past her. Not toward the exit, but toward the wet room.

Britt didn't stop until she got to the glass door. She turned around to look at Sara before going inside.

Sara hesitated before following her. Britt's energy felt frenetic. She didn't appear to be high again. She wasn't raging or wielding insults like a switchblade. If Sara had to describe her demeanor with one word, it would be *scared*.

Fear could lead to all kinds of mistakes. Sara caught the glass door before it closed. She let Britt take the lead past the showers. One of the stalls was occupied. Sara stepped around a pool of water. She could hear the hot tub bubbling, the low murmur of women talking. Britt glanced through the glass door of the sauna. There were two occupants. She opened the door to the steam room. A dense fog wafted out. Britt grabbed a towel off the rack. She glanced back at Sara before going inside.

Sara reached for a towel, but hesitated again. Was it stupid to follow Britt into the one space where they wouldn't be overheard? Was this some kind of ruse on Britt's part to gain the advantage?

The only way to find out was to go inside.

The warm, wet air felt heavy inside Sara's lungs. Iridescent tiles covered every surface. The overhead lights didn't reach far. She could barely make out Britt placing a towel on the corner section of the bench. Sara dropped her towel closer to the door. She remained standing as Britt sat down.

"I—an email—" Britt's voice caught. "I got an email."

Sara could hear a muffled echo through the fog. She stepped closer so she could see Britt's face. Her head was in her hands. She was shaking again. It was almost exactly the same as two days ago at the courthouse.

"It was fr-from our—" Britt was clearly rattled. Steam swirled around her as she looked up at Sara. "The Coopers accepted our settlement offer."

Sara touched her fingers to the wall to steady herself. "You're lying."

Britt was not lying. Tears ran down her face like condensation on a glass of cold water.

Sara didn't want her tears. She wanted answers. "Why would they take your money?"

Britt shook her head. She didn't want to say it out loud.

"Tell me," Sara said. "What did you do to them?"

"I didn't do anything!" Her shrill voice bounced into the high corners. She put her hand to her mouth as if to rein it back in. "It was a boy who dated Dani in high school. He found an old phone with some photos. He came to us for money. They always want money."

Sara knew what kind of photos she was talking about. Back when she'd worked in pediatrics, she had lectured every girl who walked through her door about sending nude pictures. Very few of them ever listened.

She asked Britt, "How bad are they?"

Britt gave her an incredulous look, because you didn't ask for money unless they were bad. "Close-ups of her squeezing her breasts. Spreading open her labia. You can see her face in most of them. Her eyes are closed, and—"

Sara didn't need to hear the rest. Britt had seen the pictures. Mac. Their lawyers. Tommy. Who else?

Britt said, "I doubt the judge would've allowed the

photos in as evidence, but those kinds of things always end up online."

Sara sank down to the bench. She had thought her heart was incapable of breaking anymore for Dani's parents, but Britt had found a way shatter it into pieces. "Please tell me that the Coopers didn't see them."

"The photos were sent to their lawyer."

"Did they see them?"

Britt was silent, which meant that Dani's parents had twice witnessed their daughter at her most vulnerable—once when they had looked at her on the autopsy table and again when Douglas Fanning had sent them the nude photos.

Sara said, "You threatened to leak the photos. That's why they settled."

Britt stared at Sara through the lingering steam. "Do you really think Mac consults with me before he does anything?"

"Are you telling me you would've stopped him?"

"I can't stop him. Mac does what he wants. I have no say in anything."

"Is that your excuse? Poor Britt in her gilded cage?" Sara hadn't forgotten why she was here. Now it mattered more than ever. "What's the connection? How does what happened to me fifteen years ago have anything to do with Dani?"

Britt murmured, "Saint Sara to the rescue."

"Shut up." Sara was tired of her sniveling self-pity. "You told me that you wanted Tommy to stop. Tell me how to stop him."

"I won't let you hurt my son."

Sara remembered what she'd just seen on the lounge TV. "There's another girl missing. A student."

"Tommy was home last night. He doesn't have anything to do with that."

"But you saw it on the news. You were worried it was Tommy, too. He's not going to stop, Britt. Especially not now."

Britt didn't answer.

"What about Mac? Was he home last night?"

Her laughter had an edge to it. "Mac hasn't gotten it up in years. He sucks on his asthma inhaler more than me. I'm surprised my vagina hasn't closed up."

"Britt." Sara didn't know how to reason with her. She was so changeable. "What happened fifteen years ago? What did I miss?"

She would not answer.

"Please," Sara begged. "You don't have to tell me outright. Just give me a clue. A name. Something to follow. Something that helps me figure it out."

Britt's head tilted back. Her skin had a fine sheen of moisture mixed with sweat and tears. She was thinking about it. And then she had decided. Her head started to shake. "I can't help you."

Sara desperately searched for a way to break through. She could only come up with Will's conversation with Mac and Richie. The either/or. Richie had brought it up twice.

Why is Cam rotting in his grave while Sara gets all the pity?

She asked, "Does it have something to do with Cam?"

Britt's head turned toward Sara. Her lips parted, but like the last time, she retreated. "Leave it alone, Sara. Cam's dead. Don't dance on his grave."

Sara didn't ask her about Dani Cooper's grave. "What happened to Cam?"

"He wrapped his lips around the muzzle of a gun and pulled the trigger." Britt was watching her for a response. "I'm sure you've dealt with that before in your line of work."

"Tell me what I'm missing."

Britt gave a heavy sigh as she started to stand. "I'm late for my match."

"Britt, goddammit, how are you going to feel if Tommy hurts someone else?"

"He's not going to hurt anyone."

"You know he is." Sara struggled to keep herself

from shouting. "What happened at the mixer? I know Cam was there. What was he doing?"

Britt paused again, but this time, she gave a little. "His head was either in a bottle or in the toilet all night."

Sara felt a memory start to itch at her brain. "He was drunk?"

"He was on the fucking floor. That's one thing you always had over him. He never had the balls for emergency medicine."

"Why was he—"

"He lost a patient."

Sara felt herself nodding. She could remember Cam careening around the bar, grabbing onto people, begging them to listen. "He was devastated. He wouldn't stop drinking. Mason had to take away his car keys."

"Too bad Mason didn't hand him a Glock. Could've saved us all nearly a decade of his whining." Britt grabbed the towel off the bench and started to leave.

Sara blocked her way.

Britt didn't look intimidated. She looked challenged. "Is this payback for the courthouse?"

Sara knew that she couldn't reason with Britt as a woman, but she could talk to her as a doctor. "Dani scored a 515 on the MCAT in high school."

Britt's shock was genuine. Even college students

struggled to score that high on the Medical College Admissions test. Sara doubted Tommy had done as well.

"Dani was valedictorian of her high school. Her speech was about improving health outcomes in minority communities. She loved organic chemistry. She was volunteering at the women's health center. She wanted to go into obstetrics." Sara could tell that Britt was affected by her words. They were familiar to her own path toward medicine. "Dani drove herself to Grady that night because she knew that she needed help. Her life was slipping away. She knew exactly what was going on. She made me promise to stop him, Britt. Help me stop him. Tell me how it's connected."

Britt clenched her jaw so tight that Sara could practically hear her teeth gritting.

They were silently staring at each other, trapped in a stand-off, when the door opened. Steam swirled against the sudden influx of cool air. A woman was standing in her bathing suit waiting to come in. She had a strange look on her face, probably because she didn't expect to find Britt and Sara fully clothed inside the steam room.

"Darcy!" Britt put on a fake happy voice. "Look at you. I can barely tell you had a baby."

Darcy's face broke out into a smile. "She's finally hitting her milestones. Thank you so much for talking to me about it. Zander and I were very worried."

"My pleasure. Where are my manners?" Britt turned to Sara. "Darcy, this is Merit Barrowe. She used to work with me at Grady."

"Merit." Darcy shook Sara's hand. "What a lovely name."

Sara didn't correct her. She was too distracted by a crystal-clear memory from the Friday mixer. Cam had been obnoxiously drunk, slurring his words, begging for people to listen to him. He'd managed to trap Sara by the bar. His breath had reeked of whiskey and cigarettes. Spit kept flying out of his mouth. Cam usually drank too much, but this time was different. He was self-medicating, trying to numb the pain. He'd wanted to talk to Sara about what had happened in the ED two weeks before. They had both been working an overnight shift when tragedy struck.

Cam had lost a patient.

Twenty years old. Thready pulse. Altered state. The woman had suddenly collapsed in the patient bathroom. Her seizures were so intense that her leg had violently kicked out against the toilet. The sound of the porcelain cracking in two had been like a rifle shot inside the emergency department. The kick was hard enough to break the woman's ankle.

Sara was two curtains over when it happened. She couldn't remember what her patient was being treated for, but she remembered the details about the death of Cam's patient from the morbidity and mortality conference.

Drugged. Bound. Possible sexual assault.

Her name was Merit Barrowe.

8

Martin Barrowe had suggested Prime Craft Coffee on Atlanta's West Side as a place to meet to discuss his sister's death. Will was familiar with the area. He had spent most of his teenage years in the industrial warehouses working steel fabrication and building displays for tradeshows. Those businesses were long gone. The carpentry and machine shops had been torn down and replaced with mixed-use developments. Pricey apartments on top, even pricier home goods, restaurants, and clothing stores on bottom.

Given how he was dressed, Will fit in seamlessly with the professionals inside the sleek coffee shop. He was wearing the perfunctory pair of white earbuds, though he was the only customer who wasn't bent over a laptop. He followed the lines of text on his phone as he listened to the AI in his text-to-speech app read the

fifteen-year-old detective's report on the death of Merit
Alexandria Barrowe.

...parents positively identified twenty-year-old
female decedent at Fulton County Medical Examiner's
office. See affidavit. Initial impression: suspected
overdose. Female claimed sexual assault; findings inconclusive. See ME's report. Female was last seen at
a party on the campus of Georgia State University.
See witness statements. CCTV between party location and Grady Hospital non-functioning. Female
arrived through the west side entrance of Grady and
flagged down a security guard. See Alvarez, Hector,
witness statement. Alvarez escorted female to ED.
Female appeared intoxicated: slurring words, unable
to walk without assistance. Claimed sexual assault
but was unclear on details. After admission to the ED,
female asked to use bathroom. While in bathroom,
female experienced a seizure that resulted in break to
R ankle. See hospital incident report. Cause of death:
suspected post-hypoxic status epilepticus/SUDEP;
undetermined pending toxicology report.

Will paused the TTS app.
Sara had told him SUDEP meant sudden unexpected
death in epilepsy. Barrowe's breathing had paused too

long during a convulsive seizure. She'd basically suffo-
cated.

According to the medical examiner's report, Merit
Barrowe did not have a history of epilepsy, which
pointed to drug toxicity being the reason behind her
seizure. Will had worked cases where cocaine, meth,
MDMA and, in one instance, smoking too much pot
had caused a seizure. Any and all of those would probably be available at a campus party.

He scrolled down his phone, letting the TTS read
the autopsy report. There wasn't much to go on. The
medical examiner had elected to do what was sometimes called a partial autopsy, which meant he hadn't
cut open the body. An external examination was performed instead: X-rays, photographs, body diagram.

Will paused the reader. He looked at the diagram.
The break to the ankle and the bump to the head were
explained by the seizure. There was no contusion or
stab wound on the left side that would connect Merit
to Sara and Dani Cooper. The only detail the medical
examiner had called out on the left was a tattoo that
was three inches below the midline of the armpit, between the fourth and fifth rib. The length was listed
as 7.62 centimeters, or around three inches. No height
provided. There was no mention of whether the tattoo
had been words or symbols or a cartoon character.

There was only a bunch of X's on the body diagram, a slightly curved line like a maniacal clown's mouth.

He tapped his phone, clicking back through to the main folder that contained all of Merit Barrowe's official police files. He opened the scan of her death certificate. State records were all computerized now, but fifteen years ago, they were still using typewriters and ink pens. The TTS was good at reading the former, but the latter represented some obstacles. The only saving grace was the fact that whoever had inked in parts of the form had written in block letters.

Merit Alexandria Barrowe. Black hair. Green eyes. Twenty years old. Cause of death: overdose. The form had three options: accident, homicide, and suicide. None of them were checked. The section that was labeled *a brief explanation of cause of death* had been left blank.

The TTS couldn't read signatures, but fortunately, the doctor's name was typed out. Will wasn't surprised that Dr. Cameron Carmichael had signed off on Merit's death. Cam was Merit's doctor of record when she'd died, so it was his responsibility to fill out the official paperwork. The lack of a check mark by accident, suicide or homicide wasn't uncommon. Nor was the absence of *a brief explanation* in the rectangular box. Cam wasn't in charge of investigating the circumstances around the overdose. That job fell to the police. The medical examiner would be the one to check the box and provide the explanation.

The fact that the lead detective had not requested a full autopsy told Will a lot of things about how the man perceived the case. He clearly hadn't suspected foul play, despite two separate witnesses, Cam and the security guard, stating that Merit had reported sexual assault. Just as clearly, the medical examiner hadn't pushed back on the assessment. Which was interesting, but as with the death certificate, not surprising.

The Fulton County Medical Examiner's office had hit three thousand cases last year. Like most any medical facility these days, they were understaffed, burned out, and nearly crushed by the backlog of cases. The situation hadn't been that much rosier fifteen years ago when Merit Barrowe had died. The economy had been on the brink of collapse. Governments were slashing budgets. Soldiers were returning from multiple tours of duty in Afghanistan and Iraq. Tempers were up, anxieties were high, and violent crime had soared.

Will searched for the autopsy photographs, but only found one. The scan was in color, but the photo looked bleached. Merit Barrow was lying on a stainless-steel gurney. A white sheet was draped to her neck. Her short hair was combed back, eyes closed. She looked very young and very much alone on the cold metal table.

He took a moment to study her face. It was easy to forget the impact that a single death could have when your job was filled with death. Merit's parents had loved her. Merit's brother had loved her. She'd had friends and possibly lovers and only twenty short years on earth before all of that was taken away.

Will returned to the autopsy report without the TTS. The forms were standardized, so he easily found the place where the toxicology results were supposed to be listed. The word *PENDING* was also familiar. If the tox screen had come back from Grady Hospital or the Fulton County pathology lab, no one had bothered to append it to Barrowe's file. The detective investigating the case had never followed up on it, either.

Normally, Will would track down the detective, but he happened to know that Eugene Edgerton had died from pancreatic cancer nine years ago.

He was the same detective who had worked on Sara's sexual assault case.

"Did you read that bullshit report?" Faith sat down across from him with two large cups and a bad attitude. "'*Female claimed possible sexual assault.*'"

Will took the cup that had whipped cream on the

top, assuming the hot chocolate was meant for him. "What am I missing?"

"Female?" Faith repeated. "Merit had a name. The only reason to use the word *female* like that in a report is if you're an asshole or an incel."

Will stirred the whipped cream into his hot chocolate. He had already told Faith that Eugene Edgerton had worked both investigations. "Edgerton made an arrest in Sara's case."

"No offense, but Sara's a white, middle-class doctor. Edgerton never called Sara *female* in his report. He never said that she *claimed* sexual assault."

"You're talking about the difference between a living witness and a dead one," Will said. "The medical examiner's report was inconclusive. Barrowe showed signs of contusions and bruising that could've come from consensual sex. There was no sperm."

"Oh shit, are you telling me a rapist wore a condom?" Faith was not expecting an answer. "I'm telling you one hundred percent that Edgerton didn't believe Merit Barrowe was raped, so he didn't pursue a suspect, and he didn't request a full autopsy, and he didn't make a connection to Sara's case, which meant that Jack Allen Wright only spent eight years in prison when he could've been in there for twenty."

Will could kind of see her point, though he didn't exactly agree with how she'd arrived at it. "Do we know Wright's whereabouts on the night Merit Barrowe walked into Grady?"

"I've put in some calls to APD, but I'm having a shit time getting anybody to return them." She looked more annoyed than usual. "I can't even get Leo Donnelly to call me back about what's the deal with that student who disappeared from the Downlow last night. Worthless asshole was my partner for almost a decade and he can't bother to pick up the phone."

They both knew why her calls weren't being answered. Will had investigated some very highly placed officers in the Atlanta Police Department. One had retired. Several were currently in prison. Instead of being thankful that Will had helped clean up their shop, he could basically get stabbed eighty times in the middle of APD headquarters and every cop in the building would claim they hadn't seen a thing.

Faith was his partner. She had Will's stink all over her.

He asked, "What's the missing student's name?"

"Leighann Park. I hate to say it, but she got lucky for disappearing on a slow news day. From what I saw on TV, she went clubbing with a friend last night. They interviewed him this morning. He told the reporter that Leighann was freaked out about some creepy texts."

"Threats?"

"He didn't say, but—" Faith shrugged. "Every time a woman interacts with an electronic device, she's either getting a dick pic or a creepy text. It's hard to tell what's a real threat and what's bullshit."

Will hoped it was bullshit. "Go back to the Merit Barrowe autopsy. She didn't have a contusion or wound on her left side. She had a tattoo higher up her ribs, but the ME didn't think it was important enough to document."

"Because Edgerton told him it was an overdose and not to waste his time because he didn't believe the *female* when she told two people that she'd been raped."

Will drank his hot chocolate to give her a moment to grumble. "It's not weird that Edgerton worked both cases?"

"Nah." Faith took the lid off her tea and blew on the liquid. "They happened two weeks apart. He was the senior detective on call both nights."

Will was familiar with on-call rotations. You worked the same schedule for a month at a time. He pulled up the calendar on his phone and dialed it back fifteen years. "Merit Barrowe came into the hospital on a Friday night. She died the next morning."

Faith stopped mid-sip. "Same with Dani Cooper."

Neither of them needed a calendar for the next part, but Will said, "Same with Sara, except she lived."

"Fuck." Faith put down the cup. "Friday mixer, Friday rape?"

"The mixer was once a month, the last Friday of the month."

"Okay, but this is probable cause to ask APD to reopen Sara's case, right?"

"It's a stretch." Will was only thinking about Amanda. She was going to be furious with them for slacking off on fraud investigation. She might suspend them. Or worse, she could refuse to let them pursue the leads. "Cam wrote on the death certificate that Merit Barrowe died of an overdose. The medical examiner listed her cause of death as undetermined pending toxicology results. The tox report was never booked. Technically, that means the case is still open, but we would need Atlanta to ask us for help, and Atlanta—"

"Won't return my fucking calls." Faith reached into her purse for her spiral notebook. "I was thinking about what Britt told Sara. Or what she didn't tell her. Why is that bitch acting like she's narrating some kind of choose-your-own-adventure story? Why can't she just say what's the what?"

"Nobody wants to be the bad guy, especially when

it's their child," Will said. "Jeremy's a good kid, but what if he wasn't? Would you protect him?"

"Wrong time to ask." She found a fresh page in her notebook. "He won't text me back about what he's wearing to the 3M dinner. I don't know what's going on, and I don't have time to peel him apart like the world's stupidest onion."

Will drank some more hot chocolate as she stared at the blank page in her notebook. She was thinking about Jeremy.

He prodded, "Britt?"

"Right." Faith started writing. "Britt told Sara that Cam was shitfaced the night of the mixer. That he was upset about Merit Barrowe's death. That he didn't have the balls for emergency medicine. That he'd been whining about it to anybody who would listen."

Will asked the obvious, "Did Cam know Merit before she ended up at the hospital?"

"Would've been nice if Detective Incel had interviewed him," Faith said. "From where I'm sitting, he barely investigated the case."

Will agreed. Edgerton had only taken three witness statements. One was from Alvarez, the security guard at Grady. The other two were from Georgia State University students who had seen Merit in class earlier that day. He hadn't tracked down any of the attendees from the party. There was nothing in Edgerton's notes that indicated he'd even tried.

Faith looked at her phone. "Martin said he'd text me when he got here. He's already five minutes late. This is the wrong day to hit me with annoying dipshittery."

Will picked up his phone, too. He paged to a photograph he'd taken at the country club. "I checked out Britt's car while she was in the locker room. This was stuck under the rear wheel well on the driver's side."

Faith stared at the photo a beat too long. "Is that a GPS tracker?"

Will saw his own confusion reflected in Faith's expression. He'd been so shocked to find the small, magnetized tracker on Britt's car that he'd actually scanned the photo into Google Lens to confirm he was correct about its purpose.

Faith asked, "If Britt's worried about her car being stolen, wouldn't she have LoJack?"

"She doesn't need it. There's an app called Alfa Connect that shows you the location of the car on a real-time map."

"You know way too much about cars," Faith said. "Why would Britt McAllister have a tracker on a car that she can already track?"

"Why would a woman who carries a forty-dollar

color-coordinated water bottle have an Apple AirTag attached to her key-fob with a cheap plastic leash?"

"Because the person who's tracking her wants her to know that he's tracking her," Faith said. "What kind of psycho tracks a car?"

Will kept his mouth shut about the tracking page he'd seen on her laptop. If he had to guess, Jeremy was being as closely monitored as Britt.

She said, "We're thinking it's the husband, right?"

"Sara told me Mac is a control freak. At the bar with Richie, he kept adjusting his glass, lining it up to the counter. Obsessive compulsive." Will placed his phone on the table, resisting the urge to align it to the edge. "My aunt told me something interesting—that Mac's like a pimp and Britt is bought and paid for. All of her power comes from Mac, and she uses it to hurt other people. Sometimes, victims make the worst abusers."

Faith got a weird look on her face. "Is this the part where you tell me about your long-lost aunt that I'd never even heard of until last night?"

"Is this the part where you tell me how the last case gave you PTSD and that's why you told me to fuck off yesterday?"

She was suddenly very interested in her notebook. "I meant to apologize for that."

Will stared at the top of her head. He guessed that

was his apology. He drank more of his hot chocolate as he looked around the room. Some of the patrons were staring back, but for once, Will was not the object of curiosity. Faith was in her GBI regs, khaki pants, and a navy polo with the GBI emblem over the pocket and her Glock strapped to her thigh. The gun in particular was catching a lot of shade. Everybody hated cops until they needed one.

"Amanda would shit an actual brick if she knew what we were doing." Faith was oblivious to the stares as she thumbed through her notebook. "I can't make sense of any of this. We need to put it up on our crazy string wall."

"It's just a crazy wall. We don't have the string. We don't know why Richie brought up Cam. We don't know what Britt was really trying to tell Sara. We still don't know the connections between the two assaults. Or three assaults, if you add in Merit Barrowe."

"We know Cam has something to do with it, which is more than we did last night," Faith said. "Do you think Sara will get anything out of Mason?"

Will shrugged, pretending like the sound of Mason's name didn't grate on him. Back at the country club, he'd been the one to tell Sara to call her former boyfriend. Mason had readily agreed to meet at his office. Will didn't know how useful the conversation would be, but he knew that Sara had to try. None of these people were straightforward. The only hope was that Mason would say something that jogged Sara's memory.

"Does that bother you?" Faith asked. "Sara talking to her extremely gorgeous and sexy ex-boyfriend?"

Will shrugged again. Sara was in Mason's office, but she would come home to Will's bed.

He asked Faith, "What'd you find out about Martin Barrowe?"

"Lawyer. Pitbull lover. Braves fan. Hawks fan. Works at the free legal clinic. Calls himself a social justice warrior. Also a Swiftie, but who isn't?" Faith tapped at her phone. She showed Will a photo. "Nice-looking guy."

Will immediately recognized the face.

Martin Barrowe was one of the professionals bent over a laptop at one of the tables.

Will said, "He's been here for about ten minutes. Over in the corner."

Faith knew not to turn around. "It's not like I'm incognito. I've got six-inch neon yellow GBI letters on the back of my shirt."

"Defense lawyers don't like cops."

"Defense lawyers are cocksuckers who help rapists and murderers walk free." Faith had her phone in her hands. Will knew she was using the front-facing camera to look behind her. "What's he up to? You think he's messing with us?"

Martin had closed his laptop. His hands were clasped together. His head was bent. His eyes were closed. Will had seen Sara's mother do this a lot.

He told Faith, "I think he's praying."

She gave a heavy sigh as she put her phone back down. "Maybe the person who doesn't look like a cop and doesn't hate defense attorneys should invite him over?"

Will thought that was a good idea. He was standing up as Martin Barrowe started shoving his things into a baseball-leather backpack. The man glanced at the door, but then he saw Will standing like a meerkat above the crowded room. There was some momentary decision-making as Martin considered leaving versus staying.

Staying won out.

He looped the backpack over his shoulder as he made his way toward the front of the cafe. Faith was right that Martin was a nice-looking guy. Suit and tie. Hair closely cropped. Thin mustache but no annoying soul patch. Will guessed he was around thirty years old. He bore a striking resemblance to the autopsy photo of Merit Barrowe, though fifteen years had put some hardness in his features. Loss had a way of showing up in your face.

"Mr. Barrowe?" Will offered his credentials since he wasn't clearly identified. "I'm Special Agent Will Trent. This is my partner, Special Agent Faith Mitchell. Thanks for meeting with us."

Martin kept his backpack over his shoulder. He didn't sit. "I want you to know that both my parents died without learning the truth about what happened to my sister. If you're anything like that worthless, lazy shithead who investigated Merit's death fifteen years ago, then do not waste my time."

Faith bristled like a porcupine over the swipe at Edgerton. Will held out his hand to stop her from responding. He had devoted his entire adult life to a vocation that often talked about brotherhood and loyalty, but he'd found out the hard way that the thin blue line didn't extend around the cops who were different.

He told Martin, "You're right. Detective Edgerton mishandled your sister's case."

Faith visibly recoiled at the admission, even though she had groused about the same thing five minutes earlier. Her mom had been a cop. Evelyn had come up with Amanda, who had helped Faith move to the GBI. Faith was so firmly inside the line that she was practically framed in blue.

Martin Barrowe had the opposite reaction. He'd

been tense before, but now a tiny part of him seemed to let go. "How did he mishandle it?"

Will thought about something Sara had told him last night about the power of honesty. "Look, man, I'm not going to bullshit you. The worst thing I could do right now is give you false hope. But we're trying to find a reason to reopen your sister's case. We think it might be connected to some others. We want to talk to you about the possibilities and see if there's enough *there* there."

Martin shifted his backpack to his other shoulder. There was a lot more in the bag besides his three-pound MacBook Air. The straps strained against the red baseball stitching. "And if there's not?"

"Then we've opened up some old wounds for nothing," Will admitted. "That's entirely possible. Just like it's possible we find something but there's nothing we can do about it. You're a lawyer. You know there's a difference between thinking somebody is guilty and proving it."

"And I'm supposed to trust two *cops* to do the right thing?"

Even Will could hear the way Martin put a spin on the word, like he was spitting it out of his mouth. Will shrugged. "I hope you do, but I can't blame you if you don't."

Martin didn't answer immediately. He looked out

the large windows at the front of the cafe, watched the cars stream by.

Will sat back down at the table. He finished the dregs of his hot chocolate. Faith had her notebook in front of her, but she'd put down her pen.

Martin made his decision. The backpack hit the floor with a heavy thud. He pulled out the chair and sat down with about a foot of space between his body and the table. He looked at Faith, then Will, then said, "Hit me with what you got."

Faith took over. "We know that your sister was at a party at Georgia State that night."

"You're already wrong," Martin said. "Merit was studying with a friend. They smoked some weed and had a beer or two, but it wasn't a party. And it wasn't at Georgia State. Merit was a student at GSU, but she was studying at one of those apartments they kept down-town for Morehouse med students who were training at Grady."

Faith had started to transcribe the information, but now she looked up. "Morehouse is a men's college. Was Merit dating a student?"

"She was dating a girl whose brother was a More-house man. Merit's dorm was at University Village over on North Avenue, so it was easier to meet up at the brother's place."

"Wait up," Faith said. "Your sister was a lesbian?"

"Yes, she was."

Will knew what Faith was thinking about. Merit Barrowe's autopsy report had called out contusions and bruising that the medical examiner had concluded were likely the result of consensual sex.

Faith asked, "Did you tell Detective Edgerton your sister was gay?"

"We all did," Martin answered. "I was with my mama and daddy when the great Detective Eugene Edgerton sat us down in our living room. He said that we might hear something about Merit being raped, but not to believe it. My mama straight up told him that Merit was gay. My parents never had a problem with it. But Edgerton did. He started lecturing us about how young girls don't know what they want, and he hated to tell us the truth, but Merit was cheating on her girl-friend with a guy, and that's why she lied and claimed that she was raped."

Faith had earned a giant I-told-you-so, but she looked livid to find her suspicion confirmed. "Did he mention the name of this alleged guy your sister was cheating with?"

"Nope. He said he wanted to protect the dude's pri-vacy. Didn't wanna ruin the young man's life." Martin crossed his arms over his chest. "You read Edgerton's report. *Female* this and *female* that. Asshole didn't even have the decency to write out Merit's name."

Will could hear it now.

Faith asked, "The brother of the girlfriend, what was his name?"

"It wasn't him," Martin said. "He was at Howard that week. Did his undergrad there, went back to serve his mentorship."

Faith said, "I'm not asking because I think he was the bogus boyfriend that Edgerton made up. I'm asking because the last place Merit was seen was at his apartment."

"Let's call him My Friend," Martin said. "You won't find his name in the witness statements, and you won't find the name of Merit's girlfriend, either. Edgerton never talked to either of them."

Will asked, "Your friend was training at Grady?"

Martin relented, "He was an intern."

Will knew getting a list of Morehouse interns from fifteen years ago wouldn't be difficult, but he was more interested in finding out the reason Martin was trying to protect the guy.

Faith had picked up on the same thing. She told Martin, "I get that you don't want to be the reason a couple of cops are knocking on your friend's door, but we need to talk to him."

"And ask him what?"

Faith said, "Who did he work with? Did his sister ever visit him at Grady and bring Merit along? Did they speak to anyone there? What were their names?"

"What names are you looking for?"

Faith exchanged a look with Will. He shrugged, because they had nothing to lose.

"They're all doctors," she said, flipping back through her notebook to find Sara's list. "Chaz Penley. Blythe Creedy. Royce Ellison. Bing Forster. Prudence Stanley. Rosaline Stone. Cam Carmichael. Sara Linton. Mason James. Richie Dougal."

Will was watching the man's face, but he gave nothing away.

Martin asked, "Are those your suspects?"

"We don't know," Faith answered. "They worked at Grady fifteen years ago. I'm being completely honest with you. That's all the information we have."

Martin kept his arms crossed. He stared out the window. Decision time again. He didn't know whether or not to trust them.

Will was surprised when he did.

Martin said, "You know that one woman, Dr. Sara Linton? She was raped two weeks after Merit died. Edgerton was assigned to both cases. But he only solved one."

"Dr. Linton gave a positive ID," Faith said. "The attacker worked at the hospital. She knew his name, his face."

Surprise broke through Martin's combative demeanor. "You already looked into Dr. Linton's case?"

"We're looking into everything," Faith said. "Did you talk to Edgerton about a possible connection between the two?"

Martin huffed a laugh. "I was a sixteen-year-old boy grieving over his dead sister. That man barely gave me the time of day. And the way he treated my mama and daddy—I will never forgive the disrespect, the contempt, he showed them. I know the asshole is dead. If I cared about finding his grave, I would go piss on it."

Will tried to take his hostility down a notch. "It sounds like you read Detective Edgerton's police report."

Martin didn't answer. Instead, he leaned down and started digging around in his backpack. He pulled out a thick stack of folders, then called them out as he dropped them on the table. "Initial complaint. Edgerton's report. Witness statements. Autopsy report. Toxicology report. Death certificate."

Faith had jumped at *toxicology report*. She grabbed the printout, traced her finger down the lines. Grady Healthcare's cross was at the top of the page, which meant the document had been generated in the hospital's lab. Merit's blood had been drawn in the ED before she'd died.

Faith read, "Positive for marijuana, alcohol, and benzodiazepine."

Martin said, "Merit never took any prescription medication. And even if she did, My Friend explained the toxicology report to me. He said that the level of benzos found in Merit's blood was so high that she would've passed out before she could've swallowed that many pills."

Faith asked, "How else would she ingest them?"

"You tell me."

"The medical examiner didn't find a needle mark."

"How hard did he look?"

Will tuned out the verbal volleys. He slid over the autopsy file, which looked like it had more pages than the official state file.

The extra pages contained several more photos from the external exam. They hadn't aged well, either. It had been a long time since he'd seen faxed pages. The print on the thermal paper was so light that the words were grayed out. The headers with the phone number the fax had been sent from were barely more than dots. The date had almost disappeared but for the last two digits. The fax was from fifteen years ago.

He thumbed through to the back pages. The photographs from the external exam were so light they could've been line drawings. The tattoo under Merit's left arm was obscured by the lines of her ribs.

Will asked Martin, "Did your sister have a tattoo?"

"According to the autopsy report she did, but I was her kid brother. She wouldn't share something like that with me. And she sure as shit wouldn't tell my mama." Martin had a sad smile on his face. "Being gay was one thing, but desecrating the body the good Lord gave you? No, ma'am."

Faith asked, "Did Detective Edgerton see the tox report?"

"I showed it to him myself," Martin said. "He told me that Merit was partying too hard and let it get out of hand. Dude had a theory in his head and wouldn't move off it no matter how much fact I threw in his face. Typical cop, thought he was smarter than everybody else."

Faith ignored the dig, tapping her pen on the table as she scanned her notes. "Do you know if your sister received any threatening messages around the time she died?"

"She never mentioned anything, but like I said, I was her kid brother." He shrugged. "We were close, but if she'd lived, we would've been a lot closer. Merit would've had kids by now. I'll never know what it's like to be an uncle. My parents died without having a grandchild to love."

Faith gave him a few seconds. "Did Merit have a phone?"

"She had an iPhone. They were mad expensive back then. My folks gave it to her for making a year of straight A's. Never seen her so excited. I was hella jealous." Martin paused, caught up in the memory. "Anyway, probably wouldn't even hold a charge after all this time."

"You didn't look at it fifteen years ago?"

Martin shook his head. "I didn't know the password, but it didn't seem like that big a deal. We didn't carry our lives on our phones back then. Merit still wrote down her contacts in an actual address book."

"Do you still have her address book?"

Martin shrugged. "Maybe I could find it."

Will couldn't help but think about how heavy the man's backpack looked. Martin had been able to locate all of Merit's files pretty quickly. Will's guess was that Martin had both the iPhone and the address book in his bag.

His other guess was that Martin was holding out on even more.

He said, "Mr. Barrowe, I'm going to lay out a hypothetical, but you don't have to respond unless you want to."

Martin huffed a laugh, probably because he knew every police tactic in the book.

Will wasn't interested in tactics. He was interested in the law. "Georgia has a sunshine law that makes government documents available to the public. But the act requires that all police records stay sealed if an investigation is ongoing. Which is the case with your sister's investigation. Technically, it was never closed. Merit's cause of death is listed as undetermined. But you have copies of all the records."

Martin kept his mouth tightly shut, but he nervously glanced at Faith as she pawed through the folders.

Will continued, "The other thing is, some of these pages were faxed. Fifteen years ago, the only people who were still using fax machines were government agencies and medical professionals. I'm ashamed to say we still use them, but the paper isn't thermal anymore because we figured out it fades."

Will gave him a moment to ponder what he'd been told.

Martin asked, "What's your hypothetical?"

"My hypothetical is, you came by this information using extralegal means. But you're a lawyer, so you know that the statute of limitations has run out on your end. So that tells me you're worried about getting someone else in trouble. Not legally, but maybe with the medical licensing board. So you should know that I don't give two shits about getting that person in trouble." Will leaned forward in his chair, closing some of the distance Martin had put between them. "What I want to know is why they shared this information with you, and what else you managed to find out."

"It wasn't My Friend," Martin said. "I asked him to get the toxicology report, but you're right. He wouldn't risk losing his license."

"Okay," Will said. "How did a sixteen-year-old kid get all of this information?"

Martin crossed his arms again. His reticence was suddenly replaced with a look of pride. "Cameron Carmichael."

Faith's head swiveled up like a turret. "Are you shitting me?"

Will asked, "How?"

Martin inhaled, holding his breath for a moment before slowly letting it out. "A lot of my extended family lives out of state or overseas. Not all of them could make it to Merit's funeral. We had a memorial service a month after she was cremated. There were about a hundred people at our church. All of them close family. And Cameron Carmichael."

"Cam showed up at the memorial?" Faith asked. "Was he invited?"

"Hell no," Martin said. "We didn't even know his name. It was Edgerton who told us she was dead. Never occurred to any of us to talk to the doctor who treated her. We were devastated. You've got no idea what that kind of loss does to a family. The wound never heals."

Faith turned to a fresh page in her spiral notebook. "Start at the beginning."

"I was talking to one of my aunties, then all the sudden, I hear some dude yelling." Martin's voice had turned terse. He was clearly still affected by the memory. "Cam was holding onto anybody he could find, crying like a baby, talking about what a fucking tragedy it was. That *fucking* sent my thermometer to hot. You do *not* use that word around my mama. No sir."

Faith asked, "You went up to Cam?"

"You bet your ass I did," Martin answered. "It was barely noon and Cam was trashed. I told him Merit was my sister and he lost it for real. Held onto me like he was drowning. Started begging me to forgive him. I had to drag him outside so he didn't upset my parents any more than they already were."

Will took a couple of things from the story. One was about Cam. The other was about a sixteen-year-old boy who was on his way to stepping up as a man.

He silently checked in with Faith. She gave him the nod to take over.

Will asked, "How did Cam introduce himself?"

"He said it straight up that he'd been Merit's doctor. That he missed the signs that she had overdosed. That it was his fault she was dead."

Will asked, "Those were Cam's words? That it was his fault she was dead?"

"Those were his exact words." Martin rested his hands on the table. His defensive posture was gone. "Look, I'm gonna be real with you, okay? My uncle Felix, he always keeps a bottle in his glove box. Old man bourbon. I went back inside the church, lifted his keys, fetched the bourbon. Cam wanted to smoke, so we sat in his piece-of-shit Honda. And we proceeded to drink all of that bourbon."

"You weren't drinking much," Will guessed. "You were helping Cam get more drunk."

"You bet your ass I was," Martin answered. "Cam told me what happened that night. Merit came into the emergency room. She was terrified. She told Cam that she'd been raped. She'd never had sex with a man before. She had dried blood on her legs. He could tell from the bruising that it happened a few hours before she landed in the hospital."

Will checked on Faith again. She was biting her lip

as she wrote down every word. Now they knew why Edgerton hadn't taken Cam's witness statement. As corroborating evidence went, a medical doctor's real-time evaluation of sexual assault was practically the gold standard.

Martin continued, "Cam told me that Merit was borderline hysterical. She didn't have any memory of being raped, but she knew it had happened. Her last recollection was leaving class at four that afternoon. She didn't remember seeing her girlfriend. Didn't remember she'd been at My Friend's apartment."

Faith turned to a new page. She kept writing.

Martin said, "Cam wanted to call the police. Merit wouldn't let him. She was worried about my parents, all right? She knew it would devastate them if they found out. Then Cam offered to do a rape kit in case Merit changed her mind about filing a report. She said no to that, too. And then she told him that she wanted to go to the bathroom. He knew she wanted to clean herself up. He begged her to do the rape kit, said he would be as gentle as possible, but she said no again. So, he walked her to the bathroom. She went inside. He went to check on another patient. You know what happened next."

They all did. Merit Barrowe had died in the bathroom.

Will asked, "Do you know if Cam told any of this to Edgerton?"

"Cam wrote it all down like a witness statement. Edgerton wouldn't take it. Told Cam that Merit was lying. Said the medical examiner didn't find any signs of rape. That if Cam stirred up shit about it, that would only be punishing the family because as far as Edgerton was concerned, the case was closed."

Faith asked, "Do you have that witness statement?"

Again, he reached into his backpack. Again, Will was sure Martin was still holding back.

Faith had put down her pen. She was reading Cam's statement.

Will asked Martin, "Cam's the one who got the toxicology report from the hospital lab, right?"

"Yeah."

Will paged through the files on the table to find Merit Barrowe's official certificate of death. He pointed to the signature line. "Cam filled out her death certificate. He listed the cause of death as an overdose, but he didn't specify whether it was accident, suicide or homicide. He left the explanation box blank. If he suspected something, he should've written it there. At the very least, the medical examiner would've performed a full autopsy."

Martin reached toward his bottomless backpack again. He found another folder. He laid it open on top of the other files. Will recognized Georgia's official

State Board of Health Bureau of Vital Statistics logo. Martin was showing them his sister's death certificate. This wasn't a fax or a copy. The border was printed in blue. The ink from the ballpoint pen was blue. The typewriter keys had punched into the paper. The original form was supposed to be stored in the records vault, not in a grieving family member's backpack.

Martin asked, "Can you spot the difference?"

Faith turned both documents in her direction. Almost immediately, she started shaking her head.

"On the original certificate, in the *brief explanation of cause of death* section, Cam wrote 'Suspicious. Non-accidental overdose. Sexual assault.' Then, you look at the certificate in Merit's file, and that same section is blank." She told Will, "Edgerton must've used Wite-Out or something to cover up what Cam wrote. Then he made a photocopy. Then he put it in Merit's file."

"No," Martin said. "Edgerton made Cam fill out a new death certificate, then he slipped the bogus one into Merit's official file. Cam got the original back from the hospital. They hadn't filed it yet. That's what you're looking at right there. My sister's actual death certificate from the night she died says that her death was suspicious."

Faith sat back in her chair. She stared at Martin. "What you're telling us is, Cameron Carmichael showed up drunk at your sister's memorial. Then you, a sixteen-year-old boy, sat with Cam in his Honda drinking bourbon. Then you somehow managed to get him to open up about everything—not just your sister's death, but the fact that he'd altered an official document, which isn't just a criminal violation but would cause him to lose his license?"

Will could see the giant hole in the story now that she'd spelled it out. "Cam didn't come to the memorial with all this paperwork. What'd you do, search his car?"

"Drove him home." Martin shrugged. "I'm not saying I looked around his place, but hypothetically, he might've had these files stashed in a locked briefcase on the top shelf of his closet."

"Holy shit," Faith said. "Respect."

Will was thinking about Martin's backpack. "That's not all you found, right?"

Martin looked out the windows again. "Hypothetically?"

"Sure," Will said.

"I might've taken his laptop."

The heft in the backpack finally had an explanation. He'd brought Cam's laptop with him, too.

Faith said, "At some point, Cam must've figured out that you stole all his shit."

"Took him forty-eight hours, but yeah. He came knocking on my door. Cussing me like a dog. Thank God my parents weren't home." Martin nodded toward the files. "I'd already read everything from the briefcase. Obviously, I had some questions."

"Did he answer them?"

"Dude was like the villain at the end of a Batman cartoon," Martin said. "He laid it all out for me. Never even asked for his shit back. He confessed, and then he walked out the door. I tried to call him a few times, but he ended up changing his number. I have no idea where he is now."

Will took that to mean that Martin didn't know Cameron Carmichael had killed himself eight years ago. He also understood that, as much as Martin seemed to despise the man, he was still protecting him. The criminal statute of limitations didn't matter. Cam's livelihood would've been in jeopardy if his multiple ethical breaches had been exposed.

Faith asked, "What was on Cam's laptop?"

"A lot of the files were password-protected. I'm not a computer guy. I didn't know any computer guys. And it's not like I could run to the police for help. Not then and not now. Edgerton's dead, but APD will still cover for him. That's just how you people are."

Will rubbed his jaw as he thought through the last

few details. Something was off about the timing. "The Batman villain confession. Did Cam tell you why he forged the new death certificate?"

"He had a DUI hanging over his head. His medical license was gonna be suspended, which meant he was definitely gonna lose his job. Edgerton offered to make it go away if Cam made the change."

"Why did Edgerton want him to change it?"

"Cam had no idea, but Edgerton scared the shit out of him. He was a big guy with a volatile temper." Martin shook his head at the memory. "Scared Cam so bad that he was leaving town. Already had a job up north. Started looking the same day Edgerton made him change the death certificate. Dude was terrified. He wanted to get as far away from Atlanta as possible."

"Let's go back to the timing," Will said. "Your sister's memorial service took place one month after she died. That same day, you came into possession of these documents along with Cam's laptop. Two days after that, Cam shows up at your door and tells you he's already got a job lined up and he's leaving town. He left his laptop and all of this paperwork with you, and you haven't seen or heard from him since. Do I have that right?"

Martin gave a single nod. "You do."

Faith tapped her pen on the table. She was looking

down at the timeline. She had bracketed it, but Will could see the obvious question. In his own way, Martin Barrowe was just as bad as Britt McAllister—dangling clues as a kind of test to see if they would grab onto them.

He asked Martin, "When Cam was doing his Batman villain confession, did he tell you how much time passed between when your sister died and when Edgerton bribed him into changing her death certificate?"

"He did, and he was real clear on it," Martin said. "Edgerton showed up at Cam's exactly two weeks and one day after my sister died."

Will felt like a fist was punching up his throat. "Two weeks and one day?"

"Yeah," Martin said. "The day after Dr. Sara Linton was raped."

9

The waiting room for the James Center for Cosmetic Surgery was expectedly sleek and modern. Black leather chairs, deep purple velvet couch, Daft Punk playing lightly from the Bose speaker atop the raw wood coffee bar that held a stainless-steel espresso machine. The matte black cups were laid out on a warmer. Even the stir sticks were a chunky, impressive metal.

Sara had always thought Mason would end up in plastics. His brand of flirty, charming reassurance was exactly what the job called for, and the money could be astronomical. Not that she blamed Mason for taking the money. Medicine was a calling, but answering the call came at a price. You spent a minimum of twenty-four years of your life in school, then you spent years making poverty wages, then you had to choose which specialty to work in, a decision that was heavily influenced by the fact that you were drowning in upwards of half a million dollars in debt. There was no better system to push new doctors into highly specialized, highly lucrative fields rather than the areas where help was really needed—general practitioners who advised you to eat healthy and exercise so you never had to see one of the specialists.

She stood up from her chair. Sara couldn't let herself start pacing, so she pretended to study a giant collage hanging by the door to the treatment rooms. Faces, body parts, teeth. She was too distracted to form an opinion, but she was certain Mason had spent several hours discussing the artist's vision with whatever high-end dealer had sold him the piece. If there was one thing Mason loved to do, it was to talk. Which was probably why he was keeping her waiting.

Sara looked at her watch.

Will and Faith were meeting with Merit Barrowe's brother right now. That fact alone had started to loosen the knot of tension inside Sara's stomach. Tommy had skated on the Dani Cooper civil suit. Sara didn't have to be a detective to know that he would find a way to rape again. Britt had in her own way provided help, but she had also managed in her own way to muddy the waters. Merit Barrowe's death was somehow connected to Sara's sexual assault was somehow connected to Dani Cooper's death, which all to some degree tied back to Cam Carmichael.

Unfortunately, the best sources for information were both dead. Cam by suicide. Eugene Edgerton by pancreatic cancer.

"My God, you still look exquisite."

Sara turned to find Mason James standing in the doorway. A roguish grin was on his face. He didn't bother to hide the appreciative once-over he gave Sara's body. The man himself was as sleek-looking as the office, his hair expertly tousled, his clothes nicely fitted, his permanent five o'clock shadow carefully sculpted. He looked like a lesser version of Will's country club persona.

Before she could think of a polite way to stop him, he kissed her cheek.

Sara gritted her teeth at the rough feel of stubble against her face.

Mason didn't seem to notice. "You can't imagine my delight when you called."

His gaze kept dipping down to her cleavage. Sara had changed out of her tennis skirt and into a belted black dress with a high slit that she now realized might be sending the wrong message. She hadn't told Mason why she'd wanted to see him after so many years had passed.

Then again, he hadn't pressed her for an explanation.

She asked, "Can we go somewhere private?"

"I'd love to take you out for a proper drink, but I've got a patient in half an hour. Real emergency. Needs Botox and filler before her husband returns from Singapore." Mason held open the door. "Don't worry, my office is sound-proofed. Wouldn't want any secrets getting out."

Sara didn't ask him which secrets he was talking about. She felt his hand press to the small of her back as she walked through the open door. A very pretty young blonde was behind the counter where payments were processed. Display cases with expensive lotions and potions were discreetly lit. The walls were filled with photographs of women and a few men posing before and after surgery. Sara was not surprised to find photos of children mixed among the face-lifts and chin implants. Mason was clearly volunteering his time to repair cleft lips and palates in medically underserved regions. Tessa was right that he was flashy and louche, but helping children in need went a long way toward redeeming his character.

He used his hand to gently steer Sara into his corner office. Sunlight came in through the floor-to-ceiling windows. More leather, velvet, wood and steel. More photographs, but these were more intimate. Mason with a teenage girl dressed for soccer. Mason and a younger girl sitting atop horses somewhere in the mountains.

She asked, "How many children do you have?"

"A baker's dozen, going by my monthly child support checks." His expression softened as he looked at the photographs. "Poppy's nine, Bess is eleven."

Sara felt an unwelcome sadness at the sight of his two beautiful girls.

"Anyway." Mason indicated the seating area in the corner. "Shall we?"

Sara chose the club chair. Mason sat on the couch, which was so low that his knees were bent almost to his chest. He didn't seem to mind. He leaned forward, asking Sara, "Tell me all about how you chose to wear that beautiful dress for me."

Sara had literally reached into her closet and pulled out the first thing that wasn't dirty. "I should've been more honest with you on the phone about why I wanted to meet."

"Saint Sara, telling a fib?" He blew air between his lips. "Tell me, when's the last time we saw each other?"

"My sister was in the hospital," she said. "You hit on me."

"Did you like it?"

Sara shouldn't have been surprised that he'd glossed over the part where Tessa had been in the hospital. "It was a long time ago."

"Not too long," he said. "I often wonder what would've happened if we'd managed to work it out."

Sara made a point of noticing his wedding band. "You've been married at least three times that I know of."

"But maybe if you'd been the first Mrs. James, I wouldn't have felt the need to find the other ones." He gave her a wolfish grin. "I thought about asking you when we moved in together. Bending down on one knee. Buying you a proper diamond."

Sara could feel the heat of his gaze on her engagement ring.

Mason's eyes slowly traveled back up to her face. "Do you know, I sit in this office for hours a day telling women all the ways I can make them more beautiful, but I'm looking at you now, and there's not a damn thing I could improve upon."

Sara couldn't let this continue. "Mason."

"Yes, yes." He laughed it off as if he'd been joking.

"I gather from that interesting ring on your finger that you're not here to rekindle our torrid sexual affair?"

Sara stopped herself from covering the ring. She couldn't bear the thought of him making fun of it. "I'm engaged. He's a special agent with the GBI."

"Ah. You're marrying another cop." He was grinning again, but there was a sharpness to it. "You always liked a man who knew how to swing his dick around. What do they call women like you? Police pals?"

Sara didn't like his biting tone. "Badge Bunnies."

"And the dick swinging?"

"When it's that big, you don't have to swing it."

Mason threw his head back and laughed. "God, I've missed your filthy sense of humor. Are you certain we can't arrange something on the side? Surely, you'll get bored."

The only thing Sara was sure about was that Will would be mortified if he could hear this conversation. "Mason, I came here to talk about something."

"Oh, that sounds serious." He pantomimed arranging himself into a listening position. "Please, do go on."

Sara had to take a breath before she could say, "I need to ask you about the Friday mixer."

Mason lifted his chin slightly. "Is that thing still happening? I haven't seen the gang since we all left Grady."

Sara noted the change in his voice. Mason had never been comfortable talking about unpleasant things. "I meant a specific Friday mixer. The one we attended the night that I was raped."

Mason sat back. He draped his arm along the back of the couch. He looked out the window. She could see the fine lines at his eyes, a slight roundness forming around his jawline. It was as if the word *rape* had immediately aged him. Sara was reminded yet again that she wasn't the only person who had suffered because of the attack.

She didn't know what to say. "I'm sorry."

He visibly worked to re-summon his charm. "Whatever happened to that little fella? Your fluffy white cat?"

"Apgar," Sara provided. "He made it to sixteen before his kidneys failed."

"Magnificent bastard. He loved a single malt." The lines around his eyes deepened as he smiled. "Named after Virginia Apgar, wasn't he? The woman who invented the Apgar score?"

"Yes." Sara let him have his small talk. "They told me at the humane society that he was a girl. I didn't think to check until after I'd named him."

"Yes, I remember now." Mason's smile was still strained. "Old Apgar was lucky to check out when he did. The world's particularly down on white men lately. Hell of a time."

"Controlling women's bodies along with the entire federal government and the federal judiciary isn't enough?"

"Come now," he said. "You know the worm has turned. Any day now, we'll all be castrated like poor Apgar."

Sara could handle small talk, but she was weary of self-pity. "Mason, I really need to talk about what happened."

He looked away again. "Not particularly proud of how I behaved around that time."

"If you're worried that I blame you for anything—don't be. Everyone reacts differently to trauma."

"You're letting me off too easy. I could've done more." He was suddenly serious. "I expect you figured out I started something with Sloan after we broke up."

Sara let the *after we broke up* part slide. "I heard something about it."

"The gang loved a good gossip," he said, as if Sara had needed help figuring it out. "Happened to Sloan, too, you know."

Sara felt a heaviness in her heart. "Sloan was raped?"

"Her first year of med school. First week, if you can

believe it. Went on a date with a fellow student. Had a bit to drink. The cad forced himself on her."

"Did she file a report or—"

"No, she didn't want to make a fuss. And the man washed out after his first year, so she never had to see him again."

"Do you know his name?"

"She never told me." Mason brushed the sleeve of his shirt. "Wanted to put it all behind her and move on. Not a bad idea, actually. She's all the better for it."

Sara bit her lip. She didn't need Sloan Bauer held up as a shining example of the proper way to recover from being raped.

She took another breath to steady herself before saying, "After medical school, Sloan matched out of state. Is that why she left town?"

"No idea. But what's that word they use now? Triggering?" He shrugged it off. "What happened to you was quite triggering for her. Hard time all around."

Sara couldn't hold herself back. "How terrible for Sloan to have to deal with my rape. She was lucky to have you."

"Don't be bitter, darling. You were always stronger than her. You had your family. All she had was boring old me." Mason leaned forward again. "I'd like to gently make a suggestion."

Sara waited.

"Why stir up the past? It can't be good for anything. You need to let this go."

Mason James didn't get to make the decision for her. "If you could remember anything from that night—anything at all."

"I attended hundreds of mixers, probably twice as many parties. They've all blended together."

"Sloan was there," Sara told him. "Do you remember getting a call before we left? You were very excited to hear she was back in town."

"She was nothing more than a friend at the time."

Sara couldn't think of a polite way to tell him how little she cared. "Cam was incredibly drunk that night. More than usual. You had to take away his keys."

"Did I?" Mason asked. "How chivalrous of me."

"He'd lost a patient two weeks before. Her name was Merit Barrowe. Do you remember?"

"I'm sorry, darling. I told you I can't remember."

"But Cam—"

"Was always drunk. He was in and out of AA until the day he killed himself. There were empty bottles all over his apartment."

Sara watched regret flood across his face. He'd said more than he intended to.

She asked, "You kept in touch with Cam?"

Mason was silent, trying to find a way to backtrack. Sara remembered this side of him now. Calculating, sneaky. There was a reason she hadn't figured out that he was cheating with Sloan until after the fact.

He said, "You know, I think I picked up those details at Cam's memorial. There was a little to-do here with the gang. Richie delivered the eulogy. He was always our archivist. Told some stories and such. Quite moving."

Sara felt a sickening sense of betrayal. Two minutes ago, Mason had looked her in the eye and told her that he hadn't seen the gang since they'd left Grady. Cam had died eight years ago. What else was Mason lying about?

"Poor Cam," he sighed. "He was always prone to depression. Not a shock that he finally did himself in, really."

Sara took another shaky breath. "I'm sorry I missed the memorial."

"You would've hated it. Just a bunch of drinking and reminiscing." Mason leaned forward on his elbows again. "Darling, why are you asking all of these questions? Has something happened?"

Sara fought the urge to move away from him. When they were living together, Mason had often lied about trivial things, embellishing stories, covering his faults.

This was different. He was lying to protect either himself or someone else.

She asked, "Are you still in touch with Richie?"

Mason took a moment to answer. "Not really. Why?"

"What you said about him. He was the archivist for the group. I bet he remembers that night."

Mason looked caught. "Probably best to leave it alone."

Sara had lost count of the number of times that he'd tried to warn her off.

She said, "That's okay. I can find a number for him online."

"No." Mason's voice was raised. He worked to moderate his tone. "I mean, of course I've got his number. Shall I send it to you?"

Sara watched him take his phone out of his pocket. Sunlight hit the screen. A bead of sweat rolled down the side of his face.

Mason stared at the phone, then he looked up at Sara. "Shall I write it down for you?"

Sara turned as Mason walked over to his desk to find pen and paper. He had Sara's number. He could've easily shared Richie's contact card from his phone. What did he have written on the card that he didn't want her to see?

She asked, "While you're at it, do you mind writing down the names of anyone you remember? Not just from that night, but from any night."

"You know the gang." His voice sounded strained. "They were all there."

"How about the hangers-on?" she asked. "There was a Nathan and a Curt and—"

"Heywood, and Don." He was bearing down so hard on the pen that she could hear it scratching through to the glass on his desk. "Anna and Jenni."

The names did not sound familiar. She watched him walk back toward her chair. He folded the paper in two. He handed it to her. "I'd better get ready for my patient. You could lose a finger in her nasolabial folds."

Sara didn't take the cue to leave. She wasn't going to wait to read the names until she got in her car. She wanted Mason right in front of her in case she had any questions.

She opened the folded note. The names were written below Richie's phone number. She assumed this was Mason's childish attempt at humor.

Heywood Jablome. Don Keydik. Anna Falaxis. Jenni Taleya.

Sara looked up at Mason.

He was grinning again, but there was no easiness to it. He wanted her gone. He knew he had said too much.

Sara remembered a comment Will had made about

his aunt Eliza. You can't get the truth from a liar. She folded the note. She slipped it into her purse. She stood to leave.

Mason waited until Sara was almost to the door. "Actually, I do remember one of their names."

Sara reached for the handle. "I don't have time for this."

He said, "John Trethewey."

Sara felt like a knife was sinking into her chest. Eliza had given Will that alias at the club. The fact that Mason was bringing it up now meant that he'd talked to either Mac or Richie in the last few hours. Did they know that Sara was meeting with Mason? Were they all somehow working together? Were Mac, Richie, and Mason the *them* that Britt had been talking about?

Mason asked, "Does the name ring a bell?"

"Trethewey?" Sara tried to rein in her emotions as she slowly turned back around. "What does he look like?"

"Tall, lanky, sandy-blond hair. Very in-your-face. A bit off-putting, actually." Mason was watching Sara as carefully as she was watching him.

Sara forced her head to start nodding. "He was in ortho, right?"

"Are you saying that you remember him?"

"I'm not surprised you don't." Sara felt an urgent

need to protect Will's cover. "John was always hitting on me. You never did anything about it."

"What would you have me do? Punch him in the snoot?"

"You could've started by not letting some Neanderthal ortho grab my ass every time he was near me."

Mason's grin was back. He'd bought Will's cover. "Fair point on the ortho."

"This is why we didn't work, Mason. You never take anything seriously."

"And your cop with the big dick who got your ring from a bubblegum machine—does he take you seriously?"

"He can take me any way he wants."

WITNESS STATEMENT OF DR. CAMERON CARMICHAEL, ED DOCTOR TO MERIT ALEXANDRIA BARROWE

My name is Dr. Cameron Davis Carmichael. I was one of four residents on duty in the Grady Hospital emergency department when Merit Alexandria Barrowe was brought in by a security guard named Hector Alvarez. Merit was triaged at around 11:30 p.m. I didn't see her in the ED until closer to midnight. The first thing I noticed about her was that she was very upset. She would not stop crying. I would call it almost uncontrollable. TO THE BEST OF MY RECOLLECTION, this is what Merit told me: The last thing she could remember was being in her Lit 201 class in Sparks Hall at GSU. The next thing she knew, it was dark and she woke up in the street, literally face down in the gutter. Her body ached all over. She thought that she might have been hit by a car. She managed to sit up, but immediately felt dizzy. She threw up. She could see a white, chalky substance in her vomit. Once the vomiting passed, she became aware of a throbbing pain deep in her abdomen. She described it as worse than her worst period. She said that she knew in her body that a man had raped her, even though she had never had sex with a man. Then she started to get flashes of her memory back: A hand covering her mouth. Her ankles and wrists somehow pinned apart. It was very dark. She could only hear his heavy breathing. She tasted tobacco on his hand. His breath smelled sweet, like cough medicine. The man got on top of her. She remembers a very sharp pain, which I believe was her hymen breaking. That was all she could remember about the assault. In the ED, she would only let me perform a visual exam. I immediately noticed dried blood and dried semen on the inside of both her thighs. I noticed bruising that was at least two hours old. Her ankles and wrists also showed bruising. I should mention she was wearing a black bra, a pair of cut-off jean shorts (mid-thigh length, not short-shorts) and a GSU T-shirt. She also had white socks, but only one sneaker. I asked her if I could call the police. She said no because she was very concerned that her parents would find out what had happened. She did not want them to know, particularly her father. She was afraid that he would do something, which is understandable. I offered twice to do a rape kit, but she refused both times. Then she said she wanted to go to the bathroom. I cautioned her against cleaning off any forensic evidence, but she told me she didn't care. I made her promise that she would at least let me keep her clothes. I would hold on to them in case she decided she wanted to use them as evidence. We both agreed to this deal. I gave her a pair of clean scrubs to change into. I escorted her to the women's bathroom. I got called away to another patient. The next thing I knew, the alarm was going off. Merit suffered a grand mal seizure that lasted more than five minutes. I led the trauma team in attempting her resuscitation. I pronounced Merit dead at approximately 12:43 a.m. Based on what Merit told me about the chalky white substance in her vomit, the blackout, and the memory loss, I believe she was drugged. Based on the bruising on her ankles and wrists, I believe she was bound. Based on her statement, her recollections, the bruising on her upper thighs, the dried blood and dried semen, I believe she was raped. I swear that this statement is accurate and true to the best of my recollection.

Cameron Carmichael, MD

10

Faith noted the date and time below Cam's signature on his witness statement. He had memorialized his observations within an hour of Merit Barrowe's death. Then he had started a shadow investigation behind Eugene Edgerton, collecting data and details because Cam had known in his gut that what was happening was wrong. Which was admirable until you got to the part where Cam had given in to blackmail, dumped a load of steaming shit into the lap of a grieving sixteen-year-old boy, then hoofed it out of town.

Faith never thought she'd see the day when she actually felt sorry for a defense attorney.

She looked down at the paperwork spread out on her kitchen table. Initial complaint. Edgerton's report. Witness statements. Autopsy report. Toxicology report. Death certificate.

Martin had allowed them to make copies of everything but getting him to part with his sister's address book and iPhone as well as Cam's laptop had taken some world-class persuasion on Will's part.

Fortunately, Martin had brought along the charging brick for the laptop. Unfortunately, he didn't have a cable for the first-generation iPhone. Neither did Faith, but she'd located one at the Best Buy ten minutes away from her house. Jeremy was supposed to be picking it up for her right now. She was also going to see if she could parlay her son's illegal hacking skills into cracking the iPhone's password and opening the protected files on Cam's laptop.

If Jeremy deigned to show up.

Faith looked at the clock on the stove. He was already fifteen minutes late.

At least she had figured out on her own that the address book was a dead end. Faith had read through every single entry without spotting anything that aroused suspicion. No obvious codes. No itemized passwords. No clues that pointed to the man who had been responsible for her death.

Merit Barrowe had been twenty years old when she'd died. Judging by the childish penmanship mixed in with a more confident script, the address book likely dated back to her tween years. The cover showed

Snoopy and Woodstock dancing. Inside, Merit had listed everyone by first names, some of them with dorm room numbers, the majority with phone numbers that were missing area codes. The most heartbreaking entry was for her family—Mama and Daddy.

Faith couldn't let herself get trapped in the terror of what it would feel like to lose a child. She looked up at the crazy string wall, skimming the red, purple and pink strips of construction paper covering her fridge and two kitchen cabinets. The Mac and Tommy headers with Britt's statements. The Connection that had more of Britt's statements, but no connections. The photographs of the gang.

A skein of red yarn she'd found in her mother's knitting basket was waiting on the counter. The band around the outside was intact because Will was right. It was just a crazy wall. They didn't have the strings to connect anything. The only thing Faith knew for certain was that her daughter would be home in four days. If Emma saw that her construction paper had been torn into strips, that her Hello Kitty tape had been used, that her drawings were gone from the fridge, she would have such a fiery meltdown that a couple of hobbits would show up to toss some rings at her.

Faith's eyes randomly picked out Britt's red missives from the courthouse bathroom.

I've lived with the fear for twenty years . . . I heard them . . . Mac is always involved . . . I can't stop the rest of them, but I can save my boy . . . don't you remember the mixer?

She looked at the clock again. Jeremy was still late. Will and Sara would not be. They were due in five minutes. Faith picked up her personal phone and dialed Aiden's number.

He bypassed a hello. "Can you tell me again why you wanted me to harass a paroled sex offender?"

Faith felt an uncharacteristic flush of shame. She had promised Sara she would leave Jack Allen Wright alone. And she had. Aiden was the one who was making sure the janitor who'd raped Sara Linton was doing what he was supposed to do.

She told Aiden, "You said I should ask you for a favor. This is a favor."

"Remind me to care less about this relationship."

"That's not a bad idea."

Aiden made a grumbling sound, but she could hear him flipping through his notebook. "Three years ago, Jack Allen Wright was still on an ankle monitor as part of his parole. His records show that he was either at home, at work or at his group therapy meetings. No deviations. They took him off GPS monitoring last year."

Faith was only mildly disappointed. Dani Cooper's three-year-old assault had been investigated to hell and back. If there was even a remote possibility that Jack Allen Wright was involved, the McAllisters' shark of a lawyer would've wrapped up Sara's rapist with a bright red bow on top.

And Britt McAllister wouldn't be spouting off cryptic quips in various Atlanta ladies' rooms.

Faith asked, "What about now? Anything on his sheet?"

"Wright is in total compliance. His parole officer spoke to him this morning."

"Spoke to him or laid eyes on him?"

"Actual eyes," Aiden said. "Wright's working at one of those places that bombards you with texts and calls to see if you want to sell your house."

Faith figured that was a too-easy level of hell for a serial rapist. "Tell the PO to surprise him with a drug test. Toss his place. Try to catch him with something. The guy needs to go back inside."

"Slow your roll, lady. I've already got the PO thinking Wright's possibly the next Unabomber."

She felt her brow furrow. "Why does he think that?"

"Because I'm part of the FBI's domestic terrorists task force for the southeastern region?" He said it like a question. "Faith, what are we doing here?"

Her gaze settled on the photographs of the gang. "I need you to run some names for me."

"Let me get this straight. I ask you why you're having me operate in some very shady legal areas, and your response is to ask me to go deeper into more shady areas?"

Faith had learned the hard way that you could not get a little pregnant. "Yes, that's exactly what I am asking you to do. More shady things. Can you do them for me or not?"

There was a long moment of silence that gave Faith just enough time to regret burning this relationship. Then she had another few seconds of panic when she realized that she'd actually been thinking about it as a relationship.

Aiden asked, "Didn't you used to work for the Atlanta Police Department?"

"Accurate."

"Isn't there a detective or a beat cop there with a strong sense of qualified immunity who can help you?"

Faith was all out of begging. "Do you want to eat the bad pancake or not?"

Aiden was silent for another stretch. "Text me the names."

She was spared expressing any gratitude by Aiden abruptly hanging up.

Faith didn't have time to sit around and ponder the meaning of it all. She typed in the names from the photos on the cabinet, making sure that she was sending them to Aiden's personal phone rather than his official FBI cell because he was right that this was very shady shit they were dipping into. If Faith had learned anything from investigating idiots over the last zillion years, it was to never put your criming on your work phone.

She sent the text to Aiden, then swiped the screen to access the GPS tracker inside Jeremy's car. He had stopped at Dunkin Donuts on his way to her house. Her stomach rumbled. She sent him a clipped text.

Where are you? You're holding me up.
@DD u want some

This was why she needed to track her son. There was no way to understand his texts without locational context.

Faith was typing in her order when a pair of bright headlights splashed through the windows. She walked down the hall, opened the front door.

Sara and Will were getting out of his Porsche.

Faith told them, "Jeremy's running late. I asked him to pick up some donuts."

Will said, "Did you—"

"Yes, I told him to get hot chocolate."

Will let Sara go ahead of him up the stairs. Sara squeezed Faith's arm as she walked into the house. Her face looked strained, and Faith was reminded for the billionth time how hard all of this was for her. And for Will, who was watching Sara so carefully that in any other context Faith would wonder if she needed to offer to file a restraining order.

She followed them into the kitchen, wishing too late that she'd bothered to clean up her Lean Cuisine mess from dinner. She dumped the plastic container in the trash and stuck the fork in the dishwasher.

She asked, "Has Amanda checked in with you guys?"

"No." Sara was reviewing the crazy wall. She worked for Amanda, too, but they had an entirely different relationship. "Why would she check in with me?"

Faith caught a look from Will. Sara had taken a personal day off work to go see Britt and Mason, while Will and Faith had gotten the fraud team to cover for them. It said a lot that the only honest person in the room was the one who couldn't arrest people.

Will indicated the files spread across the kitchen table. "Anything?"

"Not really." Faith wiped her hands on the kitchen

towel. "It seems like a lot, but if there was a case to be made from Cam's paperwork, Martin would've brought it years ago."

Will thumbed through the Snoopy address book.

Faith had long since given up trying to figure out what he could or couldn't read. She provided, "No last names. The numbers are probably too old to be useful, and we can't dig into them without authorization anyway. If Merit's girlfriend's name is in there, then I have no idea which one it is."

"Another needle in the haystack," Will said.

"All we have is hay." Sara's focus had stayed on the crazy wall. "We've still got the same questions from last night: Who was the *them* that Britt can't stop? And how the hell are they connected to what happened to me?"

Faith said, "One of the *them* could be Mason."

Sara shook her head. "I don't think so."

Faith kept her mouth shut, but her expression apparently didn't get the memo.

Sara told her, "I know what you're thinking. I'm not a good judge of who's a rapist and who isn't."

"That's not what I was thinking," Faith lied, because of course she was.

Sara said, "Mason would cover for Mac and Richie because that's his idea of what guys do for each other.

Everything is a stupid game with him. He never thinks about what that means for other people."

Faith nodded, not because she agreed but because it was easier to let it go.

"This is so fucking frustrating." Sara's hands were on her hips as she stared at the cabinets. "We still don't know what connection Britt was talking about. Is she saying the janitor raped all three of us—first Merit, then two weeks later, me, then fifteen years later, Dani?"

Faith could feel Will's eyes staring a hole into her skull. He'd clearly assumed that she would find a way to check on Jack Allen Wright. All Faith could do was give him a tight shake of her head as she told Sara, "Remove Merit Barrowe from the equation. On the first day at the courthouse, Britt said the connection was between you and Dani. The janitor doesn't fit into Dani's case. He's an outlier."

"So is Sara," Will pointed out. "Merit and Dani were both still in college when they died. Merit had a seizure from the overdose. Dani died from blunt force injuries."

"I was a few years older than both of them," Sara said. "I was stabbed. I saw his face. I remember every detail. Whatever drug Dani and Merit were given was meant to wipe their memories. Neither was able to identify their attacker. They both woke up in strange places. I was handcuffed to the rails in the toilet. The janitor made sure I knew it was him. That was part of his control."

Faith said, "I feel like we need to come out and say it. Mac, Richie, maybe Cam Carmichael, maybe the janitor, maybe-but-not-really Mason James. Maybe Royce and Chaz and Bing. They could all be involved in some kind of rape club, right?"

Sara pressed together her lips. She didn't acknowledge what Faith had said, but she didn't have to. Sara had been studying the wall since she'd walked into the kitchen. She'd obviously spent every waking hour since Britt had confronted her in the courthouse going over every detail in her mind. She had understood from the beginning that the people she'd worked with fifteen years ago, the people she had occasionally dined with, played softball and tennis with, could all to some degree be complicit in the worst thing that had ever happened to her.

Will instantly picked up on Sara's anxiety. He pivoted, suggesting, "Let's update the wall."

Faith watched Sara unclench a little bit. She reached into her purse and pulled out another index card. "The Britt stuff—I mean all that matters is she mentioned Cam and she told me Merit Barrowe's name."

"And the settlement," Faith said. "Are we sure those compromising photos of Dani were actually from an old boyfriend's phone?"

"There's no way for us to chase it down," Will said. "The end result is the same. Tommy got away with it."

Sara looked up from the index card. "I can't imagine what it's like for Dani's parents to know those compromising photos exist. They could still be leaked. There's not enough money in the world to make that dread go away."

Faith suppressed a shudder. She was so fucking glad that cell phones weren't a thing when she was a teenager. There was no chance in hell that she would not have done something stupid. She loved her son more than her own life, but Jeremy was walking proof of how reckless a fifteen-year-old girl could be.

"What else?" Will nodded toward the card in Sara's hand. "What about Mason?"

"He didn't say much worth repeating, but at the very least, he's lying about still being in touch with the gang. I assume he didn't send me Richie's contact card because he didn't want me to see where Richie is working. He asked about John Trethewey, which means that either Mac or Richie called him after talking to Will at the country club this morning."

Faith saw a flaw in her reasoning. "Do you think it

could be the other way around? Mason called Mac and Richie because you reached out to him, so he wanted to see if they knew why? And Mac and/or Richie told him they ran into John Trethewey at the club?"

Sara shrugged. "It's possible."

Will asked, "Where is Richie working?"

Faith woke up her laptop. She hadn't closed any of the tabs from the night before. "He's a consultant with a company called CMM&A."

Will stood behind her. He pointed to the logo, which showed the letters CMM&A inside a black circle. "Does that stand for anything?"

Faith shook her head as she skimmed down the page. "Not that I can find. But Cam, Mason and Mac? Is that too easy?"

Sara asked, "Is Richie a clinical consultant or another kind of consultant?"

Faith read the mission statement. "'We specialize in helping doctors facilitate the transition to funding partnerships that meet their twenty-first century needs.'"

"Oh," Sara said. "The M&A probably stands for mergers and acquisitions. Richie's helping hospitals raid physician practices."

Faith asked, "Translation?"

"Hospitals compete for patients, so if they buy out an existing physician's practice, that means they get all the lab work, imaging services, surgical support and in-network referrals. And in exchange, the doctors don't have to worry about paperwork, medical billing or managing EHR—electronic health records." Sara shrugged again. "It's really nice money, but you end up being another cog in the wheel of a massive healthcare system. They stack your schedule at fifteen-minute intervals, hold you to benchmarks, hit your patients with dynamic pricing. Then, if you try to go back out on your own, they tie you down with horrendous non-competes that put your new practice a hundred miles away from home."

Faith only got about 50 percent of what she was saying, but Will seemed to understand.

He asked, "Do hedge funds get in on that action?"

"They're worse than hospitals. They expect a quick return, so they gouge the shit out of patients, which means that insurance premiums go up, which means that care suffers, which means we all end up paying for it."

That part Faith understood. She'd had to work eighteen months of overtime when Jeremy had done something stupid on a skateboard and broken his collarbone. The best thing Will had ever done for Faith was to bring a free pediatrician into her life.

He said, "Okay, so Richie is a corporate raider. What else?"

Sara flipped over the index card. She looked up at Will. "When Mason asked about John Trethewey, I told him you were an orthopedist."

Will asked, "An orthopedist?"

"It'll help you with your cover if you ever see them again. A doctor would never talk to an orthopod about medicine."

Faith was confused. "Aren't they doctors, too?"

"Yes, but—" Sara looked embarrassed. "They're very good at sawing bones and driving in screws but if there's a serious complication, you want someone who understands internal medicine. And which direction is up on an ECG."

Will was nodding. "It's like asking a carpenter to fix your computer."

Sara looked up at him, smiling in a way that she only ever smiled at Will. "Exactly."

Faith let them have their little moment. She was used to being the wise-cracking best friend in their Hallmark movie.

She pulled over the stack of yellow construction paper and started to make another header, this one for Merit Barrowe. "What do we know about Merit?"

Will said, "That we need a subpoena for Grady's employment files."

Faith handed him the header and watched him tape it up to the right of the photos of the gang.

He said, "The Morehouse intern, the guy Martin called My Friend. He could lead us to Merit's girlfriend. The girlfriend might remember some details prior to the assault. Maybe there was a guy in Merit's class who was making her uncomfortable. Was she getting notes or texts?"

"At this moment in time, a subpoena is not going to happen." Faith turned to Sara. "What about Cam? He was overwrought about losing Merit. Is that normal doctor behavior?"

"Yes and no," Sara said. "Cam had lost patients before. We all had. Grady gets the most critical of critical patients. Sometimes, you feel the loss more deeply than others. I felt that way with Dani."

Faith said, "But you didn't get drunk out of your mind and crash her memorial."

"No, but I talked to the medical examiner and the police, and I bugged the prosecutor so many times that he politely asked me to fuck off."

"Fair," Faith said. "What about Eugene Edgerton? Why did he tank the investigation?"

"He was corrupt." Will didn't have any qualms

dissing a bad cop. "He either disappeared the case because he was incompetent, or he disappeared the case because he was paid off."

Faith had broken out into a cold sweat. She hated hearing the quiet part out loud. "Who paid him off?"

"Good question," Will said. "Write it down."

Faith chose another strip of yellow paper. She wrote and talked. "Sara, you're the only one who met Edgerton. What was he like?"

"We talked on the phone once. I only saw him in person twice. The first time was when he interviewed me at the hospital. The next time, we were in the courtroom hearing the verdict." Sara clearly did not relish the memories. "During the initial interview, he seemed angry about what happened. I wouldn't call him compassionate. Mostly, I was relieved that he was taking it seriously."

Faith said, "They had to cut off the handcuffs and surgically remove the knife. Even a bad cop would take that seriously."

Sara looked down at her hands.

"I'm so sorry," Faith apologized. "I shouldn't have—"

"It's all right. You're just saying what happened." Sara gave her a tight smile as she looked back up. "Edgerton was the first person I spoke with after the assault. I'd just come out of surgery. I couldn't stop going over and over what I could've done differently. I was nice to him. Not Edgerton, the janitor. I had a lot of guilt about that. Was I too nice? Did I give him the wrong impression? Lead him on?"

Faith watched Sara twist her engagement ring. She was a different person when she talked about that night at Grady. All her confidence evaporated.

"Also," Sara continued. "What Cam wrote in his witness statement about Merit—that she was worried about her parents finding out. That was probably the biggest fear for me, too. I had a lot of guilt about bringing this into their lives. I should've stayed home for school. I could've gone to Mercer instead of Emory. That kind of thing. But what I remember about Detective Edgerton was that he gave me a gift. He told me that it could've happened anytime or anywhere, and that I should stop blaming myself and start blaming the man who'd raped me."

Will didn't move, but something about the sudden tension in his body put Faith on alert. Sara's hand had stilled on her ring. They were both looking over Faith's shoulder.

Sara said, "Hi, Jeremy."

Dread swelled through Faith's heart as she turned around.

Jeremy was standing with a box of donuts and a drink holder. He looked shocked, which made sense. Her son had taken to Sara from the moment Faith had introduced them. They were both nerds who made obscure jokes about science and loved SEC football and math problems. And now Jeremy had just heard Sara say out loud something that had rocked him to his core.

Faith stood up. She passed the donuts and drinks off to Will, then she dragged Jeremy into the living room.

"It's okay," she told him; the same thing she always said when something unimaginably bad had happened. "Everything is okay."

"Mom, is—" Jeremy's voice cracked. His eyes glistened in the soft light from the lamp beside the couch. "Is she—"

"It's okay," Faith repeated. Her heart broke for both her son and her friend. She was seeing in real time exactly what Sara feared the most when she talked about her assault. Jeremy saw her differently now. She wasn't Aunt Sara anymore. She was Aunt Sara Who'd Been Raped.

"What she said about—" Jeremy stopped again. "Is she all right?"

"Yes, bub. She's fine. I need you to listen to me." Faith gripped his arms as if she could physically force some of her strength into him. "Aunt Sara and Uncle Will are here to work on a case. We need your help breaking into an old laptop and phone. Can you do that?"

"But what she said about—"

"It's none of your business, okay? Just pretend you didn't hear it."

"Faith." Sara was standing by the couch. The smile on her face was heartbreakingly forced. "Jeremy, I was raped fifteen years ago. The man was caught and punished. I'm okay now, but sometimes it's still hard to talk about. Especially now. We're trying to figure out if there's a connection to two other cases where women have been assaulted."

Jeremy was clearly struggling to keep his emotions in check. "Is one of them the student who went missing from the Downlow?"

Faith was prepared to lie to him like she usually did, but for some reason, she couldn't. "We don't know anything right now. That's why we need your help. Can you hack into a fifteen-year-old phone and laptop?"

His eyes darted toward Sara, then back again. He was still processing the news.

"Bub." Faith tucked his hair behind his ear. "Do you think you can help us?"

His Adam's apple dipped as he swallowed. He said, "I can try."

"That's good, bub. Thank you."

He allowed Faith to loop her arm through his as they followed Sara back into the kitchen. Will was still on alert. The space felt tight with four people in it. Sara didn't sit down. She leaned against Will, who put his arm around her waist. Jeremy's discomfort was momentarily replaced by curiosity as he took in the crazy wall. Faith tried to see it as a mother instead of a detective. He'd already been hit with a hell of a lot. Was there anything alarming or scary or too graphic?

The mother agreed with the detective. There was nothing but crazy.

Jeremy finally pulled his attention away from the wall. He looked at the laptop and phone on the counter. Will moved the box of donuts out of the way. He'd already eaten three out of the dozen. He offered the box to Jeremy.

Jeremy shook his head. He hadn't spoken since they'd entered the kitchen.

Faith asked, "Do you have the cable for the phone?"

Jeremy slid off his backpack and unzipped one of the pockets to find the cable. He was being too quiet. He was still in shock, and other than insisting that everything was all right, Faith was out of ways to make this better. She was about to tell him never mind, to go see a movie or hang out with his girlfriend, when she heard Sara take a deep breath.

"Jeremy." Sara picked up Merit Barrowe's ancient phone. "I'm curious about what will happen when you turn this on. Won't it try to register with the network?"

"Dunno." Jeremy unwrapped the cable. He wouldn't look at Sara. He had no idea how to navigate the situation. "I can look up the protocols."

Will had picked up on the tension if not the source. He asked Sara, "What are you worried about?"

She said, "If the phone tries to register, the SIM card might lock up. We'll lose access to the information. Right, Jer?"

"Yeah." Jeremy plugged the USB into the charging brick. "On these older phones, the SIM is built in. I could crack the case, but I don't have the right tools. If I try to force it, I could damage something."

Sara asked, "Where does the signal transmit? Through the front or the back?"

Jeremy hooked up the phone to the cable. "The antennae is built into the back. It conducts through the metal case."

Sara obviously knew the answer, but she kept leading Jeremy toward the solution. "Is there a way to block the signal?"

"Maybe." He was still looking at the phone instead of Sara. "I mean, you could find a dead zone. Or we could drive out to a rural area."

"That seems unpredictable," Sara said. "Isn't there an easier way to dissipate the electric currents generated from external and internal electromagnetic fields?"

Jeremy finally looked up. He was grinning. "A Faraday shield."

Sara smiled back. "Worth a try."

Jeremy started opening and closing drawers. Faith didn't know what he was looking for, but she knew she was grateful that Sara had found a way to put her son at ease. She was also heartsick that Sara was so good at something that no one should ever have to deal with.

"Password's gonna be four digits." Jeremy unrolled a sheet of aluminum foil. He started to wrap the phone, creating a kind of viewfinder for the glass screen. "I need some personal information about whoever owns the phone. We only get a few tries before it locks up. People usually choose passwords that are easy for them to remember. So, birthdays, anniversaries, that kind of thing."

Faith wasn't sure what to share. She had never wanted her son exposed to this life. She decided on Merit's Snoopy address book. "Her name was Merit Barrowe. This belonged to her."

Jeremy looked as if she'd just handed him an archeological find. He paged through the book. "Oh, it's contacts."

She told him, "The laptop belonged to a doctor named Cameron Carmichael. Some of the files are password-protected. I don't have a lot of personal information on him. I could find his birthday, maybe?"

"We probably don't need it." Jeremy flipped over the Dell laptop to review the specs. "This uses straight DES encryption. I can download a program that runs a brute force attack. That might break it."

Faith assumed he knew what he was doing. "Is there a way to brute force the phone?"

"Not unless you're the NSA. Even the older ones are pretty tight." Jeremy tapped the screen. Nothing came up, not even the depleted red battery. "We'll need to wait a few minutes to see if it can hold a charge. If it doesn't, I can reset it by holding the sleep and home button."

"And if that doesn't work?"

"It's a hard drive. I can try to boot it through my MacBook." He slid the computer out of his backpack. "Is any of this illegal?"

Faith told him the same thing her mother had always told her. "Nothing is illegal if your mom tells you to do it."

Jeremy had heard the response before. "I'll look for the attack software. I might need your credit card to buy some crypto."

None of that sounded good. Faith got her purse

anyway. She placed her Visa card beside him on the counter, though she was certain he already knew the number by heart. She stopped herself before she told him to find another place to work. Faith didn't want her son listening in on a conversation about multiple sexual assaults, but she didn't want to embarrass him by sending him to his room.

She looked at Will and Sara. "What now?"

Will had to swallow the entire donut he'd crammed into his mouth. "Timeline."

Faith could've guessed the answer. Will was big on timelines.

She said, "Friday night, Merit shows up at the ED. By Saturday morning, she's dead."

Out of the corner of her eye, Faith caught Jeremy looking up from his MacBook.

Sara had noticed, too. She said, "We know that Merit was seen at class. Then she was at the Morehouse intern apartments. Then she showed up at Grady. Faith, maybe we could plot out the route?"

Faith wasn't going to make Sara hold her hand the way she had with Jeremy. She woke up her laptop. She clicked the tab that showed a map of the area around Grady. She angled the screen toward Sara and Will. Jeremy glanced over his shoulder, but Faith had made sure that the laptop was out of his sightline.

"Here." Sara pointed to a building. "I'm pretty sure that's where the Morehouse apartments were."

Faith dropped a pin on the spot. Then she traced her finger along the three locations. "Sparks Hall, Grady and the Morehouse apartment. All within walking distance. They're basically in a triangle."

"The center of the hypotenuse." Sara tapped the line across from the ninety-degree angle. "That's De-Livers."

"Richie told me the real name was the Tenth."

"Now I remember," Sara said. "It's from a Henry Lyman Morehouse essay."

Will pushed the donuts toward Jeremy and waited for him to choose one. "Faith, what police zone is that triangle in?"

"Five." Faith needed her spiral notebook. She reached into her purse. "If APD ever calls me back, I can find out who walked that beat fifteen years ago. He might remember something."

Will asked, "Would they keep their field cards?"

"Depends." Faith had kept her cards, which were notes a patrol officer makes to keep track of incidences that don't merit an official police report. They came in handy if you kept running into the same people doing the same stupid things over and over again. Which was basically the life of a patrol officer. "This is one of those times when I really wish we had Amanda on this. She would put the fear of God into APD."

Will said, "Let's get back to the timeline."

Faith tapped her finger on the folder containing the witness statements. "Two classmates saw Merit Barrowe leave Sparks Hall around five that evening. We can assume she walked from there to the Morehouse apartment. I'd say give her four hours studying with her girlfriend. Cam noted that Merit was triaged at eleven fifteen. He didn't see her as a patient until around midnight. If the math adds up, the attack lasted around two hours."

Sara clearly didn't want to dwell on the math. She picked up one of the three witness statements that Eugene Edgerton had bothered to record and called out the pertinent details.

"Hector Alvarez, the security guard, said that Merit Barrowe stumbled in through the west entrance of the hospital around eleven p.m. She was having trouble standing, slurring her words. He found a wheelchair for her. He helped her sit down. Then, per Alvarez's exact statement, 'Miss Barrowe told me that she was raped. She was crying. She told me she had never been with a man before, which I took was her way of telling me she was a virgin before it happened. Her body was hurting she told me, and also that it hurt deep inside. I saw bruises on her wrists and also there was some blood on her lower areas. She was wearing shorts, was how I could see that. I told her that the nurses would call her parents and she got real upset. She didn't want nobody telling her folks. She was especially worried about her father, which as a father myself, I can understand. If that happened to one of my girls, I would be out there hunting that man down.'"

There was silence in the room. Jeremy had clearly noticed. His touch had gone soft on the keyboard.

Faith said, "Merit refused to file a report or do a rape kit. Cam gave her some clothes to change into. She went into the bathroom. She never came out. At least not alive."

Sara scanned Cam's witness statement. "What Cam's labeled a grand mal seizure, they're called generalized tonic-clonic seizures now. There's two stages: the tonic, where the patient loses consciousness. The muscles contract, which causes them to fall if they're standing. It's an incredible shock to the system. Sometimes there's uncontrolled screaming, or the bowels and bladder release. That stage lasts about fifteen or twenty seconds. Then the clonic stage kicks in, which is marked by rhythmic contractions. The muscles flex and relax, flex and relax. That's the longer of the two phases, usually lasting two minutes or less. Merit was in tonic-clonic for more than five minutes. There was no oxygen to her brain. Technically, that's what caused her death, but there were contributing factors if you go by the first death certificate."

Will asked, "What about Cam's inventory of Merit's clothes?"

Sara found the autopsy report and made a comparison. "Merit's underwear isn't cataloged in the inventory. She was also missing a left shoe. Air Jordan Flight 23 white/black-zest."

"The missing shoe lines up with what Cam said." Faith wrote the new details on two different pieces of yellow paper.

"Wait a minute," Sara said. "Dani was barefoot when she was brought into the resus bay. The inventory from the Mercedes listed a Stella McCartney black platform slide sandal. Right only, no left. I assumed the companion got lost between the car and the ED."

"Is that a connection?" Will asked.

Sara shrugged. "A lot of people lose shoes in the ED. And if we're trying to connect this to me, I kept both my shoes."

"All right." Faith picked out another yellow strip. "We should still put it on the wall."

Will started taping them up, telling Sara, "Stay on the autopsy report. The medical examiner didn't cut her open. Does that sound right to you?"

Sara looked dubious, but doctors weren't going to rat out each other any more than cops would. "She was in a hospital setting, so it's an attended death, and there was adequate specimen testing, which arguably means it's at the discretion of the ME."

"But?" Will asked.

"It's hard to second-guess another doctor, especially when I can't see the actual body and I don't know what Detective Edgerton said to him. My general rule as a medical examiner is that an otherwise healthy twenty-year-old woman suddenly dying from a tonic-clonic, even in a medical setting, deserves a full autopsy. But the state ME budget is higher than Fulton County's, which is chronically underfunded. And I've got Amanda's support. I don't get second-guessed a lot."

Faith would've laughed if anybody else had said that Amanda was supportive, but the truth was she always had their backs. Even if she sometimes did it at knifepoint. "What about the thing on Merit's side, the tattoo?"

"I'll admit it's sloppy to not record exactly what was seen on the body. Normally, you write out the words or draw a rough image of the tattoo. X's are typically meant to designate wounds, lacerations, scars." Sara thumbed through the faxed pages of the autopsy photos, shaking her head at the faded images. "I wish we had better photographs. Is there a way to get the original file?"

"The scan I showed you is of the original file," Will said. "Everything else would've been shredded years ago. The only clear photo we have is the one that shows Merit laid out on the table."

Sara turned to the signature page of the report. "I don't know the doctor, but even if I did, it's not like I could ask if fifteen years ago, a cop bribed or bullied him into changing his case notes. Or ask him to explain why he didn't update the tox report. That's the most surprising part to me. Even before the state implemented the GAVERS software to electronically record death records, all of the procedures were standardized. As an ME, you only have open cases in your possession. When your part is closed, you either send the originals to the prosecutor or the state records vault."

Will asked, "Anything else stick out?"

Sara shook her head as she went back to Cam's witness statement.

"What about the bruising on Merit's thighs and the contusions in and around her vagina?" Will apparently didn't care that Faith's son was standing two feet away

334 · KARIN SLAUGHTER

from him. "The ME concluded that they were consistent with consensual sexual intercourse, but Merit was a lesbian."

Sara shrugged. "You can get contusions and bruising from lesbian sex."

Jeremy's head almost spun off his neck.

Faith shot him a look that would shatter an iceberg.

Sara had caught the exchange. She redirected the conversation. "Let's go back to Cam's statement. He wrote it an hour after Merit was pronounced, so I think we can consider it accurate. Merit described, 'A hand covering her mouth. Her ankles and wrists somehow pinned apart. It was very dark. She could only hear his heavy breathing. She tasted tobacco on his hand. His breath smelled sweet, like cough medicine. The man got on top of her. She remembers a very sharp pain.'"

Faith said, "Cam was a smoker."

"A lot of the gang smoked at the bar," Sara said. "I don't remember who specifically, but definitely Cam. And never Mason, for what that's worth."

"What about the smell of cough medicine on his breath?" Faith asked. "Does that ring a bell?"

Sara shook her head. "Merit could've mistaken alcohol for medicine. Maybe a liqueur of some sort?"

Faith said, "She didn't taste it, so that means he didn't kiss her on the mouth."

Sara looked away again. Faith realized that she had inadvertently hit another nerve. The janitor must have kissed her during the assault. Faith resisted the urge to wipe her own mouth. She could not imagine how difficult it must be to live with those memories trapped inside of your senses.

Will asked, "Should we talk about Sloan?"

"Should we talk about Sloan," Sara repeated, less of a question and more of a statement. "Faith, what did you tell me two nights ago? A woman being raped is not a statistical anomaly. It happens countless times a day. The fact that Sloan was raped could be a coincidence."

"She was in her first year of medical school during the assault," Will said. "That puts her closer to the Merit Barrowe/Dani Cooper age-range."

Sara crossed her arms as she sat back in the chair. "If Mason can be believed, Sloan knew her attacker. They were out on a date. He raped her. She didn't report it. The man flunked out of school, so she put it all behind her and moved on."

Faith felt her hackles go up. "He said that—that she moved on? Like it was nothing?"

"Everyone handles it differently," Sara said. "There's no right or wrong way. There could be some women who feel it was inconsequential."

"There could be some women who walk on Mars one day."

Will asked Sara, "Do you have Sloan's phone number? Would she talk to you?"

"I don't have it, but I could find it." Sara looked up at the chandelier hanging over the table. This wasn't her usual reticence. She was thinking about something. "I'm trying to put myself in her shoes. How would I want to be approached about being raped almost two decades ago? A phone call doesn't feel right."

"We could fly up there and back in the same day," Will offered. "Connecticut's maybe a two-hour flight from Atlanta."

"I don't want to ambush her. That feels wrong, too." Sara rested her chin on her hand. "The thought of playing phone tag or waiting for the weekend—I can't drag this out much longer. It's been too disruptive to our lives. And now that Tommy's case is settled, who knows what he'll do? His own mother is terrified he'll hurt someone else. And the girl in the news—the fact that we're all worried about the worst-case scenario says something about what's at stake."

Faith glanced over at Jeremy to check in on him. As usual, his head was bent over the phone. She did a double take, realizing that it wasn't his phone he was looking at. The aluminum wrap gave it away.

"Bub?" she asked. "Did you get into Merit's phone?"

"Her password was the last four digits of her mom and dad's phone number." His voice sounded off, which meant that he'd seen more than Faith had ever wanted him to see.

She gently took the phone away from him. Before she could ask if he was okay, Jeremy had turned his attention to breaking into Cam's laptop files. His jaw was set. Faith wanted to cover the keyboard with her hands, but she knew that wouldn't help. She looked at Merit's phone. There were dozens of text balloons, each containing a single line of text.

Faith sat back down at the table. She scrolled back up to the beginning. She cleared her throat, then said, "First contact was ten days before Merit died. He said, 'Hello, Merit. Did you figure out what time the library closes on Saturday?' She wrote back, 'Yes, thank you.' Then he said, 'I'd really like to see you again. Preferably in that tight blue T-shirt.' Then she wrote, 'Who is this?' And he wrote 'Are you still living in unit 1629 at University Village?' She wrote, 'Who is this? You're scaring me.' And he wrote—"

Faith's throat strangled around the next few words. Her eyes had skipped ahead and suddenly, she was thinking about her precious little daughter and realizing that someday, eventually, inevitably, Emma would be on the receiving end of this kind of unsettling, unwanted attention.

She made herself continue, "He wrote, 'Who wants to brighten your day by telling you how beautiful you are? Who dreams about you a lot more than he should? Who is slightly more damaged than all the others? Who is someone who doesn't deserve the pleasure of your company? Who is the person who will disappoint you when you find out who I am?'"

Faith looked away from the phone. Even fifteen years on, the texts were still deeply disturbing. "No response from Merit after that. She died two days later."

"Jesus," Sara whispered. "Those remind me of the threatening texts that Dani got before she died."

Faith had read the Dani Cooper case file, but she spent most of her days reading case files. "Can you remember what they said?"

"I can get them for you, but they were more surgical, like a grown-up version of what Merit received. He mentioned that she had a mole on her leg. He knew where she lived, which apartment she was in, the name of her cat." Sara's hand had gone to her neck. "The last two lines were the worst. He said, 'Make a list of everything that terrifies you. That's me.'"

"That's me." Faith scrolled back through Merit's

phone. "Who wants to brighten your day? Who dreams about you? Who is more damaged? Who doesn't deserve your company? Who will disappoint you?"

Sara answered, "That's me."

The two words felt heavy in the crowded space. Faith thought of her children again, how her biggest worry with Jeremy was that he would fall in love with a girl who broke his heart and her biggest fear with Emma was that she would fall in love with a man who broke her bones.

Or worse.

"Mom?" Jeremy had turned Cam's Dell laptop so she could see the screen. He'd opened the old Yahoo browser. "I checked his history."

Faith could see the error message on the page.

12163 – INTERNET CONNECTION LOST

Jeremy said, "The Dell doesn't have a wi-fi card, but I manually typed the web address into my MacBook and it took me to this chat group."

"What?" Faith stood up so fast she bumped the table. "Please tell me you used a proxy to hide your IP address so we're not going to have a fucking SWAT team bust down the door."

"I went through Tor, but nobody's gonna care." He clicked open his mail. "The email address for the site owner was from AOL. I sent a test through a dummy Gmail account and it bounced back. Which means that there's no way to reset the log-in. It's a ghost page."

Faith suppressed her admiration. "Go on."

"That page was started sixteen years ago," Jeremy said. "The last time the admin tried to access the logs was eight years ago."

Will said, "Cam died eight years ago."

Jeremy continued, "There wasn't a lot of activity for sixteen years of chats. They checked in maybe four times a year. Whoever the admin was, he tried to erase all of the chat transcripts, but he didn't remove them from the backup folder, so I was able to restore them."

Faith said, "Show me."

Jeremy right-clicked to show the HTML source code.

Faith wasn't a coder, but she knew enough about it to ask a question. "What are these files?"

"Videos," Jeremy said. "The admin deleted them, too, but the backup folder couldn't store that much data. The files are corrupted."

"Can you tell how long the videos lasted? Source? Location?"

"Maybe somebody could?" Jeremy seemed doubtful. "I don't wanna screw with it because I might mess it up."

"My turn." Faith gently pushed him out of her way so she could read the chat logs. For Will's sake, she said, "The page was set up using a WordPress template for a chat group. You post something, then somebody posts back a few minutes or hours or days later."

"Like Reddit," Will said.

"Right, but private, as in only people approved by the moderator can post, and no one can read anything without a log-in." Faith scrolled down the page. "There's thirty-eight total pages of posts. No subject lines. There aren't any screen names. From what I can tell, they used numbers—001 through 007."

Will gestured toward the photos of the gang. "Seven numbers. Seven guys. What are they talking about?"

Normally, Faith would start on the first page but, given Cam's suicide, she started on the last one, which was dated eight years ago, one day after Cam's suicide. It didn't take long to find his name.

She read, "007 posted: Did you guys hear that Cam blew his brains out? The police called me. My number was in his phone. 003 answers: Fucking coward. My name had better not be in his phone. I'll tell the cops to go fuck themselves. 007 responds: I'll tell you one thing you don't want the fucking police calling you at work. The women would not shut up about it. Then 002 chimes in: Someone needs to go to NY and clean up this shit. 003 again: I think he has a sister, but she hates him like everybody else. Why couldn't he have done this sooner? Seven years ago, maybe? 004 makes an appearance: Steady on, men. What's the trouble? 007: Read from the beginning you idiot. Cam shot himself in the head. The police called me to see if I knew anything. 004: Poor old fella never had much zest for life. 002: We should take this offline. 007: Someone needs to make sure Sloan is steady. 004: Sloan is always steady. 003: You don't want her talking to the cops. 004: Out of here gents see you at brunch. 003: What the fuck are we going to do? 007: Shut our fucking mouths. No one knows anything. Ergo, if we keep our mouths shut, no one ever will. 003: What if they talk to SS? Where the fuck is she? 007: Stewing in piss and puke in South Georgia. 003: Exactly where she belongs. 002: HEY ASSHOLES TAKE THIS SHIT OFFLINE."

"SS is me." Sara was behind Faith, reading over her shoulder. "Saint Sara in South Georgia. 004 is Mason. That's his voice. And his cowardice."

Will said, "There's a total of four posters. Who are the other three?"

"I don't know," Sara said. "I'll ask Sloan when I see her tomorrow."

11

S ara thought about Sloan Bauer as she loaded the breakfast plates into the dishwasher. Back in medical school, Sloan had been incredibly competitive among a group of people known for their competitiveness. In many ways, Sara had been glad when the other woman had matched out of state, if only to free up the space. Sloan was whip-smart, darkly funny, and, except for the part where she was screwing Sara's boyfriend, had seemed like a generally nice person.

Even taking the cheating into account, the idea of getting on a plane to ambush Sloan at work still didn't feel right. Yet here Sara was planning to do exactly that. At least she wasn't going to interrupt the woman's clinical schedule. Will had suggested that Sara check Sloan's social media before booking a flight to Hartford. According to Sloan's Instagram, she was delivering a paper at a Pediatric Hematology-Oncology conference in New York city today. Distracting Sloan from her colleagues felt marginally less shitty compared to distracting her from very sick children.

Unfortunately, Sara didn't have any better options. Britt wasn't going to tell her anything. The Merit Barrowe police and autopsy reports had only opened up more questions. Faith was unable to reverse trace the fifteen-year-old number that had sent the threatening texts to Merit's iPhone. Cam's password-protected laptop files were beyond Jeremy's hacking skills. The chat website felt like the only viable lead, and both Sloan and Sara had been mentioned in the posts.

Stewing in piss and puke in South Georgia.

When Faith had read the words aloud, Sara had felt as if she'd been punched in the face. She assumed that Faith and Jeremy had passed it off as a reference to Sara's work as a pediatrician. Only Will knew the truth.

Fifteen years ago, the drug that the janitor had slipped to Sara had made her so nauseated that she'd barely made it to the bathroom. The nausea hadn't dissipated during the assault. Or after. Her bladder had been full when it started. Sara could still remember hanging from the stall railings, handcuffs pinning her arms apart, her bare knees digging into the cold tiles, her stomach constricting as she retched, her eyes tightly closed as vomit and urine spattered onto the floor.

The knife had sunk to the hilt into her side. She hadn't been able to stand. To speak above a whisper. To cry for help. She was soaked in her own effluence. Nearly ten minutes had passed before a nurse had found her. Then another nurse had rushed in. Then doctors. Then the EMTs. Then police officers. Firemen.

Everyone had seen her stewing in piss and puke.

Sara took a deep breath, inhaling for five seconds, then exhaling for five seconds, then continuing the cycle until her heart didn't feel like it was going to burst inside her chest. The breathing exercise was a version of cardiac coherence. The heart rate increases slightly when you inhale and decreases when you exhale, so timing them out could theoretically calm the parasympathetic nervous system, the central nervous system, and the brain.

She had been taught the exercise by her mother's pastor, of all people. Sara had butted heads with Preacher Bart from her first day in Sunday School, but he had known her well enough to explain the science behind the process. She had to hand it to Bart for calling out the pre-Bötzinger complex in the brain stem, particularly since he'd had to raise his voice in order to be heard through the locked door of her childhood bedroom. At the time, Sara had still been recovering from her ectopic pregnancy, reeling from the devastating loss of the future she had so carefully planned. Bart had sat in the hall for several hours across several days until Sara was finally able to look the man in the face.

The fact that Bart was a man was perhaps the most terrifying part of the process. In the months after the assault, Sara could not stand to be alone with any man but her father. Dating had been out of the question. If rape taught you anything, it was that trust and intimacy were two sides of the same coin. Sara had spent hours online reading countless posts by survivors who talked about their struggle for physical connection. They called it their recovery, as if rape was a disease. And maybe it was, but no one had the perfect cure. Some women chose celibacy. Others fucked anything that moved. Some grinded it out through sex like it was an obstacle to overcome. Some resigned themselves to never recovering. Sara had almost fallen into the latter category. Years had passed before she'd felt comfortable being with a man. That she had found her first husband, that she had eventually found Will, felt like a miracle.

Not that she would ever admit that to Pastor Bart.

Or the state medical licensing board. A doctor could lose her career for seeing a trained psychologist, but as with every facet of American life, there was a religious exception.

Sara added a tablet to the dishwasher and started the cycle. Her eyes caught the TV in the living room as she stood up. Sara had muted the sound after Will had left, but she read the closed captioning.

. . . been missing for forty-eight hours. Police urge anyone with information to come forward. Park, a student at Emory University, was last seen . . .

Sara looked away.

Her phone showed that her flight to New York was on time. She'd managed to snag the last seat on the 8:15 a.m. shuttle. She could be at Sloan's conference just after Sloan delivered her paper. Sara wasn't going to be a complete asshole and try to do it before. Her return flight was booked for 5:15 p.m., but she could go standby on any of the hourly flights back to Atlanta.

At least that was the plan. Sara couldn't imagine what Sloan's response would be after not seeing each other for fifteen years. At the very least, her reaction might tell Sara whether or not Mason had called Sloan to make sure that they were all on the same page.

Sara checked the time. Parking at the airport was a nightmare. She would need to leave soon. She dashed off a quick text to her sister—*Going to be tied up all day. Will call you later tonight.*

She waited for Tessa to tapback a heart.

Sara felt a pang of guilt for lying. She hadn't told Tessa about Dani Cooper. She hadn't told her about Britt or Merit or any of it. Sara had persuaded herself that she was protecting her family, but the truth was that she was protecting herself. She loved her sister. Tessa was her best friend. But there were some things that she would never be able to understand.

One of the most traumatizing aftereffects of being assaulted was knowing that there was only one other person on earth who knew exactly what you'd been through, and that person was the monster who'd raped you. During an assault, the victim typically panics, their fight or flight triggering a surge of adrenaline, their soul filled with terror, their body frozen by shock. The attacker does not panic. He is completely in control, because control is the point of rape. He is the one who memorizes your every movement, every sound, every expression, because unlike you, he wants to remember the details. One of you will spend the rest of your life trying to forget it. The other will spend the rest of his life deriving pleasure from the memory.

Sara looked at the television again. The weather report was playing, but she could see the scroll across the bottom.

Leighann Park was last seen at the Downlow pop-

up nightclub on Atlanta's West Side. APD encourages anyone who saw something that night to come forward.

Sara found the remote on the counter. She turned off the TV. She dialed Amanda's number from her work phone.

"Dr. Linton," Amanda answered. She was far more formal with Sara than she was with Will and Faith, probably because Sara wasn't afraid of her. "What can I do for you this morning?"

"I need to take another personal day. I'm caught up on my cases. I already spoke to Charlie about covering for me, so it shouldn't be a problem."

Amanda was silent for a beat. "I assume this is for the wedding."

Sara felt her brow furrow. The tricky thing about Amanda was that she had a weirdly complicated relationship with Will that Sara hadn't quite learned how to navigate. Telling her that they were called personal days because they were personal was not going to work.

"Yes," Sara lied. "I have some last-minute details I need to square away."

"Are you happy with your dress?" Amanda asked. "I suppose your mother and sister have been accompanying you to the fittings. Did you go with a traditional style?"

"Oh—no. I'm not wearing a wedding gown." Sara

had to take a second to reset. Normally, Amanda was rapid-firing questions about autopsy results and scheduling. "That would be a bit much, considering this isn't my first time."

"Last time, I should think." Amanda paused for a moment. "What does your dress look like? Where did you get it?"

Sara had to reset again. Amanda didn't do small talk, let alone make polite conversation. "It's a tea-length A-line with tulle lace. Off white. Princess scoop neckline. Carolina Herrera."

"Tea-length looks good on you," Amanda said. "You've got the shoulders to pull off a princess scoop. I suppose your mother has pearls, but if she doesn't, you're welcome to borrow mine."

"Pearls?" Sara had never worn pearls because she was not a debutante.

"They were passed down from my grandmother to my mother, then to me. My great-grandfather was a Flemish jeweler who profited off the pearl necklace craze inspired by the Red Cross Pearls commemorating the 1918 Armistice."

"That's amazing." Sara felt her head shaking. She could not recall a more bizarre conversation in recent memory. "Quite a history."

"Something borrowed, at least. No pressure. You

can decide when you see them. I'll bring them to work tomorrow." Amanda seemed to remember herself. "Unless you need a third personal day, Dr. Linton?"

"No, thank you. I'll see you tomorrow." Sara ended the call. She pressed the edge of the phone against her chin. She didn't know which was more shocking, Amanda talking about a princess scoop neckline or offering up her family heirlooms.

The door opened. Will was eating the last of a gas station sticky bun as he walked into the condo. Sara's greyhounds lifted their heads by way of greeting, but Betty jumped up from her pillow and pranced around his legs as Will dropped Sara's keys on the kitchen counter. He leaned down and scooped up the dog to his chest so she could lick the sugar off his fingers.

There was so much wrong with his entire entrance that Sara had to bite her tongue. Will's incessant working out was the only reason his pancreas didn't resemble a block of Swiss cheese.

He kissed her on the cheek as he walked into the kitchen. "Your gas tank is full. I topped off your washer fluid. Didn't you notice that the orange light was on?"

Sara had noticed if she ignored things like that, Will would take care of them for her. "I just had the weirdest conversation with Amanda. She was asking about the wedding."

"She brought it up the other day, too." He put Betty on the floor and washed his hands at the kitchen sink. "She said after the ceremony, you would start out dancing with your father, then he would hand you off to me."

"Hand me off? Like a sack of old clothes?"

Will dried his hands. Then he smoothed down the vest on his three-piece suit. He had that look on his face that said he'd been thinking about something that Sara wasn't going to like. "You should record your conversation with Sloan Bauer."

Sara knew that Will often recorded interviews, but he had a good reason and Sara did not. "That's legal in Georgia, but what about New York?"

"Same. It's legal so long as one party knows the conversation is being recorded." He pulled a Coke out of the fridge because he hadn't had enough sugar this morning. "Connecticut has one-party consent unless it's on the phone, then both parties have to know. Pennsylvania requires two-party consent no matter what, so if you happen to cross state lines, be careful."

Sara knew he was being serious because he'd clearly done the research. "Are you going to wire me up like in a mob movie?"

He twisted the cap of the bottle. "It's an app on your phone. The same one I use. There's an AI that can transcribe the conversation."

Sara felt a sense of unease. It was bad enough she was waylaying Sloan Bauer. Secretly recording the woman felt like an ethical breach. She knew Will wouldn't agree, so she deflected. "What am I going to ask her?"

"Didn't you spend half the night lying awake thinking about it?"

She tugged at the front of his vest. "Remind me how I spent the other half?"

Will put down the Coke. Crossed his arms. Leaned back against the counter. There had been a time early in their relationship when she could easily distract him. That time had passed.

Sara told him, "Sloan could refuse to talk to me."

"She could," Will agreed. "But what if she doesn't?"

Sara gave an audible sigh, because he was right about how she'd spent the other half of the night. Her mind had played ping-pong with how the meeting with Sloan might or might not go. "She never got along with Britt. I'm pretty sure they hated each other. And what Britt said to me—both times, there was a lot of stuff in there that resonates with me personally because of my connection to Dani Cooper. And because of what happened to me fifteen years ago. I don't know that Sloan will feel the same urgency."

"Are you worried she'll think you're crazy?"

"I don't know what I'm worried about," Sara admitted. "Part of me thinks flying up there is the right thing to do, but another part of me thinks this is incredibly cruel. I looked back at Sloan's Insta. She's married with a kid. What if Mason wasn't full of his usual shit? What if Sloan's really managed to move on? What if my showing up and saying, 'Hey, I heard you were raped, too' throws her into some kind of tailspin?"

"Britt put you into a tailspin."

"So I should pay it forward?"

"No," he said. "You can cancel the flight. We can try to find another way."

Sara's eyes found the television. The black screen stared back. A young woman was missing. She was very attractive and had an active social media account, which had translated into her disappearance receiving widespread coverage.

She told Will, "I keep thinking about Tommy McAllister. I saw what he did to Dani. He didn't just rape her. He drugged her. He beat the life out of her. I literally held her heart. I could feel the shards of her broken ribs on my fingers."

Will had been following the news, too. "Britt said Tommy was home the night Leighann Park disappeared."

"Britt wouldn't know the truth if it bit her in the ass. And she didn't answer me about where Mac was that night. She told me he was impotent."

"Impotent in general or just impotent with her?"

"I didn't push for an explanation, but God, would you want to fuck that?"

Will shook his head. "Answer your own question. What do you want to ask Sloan?"

Sara finally relented. "I want to know the name of the man who raped her."

"Do you think he's part of the gang?"

Sara shrugged, asking, "Who knows?"

"Sloan told Mason that the guy washed out of medical school."

"Mason isn't a reliable narrator." Sara had noticed last night that Will got a set to his jaw whenever Mason's name came up. "It's possible Sloan lied to him about the details because she knew that Mason doesn't like complications. I told you, he's a flake."

Will clearly wasn't mollified. But just as clearly, he didn't want to talk about it. "What else do you want to ask Sloan?"

As with Britt yesterday morning, Sara had memorized a list of questions. "Britt picked up on something that happened at the mixer. Did Sloan pick up on it, too?"

"Considering Sloan was also assaulted, would she keep an important detail to herself if another woman was raped?"

"It's not the sisterhood you'd think it is. Even women who are raped can be assholes about other women who are raped."

"Okay." Will didn't need an explanation. He'd seen his share of assholes in the child welfare system. "What else?"

She continued down her list. "Did Sloan remember hearing anything that night or even that week? Or did Cam tell her something? Even if she didn't think it was important at the time, maybe it stuck in her head. Maybe my asking the question will help something click into place. Or maybe seeing me will trigger old memories and she'll end up in the fetal position on the floor."

Will's expression had softened. "Let me ask you something—if you were on social media, you'd have pictures of us together, right? And the dogs, and your family. From the outside, we'd look happy."

"We *are* happy." She pressed her hand to his cheek. "I adore you. You're my heart."

He turned her hand and kissed her palm. Then he held onto it. "Talking to Sloan is gonna be different than it was with Britt. More stressful. More complicated. A different kind of emotional."

Sara understood what he was saying. She had her guard up around Britt because she expected the worst.

Sloan was not the same. She had been assaulted. She had been on the periphery of Sara's assault. They both had a shared history that neither of them particularly wanted. They both knew how to hurt each other in ways that Britt could never dream of.

He said, "If you do the recording, that's not for me. It's so when you're in the moment, you can focus on what Sloan's saying, not on trying to memorize everything that comes out of her mouth. You can erase it afterward if you want. I'm just trying to help take off some of the stress. The last few days have been a lot."

"They've been a lot for you, too." She stroked back his hair. "I'm sorry I dragged you into this."

"I'm sorry that Mason won't help you." His jaw was set again. "Even if he's not involved, he knows something's going on, and he's choosing to look the other way."

"Don't worry about him. He knows I'm taken."

"I'm not worried about him." Will's jaw told a different story. "Did he make fun of your ring?"

"He made fun of me for being a badge bunny." Sara stroked her fingers along the side of his face. "And I told him that you have an enormous cock and I can't get enough of it."

His lips twitched in a smile. "Saint Sara. Always has to tell the truth."

Sara smiled back, because he had no idea. She gave him a quick kiss on the mouth, then said, "Download the recording app. Show me how it works."

Will picked up her personal phone from the kitchen counter. Sara watched his hands as he entered her password to install the app. Three years ago, she had daydreamed about kissing him, but the thing that had really gotten her was the first time Will had held onto her hand. He'd stroked her fingers with his thumb, and Sara had felt such a rush of heat that she'd had to go to the bathroom to splash cold water on her face. Finishing the rest of her shift had been a hardship.

He said, "I can go with you to New York if you want. Hang out on the street. I'm sure there's a park."

"No, I've got this."

"I know you do." He glanced up from the phone. "But I'm here if you need me."

Sara felt a sudden swell of emotion. This was the miracle of her recovery. She trusted with every fiber of her being that Will would always be there.

As usual, he picked up on her mood. "You okay?"

Sara nodded. "With the app, does the transcription save to the cloud?"

"I backed it up to your Google Drive, so if you want to erase it, check there, too." He handed back the phone. "I programmed the button on the side. Press it twice to start the recording."

Sara pressed twice. The thin red line started spooling like a bad ECG. "What if I want to stop it?"

He placed his hand over hers and tapped the button twice again. Then he let his fingers lightly trace along her arm. She could feel her skin reacting to his touch. He was leaning down, their faces close. Sara's heart did that familiar little flip when his lips brushed against hers. The scar above his mouth still felt just as electric as she had imagined.

His hands moved to her hips. "When do you have to leave?"

She looked at his watch. She had ten minutes. "Just enough time to tell you goodbye."

"How are you going to tell me goodbye?"

"With my mouth."

Will gave her a deep, sensual kiss. She started unbuttoning his pants. He started to unpin her hair. They both froze at the sound of a firm knock on the front door.

He said, "I'm gonna kill your sister."

"Don't move. I'll get rid of her."

Sara was trying to think of the fastest way to get rid of Tessa without embarrassing the hell out of Will when she opened the door.

But it wasn't Tessa who'd knocked.

A frail-looking older woman stood in the hallway. Her designer clothes couldn't hide the wasted, skeletal frame of her body. Her back was crooked like a Halloween cat. There was a sway to her stand. She wasn't smoking, but a fog of menthol cigarettes lingered in the air. Her long, bleached-blonde hair looked as fake as the tight skin that stretched across her skull.

Sara's body realized who she was looking at before her brain did. A bead of sweat rolled down her neck. She said, "Eliza."

The woman's rheumy eyes went to Sara's ring. "That was her favorite piece of jewelry. She wore it all the time."

Sara covered the ring with her hand.

"She was heartbroken over the scratch. Caught it on the edge of a car door." Eliza waved her gnarled fingers toward the ring. "She was going to trade a trick with a jeweler to get it out. You should look into that. Removing the scratch, not turning a trick. Your mother would want the glass repaired."

She had said the last part to Will. He was standing behind Sara. There was a heat coming off him, a kind of boiling rage. She reached back her hand, but he didn't take it.

Eliza's head dipped in a slight nod. "Nephew."

"What the fuck are you doing here?" His voice had a low growl that made the fine hairs on the back of Sara's neck stand up. "How do you know where I live?"

Eliza started to answer, but she was racked by a sudden, rattling cough. She smacked her lips, swallowing down whatever bile had filled her mouth. She told Will, "You own a house four streets over. You both spend your weekends there, but your weekdays are here."

He asked, "Am I supposed to be surprised that you hired a PI to look into me?"

"One must always keep tabs on family."

"I don't have a family," Will said. "What are you doing here?"

"You visited me. I thought I should return the favor."

Will started to close the door.

Eliza said, "Someone at the club is trying to get in touch with you."

Will caught the door before it latched.

Eliza smiled like a witch, her teeth unnaturally straight and bright in her skeletal face. "This person is very eager to speak."

"Who?" Will asked.

Eliza did not answer. "Won't you invite me in?"

Sara looked at Will. The hard look on his face could've been carved from granite. She silently begged him to refuse Eliza's request.

He barely acknowledged the entreaty. He held open the door, inviting the devil inside.

The air in the condo felt thicker as Eliza crossed the threshold. Her heels scratched at the hardwood floor like cat's claws. She pulled her heavy purse up to her shoulder. There was a wet wheeze from her lungs every time she exhaled. The sunlight did her no favors. Sara guessed from the wasted state of her body that the woman was dealing with an aggressive form of cancer. Judging by the wheeze and stench of cigarettes, her lungs were probably riddled with tumors. If there was a God in heaven, they'd eaten into her bones.

"What the hell is that?" Eliza was giving Betty a disgusted look.

Sara picked up the dog before Will could. She clicked her tongue for the greyhounds, then locked them all in the large pantry off the kitchen. When she turned back around, the tension had only amplified.

Eliza was staring out the floor-to-ceiling windows like a tourist taking in the view.

Will was glaring at Eliza. His fists were clenching and unclenching. His body practically vibrated with anger.

Sara told Eliza, "You got your tour. Who's trying to get in touch with Will?"

Eliza pulled her gaze from the Atlanta skyline and

focused it on Sara. "Your eyes are the exact shade of green that hers were."

Sara could feel Will's sudden, unexpected anguish. He'd never seen a photograph of his mother. The only documentation of her existence was a birth certificate and a faded autopsy report.

"Green was her favorite color." Eliza hacked out another sickly cough. "She was tall like you. Funny, I guess boys really do marry their mothers."

"Stop talking to her." Will sounded coiled, an animal wanting to strike. "Who asked you to get in touch with me?"

Eliza reached into her purse, but she didn't pull out a business card or a note. She held up a thick stack of papers. "This is your copy of a trust I've set up. You'll have to wait until I'm dead, but don't worry, that won't be long."

Will's head was shaking before she'd even finished. "I told you I don't want your money."

"I'm not giving it to you. The trust is for the benefit of children leaving foster care. A cushion to help the little waifs find their way to school or technical college or whatever the fuck you decide."

"I'm not deciding anything," Will said. "Your money's got nothing to do with me."

"Unfortunately, it does. You're listed as one of the

trustees." Eliza dropped the documents on the coffee table with a heavy thunk. She told Sara, "You're the other trustee. Obviously, you understand money better than he does."

Sara struggled to keep her mouth closed. She could see the bold print at the top of the page. THE WILBUR AND SARA TRENT FOUNDATION.

Eliza said, "I assumed you'd take his name."

Sara bit her tongue so hard that she tasted blood. Amanda was the only reason Will even had a name. He'd been Baby Boy Doe until she'd intervened.

"At any rate." Eliza closed her purse. "You can read about it in the documents."

"You can shove them up your ass," Will said. "I'm not doing it. We're not doing it."

"Then the money will sit in the bank making more money. I can't take it where I'm going, and frankly, I'll have no idea what you end up doing, so fuck me or fuck your fellow orphans. I really don't care." Eliza directed her focus back toward Sara. "I'm glad he found someone."

Sara couldn't hold back any longer. "I hope that cancer in your lungs metastasizes to your brain."

"Your wish has been granted." Despite the news, Eliza was smiling. "Well done, nephew. This one's a keeper."

Will took a menacing step toward her. "You can leave through the door, or I can throw you through the window."

"My body would break before the glass does."

"Don't threaten me with a good time."

Without thinking, Sara had taken a step back. She wasn't sure what either of them was going to do.

Eliza broke the stand-off with a bark of laughter. She reached into her purse again. She handed Will a folded sheet of paper. "As I said, this person is very eager to speak with you. Made it sound quite urgent."

Will opened the note, pausing long enough to give the impression that he could read the words before shoving it into his pocket. He nodded toward the trust documents. "Pick up your shit and go."

"With my osteoporosis? I don't think so." She started to leave, but not without taking one last look at Sara's ring. Her expression changed. There was a sense of sadness. "It really did break her heart when the glass got scratched. Fix it for her, will you?"

Sara wasn't going to give her the satisfaction of an answer.

Eliza slipped her purse up to her bony shoulder. She nodded toward Will before beginning a painfully slow shamble toward the front door. Her balance was off. The tumors in her brain were likely pressing against cranial nerves. Eliza held out her hand to the side, a use-less counterweight to a sinking ship. When she reached for the door, her arthritic fingers missed the handle. She tried a second time. The door opened. She didn't look back. Eliza's days of dramatic exits were over. The only thing she left in her wake was the odor of stale cigarettes and the white-hot fury of Will's temper.

The door had barely latched when he yelled, "Fuck!"

He kicked the coffee table so hard that it splintered against the wall. Papers scattered, journals, the trust documents.

Sara's heart jumped into her throat.

"Goddammit!" He punched his fist into the wall. The sheetrock splintered. So did the skin on the back of his hand. Blood seeped from his knuckles.

"Will—"

"Fuck!" He tried to shake the pain out of his hand. "Fuck!"

Sara watched him pace the room. Her heart was racing. The dogs had started howling. They were scratching at the pantry door.

She started to go to them, but Will beat her to it. He threw open the door. The dogs didn't run out. Billy and Bob slinked into the kitchen, heads bowed, eyes nervously glancing up at Will. Betty started whimper-ing. She didn't want to leave the dark pantry.

Their fear managed to shake him back to his senses. The hardness slowly drained from his face. He saw the splintered table. The hole in the wall. He could only hold Sara's gaze for a second. He knelt down in front of the dogs. He made soothing noises as he stroked their whiskered faces. The greyhounds leaned against him. Betty finally stopped whimpering. She flopped onto her side, showing her belly so that he could rub it.

Will's hand was nearly half the size of the dog. Sara often forgot how big he was. Will tended to slouch. He didn't like attention. He would rather listen than speak. He had a lingering and unfounded shame about his dyslexia. His tumultuous childhood had given him a desire for calm and peace. He had spent his entire life in search of safety.

Eliza had shattered that in minutes.

He told Sara, "That shouldn't have happened. I'm sorry."

She patted her hand to her chest, trying to calm her heart. "It's okay."

"It's not okay." Will stood up, holding Betty in his arms like a baby. The greyhounds walked alongside him as he carefully placed her back on her pillow. He waited for Billy, then Bob, to climb onto the couch. He scratched behind their ears, telling Sara, "I let her get to me. I'm sorry."

Sara pressed her lips together. He kept apologizing when it was Sara's fault. She had brought Eliza into his life. The only reason he'd gone to the country club was to help Sara.

She asked, "Do you want me to look at your hand?"

"No." He flexed his fingers, wincing from the pain. "Are you all right?"

"Yes." Sara wiped tears from her eyes. She had been shaken by the sudden outburst. She hated seeing Will in distress. "Are you all right?"

"I can glue it back together." He meant the coffee table. "I'll patch the wall this weekend."

"I don't care."

Will took out his handkerchief, wiped the blood from his hand. The sleeve of his suit jacket was stained dark red. He was rattled, just as uneasy as she was.

"Let me look at your hand." Sara waited for him to come to her. She gently examined the damage to his beautiful hand. The fifth metacarpal had caught the impact against the wall. She couldn't tell if there was a fracture. The bleeding was not going to clot. He would need sutures, a week of antibiotics. "I want us to stop this. All of it. I'll cancel my flight. We have more important things in our lives."

"Eliza has nothing to do with anything we're looking into."

"She's made herself a part of it," Sara told him. "She's hired a PI. You're being followed. She knows the person who's trying to get in touch with you at the club. She could do something, Will. She might—"

"Look at me." Will cupped her face in his hands. "I told you when we met that I don't have any quit in me. We can't let her win."

"Look at what just happened." Sara worked to keep her voice from cracking. "It's not about her winning. It's about us losing."

"Have I lost you?"

"Of course not. You're never going to lose me. Don't ever ask me that again."

"Then listen to what I'm saying." He used his thumb to wipe her tears. "Eliza wants to fuck with our lives. She got eighteen years out of me. I'm not gonna give her another day. You're sure as hell not, either. Agreed?"

"Will—"

"Agreed?"

He looked at her with such need that Sara felt a physical ache in her heart. She knew what he was doing because she was guilty of doing the same thing. Fifteen years ago, deep breathing wasn't the only coping mechanism that Preacher Bart had advocated through Sara's locked bedroom door. Get out of bed. Shower. Dress. Leave the house. Go to work. Do your job. Let denial blunt memory's razor-sharp edges. Let the passage of time give you some distance. Then, when you were ready to face what happened, the cuts wouldn't feel so deep.

Sara nodded her head. "Agreed."

Will let out a slow breath of relief. He reached into his pocket and found Eliza's folded note. Blood stained the white paper. Everywhere he touched, he left rust-colored fingerprints.

Sara's hands were steady when she unfolded the page. The name was in cursive, clearly a doctor's scrawl, with a phone number that was not the same one that Mason had given Sara the day before.

She told Will, "Richie Dougal. He wrote—*looking for you.*"

"He's not looking for me," Will said. "He's looking for John Trethewey."

Outside the Windsong Apartments— Midtown Atlanta

They had a cat whose government name was Pepper, but like every cat, he had several aliases. Mr. Frisk. Bubbly-boy. Then, when he had gotten older, Paunch de Leon.

He was mercurial, going from family member to family member during the day, but every night, he would find his way to the foot of Leighann's bed. In his later years, he'd developed a pronounced snore. Sometimes, the honking sound would wake up Leighann. Sometimes, he would have dreams of chasing squirrels or rabbits, and she would feel his tiny paws kicking against her leg as he chased after them in his sleep.

Leighann reached down her hand to stroke his furry head, but Paunch was not there. She tried to roll over in bed. Pain shot into her face. Her eyelids were closed with a crusty film. She reached up to her face, trying to wipe it away. Her fingertips were gritty. She blinked several times.

Tiny green specks kaleidoscoped through her vision. Her eyelids would not fully open. She wanted to go back to sleep. She wanted Paunch to snuggle against her. She felt cold. Her skin was tingly. She had to pee. A breeze frosted her nerves.

This wasn't right.

Leighann gasped a deep breath like she was coming back from the dead. The green specks were tiny leaves in various shades of emerald. She saw limbs, twigs, and a slice of light coming from above. She touched her fingers to her mouth. Her lip was cracked. She was bleeding.

There was no way to sit up. She had to inch her way across the dirt on her butt and elbows to get out from under the thick row of bushes. Arborvitae. Leighann only knew the name because her mother had told her when she was helping Leighann move into her first apartment.

Look at that beautiful hedge, sweetie. That's arborvitae.

A sudden burst of sunlight cut into her eyes. Her brain throbbed inside her skull, keeping time with her heartbeat. She heard birdsong. Car engines. Leighann cringed, using her hand to block the unrelenting sun.

Her apartment building rose up in front of her. Cars filled the street, waiting at the traffic light. It was morning rush hour. She could tell from the drivers. Some were drinking coffee. A woman was putting on eyeliner as she waited for the light to change.

What the fuck was happening?

Leighann looked down at her legs. Tiny streaks of blood sliced across the skin. From crawling under the hedge? From lying on the ground? She had no memory of how she'd gotten here. She'd been at Jake's. Hiding out. Avoiding the Creeper. Sleeping on the couch. Jake had told her to go out clubbing with him. She had wanted to, but she'd made him beg anyway. Then they had driven to the new spot for the Downlow. And then—

Leighann put her head in her hands. The pounding wasn't stopping. She looked for her purse. She found it under the hedge. She did a quick inventory, not from memory but from habit. She always pared down her purse whenever she went out: driver's license, credit card, a five and a twenty, lipstick, hand lotion, tampon, phone. The only thing missing was the emergency condom.

Her heart stopped. She put her hand between her legs.

Her underwear was missing.

Leighann's eyes closed. Vomit swelled into her mouth.

What the fuck had she done?

The sudden blare of a car horn exploded into her brain. Leighann scrambled to stand up. Her feet were bare. She grabbed her right shoe, couldn't find the left one and didn't care. She had to get inside. Pine needles dug into the soles of her bare feet. A warm liquid ran down the inside of her thighs. She tugged down the hem of her short skirt. She was wearing her club dress, a form-fitting mini with bishop sleeves and a plunging neckline. Leighann's brain flooded with recriminations—

What did you think would happen why were you wearing that dress why did you talk to him why did you dance with him why did you trust him why why why—

She pressed her fingers into her eyelids.

Him.

The memory was fleeting. A mirror ball spinning. Bass pulsing through the speakers. Sweaty bodies on the dance floor. His face. Why couldn't she remember his face?

She heard a car door open. A man was getting into a blue Kia. Obviously, he had seen her, but just as obviously he was deliberately avoiding her.

What did you expect?

Leighann gripped her purse and shoe as she walked across the grass. The asphalt in the parking lot was cold beneath her feet. She saw her Toyota RAV-4 parked in her usual space. Instead of going into the lobby of her building, she walked around the side. The door to the stairs was always propped open. She went into the vestibule. She leaned her back against the wall. Her body shivered from the cold. Or maybe from the memory.

Jake with his hands in the air. Bouncing to the music. Girls surrounding him. Bodies pressing in. Lights flashing. A stranger's lips brushing against Leighann's ear—do you want a drink?

Her throat felt raw when she swallowed. Her jaw ached. Vomit pressed back into her mouth. She couldn't hold it down this time. She leaned over and retched so hard that her eyes watered. Bile splattered the raw concrete. She could feel the hot liquid hitting her bare legs like pinpricks. She gripped the railing to keep herself from doubling over.

Leighann forced herself to stand back up. Placed her foot on the stair. The overhead lights flickered against the dark concrete block walls. Without warning, her body came alive with pain. Her breasts were sore. The muscles in her lower back and legs felt like she'd fin-

376 • KARIN SLAUGHTER

ished a marathon. Worse, she had a deep ache inside her. Worse than cramps. Worse than a rough night.

She had to take a shower. Her skin was crawling off her bones.

Leighann held tight to the railing, pulling herself up the stairs. Her apartment was on the third floor. The climb felt like Everest. The treads were razors cutting into her bare feet. The liquid between her legs kept dripping. She wouldn't look down. She couldn't look down.

The door was so heavy she had to use the weight of her body to open it. Leighann stumbled down the hall. She still didn't look down, but she knew she was leaving a path of blood. She nearly cried out when she reached the door to her apartment. She punched the code into the electronic lock.

"Leighann!" Her mother jumped up from the couch. "Where have you been?"

Leighann winced at the booming sound of her voice. She dropped her purse and shoe on the floor. "Mom—I need—"

"We've been worried sick!" her mother wailed. She was sobbing, jogging across the room. She wrapped Leighann in a tight hug. "Where have you been?"

"Mom, I—" Leighann clamped her hand to her

mouth. She was going to throw up again. She peeled herself away from her mother as she sprinted toward the bathroom. She barely managed to lock the door. Leighann fell to her knees in front of the toilet. She gagged so hard that she felt like a knife was stabbing her in the gut. Her bowels clenched. Piss dribbled down her legs.

"Leighann!" Her mother was banging on the door. "Please! Open the door! Baby! Where have you been? What happened?"

"I'm fine!" she screamed. "Leave me alone!"

"No!" her mother yelled back. "Talk to me! Please!"

Leighann clutched her hands to her head. Her brain gonged inside her head. She had twigs in her hair. Leaves. Pieces of dirt. Her skin felt thick and nasty. She reached up into the shower, fumbling for the handle to turn it on. A blast of water shushed against the tiles.

"Leigh, what are you doing?" Her mother was crying, her fingers tapping hard on the door. "Honey— please. Let me in. You have to let me in."

Leighann's eyes avoided the mirror on the medicine cabinet as she pulled herself up from the floor. She inched the tight dress down over her hips, down her legs. Her thighs were dotted with black and blue dots. The liquid dribbling out of her was blood. Urine.

Something else. She reached behind to her ass. When she looked at her fingers, they were stained with blood and shit.

She gagged again, but nothing was left in her stomach.

"Leighann?" Her mother's voice was strained. She was begging. Pleading. "What happened, baby? What happened?"

Mirror ball. Dancing. Pulsing. Hot breath in her ear—are you teasing me or what?

"Baby, I know it's hard but—" Her mother's voice caught. "You can't take a shower, okay? Don't wash it off."

It.

Blood. Piss. Shit. Saliva. Sperm.

Evidence.

Her mother knew which meant her father knew which meant—

Leighann squeezed her eyes closed. Blackness enshrouded her. The pain started to recede. Her body was going numb. Her brain clouded with silence. She was overwhelmed by the desire to fade away, to stop being herself, to become a disappearing woman. A weightlessness took hold. Her arms felt like she was floating. Her feet wanted to lift off the floor.

His mouth so close—Let's get out of here.

No.

Leighann forced her eyes to open. She returned to her body. Lungs drawing in air, feet absorbing the cold from the floor, skin soaking in the steam from the shower. She was standing naked in the middle of the bathroom. The water was still shushing. Her mother was still begging to be let in. There was a full-length mirror on the back of the door. Leighann didn't want to see herself, but she needed to see herself, to make sure that she was still there.

Slowly, she turned.

She looked at her naked body in the mirror.

She started screaming.

12

Faith knew better than to look in the kitchen mirror as she tidied up from breakfast. Her eyes had bags under bags. She'd spent hours last night reading through every line of text from the chat group website Jeremy had found on Cam's laptop. Then she'd printed everything out and read it again. Then she'd made notes. Then she'd fallen asleep sitting up on the couch. She was so exhausted this morning that she'd turned on the stove and cooked air for ten minutes before she'd realized the egg poacher was still on the counter.

As with everything else in this case that wasn't a case, she had too much crazy and not enough string. She longed for all the things she took for granted in an official investigation, and not just the ability to subpoena. There was an entire back office at the GBI filled with agents who spent their time hunched over computers trying to crack files. Cam had six password-protected PDFs on his laptop. There was also the matter of the corrupted video files from the chat website. Who knew what else was in the hard drive. Or on Merit Barrowe's iPhone.

The worst part, the part that Faith would only admit in her hours of desperation, was that she really missed Amanda's ability to cut through the shit.

And there was a lot of shit.

For every small detail Faith had gleaned last night, she had ten more questions, the main one being who was still paying for the chat website to be hosted. The AOL email was a bust, but someone had put down a credit card at GoDaddy to keep the site active for sixteen years. Was this an oversight? Did the renewal get swept up with a bunch of other registered domains? There was no way to know because Whois, the site that provided the identities of website owners, listed the registration as private.

Another situation where a subpoena would come in handy.

Faith looked at her kitchen table. Martin Barrowe's purloined files had been neatly stacked beside the chat transcripts beside the other crap that she had printed out last night and early this morning in the hopes that something, anything, would click.

Nothing had clicked.

She stared at the crazy wall. Still no string.

Faith had added a new section to another set of cabinets. The construction paper strips were blue. The header read RAPE CLUB, which was what she was calling the chat website, though technically, the domain name was CMMCRBR.com

Chaz, Mac, Mason, Cam, Royce, Bing, Richie?

Seven men. Seven screen names. Seven numbers, from 001 to 007.

Faith had generated a profile for four of the numbers, which were the same numbers who'd made an appearance in the last exchange about Cam.

002, 003, 004, 007.

If Sara was right, 004 was Mason James. Based on what Faith had heard about the cowardly asshole, the profile fit. 004 would routinely laugh at crude jokes, provide a few of his own, then when things took a dark turn, he would take himself out of the conversation.

007 and 003 were obviously pals in real life. They were always making sarcastic remarks toward each other—003: hold your fire for the golf course you stupid twat. 007: speaking of stupid twats, how's your sex life?

Considering 007 was the coolest handle because of James Bond, Faith had to think that Richie Dougal was 003. You couldn't be cool if you wore a bow tie.

As for Mac McAllister, his personality put him squarely in 002 territory. His posts were the most cautious and controlling—HEY ASSHOLES TAKE THIS OFFLINE.

Which left 007 as the mystery man.

Faith looked at the photos of the gang. The only living suspects left were Chaz Penley, Royce Ellison, and Bing Forster. A hospitalist, an ENT and a nephrologist, or kidney specialist. Based on their postings, they were all pricks, but one of them was a particularly nasty motherfucker. To the delight of the other men, he was constantly talking about his sexual conquests, the size of his penis, whether a woman had been *horny as fuck* or a *block of ice* or was *tight* or *loose* or *clamped down like a fucking boa constrictor* or his dick felt like he was *clanging a cowbell*. Even the women he seemed to like didn't come across well—they were *needy bitches, hysterical cunts, fucking psychos, cocksleeves*.

He never provided their names, but there was one occasion when he took a swipe at one of the women in the gang:

007: Did anyone hear what Pru said tonight? Took all of my self-control to keep from gagging my dick down her throat. 003: Not sure your pencil dick is big enough to shut her up? 004: Come now gents I think Pru was kidding. 007: She needs a stiff fuck to loosen her up. 002: Are we seriously doing this again? 004: Not with me. Tapping out. 007: Would love to smash her vag to pieces. Part her like the Red Sea. 003: Blood is a lubricant, Master. 007: Friendly reminder not all urine is sterile. 003: Ouch.

Faith took the urine comment as a clue that pointed toward Bing Forster, though she doubted you had to be a kidney specialist to know about urine. The mention of Pru had to mean Prudence Stanley, a breast cancer specialist in South Carolina. Interestingly, Blythe Creedy's name had never come up, though she'd been married to Royce Ellison and had cheated on him with Mason James—another detail that hadn't made it into the chats. Rosaline Stone, the OB/GYN in Alabama, was likewise ignored. Sloan Bauer had made one appearance alongside Saint Sara. Both women were mentioned when the core group was panicking about the possible fallout from Cam's suicide.

007: Someone needs to make sure Sloan is steady. 003: You don't want her talking to the cops. 003: What if they talk to SS? Where the fuck is she?

007: Stewing in piss and puke in South Georgia.

003: Exactly where she belongs.

Faith looked back at the wall, letting her eyes travel to the incomplete blue strips: 001, 005, 006. She hadn't been able to definitively assign names to the numbers, but she had some hunches. By process of elimination, one of them had to be Cam Carmichael. Faith thought that he was 006, the man who'd posted the least. Though the site was sixteen years old, the posters had only been active for eight years. 006 made multiple appearances early on, usually to complain about patients, usually female, but he'd disappeared completely after eighteen months. After Merit Barrowe and Sara Linton had been raped.

Which left 001 and 005.

Their posts sounded like they belonged in a manual on How to Make Women Despise You. Their first exchange had appeared on the very first page of the thirty-eight-page chat transcripts.

005: Bitches should be honest about what they want from men, which is money and security. As long as I'm providing those two things, then I should be able to do whatever the fuck I want. 001: OK but with the understanding that it's your money. 005: Obviously if she leaves me she leaves with nothing. Not even her clothes, which I paid for. 001: They'll say we hate women, but we only hate the stuck-up cunts.

Faith had felt her Spidey Senses start to tingle when she'd first read the word *cunt*. Two days before Sara was raped, the same disgusting slur had been carved into the paint on the side of her car. Then Faith had read the word in the chats again and again, and realized that they used it so prolifically that it had almost lost any meaning.

She was reminded of her patrol days, when she'd been called *bitch* so often that she'd actually started responding to it.

She stacked together the pages, lined them up on the table. Again, she longed for the GBI's data resources. They could analyze every post, look for identifiers, and more importantly, isolate word usage so that they could run a comparison against the creepy, threatening texts that had been sent to Merit Barrowe's iPhone.

Faith found the printout of the screenshot. She read the missives again:

Who wants to brighten your day by telling you how beautiful you are? Who dreams about you a lot more

*than he should? Who is slightly more damaged than
all the others? Who is someone who probably doesn't
deserve the pleasure of your company? Who is the
person who will disappoint you when you find out
who I am?*

She was racked by an involuntary shudder. The note
was clever because of the inherent deniability. You
could read it one way—that someone had a crush—or
you could read it another way—that someone was obsessed and dangerous.

Faith had been a cop long enough to know how a
cop would read it, especially fifteen years ago. It was
easy to see the red flags in retrospect, but people sent
up red flags all the time. Death threats, rape threats,
bomb threats—people tossed around words like they
were nothing. Most of the time, they were stupid assholes blowing off steam. Sometimes, they were serious.
Figuring out the difference was nearly impossible, particularly when you had ten other calls stacked up on
your radio.

She returned the screenshot from Merit's phone back
to the pile. She stared down at the text bubbles. Had
Eugene Edgerton seen these? Did he know that Merit
Barrowe had been stalked? He'd clearly come into the
case with a result in mind. Will had called it last night.
Edgerton was either bad or corrupt or both. He had

also been dead for years, but his bank records would still exist. If someone had paid Edgerton to make the case go away, there would be a paper trail.

Another excellent time to have the power of a subpoena.

Her personal cell phone started to ring. Faith prayed that someone from APD was finally calling her back, but it was Aiden. She ignored the fact that a very tiny, non-investigative part of her thought that it was very nice to see his name.

"Good morning," he said. "I've done your shady things."

Faith looked at the photos of the gang. She had not forgotten about asking Aiden to covertly run their backgrounds. "And?"

"Various shades of gray," he said. "Chaz Penley logged a DUI in City of Atlanta sixteen years ago. Got knocked down to recklessly operating a motor vehicle. Ended up in anger management classes as part of his plea. Royce Ellison declared bankruptcy four years ago, but it looks like he came out of it okay. Bing Forster is clean. Richie Dougal settled a harassment lawsuit last year, but obviously that's sealed. Mason James is clean, but is a gazillionaire. Same with Mac McAllister."

"Penley." Faith had keyed in on the timing and the charge. Fifteen years ago, Edgerton had made Cam's

DUI go away. Maybe Penley had gotten a similar deal a year before. "Can you get me a copy of the case file?"

"You can't get a copy on your own?"

Faith kept her mouth shut.

"All right," Aiden said. "Dougal's interesting. He lost his job over the harassment suit, but his credit didn't take a hit. As a matter of fact, he seemed to profit from it."

Faith could tell there was more. "And?"

"He works for this company, CMM&A. They act as a go-between for hospitals and hedge funds that want to buy out medical practices. Big money. I looked them up, but I couldn't find anything on them. Their website's a bust. Filled with pabulum and a phone number. No office space. Their address is a PO box."

Faith had found roughly the same thing. "Thanks for looking. I really appreciate it."

He didn't respond, which was unusual. Aiden was not a man who liked a lengthy silence. Faith sat down at the kitchen table. She put her head in her hand. He was going to break up with her. Not that there was a lot to break up. She had done everything in her power to push him away. Why had he let her push him away?

He said, "You should know something about me, okay? I'm like the most annoying beagle you've ever met."

She looked up. "What?"

"I'm a beagle," he repeated. "You try to hide something from me, I'm gonna find it. And I'm gonna bark my head off until I do."

Aiden had gone rogue on his shadiness. Faith had never been more attracted to him than she was right now. "What did you find out?"

"The company, CMM&A. They've got it shielded by a couple of LLCs, but the three board members, they're on your list." Aiden had earned the dramatic pause. "Charles 'Chaz' Penley, Thomas 'Mac' McAllister and Mason James."

Faith said, "Huhn."

"That's all I get, a huhn?" Aiden also had a right to sound disappointed. "I thought you'd be impressed with my mad skills."

"I am," Faith said. "It's just that knowing these rich white guys bailed out another rich white guy and they're all getting richer doesn't get me anywhere."

"What if I told you I went by their place of business?"

He was being sexy again. "And?"

"It's in a building called the Triple Nickel—555 Warren Drive. Off Buford Highway near the airport. There's a desk in the lobby, some chairs, alley at the back. Burglar bars everywhere. Cameras on the exit and entrance, plus the parking lot and alley. Place is locked down. I chatted up the folks next door at the nail salon, and they told me that they never see anybody in or out. And that I should stop picking at my cuticles."

Faith felt herself shrugging, but she had to say something about his initiative, which had saved her the trouble. "Thanks for checking, but it's still not getting me anywhere."

"Huhn," he echoed. "Did it occur to you that if you told me where you wanted to get to, I'd be able to help you get there?"

The thought had literally never crossed her mind.

He said, "Okey-doke, maybe you'll be happier with my last bit of shady. I got Jack Allen Wright's PO to do a surprise inspection. Dude had porn mags under his mattress."

Now Faith really did have something to celebrate. Georgia's terms of parole for sex offenders forbade them from purchasing or possessing any pornographic or sexually explicit material. If you were busted, your parole got revoked and your ass went back to prison.

She only had one question. "Magazines?"

"It's easier to get rid of a dirty magazine than to scrub a hard drive."

Faith thought of something. "Did Wright have a computer?"

"He did. No porn, but unsurprisingly, he's a fan of incel sites."

Faith had spent nearly her entire evening reading what could've passed for an incel site. "What do you know about incels?"

"Involuntary celibates. The movement was started in the nineties by a Canadian university student who created a website for lonely, socially awkward, usually virginal, anonymous posters called 'Alana's Involuntary Celibacy Project.'"

"Alana?" Faith said. "A woman?"

"Yeah, ironic, right? A lady started out doing something nice to help people, then a bunch of men fucked it up."

"I've never heard of that happening before." Faith laid on the sarcasm. "That's bananas."

"It's the whole Chiquita factory," he said. "The current incel movement is the main cog driving the online male supremacist machine. Mostly white, mostly young, all males, all expressing hatred, misogyny, self-pity, self-loathing, a sense of entitlement to sex, a love of violence against women, and the obligatory side of racism."

"How do you know so much about this?"

"Because occasionally, they murder people. And usually, their first victim, if not all of their victims, is a woman." Aiden paused. "Hey, did I ever tell you I'm part of the FBI's domestic terrorist task force for the southeastern region?"

Faith felt herself smiling. "Are you really?"

"Yeah, chicks usually dig that. They find me real sexy."

She laughed despite herself.

"I could come by tonight and flash my badge."

Faith's work phone started to ring.

She told Aiden, "I'll text you when I'm on my way home."

Her work phone was buried somewhere inside her feedbag of a purse. Faith had to dig around for it. When she saw the screen, she felt a scowl on her face. She tapped the screen to answer.

"Leo, what the fuck? I've called you ninety times."

"You don't think I gotta life?"

"I know you don't," she shot back. "I was your partner for ten years. Has your personality changed since then?"

"I'm working on it," he said. "It's a process."

Faith looked at the clock on the stove. She would need to report to the fraud squad soon. "Did you listen to any of my messages?"

"That's why I'm calling. You were looking for Leighann Park, yeah?"

Faith pressed her hand to the counter. She realized now that she had been carrying around a sense of dread from the moment she'd heard that the girl was missing. Another murdered college student. Another parent without a child. Another woman whose name would be forgotten the second another woman went missing.

She asked, "Where did you find her?"

"Here," Leo said. "She just showed up at the station."

The sound of jail detainees screaming was so familiar to Faith that she barely registered the racket. Leo had parked both her and Will on a metal bench across from the jailer's desk. The bench was torturous by design. The seat wasn't wide enough. The metal was so cold Faith could feel it in her colon. There were hooks at three-feet intervals for handcuffs because this was where arrestees usually sat while they waited to be processed. It was not lost on Faith that Leo hadn't taken them to the marginally more comfortable squad room. The glowering man sitting beside her was the reason neither of them were welcome.

She glanced at Will's profile. He was hunched down, his back to the wall, otherwise her eyeline would've been at his shoulder. She couldn't get a read off of him other than that something was wrong. Will wasn't generally chatty, but this morning, he was even less so. His hands rested in his lap as he stared straight ahead. There was a bandage wrapped around his left hand, winding up to his pinky finger. He hadn't explained the provenance of the injury when Faith had asked about it. He'd looked at his hand, then looked at her, then asked her if she'd figured out anything from reading the chat transcripts.

Faith couldn't sit on the bench anymore. Lack of sleep, anxiety, frustration—all of it was making her as jittery as a speed freak. She stood up. There was a keypad by the door that led to the back. She still remembered her code from four years ago. She punched it in. Waited. The red light flashed three times. The door did not buzz open.

She told Will, "This could be a waste of time on top of a waste of time. We have no idea if Tommy McAllister had anything to do with this. Or Mac. Or any of the other assholes from the Rape Club."

Will said nothing, but a raised eyebrow meant he'd clocked the Rape Club moniker.

"We have real jobs we're supposed to be doing." She looked at her watch. "The fraud team can't keep covering for us like this. Amanda's gonna find out. I say we give Leo five more minutes, then we're out of here."

Will returned to his thousand-yard stare.

Faith paced, concentrating on the one puzzle she might be able to solve. There was a short list of things that could make Will unhappy, ending with the vending machine being out of sticky buns and beginning with anything that made Sara unhappy. Faith knew that Sara was on a plane right now. There was no telling how the surprise meeting with Sloan Bauer would go. The only hope was that the woman would remember something from that fucking mixer.

Will asked, "Did Sara forward you the threatening texts that were sent to Dani Cooper before she died?"

"She had the lawyer send them. First impression is that the dude is older because he used punctuation. Or he's trying to make us think he's older." Faith was glad for something to do. She retrieved her personal phone from her purse. "He starts off kind of neutral, then there's all this personal shit about what she's doing, where she lives, the name of her cat. She keeps asking who he is. He keeps escalating. Safe to say he gets off on terrifying women."

Will waited.

Faith looked down at her phone, reading, "'I keep thinking about that mole on your leg and how I want to kiss it . . . again . . .'"

Will asked, "Did Dani have a mole on her leg?"

"The autopsy report called it out. Inside her right

thigh, high up, close to her bikini line, a few centimeters from a small scar she probably got in childhood. You wouldn't see it if she was wearing shorts. Maybe a bathing suit?"

Will nodded for her to continue reading the texts.

"Dani responded, 'This isn't funny. Tell me who the fuck you are.'" Faith scrolled down. "He answered, 'There's a pen and paper in the drawer beside your bed. Make a list of everything that terrifies you. That's me.'"

"'That's me.'" Will rubbed his jaw with his fingers. His pinky stuck out like he was making fun of British people drinking tea. "Was there a pen and paper inside the drawer?"

"Dunno, but it's likely."

"He had access to her apartment. He searched it when she wasn't there."

Faith knew where this was going. Jack Allen Wright had been a janitor. It would make sense that he would work in an apartment building.

She told Will, "Wright was in jail when Dani died. Since then, he's been working in a call center, clocking in and out every day. You'll be happy to hear that he violated parole yesterday. He's in Dekalb County holding until his hearing. I imagine his PO will advocate sending him back to for-real prison."

Will said, "You told Sara that you wouldn't do any-thing."

"I think we've established that I'm a terrible liar."

Will gave her a look.

"Okay, a terrible person who's an amazing liar." She paused. "You're glad he's locked up, though."

Will nodded, asking, "What else did you find out?"

"Richie's employer, the mergers and acquisitions company. The owners pretzeled themselves behind a bunch of entities, but it's owned by Chaz Penley, Mac McAllister and Mason James."

Will looked surprised, but not because of the infor-mation. He knew Faith didn't have the tools to dig that deep. "Richie asked my aunt to get in touch with me. I'm meeting him for lunch at the club."

Faith felt her jaw wanting to hit the floor. "You didn't think to tell me that during the last ten minutes of uncomfortable silence?"

"Was it uncomfortable?"

Faith shrugged. She was used to it. She dropped her phone back into her purse. "What do you think Richie wants?"

"I have no idea." Will rested his hand on the bench, then thought better of it. He looked at his damaged pinky, tried to move it around.

She asked, "You gonna tell me how that happened?"

"You gonna tell me about your PTSD?"

"You gonna tell me about your aunt?"

"You gonna tell me who's doing your shadow investigation?"

Faith was out of *you gonnas*. "Technically, it's *our* shadow investigation."

"Should I respond, or do you want to keep doing all the talking?"

"The second one." Faith resumed her pacing. "I hate to say this, but I wish we could tap into Amanda's brain. We're too close. We're not seeing the big picture."

"Like what?"

Faith had one top of mind. "Edgerton. He made Merit Barrowe's case go away. Was that because he didn't want anyone to connect it to Sara two weeks later?"

"Martin Barrowe's timeline has him knocking on Cam's door the day after Sara was assaulted," Will said. "Edgerton forced Cam to change Merit's death certificate so there was nothing suspicious. That doesn't feel like a coincidence."

"Which takes us back to Britt. She told Sara there was a connection between what happened at the mixer and what happened to Sara. Cam is at the center of that. He must've said something at the mixer."

"Maybe Sloan Bauer can help clear that up." Will did not sound hopeful. "Can your shadow investigator take a swing at breaking those password-protected files on Cam's laptop?"

Faith shook her head. There was a fine line between shady and criminal, and she wasn't going to ask Aiden to cross it. At least not right now. "What I really want to know is what's on those corrupted videos from the website."

"You couldn't figure that out from the chats?"

"Nope. Best guess is porn, but the videos were never referred to in any of the chats."

"Porn's been around almost as long as the internet," Will said. "Tell me about the chat transcripts. Any clues?"

"Nope. It was mostly 007 bragging about all the stupid bitches he gagged with his cock." She caught Will's surprise. "I'm quoting him. Those aren't my words."

"How did the rest of the group respond?"

"Vigorously egging him on. Exactly the kind of crap you'd expect."

"What about 004?"

He meant Mason James. "You ask me, he's just as bad as the rest of them. Maybe worse. He reads their shit talk, laughs at it sometimes, then when they get really nasty, he peaces out."

Will said, "He doesn't have the balls to call them on it."

"Exactly." Faith crossed her arms as she leaned against the wall. "A few years ago, I overheard one of Jeremy's friends talking shit about a girl, and I was so proud of Jer because he told the guy to shut the fuck up. Why is that so difficult? My kid was nineteen. These guys are grown-ass men."

"When you're part of a group, it's hard being the only person who disagrees with what the group is doing. Easier to go along to get along. Otherwise, you're completely isolated." Will shrugged. "Not to mention they can turn on you. People who are doing bad things don't like being told they're doing bad things. You call them out on their bullshit, they'll try to destroy you."

Faith got the feeling they weren't talking about Mason James anymore. The first time she'd met Will, his car had been spraypainted with the words RAT MOTHER on one side and FUCKER on the other. Nobody was going to investigate the crime because the investigators were responsible. Will was the reason they had been relegated to a hard metal bench in holding rather than hard plastic chairs in the squad room.

Faith looked at her watch again. "What time does Sara's flight land?"

"Ten-thirty." He looked at his watch, too. "She'll take the train to the conference where Sloan's speaking. It's in Times Square, easy to find. She'll call me on her way back to the airport."

"You'll probably still be tied up with John Trethewey's new best friend Richie Dougal."

"Probably."

They both turned when the door buzzed.

"Mitchell." Leo Donnelly had gotten rounder and more beady-eyed since their partnership had ended. "You still here?"

"Obviously," she said. "What the fuck with making us wait?"

"You understand the word *courtesy*, as in the APD is extending the GBI the *courtesy* of including you in our investigation?" Leo glanced at Will like he'd just spotted a festering sore on another man's ball sac. "Especially with Lurch over here."

Will turned his head, keeping to his low slouch on the metal bench. "Did you know a detective from zone five named Eugene Edgerton?"

Leo looked offended. "What're you gonna do, dig him up from his grave and investigate him?"

Will said, "I think he was cremated."

"You fucking fuck," Leo said. "Edgerton was good police. Had his issues, but he got the job done."

"So, you knew him?"

Leo opened his mouth, then shut it.

"What about Merit Barrowe?" Will asked. "Twenty, student at Georgia State. Died fifteen years ago."

"This guy," Leo told Faith.

Will asked, "What about beat cops from zone five around the same time? Do you have any names?"

Leo asked Faith, "Tell your rat to stop squeaking at me. I got the whole squad hiding the cheese in their sandwiches so he don't steal it."

Will stood up. He towered over Leo. He was younger and fitter and he didn't have failure wafting off him like a wet fart.

Will said, "Leighann Park. What happened?"

The fat at the back of Leo's neck folded like a duvet as he looked up at Will. "Whole lot of noise over nothing. Her mom's a producer at WSB radio. Pulled some strings when her little girl didn't show up after a night partying."

That explained why the case had made the news so quickly. Faith asked, "What did Leighann say happened?"

"That she woke up in the bushes outside her apartment this morning. Can't remember how she got there.

Took a shower, got dolled up, rolled with her mom into the station. My take is she partied too hard. Freaked out when she realized Mommy called the cops. Didn't wanna lose her allowance. Came up with a story to get herself outta trouble."

Faith chewed at the tip of her tongue for a few seconds to try to quell the sudden desire to slap him across the face. "Leighann's been missing for thirty-six hours. She voluntarily came into a police station this morning. Was she dropping by to say hello? Or did she have an actual crime she wanted to report, like abduction and rape?"

"Smart ass," Leo said. "I gotta easy test for these girls. I walk into the room, they look relieved to see me, that means something bad happened. Park didn't look relieved."

Faith was incredulous. "What the hell does that even mean?"

"I'm a big guy with a gun on my belt. If something bad happened to her, she'd be relieved to see me because she knows that means she's safe."

Faith hadn't heard anything this stupid in weeks. "Did it ever occur to you that a woman might feel scared because the man who raped her was a big guy with a gun?"

"This broad ain't scared of nothing but her mama

pulling her pocket money," he insisted. "You should see how she's dressed. Looks like she's ready for another night on the town."

Will said, "Donnelly, I forget. How did you dress after you were raped?"

Leo gave him a churlish look.

Faith wasn't one to hold her tongue, but she tried it out for a change. Will did the same, though it took no effort. They both knew that Leo was right that this was a courtesy. If they escalated things, it could get back to his bosses, which meant it could get back to Amanda, which meant that Will and Faith would be lucky if they found jobs rounding up carts at the grocery store for ten dollars an hour.

Leo broke first, sputtering out air between his wet lips. "We gonna talk to her or not?"

"Who is *we*?" Faith asked. "You and who else? You gotta mouse in your pocket?"

He did the lip sputtering thing again, but he finally punched the code into the door.

The screams from the holding cells faded as they went deeper into the building. Faith glanced into the squad room on her way by. Ten years of her life had been spent at the desk over by the elevator. She saw the same wave of expressions play out on every single face. A smile of recognition for Faith, a look of burning hatred for Will. It was like watching a magic trick if your magic came from a need for ritualistic sacrifice.

Leo stopped in front of the door to the interrogation room. The OCCUPIED sign was posted. "You gonna say thank you before you tell me to fuck off or what?"

"Thank you," Faith said. "Fuck off."

Leo gave her a salute, then headed back toward the squad room.

Will told Faith, "We need to go in clean."

Faith had been thinking the same thing. They couldn't look at Leighann Park as only a possible lead. She was a young woman whose life had been changed over the course of thirty-six hours. Statistically, there was around a 5 percent chance that Leo was right about her motivations. That left a 95 percent chance that the young woman had been abducted and assaulted. Whether or not that had anything to do with the McAllisters, the Rape Club, or the deaths of Merit Barrowe and Dani Cooper, was immaterial. She was a victim who deserved justice. Or at least what passed for justice.

Will knocked on the door before opening it. He let Faith go into the room ahead of him.

Leighann Park was sitting alone at the table. Her hands were gripped in front of her. She had startled when the door opened. Heavy mascara raccooned her bloodshot eyes. Her lips were shiny with candy-pink gloss. Contouring hollowed her cheeks. Blue eyeshadow rimmed her lids. She'd teased out her hair. Her tight, white shirt was opened to show her cleavage and the lace of a black bra. Faith could see her shapely, bare legs under the table. Her form-fitting black skirt hit mid-thigh. Her four-inch heels were flat to the floor. She wasn't crossing her legs. She was keeping them a few inches apart. Even in the shadow of the table, Faith could see a scattershot of bruises on her thigh that looked like someone had dipped their fingers in ink, then pressed them into her skin.

Faith took out her credentials. "I'm Special Agent Faith Mitchell with the GBI. This is my partner, Will Trent. May I sit down?"

The woman didn't answer. She snatched Faith's ID wallet out of her hands. She studied the photo carefully. She traced her finger under Faith's name.

Faith stared at her teased-out hair. Leo was right that Leighann looked like she was heading back out to the club. But it was ten in the morning. No clubs were open. Men often assumed that women only dressed up to attract men when the fact was that sometimes women wanted to look shit-hot for themselves. It was a kind of armor against the world.

The set to Leighann's mouth, the stiffness to her posture, told Faith that the woman needed it.

Leighann handed Faith back her wallet. She nervously glanced at Will. "Where's Shitlips?"

Faith gave her silent props for the nickname. "Detective Donnelly's been pulled away. If you don't mind, I'd like to talk to you about what happened."

"Fine." Leighann sat back in her chair, arms crossed. Her hostility was like a third person in the room. "I already told Shitlips what happened. I was at the club. My memory blanks after that. Literally. I woke up under a hedge. Do you really need to hear it again?"

Faith indicated the chair. "May I sit, or would you prefer that I stand?"

"What is this 'may I' shit?" Leighann looked at Will again. "Why isn't he saying anything?"

Will told her, "We're performing what's called a trauma-informed interview. The goal is to build trust between the three of us so that you feel comfortable telling us about your experience."

"Well it's not fucking working," she said. "Jesus, lady, sit the fuck down. How tall are you?"

The last question was for Will. He said, "Six-three."

"You're like fucking Hodor. I mean, not like him as in ugly, but big and—fuck. Jesus Christ, I'm not flirting with you, okay? I just need a fucking minute."

Faith sat in the chair across from Leighann as the woman furiously wiped tears from her eyes. This wasn't the first time Faith had sat across from the victim of a sexual assault. She had learned to harden herself against their stories, but this time was different. Faith was thinking about how hostile and angry Leighann sounded and wondering if that was how she herself would come across if something horrible happened to her.

Leighann said, "Shitlips told me my mom couldn't be in here with me."

Faith asked, "Would you feel more comfortable if your mother was here?"

"Fuck no. She's already—" Leighann stopped. Her teeth were clenched as she tried to hold back tears. "What do you need from me?"

"Where would you like to start?"

"How about that I lost nearly two days of my fucking life?" she demanded. "I mean, shit. I've got no memory of what happened—just these flashes and shit. And no, I don't remember his face. He was white, but so what? Everybody's white. He's white."

She had angrily gestured toward Will. Faith couldn't tell if Leighann wanted him gone or wanted him to stay so that she could prove a point.

Leighann said, "I don't know what color his hair

was, his eyes. I don't remember if he was short or tall or—I mean, he wasn't as tall as this fucking dude."

Will offered, "I can leave if you like."

"If I like? What is this, the woke-ass police station?" Leighann wiped her eyes with her fist. Mascara smeared across her cheeks. "I was drinking. I wasn't doing drugs, but I tried to. I would have taken Molly. I wanted to take it. And I was dressed like a slut. Like this—do you see what I'm wearing? This is pretty close to what I was wearing the night it happened, only I put my fucking dress in the washer already. My mom told me not to, but I did it anyway."

"Your dress?" Faith asked. "Anything else?"

"I wasn't wearing any fucking underwear if that's what you mean." She wiped her eyes again. "I mean, yes, I had a bra on, but no underwear. I put on a pair before I left for the club, but—fuck, I don't know. And my shoe is missing. One of my shoes."

Faith worked to keep her tone even. Both Merit Barrowe and Dani Cooper had been missing a left shoe. "Do you know if it was the right shoe or the left one that's missing?"

"The left, and it was six-hundred-dollar Marc Jacobs in blue velvet with a square heel and laces. Same color as my dress." She wiped her nose with the back of her hand. "I washed the dress on hot, which was a stupid fucking thing to do."

"That's okay," Faith said. "Sometimes, we can still get evidence from clothes after they've been washed. We can pick them up whenever you like."

"Whenever I like?" she asked.

"It's up to you."

"You're leaving shit up to me?" Her anger ignited. She slapped her hands on the table. "I did all the wrong things, okay? I took a shower. I scrubbed the shit out of myself. I sprayed the shower thingy into every fucking hole I have. I couldn't—I felt dirty, okay? I couldn't *not* clean myself. And I puked my guts out. And pissed myself. Blood was coming out of my ass. I felt like somebody jammed a knife up there. And I still got down on my hands and knees and cleaned up the bathroom. I used bleach, so that's another fucking giant mistake. I wiped away all the evidence. What kind of fucking moron does that?"

Faith tried, "There's no right or wrong way to—"

"Bitch, do you think I've never seen a *Dateline*?" Leighann banged her fist on the table. She was furious. "I cleaned up my own fucking crime scene. What the fuck is wrong with me?"

Faith remembered something that Sara had told them

about her interview with Eugene Edgerton. The man had at least one good page in his playbook. "Leighann, what you're feeling right now? That anger? The recriminations? Direct that rage away from yourself and put it where it belongs: on the man who raped you."

Leighann looked astonished. Then horrified. She covered her face with her hand. She started to cry.

It was the word *rape*. No woman wanted to hear it.

Faith said, "Leighann, it's okay. You're safe now."

Leighann tried to pull herself together. She sniffed. She wiped her eyes again. "Is that part of the trauma interview? Telling me it's not my fault?"

Faith said, "It's something I would say to my own daughter if I was sitting across from her in this room. It's not your fault. You did nothing wrong. You have every right to go to a club and drink and dance and have fun. The cocksucker who hurt you—he's the monster. Not you."

Leighann wiped her eyes again. Black streaks radiated from her eyes. "I always thought I would be smarter. I *am* smart. I don't do stupid things. But I did all the stupid things."

Faith reached into her purse. She found a pack of Kleenex. She placed it on the table.

Leighann pulled a few tissues but didn't use them. "I keep having these flashes, like an old movie flickering. I see the club, then I see this—this blanket. It's white fur, like a sheepskin? But I don't know."

Faith caught Will reaching into his pocket to turn on his recording app.

She asked, "Would you tell me more about the sheepskin blanket?"

"Maybe it was a rug? My face was in it. I remember it—it was up my nose. The hairs or sheep fur or whatever you call it." Leighann wiped her nose. "I smelled something."

"Would you describe it for me?"

"Sweet? Like, maybe cherry Mountain Dew?"

Faith clenched her teeth so she didn't put words in the woman's mouth. Merit Barrowe had told Cam that her attacker's breath had smelled like cold medicine. "Can you recall anything else about the smell?"

Leighann shook her head. "Ask me something else."

"What about your thoughts? Do have any memory of what you were thinking while the assault was happening?"

"Which time?" she asked. "It was two fucking days. I mean, fuck, lady, do you know how many times a dude can fuck you in two days? Because I sure as hell don't. I don't fucking remember."

Faith watched her start pulling apart the tissue.

"I kept forgetting how to breathe," Leighann said.

"I would be asleep, and I would wake up thinking I was suffocating, but it was because my brain had stopped telling my lungs to breathe."

Faith resisted the urge to reach for her notebook. She didn't want to stop the flow.

"My arms and legs—I couldn't move them. Control them, I mean. They were moving. I could feel them moving, but like, I was asleep, but I was also a mannequin. He kept moving me. Posing me, I guess?" She put her hand to her forehead. "What else? Help me remember."

"Were you able to hear something while it was happening?"

She shook her head, but said, "A purring kind of sound? I don't know. Not like a cat, but an electronic purring sound. *Zzzzt. Zzzzt.* Fuck, what was it?"

Faith couldn't place the sound, but she wanted to keep the momentum. "What about your feelings while it was happening? Where were you emotionally?"

"My feelings?" Her hostility looked like it was about to flare, but it sputtered out quickly. "I wasn't afraid."

Faith caught the girl's shock of anxiety. "Remember, there's no right or wrong."

"But, I don't understand. Like, when it was happening, why wasn't I afraid? I should've been terrified, but

I was kind of numb? Or out of it? Like, not just in my head but out of my body? I felt like I was disappearing. There was this white noise in my brain, and my arms and legs—I thought they were going to detach from my body. I don't understand. Was I watching it happen? Did it really happen to me?"

Faith noticed that Leighann's hand had moved to her left side. Her palm was pressed just along the line of her last rib. "Leighann, can you tell me why your hand is there?"

She looked down. She turned her hand upward as if the answer was written on her palm. She looked at Faith. "He drugged me. This is where the needle went in. Right here."

"How many times?"

"I don't know." She pressed her hand back to her side. "At the club, at least. I felt the pinch, but it was more like a sharp sting. And then later—I remember it happening later, but not how many times or where I was or what was happening. Is that why my memory is so fucked? He drugged me?"

Faith wasn't supposed to draw conclusions, but she couldn't hold back. "That's what it sounds like."

"It makes sense," Leighann said. "Because— because I couldn't remember. But if he drugged me, like kept shooting me up, then that would make sense. Like, I wasn't scared. So maybe it was Xanax or Valium or something like that?"

Faith could feel Leighann retreating, as if now that she had an explanation for her memory loss, nothing else mattered. She asked, "Leighann, what about before you were at the club. Is there anything from that time that you can tell us about?"

She smoothed her lips together. She was clearly holding back.

Faith couldn't let her close down again. "If you want, we can find another time to speak. You're in control here."

Leighann nodded, but she didn't ask to leave. "I was sleeping on Jake's couch. I was scared to be at my place."

"Why?"

"The texts," Leighann said. "Didn't Shitlips tell you about them?"

Faith was going to murder Leo Donnelly. "Can you show me?"

"No, I erased them. I don't know why, but I erased them." She ran her fingers through her hair. "That's another stupid thing I did. I could see it in Shitlips' stupid eyes when I told him, like *you stupid fucking bitch*. And that's the correct response. I don't know why I erased them. It felt like I was taking back control, you know? Like *Fuck you, asshole, I'm erasing your shit.*"

"Are you able to remember anything about the texts?"

"He knew things," Leighann said. "He knew that I was looking for a book at the library on the Protestant Reformation. And he knew where I lived, down to my apartment number. He said something about what I was wearing, like, the color of my underwear, even, but he was gross, he called them panties. And he knew where my dad works and—"

Leighann put her hand to her mouth. She squeezed her eyes shut. Tears seeped out.

Faith let herself check in on Will. He was watching Leighann. They both knew that the girl was fragile. Even a gentle push might be too much. All they could do was wait.

Leighann took almost a full minute before she was able to speak again. She ripped more tissues from the pack. She dabbed at her eyes. She took a quick breath. "He told me to get the mirror out of my make-up drawer. Like, he knew it was there. That's where I keep it. And he told me to look at the back of my left knee. That there was a circle there. And I looked. I did what he said. I got the mirror. I twisted around on my bed. There was a circle drawn on the back of my knee, right in the center, a perfect, round circle."

Faith took her notebook out of her purse. She opened it to a fresh page, clicked her pen, then put both in front of Leighann. "Draw it for me."

Leighann picked up the pen with her left hand. She drew a circle that was about the size of a dime. Then she carefully filled it in without crossing the line.

"Is that how big it was?" Faith asked.

"Maybe it was a little smaller? But it was perfect, completely round, like he traced a pen around something. And it was in the exact center." Leighann shook her head. "I don't know. I should've taken a picture, but I scrubbed the hell out of it until it faded. It freaked me the fuck out, and Jake—he told me that probably somebody was playing a joke on me. We got drunk a couple of nights before I saw it. I mean, it's stupid, but maybe one of my friends drew it?"

"What about Jake?" Faith asked. "Could he be the one who drew it?"

"You sound like Shitlips now. He said I was out banging Jake and I didn't want my mom to know I'm not a virgin." She threw her hands into the air. "News flash, my mom knows I'm not a virgin. She took me to get a fucking IUD when I was fifteen. She held my hand while they stuck a needle up my cooch."

Faith tried to tread carefully. "How long have you known Jake?"

"Two years. What does that matter?"

"I know Jake is your friend, but—"

"There's no *but* about it, lady. Jake didn't do this shit to me. He was at the club with me. I literally saw him with my own eyes dancing with some girl when I was getting texts from the Creeper."

"The Creeper?"

"That's what we called him."

"Jake saw the texts, too?"

"Yeah, but you're not listening to the important part. I was getting texts from the Creeper while I was watching Jake on the dance floor. That's how I know it wasn't him."

"Okay."

"Don't okay me like I'm fucking crazy," she said. "The Creeper is the one who texted me. He's the one who did this to me. It's the exact same guy."

"I hear you."

"You'd better fucking hear me. I don't want you assholes going after Jake. That's how unarmed men get shot in the back by cops."

Faith tried to steer her back on topic. "Can we talk a little bit more about the texts? Was there anything else the Creeper said that you think is important?"

"Yeah, I kept asking him who the fuck he was, and he said look at the fucking circle. That's who I am."

"'That's who I am'?" Faith's brain flashed up the transcript of the threatening texts that Dani Cooper had received. "Those were his exact words? 'That's who I am'?"

"No, it was—" Her voice caught again. She pressed her fingers to her eyelids. Her anger gave way to devastation. She started to sob. She pressed her forehead to the top of the table, her hands cupping her face.

Faith felt like a vise was squeezing down on her heart. Emma would sometimes do the same thing at her kitchen table.

"Can—" Leighann whispered. "Can you make him leave? Please, just make him leave. I need him to go. Please."

Will dropped his phone into Faith's purse on his way out the door. He closed it softly. Faith could barely hear the click.

"Leighann," she said. "He's gone. You're all right. You're safe."

She kept her forehead on the table, her face still cupped by her palms. Tears spread across the metal surface. Leighann silently reached out her hand.

Faith grabbed onto it. She could feel the girl shaking.

"I'm sorry," Leighann whispered. "I got scared."

"It's all right, sweetheart." Faith held on tight to her hand. "Do you want to stop? I can get your mom. I can take you home. We don't have to do any of this."

"I need to," she said. "I know that I need to."

"What you need to do is take care of yourself," Faith told her. "That's all that matters."

Leighann's grip tightened. "I couldn't get rid of it. I tried and tried but it wouldn't go away."

"What wouldn't go away?" Faith waited, but there was no response. She reminded herself not to push, to let Leighann take the lead. She silently counted the seconds in her head, waiting, praying that the girl would continue.

Leighann slowly sat up. Her fingers slipped from Faith's grasp.

There was a look of resolve on the young woman's face. She didn't speak. She bowed her head. Her hands shook as she worked the small pearl buttons on her tight white shirt. As the material parted, Faith saw bruises, teeth marks, broken blood vessels pressing red dots into her skin.

Leighann pulled the shirt back off her shoulders. Her black push-up bra was sheer lace. Her areolae were dark circles underneath the see-through material. The clasp was in the front. Her fingers were still shaking when she separated the hooks. She held the bra closed with her thumb and fingers.

She said, "This is what he texted me."

Faith watched her pull the bra away from her left breast.

There were two words written around the arc of her nipple—

That's me.

13

"That's me," Sara repeated into the phone. Will's call had pulled her out of Sloan's presentation. She looked up at the soaring glass atrium of the Times Square Marriott Marquis. Her brain visually broke down the two words into three—*that is me*. Subject, verb, object. Relative pronoun and verb forming the contraction. The pronoun *me* answering the questions posed to Merit Barrowe fifteen years ago—Who wants to brighten your day? Who dreams about you? Who is more damaged? Who doesn't deserve your company? Who will disappoint you when you find out who I am?

That's me.

She asked Will, "Did you see the photograph of Leighann's breast?"

"There are three. One front-facing, one close-up, one from the side," he said. "Faith described them to me. Leighann didn't want me to see it. Which is understandable. And I'm not sure what I could bring to the table."

Sara knew that Will's dyslexia sometimes gave him insight into clues that other people missed. She also knew that sometimes he erroneously assumed it would hold him back.

She told him, "Leighann said that she scrubbed herself in the shower. Do you know what was used to write the words?"

"Bullet-tipped permanent marker in black ink," he supplied. "Maybe a Sharpie. She scrubbed so hard she bled, apparently."

Sara closed her eyes at the thought of Leighann's panic. She knew what it was like to realize that your body no longer belonged solely to you. "Rubbing alcohol would be better."

"I'll make sure Faith tells her that," Will said. "She got Donnelly to move the case to sex crimes. They're taking it seriously now. Talking to Leighann's friend, Jake Calley. He corroborated seeing the texts. APD's got their tech people digging into her phone to see if they can find the backups."

"They've sent her shoe and her dress to the lab?"

"As far as I know," he said. "Faith got a description on both."

"Were there any needle marks from the injections?"

"We've got to wait for the physical exam."

"What about that mechanical purring noise that Leighann heard?" Sara asked. "Does that mean anything?"

"I'll send you the audio of her interview so you can listen on the plane. It's hard to pin down. A lot of machines make noises like that. Could be a compressor, a heater, static from a radio, a white noise machine?"

"I'm thinking about the tattoo that was called out in Merit Barrowe's autopsy," Sara said. "Maybe it was permanent marker, not a tattoo. Maybe he wrote *that's me* on her side."

"Maybe," Will said. "You didn't see anything written on Dani, though."

"I didn't," Sara confirmed.

"What about a white sheepskin rug?" Will asked. "Leighann said she remembered her face pressing into a rug."

"Dani wasn't conscious long enough to go into detail."

Sara blinked, and she was back at Grady, her hand squeezing life into Dani's heart.

She told Will, "Even without a sheepskin rug, Leighann's attack overlaps a lot of the details from Dani Cooper and Merit Barrowe. The threatening texts.

The drugging and abduction. The memory loss. The sweet-smelling odor on his breath. Then you have the writing on Leighann's breast matching the same words in the texts to Dani. And the missing underwear and the missing left shoes. Those aren't guesses. They're clear connections."

"They are. And we laid it all out for APD, but they're staying away from Merit Barrowe. Eugene Edgerton's probable corruption could open a lot of his old cases. Add in the dirty medical examiner and you're talking about hundreds of convictions being overturned." He sounded more frustrated than angry. Will knew how politics could impede an investigation. "Dani's case is off-limits, too. They're terrified of the McAllisters and their lawyers and their money. Which is fair, I guess. Nobody wants to be sued."

"Does that mean they're not going to show Leighann a photo array with Tommy McAllister?"

"You really think Faith didn't manage to sneak that in?" he asked. "Leighann's memory is wiped. She didn't recognize him."

"Some of the symptoms she described point to Rohypnol—the memory loss, the disorientation, the respiratory depression. But thirty-six hours is a long time to be under. I wouldn't be surprised if it was augmented with ketamine. That has a more hallucinogenic property, but it increases the heart rate and blood pressure. It's a delicate balance if you're trying to knock someone out but keep them alive."

"So, you'd need medical knowledge?"

"In my opinion." Sara watched a group of doctors milling around the coffee bar. The conference on Pediatric Hematology-Oncology was in full swing. Sloan was presenting her paper, *Exploring the Genesis of Sex Differences in Pain Management in Pediatric Hematological Cases,* in the main room. The research had been fascinating as well as a welcome distraction. Sara had started taking notes.

Will said, "Faith wants us to read Amanda into what we're doing."

Sara pressed together her lips. Reading Amanda in meant giving her the whole story, meant telling yet another person about what had happened fifteen years ago. The irony was not lost on her that the very thing she was dreading was the very thing she was about to put on Sloan Bauer.

He said, "The press is going to be all over this. Leighann's mother will make sure the cops feel the pressure. There's going to be a lot of attention. Maybe some witnesses from the dance club will come forward."

"Isn't there CCTV?"

"It was a pop-up club in a warehouse that's slated for demolition. There were two security guards. No cameras. No extra staff. They were credit card only, so at least there's a way to trace possible witnesses."

"That's good."

As usual, Will could tell that something was off. "Are you okay?"

"Didn't you send me a pointed text two hours ago telling me to stop asking you if you're okay?"

"That's different," he said. "I know I'm okay."

She felt herself smiling.

He told her, "I dropped by Ace and got a patch kit for the wall. I think I'll be able to have the first coat on before your plane lands."

"You'd better," she joked. But then she turned serious. "I'm sorry that I brought Eliza back into your life."

"She was never in my life and she still isn't," he corrected. "Were you worried I was going to throw her out the window?"

"A little, but only because she was probably right about her body breaking before the glass did. It would be hard to explain those bruises to the Fulton County Medical Examiner."

He laughed.

"Do you want me to read the trust documents?"

Instead of telling her no, he asked, "Are you still on the fence about talking to Sloan?"

Sara made herself stop twisting her ring. "My mother always says *be careful chasing ghosts because you might find demons.*"

"You could always catch an earlier flight."

Sara appreciated that he kept giving her chances to back out. "That might happen anyway. Sloan doesn't have to talk to me. I'm not sure I would."

"You would if it meant possibly helping someone. And from what you've told me about Sloan, she wants to help people, too."

"Maybe." Sara watched as a few doctors started filing out of the main room. Sloan's presentation was wrapping up. "I'm sorry I didn't get to tell you good-bye this morning."

"You can make it up to me by letting me tell you hello tonight."

"How about I tell you goodbye while you're telling me hello?"

"Deal."

Sara ended the call. She took a deep breath, trying to calm her nerves. It wasn't just the prospect of talking to Sloan. She was still reeling from Eliza's shocking visit, Will's even more shocking blow-up, having to pop three sutures into his knuckle, anxiously waiting for a taxi to take her to the airport, running like a mad-woman through the terminal, and reaching her gate moments before they were shutting the door.

The double gin and tonic she'd slammed back before take-off had not been one of her better decisions. Sara had contemplated a second one, but like every doctor ever, she dreaded the sound of the pilot coming on over the PA and asking if someone could help with a medi-cal emergency.

Rather than using the time in the air to focus her mind or drink herself into oblivion, she'd ended up lis-tening to the playlist Will had made her for the trip. Alabama Shakes. Luscious Jackson. P!nk. There was something to be said for a man who made you a playlist of songs you liked instead of foisting his favorite music on you. There was no way Sara would've been able to endure two hours of Bruce Springsteen B-sides.

A sudden burst of conversation pulled her away from her thoughts. The main room had started to empty out. Sara stood up, adjusting the badge hanging from her neck so that it faced inward. She'd clipped her GBI cre-dentials onto a bright yellow HEM-ONC NYC lanyard she'd found on the floor of the women's bathroom. If there was one thing she'd learned over the years, no one could argue with a lanyard.

Sara checked the line at the coffee bar to make sure

she hadn't missed Sloan. She could trace the generations of women in medicine by dress alone: the older
women were in sharply tailored black, navy or red
pantsuits with high heels. The women around Sara's
age had stepped out with a colorful blouse and a navy
or black skirt with low heels. The newly minted young
docs were in whatever they found most comfortable—
beautiful, flowing dresses, fitted shirts, even jeans and
sneakers. 2017 had been the first year that more women
than men had entered medical school. Sara gathered
they had been spared the ancient practice of advising
female doctors that they had to dress conservatively if
they wanted their patients to take them seriously.

Sloan Bauer had been on the receiving end of the
same advice, but she was wearing far more accessories
than the regressive policy dictated. Hoop earrings,
bangles, a gold locket around her neck. Her wedding
band was unexpectedly understated, a slim, gold band
that didn't cry out for attention like the giant rock that
Britt McAllister sported.

Sara watched Sloan move with the line toward the
hissing espresso machine. People kept coming up to
her to ask questions or comment on her presentation.
Sloan had earned the accolades. Her CV was the most
impressive of all the gang, including Mac. She'd gotten
her undergrad from Boston College, completed medical

school at Emory University, matched at NYU Langone Medical Center, completed her hematology fellowship at Johns Hopkins and was currently head of pediatric hematology at Children's Hospital in Connecticut. The conference was a huge deal for her, a highlight in an incredibly impressive career.

Which explained the knot in Sara's stomach. The feeling that this was wrong hadn't just returned. It had started eating her resolve. She turned away from Sloan, looking back at the elevators. The atrium was on the eighth floor. Sara could change her flight and be back in Atlanta before rush hour. Will had told her that they could find another way.

"Sara Linton?"

Sara felt the knot tighten. She had no choice but to turn back around.

"I thought that was you." Sloan was walking toward her, a big grin on her face. "My God, you haven't changed a bit."

"You were great in there." Sara nodded toward the conference room. "The sequela to undermanaged pain in sickle cell was eye-opening."

"Oh—" Sloan waved away the compliment, but Sara could tell she was pleased. "What are you doing in New York? Shit, you're not thinking of moving up here, are you? I can't handle the competition."

"No, I'm still in Atlanta." Sara gripped her hands together. She could still back out of this. So many years had passed since Sloan had been in medical school. If she was anything like Sara, what had happened to her at Emory, the pain of being sexually assaulted, was probably something she had worked very hard to put behind her.

"Sara?" Sloan was giving her a curious look. "Don't tell me you're up here for fun. Even I wouldn't go to a medical conference on vacation."

"No, I—" Sara worked to find her voice. She had come all this way at the emotional expense of so many people. And she had promised Dani Cooper that she would not give up. "I want to talk to you about what happened to me at Grady. And about what happened to you at Emory."

Sloan's welcoming expression changed so quickly that it was like watching a door slam shut. "What do you mean?"

Sara was mindful they were in a public space. She made her voice low. "Mason told me that—"

"Cocksucker." Sloan hadn't bothered to whisper. She caught the nosy glances from the coffee line. She nodded for Sara to follow her away from the crowd.

Sloan stopped by the towering windows. Cold whistled in between the glass. She didn't give Sara a chance to explain. "This is the wrong place for this bullshit."

"I know. I'm so sorry."

Sloan started shaking her head. She was clearly furious. "I'm not doing it. You can leave. I'm leaving."

Sara felt her heart sink as Sloan walked away. She couldn't blame the woman. Sara had known from the beginning that this was an incredibly shitty thing to do. Sloan had headed toward the elevators. Following her felt like a second offense. Sara searched for the stairs, her eyes skipping around the room.

"What did he say?" Sloan had returned, her anger still on full display. "Is it some kind of fucking joke he tells at cocktail parties? 'You won't believe this, gents, but I ended up fucking two gals who've been—'"

Sara battled against her own sorrow as Sloan stopped before saying the word.

Raped.

She told Sloan, "I don't know what Mason's doing at parties, but I wouldn't put it past him. I only talked to him because Britt—"

"Britt? Why are you still talking to these toxic assholes?" Sloan demanded. "Sara, they were never your friends. They laughed about you behind your back. They called you—"

"Saint Sara," she said. "I know."

Sloan crossed her arms. She was clearly trying to regain her composure. "What is this? What are you hoping to accomplish? Do you want to embarrass me? Is this some kind of payback for taking Mason away from you?"

"Of course not. There was nothing to take." Sara felt her resolve finally crumble. She had to get out of here. "Sloan, I apologize. You're right that I shouldn't have come. I'm going to leave now. Your research is amazing. It's really going to help patients. You have a lot to be proud of. I'm sorry that I stepped on your moment."

This time, Sara was the one to walk away. She twisted her ring around her finger as she looked for a glowing exit sign. The hotel was massive, with two different wings that fronted two different streets. Sara felt turned around, out of sorts. The self-recriminations flooded in as she finally gave up on the stairs and headed toward the minaret-shaped elevator column.

Why had she made this stupid trip? What did she think was going to happen?

Her hands shook as she tried to figure out the stupid elevators. There was no up or down button. You had to enter your desired floor into a panel. Sara was searching for the lobby when a hand reached past hers and tapped the numbers for the thirty-first floor. The gold bangle around Sloan's wrist hit the console as she pulled back her hand.

"All right." Sloan tossed her full cup of coffee into the trash. "We'll finish this up in my room."

Sara could not do this. She could see tears in Sloan's eyes. The woman's carefully applied make-up was going to run. She'd been given the main room to deliver her paper, the audience had been riveted, her research had been compelling—she should be celebrating her triumph right now, not taking Sara up to her hotel room to talk about something she'd probably spent nearly two decades trying to forget.

"Sloan," Sara tried. "I'm leaving. You don't have to—"

There was a loud ding as their elevator arrived. Sloan joined the crowd that flooded into the car. Sara reluctantly followed. She was shoved against sweaty tourists in puffy coats who were going to the restaurant on the top floor. She tried to catch Sloan's eye, but Sloan was turned away from her.

There were nervous giggles as the car lurched. The concrete elevator core ran up the center of the building, creating a soaring atrium from the lobby to the top of the restaurant. Each floor was ringed by a white concrete balcony. Sara could see the guest room doors as they whizzed by in the glass elevator. The place reminded her of a supermax. She tried to catch Sloan's eye again, but Sloan was looking at her phone as if she was studying a blood smear under a microscope.

The car finally stopped at the thirty-first floor. Sara waited for Sloan to extricate herself from the back. The woman's expression was steely. Her jaw was clenched. She stalked through the elevator vestibule, took a left down the long balcony. Sara followed at a distance. She watched Sloan pause outside one of the rooms. Her hand was in her purse as if she was still deciding whether or not to do this. Finally, she pulled out her keycard and opened the door.

From the hall, Sara could see the suite had a sitting room off the bedroom. The view looked straight across to the Hudson River where the *Intrepid* was berthed. The coffee table had champagne chilling in a bucket of ice. Flowers. Chocolate-covered strawberries.

Sloan waved her into the room, saying, "It's my anniversary. My husband's joining me tonight. We were going to have a romantic evening in the city."

Sara caught the implication: all of that was ruined now. "Every bad thing you're thinking about me right now—I'm thinking the same thing."

"Is that supposed to be a consolation?"

"No, but it's the truth."

Sloan dropped her purse on the floor. She walked

into the other room, telling Sara, "Pour me something from the minibar. I need to use the bathroom."

Sara didn't bother to look at her watch as she opened the small fridge and selected four mini bottles of Bombay Sapphire and a Fever Tree. She'd had more to drink today than she'd had in months. Will had spent his childhood making the connection between the smell of alcohol and untold violence much in the same way that Sara had spent the last fifteen years shuddering at the thought of a man's beard scratching against her face. They both tried to respect each other's boundaries. There were roughly eight hundred miles between them right now. That was boundary enough.

She was pouring the drinks when Sloan returned from the bathroom.

Sloan looked shaky. She had clearly been sick in the toilet. Still, she grabbed one of the glasses. She took in a healthy mouthful and swished it around before swallowing. "Do you still throw up sometimes when you think about it?"

Sara nodded. "Yes."

"Sit down." Sloan slumped into the chair.

Sara sat on the couch. Her phone was in her pocket. She thought about the recording app, but she couldn't bring herself to do it. All she could say was, "I'm sorry."

"I know you are. Let that be your last apology."

Sloan finished her drink. She reached over to the fridge and found another mini bottle of gin. "What I said downstairs—I know you wouldn't be here on a whim. And I know you wouldn't be here because of Mason."

"Your impression of him bloviating about rape at a dinner party was spot-on."

"He's such a feckless turd." She tossed back the gin directly from the bottle. It was empty in two gulps. Then she stared at the champagne chilling in the bucket. "My husband read somewhere that you're supposed to drink champagne when you're sad so that it makes you happy."

Sara shrugged. "Worth a shot."

Sloan picked up the bottle and started on the foil. "I should've been more generous to you when it happened."

"When I was raped?" Sara felt a jolt of shock that the question had slipped out so easily. "I usually do everything I can to avoid saying that word."

"We're both in the worst club ever." Sloan popped the cork, catching it in her hand. "It's easier to talk about rape with someone who's been through it. You don't have to explain yourself, or worry about managing their feelings or their responses, or—pass that over."

Sara downed the rest of her glass so that Sloan could

fill it with champagne. "When is your husband supposed to be here?"

"He has to pick up our daughter from soccer practice, then he'll catch the train." Sloan filled both glasses to the rim. "He knows, but she doesn't. I keep telling myself I need to find the right time, but the truth is, I don't know if I want her to know. Or if I want to deal with her knowing, which is a completely separate burden."

Sara didn't have the answer. "How old is she?"

"She's at that age where she's realized that I am the stupidest motherfucker who has ever walked the face of the earth."

"Thirteen?"

Sloan nodded as she sipped from her glass. "Molly's the only good thing I ever got out of a one-night stand. I hate when women talk about their kids like their magical beings, but she really helped heal me."

Sara sipped her champagne, though the taste was too sweet.

"Fuck me, I'm sorry. I know you can't—"

"It's all right. I've had fifteen years to get used to it." She shrugged. "And I'm at that age where it doesn't matter anyway."

"Don't bullshit me, Sara. You're not too old and

you're not used to it," Sloan said. "I don't know you well, but I know that."

Sara figured if they were going to do this, she might as well get comfortable. She curled back on the couch with her glass, saying, "My fiancé has this little dog he rescued from the pound. And I love her—I mean, she's a dog, obviously I love her. But sometimes I see him being so sweet and patient with her and I feel this emptiness inside, like, 'What right do I have to deprive him of being a father?'"

"Does he want to be a father?"

"He says no, but—" Sara wasn't going to share Will's private feelings. He had told her more than once that he knew too much about all the bad things that could happen to a child to feel comfortable bringing one into the world.

And yet.

"You know what I hate?" Sloan asked. "Honestly, I hate a lot of things, but I really hate when people say, 'Everything happens for a reason.' I mean—seriously? What's the reason?"

Sara shook her head, because she was just as clueless. "I like, 'Time heals all wounds.'"

"Unfortunately, it doesn't keep you from puking out your guts in a Marriott."

Sara raised her glass in a toast.

Sloan toasted back. "How about 'At least it made you stronger'?"

"Yep, one of my favorites. Rape as a character-building exercise."

They toasted each other again.

Sloan said, "My favorite question is, 'Did you tell him no?'"

"It's crazy, but it's hard to speak through duct tape."

"Sorry, it's not rape unless he hears you give a firm no."

Sara laughed. "What about, 'Did you try to fight him off?'"

"That is my absolute favorite," Sloan said. "Everybody always thinks it's easy to kick a guy in the nuts, but they're harder to find than you think."

"'How about screaming? Did you try that?'"

"Sure, that's an easy one. Except when your vocal cords freeze."

"'What were you doing there in the first place?'"

"'What were you wearing?'"

"'Did you send the wrong signals?'"

Sloan laughed. "'If that had happened to me, I would've scratched out his eyes.'"

"Yeah, but I was handcuffed."

"My wrists were tied to the bed."

Sara knew they had stopped playing the game.

Sloan put the glass to her mouth but didn't drink. "Maybe I should've bitten him, pulled a Mike Tyson on his ear. Nose. Face. Anything. But I didn't. I just laid there and waited for it to be over."

Sara watched Sloan roll the glass between her hands.

"I voluntarily went out with him. We were officially on a date. I had too much to drink. We both did." Sloan placed her empty glass on the table. "You know, if you get drunk and you get behind the wheel of a car and you kill somebody, they don't give you a pass, like, oh you would never kill somebody when you were sober. You can't possibly be a murderer. Go with God."

"No," Sara said. "They don't."

Sloan let her head drop back in the chair. She stared up at the ceiling. "I wouldn't have met my husband if I hadn't been raped. I would've stayed in Atlanta. I would've probably been the first or second Mrs. Mason James."

Sara waited.

"His name is Paul," she said. "I know a wife loving her husband is not the thing to do, but I do love him. He's supportive. He listens to me. And he does this thing that's so astonishing. Sometimes, we'll be talking, and he'll say, 'you're right.'"

"Mine does that, too." Sara felt herself wanting to

smile at the thought of Will. "I've never understood women who would rather be tolerated than loved."

"You're talking about me with my first husband." Sloan sat back up. She poured more champagne into her glass. "And my second one. Almost my third. I have no idea why I kept agreeing to marry them. I had to fuck a lot of frogs before I met Paul."

"After it happened, I never thought I'd fuck another frog again."

Sloan gave a wry smile. "Mason called me when his first daughter was born. He wanted to apologize. He said that now that he was a father, he got it."

Sara felt a massive eye roll. It was an internet joke— men who had daughters and suddenly realized that rape, sexual harassment and assault were actually kind of bad. "He never apologized to me."

"I wouldn't technically call it an apology. He told me that he *wanted* to apologize. He didn't actually *make* the apology." She cleared her throat to mimic Mason again. "I'll tell you, Sloany, it's quite moving to look into my little girl's eyes. Makes my chest swell with the urgent need to protect her. I've now realized that what happened to you was rather terrible."

Sara tried to keep the bitterness out of her laugh. "If you ever give up medicine, you could work as Mason's voice double."

"Well." Sloan had turned circumspect. She was still considering whether or not she could do this. Finally, she looked at Sara. "I'm not completely disconnected from the gossip. I know about Mac and Britt's kid being on trial for rape."

"Were you surprised?"

"I'm never surprised when someone is raped."

Sara felt the same. "They settled the case yesterday morning. He got away with it."

"They generally do." Sloan dropped back her head again and stared at the ceiling. "Before you even opened your mouth downstairs, I had this feeling in my gut that Britt was the reason you were here."

"Why?"

"She's such a vicious cunt. You went after her son. She had to extract her pound of flesh." Sloan looked Sara in the eye again. "I never knowingly hid anything from you. I need you to know that."

Sara thought about the recording app again. Her phone was still in her pocket. She left it there, saying, "Okay."

"I was really fucked up after what happened to me. You get that."

"I do."

"I matched out of state to get away from him."

"Mason told me that the man washed out of medical school."

"No." Sloan shook her head. "He was still at Emory. I had to see him every day, all through med school. We did rounds together. It was a slow, wearing kind of torture pretending to laugh at his jokes, trying not to scream at the top of my lungs."

Sara bit her lip to keep from asking for the man's name. She had to let Sloan do this in her own time.

"After I was raped, that's when I really started drinking." She waved her hand at the nearly empty champagne bottle. "This used to be breakfast for me."

"Sloan—"

"Don't you dare feel sorry for me," she warned. "I fucking mean it."

Sara nodded, though the guilt was unavoidable. Her worst fear about knocking Sloan to the floor was happening in real time.

Sloan said, "I wanted to reach out to you when you were raped. Mason told me to leave you alone. Probably right. I mean I was fucking him behind your back. But I had this fantasy that I could be—I don't know, your rape mentor?"

They both smiled. Everybody wanted to do something. No one really knew what to do.

Sloan asked, "What did Britt tell you?"

"That my being raped was connected to something that happened the night of the mixer."

Sloan looked genuinely surprised. "Did she tell you how it was connected?"

Sara opened her mouth, but Sloan answered the question.

"Britt wouldn't tell you how. She's such a mind-fucker. She puts on this feminist front, but she can only be strong when someone else is weak. You know Mac was abusing her, right?"

Sara felt something click into place. She had always found it slightly unnerving the way that Britt had never left Mac's side, but now she could see that Mac had wanted it that way. "Emotionally?"

"And physically," Sloan said. "You never noticed the bruises?"

Sara hadn't noticed a lot of things. "I didn't spend that much time around her."

"She left medicine after she herniated a disc at C-6. I don't know exactly what happened, but I think Mac pushed her down the stairs. The timing made sense. Britt was bringing in a salary while Mac was struggling through his training, but once he finished the fellow-ship, he made sure Britt stayed at home. Not that any-body felt sorry for her." Sloan gave a dry laugh. "She's a bad victim, you know?"

Sara knew. People had endless amounts of compassion for women who were the *right* kind of victim—

sympathetic, stoic, slightly tragic. Britt was too angry, too cruel, for anyone to feel anything but a sense of karma that she was getting what was coming to her.

But Sara had not come here to talk about whether or not Britt McAllister deserved pity. She took a deep breath before asking, "Can you tell me what you remember about the mixer? Or anything that happened around that time?"

Sloan was understandably reticent, but she pushed through. "Cam was drunk. He was slurring his words. He would go to the toilet, throw up, then come back and drink some more. Not that much different from what he normally did on a weekend, but this time, it was noticeably worse. I would call it binging and purging."

Sara nodded. "That's what I remember, too."

"I kept asking Mason to deal with him. Make him leave."

"Mason took away his car keys."

"My hero," Sloan said. "Cam was upset about losing a patient."

"Merit Barrowe," Sara supplied. "Two weeks before the mixer, she came into the ED. She was drugged and raped. She had a tonic-clonic in the bathroom. She died."

"I've never forgotten her name," Sloan said. "Cam was angry about her death. He told me that the police hadn't even bothered to investigate what had happened. The cop in charge was a prick. Cam told him the girl was drugged and raped, but the guy either didn't believe him or he didn't care."

Sara waited for her to continue.

"Cam was collecting paperwork and files and all this stuff to prove that Merit had been raped and murdered. I mean, he was manic about it. He wanted to show me the evidence. He kept begging me to go back to his apartment with him. I told him absolutely not." Sloan looked directly at Sara. "Fool me once, right?"

Sara nearly dropped the glass in her hand. "Cam was the man who raped you?"

Sloan was watching her closely. "Mason didn't tell you?"

Sara could only shake her head.

"That's surprising. He gossips more than my thirteen-year-old. Then again, maybe it's not. He'll protect anyone in the gang. It's their code." Sloan leaned forward, reaching for the champagne bottle. Then she thought better of it and sat back in the chair again. "First week of med school. Cam asked me out. He wasn't my type. Doughy, sad-sacky, alcoholic chain smoker. Still, I was excited. You know what it's like. Your standards drop to whatever warm body can fit into your schedule."

Sara was still in shock over the news. She forced herself to nod so that Sloan would continue.

"I bought a new dress. Low-cut, obviously. Thigh-high leather boots. He took me to Everybody's pizza. Is that place still around?"

Sara shook her head. "It closed a few years ago."

"We had a lot of beer." Sloan was staring at the bottle of champagne. "He asked me back to his place. I was having a nice time. That's what gets me. Once you cut through Cam's bullshit, he was funny and came across as sweetly earnest. We were walking back to his apartment, and I remember feeling a little tingle when he held my hand."

Sara watched as Sloan started twisting her wedding band around her finger.

"We made out on the couch. I liked it. I realized I wanted to see him again, and they never call you back if you put out on the first date, so—" Sloan took a deep breath. "I told him I was going to leave. He started kissing me again, telling me he wanted me to stay the night, that he was serious about me. And I believed him. So, I went to the bedroom with him."

Sara watched Sloan stand. She started pacing the room, hands on her hips.

"Everything was very neat in his apartment. That's what stuck out the most. I grew up with brothers.

They throw shit around, leave clothes on the floor, but not Cam. He'd even turned down his bed, like you see at a hotel. I made a joke about him expecting me to cave to his charms." She had stopped by the window. She looked out at the view to the river. Her demeanor had changed. She was trying to talk about what had happened without putting herself back in that dark place. "We started kissing again. Things got hot and heavy. And then he pinned both my hands above my head. Really pinned them so I couldn't move. I don't like that, not before and sure as hell not now. I told him to let me go. His grip got tighter. I tried to squirm away but—"

Sara watched Sloan's right hand go to her left wrist. Her voice was quiet in the large room.

"His face changed completely. It was like watching a mask slip away. One second he was this sweet, charming guy, and the next minute his face was gnarled like a monster. He kicked my legs apart. He used his weight to pin me down. I could barely breathe. He had at least fifty pounds on me."

Sloan turned to face Sara, pressing her back to the window.

"It's weird, because, initially, I didn't panic. Instead, I had this flash of when I first walked into the bedroom and he turned on the lights. I saw a long, black silk rope hanging from the headboard. There was a noose tied on the end, some kind of slip knot. So that's what I was thinking when he tied me up—you fucking idiot, why didn't you notice that fucking rope?"

Sara pressed together her lips. She knew how useless it would be to tell Sloan it wasn't her fault.

"He kept trying to—I can't call it kissing. He jammed his tongue down my throat. Just like, I don't know—fucking my face. My jaw hurt from it. Our teeth kept clashing. Did your guy do that?"

Sara nodded.

"That's a great memory to carry for the rest of your life, isn't it?" Sloan touched her fingers to her neck. "Paul was the first man I could kiss without thinking about the taste of Cam's fucking amoxicillin. Do you remember him carrying it around like a water bottle? He drank it for his acne."

Sara had forgotten that detail, but now she remembered Cam swilling the antibiotic straight from the bottle. It had a sickly-sweet flavor, almost like cough medicine.

"I did tell him no, at least. Every time I tried to scream, he would stick his tongue in my mouth. He bit me, scratched me. He even ripped out some of my hair." Sloan's hand went to the back of her head. "He raped me. No condom, thanks a lot. At least it was only vaginal penetration, but Jesus, it hurt. He never closed his eyes. He barely blinked. He kept grunting like a pig, banging against me so hard that my head kept slamming into the headboard. He didn't last long, which I guess was a blessing. He jerked off in my face. Then he untied my wrists. Then he thanked me. Can you believe that part? 'Thank you. I needed that.' Then he went outside to smoke a cigarette."

Sara watched Sloan nervously wring her hands.

"I didn't know what to do except wipe myself off and get dressed." She lifted one shoulder in a shrug. "I was in shock. Numb. Desperate to leave before he returned for another go. He was on the front stoop of his apartment building when I left. He kissed me on the mouth, and I let him. I didn't say anything. I didn't push him away. All I could think about was doing a blood test. I was legitimately concerned about catching something from him. Or being pregnant. Or both. But I told him I'd see him later, and he said, 'I had fun tonight. I'll call you tomorrow.'"

Sara could practically hear the silent recriminations racing through Sloan's mind. They probably echoed her own. All these years later, she could still carousel through the *I should haves*, as if there had somehow been a magic word, a magic action, that would've stopped him.

Sloan wiped her eyes. "I had this idea that I was a strong person. Cam shattered that. It was actually a murder, really, because I was never me again after he raped me. I've never felt completely safe. I've never been able to completely trust someone. Even my husband, who I trust the most in the world—that's only ninety-nine percent. That one percent is gone forever."

Sara was uniquely qualified to understand.

"I couldn't let myself admit that I was raped," Sloan said. "It took about a week before I accepted what had happened, and by then, too much time had passed. That's what they always say, right? Why did you wait so long to go to the police? And then what would I say to the cops? I got drunk with him. I went back to his place with every intention of letting him fuck me. I changed my mind. He forced me anyway. This was nearly twenty years ago. There's no way anyone would've believed me."

Sara knew that the passage of time hadn't changed that much. Everyone called it he said/she said, as if a woman's word carried the same weight as a man's.

"He actually called me the day after. He asked me out. I panicked. I said I already had plans. He called a few days later. Asked me out again. I kept making excuses—I had to go to the library, had to study, had a birthday party or a family obligation. He was very persistent. I almost said yes just so he would stop."

Sara knew that she wasn't exaggerating.

"I put up with it for over a month. Then he started flirting with me in class. People were teasing me about him being lovesick. He followed me back to my apartment one day, and I exploded. I screamed at him, 'Why would I go out with you when you raped me?'"

Sara watched her wipe away tears.

"He looked horrified. Or at least that's how he acted. He started crying. Which really pissed me off. The entire fucking time, I had never cried. And here was this fucking rapist whining like a baby in the street, actually expecting me to comfort him?"

Sara felt her own outrage echoed in Sloan's voice.

"He kept saying it was a misunderstanding. He thought I was into him. He really liked me. He'd assumed that's what I wanted. I mean, I went home with him. I was the one who kissed him. I was the one who followed him back to his bedroom. That part where I kept saying no, when I tried to scream, when I struggled to get away because it felt like he was using sandpaper inside of me—he couldn't remember any of that. Too much to drink."

Sara watched Sloan sit back down in the chair. She

was staring at the bottle of champagne, clearly wanting to finish it.

"In retrospect, I'm kind of glad he tied me up, right? Because otherwise, it feels squishy."

Sara thought she knew what Sloan meant, but asked, "Squishy?"

"You can argue away all the other stuff, but you can't argue with someone being tied up against their will. It's not nearly as clear-cut as what happened to you, but it's something to hang your hat on."

Sara felt herself nodding. There was a weird sort of hierarchy among rape victims. Sara was considered one of the lucky ones. The crime was blatantly obvious. Sara was a white, middle-class doctor with a good reputation and strong familial support. The detective had been sympathetic, the prosecutor had been self-righteous, and the jury had delivered some form of justice.

Fewer than 1 percent of rapes led to a felony conviction.

"That's how I got him," Sloan said. "When I confronted Cam, he had an excuse for everything, but then I asked, 'If you thought that's what I wanted, then why did you have to tie me up?'"

"Did he have an answer?"

"Nothing. He was genuinely stunned. I could see it in his face. He really didn't know the difference between sex and rape." Sloan started rubbing her wrists again. "I tried to walk away, but he followed me. He kept asking me, 'Did I rape you? Did I really rape you?' It got to the point where I told him I was going to call the police if he didn't leave me alone. I wasn't going to reassure him. He expected me to make it all better. Honestly, that's why I left Atlanta. I could almost handle being raped. But I couldn't handle Cam pretending to be the fucking victim."

Sara watched her try to shrug it off, but she was clearly still angry.

"That's it. That's what happened." Sloan clasped her hands together. "After I left Emory, I saw Cam a handful of times, but never alone. I'd sneak back into Atlanta to see Mason, and he'd take me to dinner or something, and Cam would just happen to be there. I can't believe how long it took me to stand up for myself. I was so fucking stupid."

"What made you finally break away?"

"You," Sloan said. "They were so nasty about what happened to you. I never joined in, but I didn't defend you, which feels a lot worse."

Sara wasn't going to blame her. "Do you remember how they were nasty? Did they say anything specific?"

"Not really. And I was drinking so much back then. I can't remember."

"Can you tell me anything about the mixer?"

"Cam wouldn't leave me alone. I kept begging Mason to do something, but Mason had it in his head that we could *solve the misunderstanding.*"

That sounded exactly like Mason. "You said earlier that Cam wanted you to know that he was looking into Merit Barrowe's death?"

"Yes. He was holding it up like it could redeem him. Then he started sobbing again, telling me that he had always loved me."

Sara felt the alcohol in her stomach start to turn. "He said that—that he loved you?"

"Yeah." She slowly nodded, lost in the memory. "I can't describe how disgusted I was. He kept talking about his crusade to get Merit justice, acting like one thing could cancel out the other. And it can't. Being a good guy for once in your life doesn't erase being an asshole rapist for the rest of it. Especially if you can't fucking own it."

"If it's any consolation, Cam's crusade barely lasted more than two weeks." Sara explained, "He stopped looking into Merit's rape when the detective on her case offered to make a DUI go away."

"Are you sure it was only a DUI?"

Sara felt another piece click into place. "You don't think that you were the first woman Cam raped."

"The rope was tied to the headboard when I got there," Sloan said. "The way he grabbed me, rolled me onto the bed, tied me up—that took practice."

Sara had thought the same thing about the man who had raped her. He was too fast, too focused, for it to have been his first time. "Did Cam ever write anything down, or send you notes or texts?"

"Why?"

Sara realized she hadn't answered the question, but she still provided, "Merit Barrowe got threatening text messages. Dani Cooper, the girl that Mac and Britt's kid was accused of raping, got threatening text messages. There's some overlap to what happened to me."

"Cam is dead."

"I know."

Sloan leaned forward, her elbows on her knees. "Cam called me before he killed himself."

Sara asked, "When?"

"Right before he pulled the trigger, according to the police." She clenched her hands together. "My number was the last one he dialed. The detectives showed up at my work. I think they were expecting me to burst into tears, but I have never laughed so hard in my life. The relief flooded through my brain like helium. I actually felt like I was floating off of the floor. I didn't realize until that moment the weight I carried around, knowing that Cam Carmichael was still out there in the world."

Sara longed for that kind of relief. "What did Cam tell you on the phone?"

"The same bullshit from before about being in love with me, wanting to marry me and some other bullshit. Then he apologized. He said that he wanted me to know that he had never forgiven himself. I mean— good. He shouldn't forgive himself. He very nearly destroyed me." Sloan crossed her arms again. "Then he told me that he'd mailed a box to my work. He said, 'Do what you think is right.'"

Sara had moved to the edge of the couch. "What was in the box?"

"A thumb drive."

Sara felt her lips part in surprise. Cam's laptop. The password-protected files. The corrupted links of the chat website. He had left data in his wake.

"I never looked at the contents. I'm sorry, but I thought—" The muscles in her neck strained as she battled her emotion. "Cam was dead. I thought if I looked at the drive, if there was something terrible on it, I was giving him another way to keep hurting me."

Sara could not fault her logic. "Did Cam give you any idea what was on the drive?"

"No. I'm sorry."

Sara remembered that Sloan hadn't answered her earlier question. "Did he leave a note?"

"Yes."

"What did it say?"

"Personal stuff. Stuff about that night." Sloan needed a moment. She looked up at the ceiling again. "He said that he had always loved me. And he wished that things had been different. And that I was a beautiful person and he knew that I would do the right thing."

"What's the right thing?"

Sloan closed her eyes for a moment. "Are you sure you want to do this?"

For the first time, Sara got the feeling that Sloan was holding back. She silently ran through the last few minutes of the conversation. Sloan had said that Cam had mailed her a box. An eight-year-old thumb drive was about half the width of a business card and slightly thicker than a smartphone.

She told Sloan, "I don't think I understand your question. What would I be unsure of?"

"You can never unring the bell," Sloan said. "It's the same choice I had with the thumb drive. Do you look at it, do you risk getting hurt in a new way, or do you get on with your life?"

Sara didn't see it as a choice. "Now you really sound like Mason."

"There's some value to moving on."

"That's very easy for you to say. Cam is dead."

Sloan sat back. "Nothing is easy."

"You were right before. I didn't fly up here on a whim. Don't you think I've considered the toll this is taking on me? On my friends? On the man I'm going to marry?" Sara had no choice left but to beg. "Sloan, please. What else did Cam send you?"

Sloan took a deep breath and held onto it for a few seconds. Instead of responding, she picked up her purse from the floor. She took out her phone. Dialed a number. Pressed the device to her ear. Waited for someone to answer on the other end.

"Paul, there's a Ziploc bag in the bottom drawer of my black filing cabinet in the basement. I need you to bring it to me when you come into the city." She paused a moment. "Yes, that one."

Sara waited until Sloan had ended the call.

She asked, "What's in the bag?"

"Merit Barrowe's underwear."

14

Will waited at the entrance to the country club's Riverside Dining Room, which, as advertised, offered a commanding view of the Chattahoochee River. There were mostly men at the round dining tables, mostly in business casual, some in golf outfits, a few wearing suits and ties. Lawyers, doctors, bankers, trust fund spenders. Will wasn't looking forward to slipping back into his John Trethewey cover. He was much more comfortable pretending to be a thug or a thief. You got to flash the same level of entitlement, but it came from knowing you could beat the shit out of anybody rather than knowing you could buy them off.

The difference was not subtle.

At least thugs got to dress more comfortably. Will had swung by the mall after the Leighann Park interview to return his previous douchey clothes and pick up some new ones. The tight jeans were by some Italian designer this time and Will was having to actively work it out of his mind that he looked like he was wearing a codpiece. The Diesel boots were apparently part of his wardrobe now. As for the shirt, he'd gone with a similar model to the cashmere polo Sara had picked out for him. The cost had been astonishing. Will had left sweat on the machine when he'd put his debit card into the reader.

The door opened behind him. Will turned around. Men in loud golf pants. No Richie, though they were supposed to meet five minutes ago. Will guessed it was a rich people thing to keep people waiting. He scanned the dining room again, searching for the hostess. All he could see were waitresses bustling around. If one of them had noticed Will waiting, they hadn't passed along the word. They bustled silently back and forth across the loudly patterned carpet. The tufted cream and brown swirls were meant to hide the stains, but there was nothing that could be done about the splash of red wine that looked like blood had splattered in the corner. One thing Will was learning about incredibly expensive country clubs was that they were not as well-maintained as an average Holiday Inn.

He rubbed the scar along his jaw. The stubble felt prickly. He would need to shave before Sara got home. He'd also have to pressure-wash the gunk out of his hair. He looked at his watch. He had to assume Sloan had agreed to talk to Sara. Part of him had expected her to call him ten minutes after their last call to say it was a bust. Another part of him knew that Sara was really good at getting people to do the right thing.

His phone buzzed. Will looked at the text from Faith. She'd sent him a thumbs up. She was working with the fraud team this afternoon. There was going to come a point in time when Amanda found out what they were doing. In a lot of instances, it was easier to ask for forgiveness rather than permission. Amanda had never enjoyed being on the receiving end of one of those instances.

"Mr. Trethewey?" The hostess had finally appeared. She was thin and very young, dressed in a black skirt and white shirt, just like at a Holiday Inn.

She told Will, "This way, please."

He followed her through the dining room, trying to remind himself why he was here. Between his sutured hand, the slow-healing papercut at the corner of his eye from the militia man's pinky ring, and the sales tags that were stuck down the back of the clothes, every step felt like a slow kind of torture. He worked to block it all from his mind. He let John Trethewey click into place. A refugee from a MeToo charge. A father to a surly son named Eddie, who shared a remarkably similar trajectory with Faith's son, Jeremy. A husband to a disappointed wife. An asshole looking to make a fresh start.

The hostess didn't seat him at one of the round tables. Instead, she opened a door in the back. There was a gold plaque beside it that Will didn't bother to decipher. He was more curious about the men in the private area of the dining room.

Richie Dougal had brought some friends.

Mac McAllister was seated at the square table. Chaz Penley was beside him.

"John." Richie stood to shake Will's hand. "You remember—"

"Chaz," Will said. He'd seen the man's picture on Faith's crazy wall. Blond hair. Blue eyes. Gone to seed. She'd made a joke about him turning the Von Trapps into the Nazis. "I barely recognized you. Guess you're not working out much these days."

"I see you're still an asshole, Trethewey." Chaz was grinning as he gave Will a firm handshake. "Where've you been?"

"Here and there." Will took a seat across from Mac. He put his phone face down, making sure to click the button to turn on the recording app. A waitress appeared out of nowhere and placed a glass of liquor in front of him. She started to fill his water glass. The other men ignored her, so Will did, too.

He said, "I was in Texas. What a hellhole. One day you don't have power, the next day they're telling you to boil your water. The whole country's going to shit."

"No kidding," Richie said. "You should see the potholes on my street."

Chaz asked, "What's the story with your hand?"

Will looked down at the bandage. Sara had prepped him on the language to use. "Dodged a Boxer's Fracture. Thankfully, I can still wrangle a syringe."

Chaz glanced at Mac, a tacit acknowledgment that Will hadn't really answered the question.

The waitress asked, "Gentlemen, can I get you anything else?"

Richie kept ignoring her, telling Will, "We took the liberty of ordering steaks. You good with that?"

Will asked Chaz, "Sure you wouldn't rather have a salad?"

They all laughed, but Chaz's stiff posture showed the blow had landed.

Mac's head dipped down, dismissing the waitress. She backed out of the room, closing the door behind her.

"Nice tits on that one," Chaz said.

"Indeed." Richie finished his glass of Scotch. He had

a second waiting on the table in front of him. "John, thanks for coming on such short notice. I'm only sorry we couldn't do this on the course. Have you played here?"

"Not much. I prefer tennis, basketball. Something that gets your heart rate going."

"Typical ortho jock," Chaz said, but the joke fell flat.

Will used his silence to let the joke sputter a bit more. He took his time unrolling the cloth napkin and placing it in his lap. The dynamic between the three men wasn't hard to figure out. Mac was in charge. He hadn't spoken since Will had entered the room. Richie was like a Labrador, eager to please, making all the small talk. Chaz was acting with more precision, trying to get information. He was clearly higher up the chain of command. Just as clearly, Mac enjoyed watching him get bullied.

"All right," Will said. "As much as I enjoy a free steak, why am I here?"

Mac still said nothing, but Richie and Chaz smiled like crocodiles.

Richie offered, "We thought we'd welcome you back to Atlanta."

Chaz added, "I didn't know Eliza had any living relatives."

Will shrugged. "Never a bad idea to suck up to a rich aunt."

"She's at death's door," Chaz said.

Will sat back in his chair, waiting for them to continue.

Richie started on his second glass.

Mac finally spoke. "What happened to your hand?"

Will looked down at the bandage again. "I failed to step away from a triggering situation."

Chaz sputtered a laugh. Will knew that the man had been forced to take anger management classes as part of a DUI plea deal sixteen years ago. The line was straight out of Controlling Your Temper 101.

Mac asked, "Wife? Kid?"

Will drank from his water glass, feigning the need to quell his irritation. "Eddie is a little younger than Tommy. You know how they get. Start to think they can take on the old man. Primal shit. You've got to put them back in their place."

The three men took the opportunity to exchange another look. They weren't disapproving. They were calculating.

Will put down his glass. "Speaking of sons, I heard Tommy dodged a bullet on the trial."

Mac stared at Will for a beat before answering. "If

you call me having to write a check for two million dollars dodging a bullet."

"Small price to pay to keep Britt from whining about her precious baby's reputation."

Mac allowed a smile. "It is indeed."

Will pushed his Scotch toward Richie. "I'm on Percocet for the hand. Help yourself."

Richie scooped up the glass like a bear dipping his paw into honey.

Chaz said, "I tried to look you up on social, Trethewey. You're a ghost."

"Good," Will said. "I paid a hell of a lot of money for that."

Mac asked, "What happened in Texas?"

Will gave him a steely look. "Why the curiosity?"

"Making conversation," Mac said. "We're all friends."

"Are we?" Will threw the cloth napkin back onto the table. "You've gone to a lot of trouble to get me here. I'll admit I was curious, but this is starting to feel like a fucking interrogation."

"Hold on." Mac patted his palms in the air, urging Will to stay seated. "Sorry for the third degree. It's been a while since we've seen you."

"Don't think I didn't notice," Will said. "I found out about Cam at a fucking conference. Would've been nice to be invited to the memorial. He's the one who brought me into the gang in the first place."

Richie had stuck his tongue into his cheek.

"Cam brought you in?" Mac asked. "I didn't remember that detail."

"You seem to be forgetting a lot of details," Will said. "I know I've always been on the sidelines, but who do you think got him the job at Bellevue? Not one word of thanks from any of you assholes for getting him the hell out of town. Do you know how bad it would've been if he'd stayed here?"

"Apologies," Richie mumbled. "Tough times."

Will tapped his hand on the table, openly conveying hostility. "I had to put sixteen hundred miles between my family and Cam's fucking mouth. What a shitshow."

No one spoke.

Will said, "So, what is this? You're all trying to make sure I kept your secret? Do you think I'd show my face back to Atlanta if I hadn't?"

The men went completely silent. Will couldn't tell if he'd gone too far. All that he could hear were knives and forks hitting china in the main dining room. He kept his nerve, looking them each in the eye. They all stared back, their eyes scanning his face as if they could read his thoughts.

What did he know? What did he want? How much had Cam shared?

"No," Richie finally said. "We're not worried about you."

Will could tell they were all very worried.

Mac asked, "How is it that you met Cam again?"

Will gave an audible groan. "Come on, what Cam told me died with Cam, as far as I'm concerned. I've got a hell of a lot more problems in the immediate than some sad sack drunk who couldn't handle a little rough play."

Mac's gaze had not left Will. There was a coldness to him that hadn't come across as clearly before. Will thought about Sara describing the profound joy of seeing a living heart for the first time. Mac McAllister had never looked on anything with joy in his entire life.

"Anyway." Will tapped the table again. "What do you want with me? Was that it?"

The door opened before anyone could answer. Two waitresses brought in their lunch. Steaks with loaded baked potatoes. More Scotch. Glasses of iced tea. The silence was uncomfortable as the food and drink was laid out. Empty glasses were removed. The women backed out through the door like they were leaving the throne room.

Chaz and Richie picked up their silverware and started to eat. Only Mac and Will didn't move.

Mac asked, "What are your plans in Atlanta, John?"

Will shrugged. "Find a job. Support my family. What else would I do?"

Chaz smacked his lips around his fork, asking, "Eliza's not helping with that?"

"I'd rather not live with that old bitch's foot on my neck, thank you very much." Will remembered something Faith had called out from the chat group website. "You ask me, somebody needs to gag her mouth shut with his cock."

Richie barked a laugh, which wasn't surprising. But then Chaz laughed. Then Mac started laughing, too. He actually leaned over, gripping the table as if he needed to keep himself from rolling on the floor. They were all laughing so hard that Will felt the need to force himself to join in.

"Fucking hell." Chaz banged his hand on the table. "Well done."

Mac said, "Cam really did bring you in, didn't he?"

Will kept grinning, not sure about what had just happened but knowing he'd hit very close to the darkness that ran like a river through these wealthy, entitled men.

Richie held up his glass. "To Cam."

Chaz said, "Cam."

Mac raised his glass. "One of the great Masters."

"Before the fucker lost his nerve." Richie downed his drink.

Will joined in, silently searching his brain for a way to bring up the word *master* again. What did they mean about Cam losing his nerve? Did it have something to do with Merit Barrowe? Will couldn't see a way into the question. He had to take the win. They had all relaxed. The interrogation of John Trethewey was over. He wasn't sure what had caused the sudden show of trust, but he knew not to push it. Will picked up his knife and fork, trying to navigate cutting the steak with his injured hand.

Mac started eating, too. "You told us that your son's about to graduate Tech?"

"If he can get his head out of his ass." Will took a bite of steak and tried not to gag. There was a weird seasoning. The meat was filled with gristle. He'd had better food at the orphanage. "Eddie's doing something with polymers. Frankly, all I care about is what the headhunters are willing to pay."

"3M, right?" Richie had been paying attention yesterday morning, too. "That's not bad."

"Wants to travel the world." Will had listened to

Faith talk about the company enough to give a lecture. "They've got an HQ in Sydney. Not a bad idea to keep him at arm's length. Let him become his own man."

"Good money?" Chaz licked food off his fork, his tongue flickering out like a reptile.

"Good enough to get him to Sydney." Will had to force himself to swallow the meat. He went for the potato, thinking no one could fuck up a loaded baked potato. He was wrong. "His mother, too. I'll get at least a month of peace when she visits him."

"Got it all planned out," Mac said.

"Let's hope the shithead aces the interview."

Richie said, "What about—"

There was a sudden noise, like a dog whimpering. Will felt John Trethewey start to slip. The sound reminded him of the dogs this morning when he'd lost it over Eliza. He looked around the table, but no one had noticed the slip. No one was even paying attention to him. All three men were looking at each other like a group of teenage boys who'd just discovered porn existed.

The whimpering came again. It was from Mac's end of the table.

Richie said, "You want to show him?"

Chaz picked some meat out of his teeth. "You should show him."

Will said, "Show me what?"

Mac reached into his jacket pocket and found his iPhone. The whimpering continued until he opened the lock screen. He tapped through to something, then handed the phone to Richie.

Will kept his mouth closed as Richie scooted his chair closer. He showed Will the screen. There were four panels, each offering a view of the interior of a house. Will guessed the app was connected to a security system, but the cameras were in intimate spaces: a bedroom, a bathroom, a living room and a kitchen.

This had to be the McAllister house, the mansion with the gate and the full staff. The rooms were palatial, styled in a muted white like in an architectural magazine. The lens had a bubble effect, which meant that the cameras were concealed, which meant that Mac was straddling a fine line. It was illegal in Georgia to record anyone in a private area out of public view without consent.

Will thought about the GPS on Britt's car, the AirTag on her keys. She knew that Mac was tracking her. She would know about the cameras, too.

"Watch this." Richie tapped one of the bottom panels to zoom in on the kitchen. The sound was up as loud as it would go. Will could hear running water.

The camera was over the kitchen sink, pointed straight down at Britt McAllister.

Her face was expressionless, almost too flat. Will thought about all the Valium that Sara had seen on the bathroom floor of the courthouse. Britt was definitely on something. Her eyelids were heavy, her mouth slack, as she washed dishes by hand. She was wearing a slinky black slip like the bored housewife in an adult movie. Except she was coated in sweat. The satin material was stuck to her skin. Her hair was lank. She used a kitchen towel to wipe her face.

"Mac turned up the heat an hour ago." Chaz brushed away the food that dropped out of his mouth. He looked almost gleeful. "The alert comes on the phone when she's in view of the cameras."

Will asked, "She can't open a window?"

"Not without Mac hitting the panic button on the alarm." Richie was laughing. "He controls the lights, the window shades, the locks."

"What about the staff?"

Mac said, "They're in twice a week. Britt doesn't work. She's got plenty of time to take care of the house."

Will plastered a nasty grin on his face, a mirror image of the one on Mac's. Eliza had called it before.

He was like a pimp, and like every pimp on the planet, he wanted total control.

Chaz said, "Show him how to do the thing, Rich."

Richie looked to Mac for permission.

Mac gave a slight nod of his head.

"Here." Richie pointed at an icon of a musical note at the bottom of the screen. "Tap it."

Will looked at Mac again. His chin was slightly tilted up. His smug expression was the same one he'd showed when Will had bullied Richie, the same he'd showed when Will had jabbed Chaz about his weight. Whatever was going on with the gang, Mac was at the center of it. He got off on watching people suffer.

Mac said, "Go on. Hit the note at the bottom."

Will tapped the note.

The sudden, ear-shattering blast of music made him flinch. The real-time reaction inside the house was more pronounced. Britt jumped back from the sink. Her mouth gaped open as she screamed at the sudden screech of death metal. The sound fried out of the phone's small speaker as it reverberated through the kitchen. Britt's hands covered her ears. She continued to scream as she fell to the floor, crouching against the cabinets, mouth open in terror.

Will could feel Mac watching him, gauging his reaction. Will forced his mouth to contort into a smile, an approximation of Mac's smugness, his smarminess, his disgusting delight at the abuse of his wife.

On the screen, Britt's head was between her knees. Her shoulders were lurching up and down. She was trying not to hyperventilate.

Richie started to take the phone away. Will clamped his hand around the man's wrist. He tapped the music note, and the death metal stopped. He stared at the phone, making his eyes blur so that he couldn't see Britt's lingering terror. There was nothing to block out the sound. Britt was crying so hard that she was making a whooping sound as she tried to catch her breath.

Will licked his lips. He glanced up at Mac. Then he looked down at the phone again. "How long will she stay like that?"

"Not long," Mac said. "Ten, maybe fifteen minutes."

Ten, maybe fifteen minutes.

Will had been panicked like that before, but not since he was a boy. Ten minutes. Fifteen minutes. Even one minute felt like you were going to die. How many times had Mac done this to Britt? How many men had laughed at her suffering?

Britt had started gulping for air, trying to make herself calm. Will looked at the other icons at the bottom of the screen. A thermometer. A hasp lock. An automobile.

He asked, "You control the locks?"

"I control everything," Mac said. "Including her car."

"Fucker cut off her engine on 285. She was going eighty," Richie said. "She literally shit herself."

"She wouldn't get back into the car because of the smell." Chaz chuckled as he folded the skin of the baked potato and shoved it into his mouth. "Bitch went to the car dealership the next day and paid cash for a new one."

"Mac's cash," Richie said.

Will forced his grin to stay in place, asking Mac, "She can't figure out how to stop you from messing with her?"

"You know women." Mac said. "She doesn't have a mind for technology."

"She doesn't want him to stop," Richie said. "She likes it."

Will looked at Britt on the screen again. She was clinging to the counter, still trying to calm herself. If she liked it, she was doing a damn good job of hiding it.

"She'll get him back on the Amex," Chaz said. "What did that purse cost the last time, Mac? A hundred grand?"

"One-ten," Mac said.

"Worth it."

Will slid the phone back toward Richie, trying to pretend like he didn't want to turn over the table and beat the shit out of every single asshole in this room. "I feel your pain, man. The wife maxed out all of her cards after Texas."

"*Her* cards?" Richie asked.

Will laughed like a man who did not make half the salary of his soon-to-be-wife. "Good point."

"How'd you manage to keep her on side with your—" Richie waved his hand.

Will waited for him to finish the sentence.

Richie looked uncomfortable. "You said you experienced a MeToo issue."

Chaz asked, "What was that about?"

Will turned hostile again. "It was about my dick. You want to see it?"

"No, no, no." Chaz held up his hands. "Just making sure it was taken care of. You got the NDA, buttoned it all up?"

"Do I look like I'm in prison, you stupid mother-fucker?"

Richie laughed uncomfortably, but asked, "It was that bad?"

Will drank some tea, not answering.

Mac asked, "What about your wife?"

Will shrugged. "Spousal privilege. She couldn't testify."

"Texas is a community property state. She would've gotten half if she'd left."

"Not with the prenup," Will said. "That's one good thing Eliza taught me. Never let a bitch control your money."

"You'll inherit?" Mac asked. "Is that why you're back in town?"

"I fucking better." Will didn't know where the questioning was going, but he was close to pushing back. "Unless she wants to die in the shittiest nursing home I can find."

"I parked my mother-in-law in one of those places," Chaz said. "Reeked of urine. The one time I walked into the place, I actually gagged."

Mac smirked. "Some women deserve to stew in their own piss."

Another sudden burst of laughter shook the air.

Of all the things they had laughed at, this one did the most damage to Will. They were talking about Sara. His skin was suddenly hot. His muscles tensed. He felt a sharp pain as his hand reflexively curled into a fist. He couldn't beat these men to death—not without ruining his cover. But he could get them to keep talking, because every word out of their mouths could lead them toward a prison cell.

"Speaking of piss," Will said. "I would've paid to see the look on Linton's face when she heard about Tommy's settlement."

"Shit," Mac said. "I would've thrown in an extra mil to watch her get the news."

"Count me in," Chaz said. "Let's hope this is the end of it."

"It had fucking better be," Richie said. "Unless Saint Sara wants to find herself chained up in a toilet stall again."

There was another round of boisterous laughter. Again, Will forced himself to join them, but his hand had clenched so tight that he could feel blood seeping out between the sutures.

Chaz asked Will, "Why did you come back to Atlanta? Surely you had other options."

Will tasted blood in his mouth. He had bitten the inside of his cheek. "Eddie was already at Tech. The wife wanted to be close to him. I had to give her something."

"You should take her in hand," Mac advised. "You know she's not going to leave you. Why not have a little fun?"

Will made himself nod. "Maybe you can hook me up with your security company."

Mac raised an eyebrow. "I wouldn't risk that kind of exposure. It was a father–son project."

Will shouldn't have been surprised by the information. He had seen the autopsy report on Dani Cooper. Tommy was the proverbial apple who hadn't fallen far from the tree.

Will asked Chaz, "You got a kid?"

"Chuck, he's a little younger than Tommy, but they've always gotten along." Chaz asked Richie, "What about Megan, has she come round?"

"Only for my money," Richie said. "You have no idea how lucky you are to have sons. I'm all for women's rights, but they've taken it way too far."

"Tell me about it." Chaz kept looking at Will. "You said you can still hold a syringe. You're not doing surgery?"

Will drank some tea to wash the taste of blood out of his mouth. He made himself lock into John Trethewey again, launching into the prep that Sara had given him. "I was doing PRP, stem cells, some cortisone, tramadol. No insurance. Cash up front. Extra if I bring in the mobile anesthesiologist, which all of them want. It's a good business."

"We do a lot of that in metro Atlanta," Chaz said.

"Mostly through the private practices, but more hospitals are getting into it. Very lucrative, as you say."

Will held onto his glass. "You guys thinking of slumming it in ortho?"

"We're investors," Mac said. "We look for practices that need a quick turnaround, locate new income streams, monetize existing services with a concierge model."

"Concierge ortho?" This was the real reason they had invited John Trethewey to lunch. It was why they were asking such pointed questions. They wanted to make sure his MeToo case in Texas was a closed book because they saw the opportunity to make more money.

He said, "Not much of a profit in boots and splints."

"That's where the membership fee comes in," Richie said. "Chaz?"

Chaz took over, spouting off about high-net-worth clients, the never-ending supply of Baby Boomers searching for magical cures to make them feel younger. Will feigned interest, trying to ignore the pulse of blood rushing through his ears. He had worked undercover more times than he could count. He'd had the shit beaten out of him, a gun forced into his mouth, been given a strip search to check for wires and once almost had his hand chopped off, but he had never,

ever felt the desire to break cover the way he did now. If he thought he could get away with it, he would've shot every single one of these psychotic fuckers in the face.

Chaz said, "We realize it's a lot. Take your time."

Mac said, "But not too much time."

Richie added, "We know you'll need to think about it."

"What am I thinking about?" Will asked. "You're all wind-up and no pitch."

"The pitch," Mac said, "is we put you at one of these practices. You'd be our guy on the inside. Get to know the organization. Let us know where we need to cut the fat."

Will forced his hands to unclench. One of the sutures had ripped out. He'd dripped blood on the Italian jeans. "Like a spy?"

"Not *like* a spy, an *actual* spy," Richie said. "We're looking to maximize our returns. You go in, tell us where to trim, where to beef up. Don't think long-term, think immediate—what can we do right now to make this place look good on paper?"

"We don't care if it goes to shit after the sale," Chaz said. "Not our problem."

"What do I get?" Will asked. "You're asking me to do two jobs, basically."

"You'll be compensated," Mac said. "Say, two percent of the sale?"

Will laughed. "Two percent is a joke. And where do I go once you sell?"

"Go to the next one," Chaz said. "Get another two percent. You wouldn't be the first. We've found the model to be very successful for all parties."

Will shook his head. "Two percent is a non-starter. I need to see some hard numbers. And don't forget who my aunt is. Her lawyers will gut you if you cross me."

Mac looked impressed. "We're all here to make money. We take care of our people."

"I'm not your people," Will said. "I'd want meaningful participation. I think I've earned that. And not just because of Cam. Sixteen years ago, I was content to be on the outside looking in. Not anymore."

There was another prolonged silence. He had touched a nerve.

Mac said, "Come through the fire after your ordeal in Texas, have you?"

Will sat back in his chair. "I have. It made me stronger. Smarter."

"Is that so?"

"Were you able to find anything about me or my case online?" Will asked. "I'm a ghost because I know what I'm doing."

Chaz said, "He's not wrong about that. Our people couldn't find anything."

Will guessed that gave him the room to go harder. "I've been a good boy long enough. I deserve to have some fun."

Mac huffed a laugh. "That's quite an ask."

"I don't ask for things," Will said. "I take them."

Chaz and Richie were poised, practically on the edge of their seats.

Will kept his eyes on Mac, because Mac McAllister was the person in charge.

"This should be an ongoing conversation," Mac said. "Why don't you meet up with us at the Friday mixer? Bring Eddie. He can meet Tommy. Chaz is bringing Chuck."

Will asked Richie, "What's your girl's name? Maggie?"

"Megan will not be there." Richie had never spoken so clearly before now. He was a shit father, but he felt the need to protect his daughter. "She's not part of this."

"Quite right," Chaz said, as if this had been agreed to.

"So," Mac said. "We'll see you and Eddie at the Friday mixer?"

Will studied each of them: Mac with the imperious tilt to his chin, Richie with his rheumy, alcoholic eyes,

Chaz with his wet, reptilian mouth. They had opened up to Will, but not enough. He needed to show them that he could be trusted. He was still looking in on their darkness. If he was going to bring a case against them, he needed to see it from the inside.

"Sure," Will said.

Now all he needed was a son.

15

"My son." Faith grabbed Jeremy by the shoulders and turned him away from the kitchen crazy wall. "Hear me when I tell you that this is none of your business."

Jeremy tried to look anyway. "It was my business when you needed my help."

"No, it was not." Faith pulled a box of cookies out of the pantry to distract him. "I needed your help with the computer and the phone, and you did a bang-up job."

"I did a half-ass job." He opened the cookies. "I can crack those password-protected files if you give me more time."

"The only way you should be spending your time is thinking about what you're going to wear to the 3M dinner tomorrow night." She tried to fix his mop of hair. "Maybe I could give you a quick trim?"

He batted away her hands. "Mom."

"I'm just trying to help. These corporate guys have giant sticks up their asses. Your adorable tousled hair with a hoodie and jeans look isn't going to cut it."

"What do you know about corporate guys?"

"I've arrested enough of them." Faith patted his shoulder. "Come on, bub. I need the room so I can work. Get going."

Jeremy still wouldn't budge. "I've got half an hour before I'm supposed to meet up with Trevor and Phoenix. I thought I'd hang out on the couch."

Normally, hearing that her son actually wanted to stay under her roof would be a gift, but Faith was wary of him being so close to the kitchen. "Okay, but only until Will and Sara get here. I don't want you involved in this, all right?"

"Sure." Jeremy took the cookies with him as he loped out of the room.

Faith counted to twenty, then craned her head around the corner. He was on the couch in what she called The Position: spine curved into the couch, Beats headphones covering his ears, socked feet hooked on the edge of the coffee table, Xbox controller in his hands. Technically Faith's Beats headphones and Faith's Xbox controller, but that was the thing about being a mother—nothing was ever truly yours.

She turned back around to the kitchen. She sent a quick text to Aiden telling him that she would have to give him a rain check on tonight. Then she ignored the very real feeling of disappointment, because Faith was not the type of woman who ever cared about being the only person snoring in her bed.

She looked at the crazy wall, which remained without string, but only because Faith was going to let Will do the honors. They had two connections to make:

One: Dani Cooper was texted the words, "that's me." Those same words had been written on Leighann Park's left breast.

Two: Merit Barrowe, Dani Cooper and Leighann Park were all missing left shoes.

Faith had printed out photos of Merit's Air Jordan Flight 23 in white/black-zest, Dani's Stella McCartney black platform slide sandal, and Leighann's Marc Jacobs midnight blue velvet lace-up with a square heel.

The one thing Faith knew for sure was that these young women had more money for shoes at that age than Faith had had for food.

She forced herself to stop looking at the crazy-soon-to-be-string-wall. She mentally cataloged the work she'd done over the last two hours. The stacks of print-outs on the table were in good order: Rape Club chat room transcripts, Martin Barrowe's files that he'd stolen from Cam Carmichael, a copy of Leighann Park's witness statement, Dani Cooper's case file, text messages and autopsy report, a thumb drive that contained the audio recording Will had made of Leighann's interview, copies of the three photos from different angles that Faith had taken of the words that had been written on Leighann's breast.

Faith shuddered, burying the photos deeper into the stack in case Jeremy walked back in.

Cam's laptop was still on the counter. The password-protected files needed to be opened. Maybe the GBI's data processors could restore the corrupted video files from the chat website. Maybe they could find some hidden information on Merit Barrowe's ancient iPhone.

Maybe.

The most important item was Faith's running wish list of subpoenas: GoDaddy's records to find out who owned the Rape Club website, Grady's employment records from fifteen years ago, Morehouse's list of interns from the same time period, Eugene Edgerton's bank records, bank records from the medical examiner who had botched Merit's autopsy, phone numbers from Merit's iPhone.

Everything was ready to show to Amanda. All they

had to figure out now was how to present the case without her gutting them like a feral hog.

Faith checked on Jeremy again. He was still wearing her headphones as he played Grand Theft Auto. She knew for a fact that he kept the volume up loud enough to break his eardrums, but she wasn't going to risk her son hearing something that he should not. She turned the sound down low on her laptop as she sat at the table.

Her spiral notebook and pen were already out. She opened her email. She found the audio recording Will had made of his lunch with Mac, Richie, and Chaz at the country club. He'd prepped her for some of the worst parts, but Faith had a feeling that wasn't going to help make what she was about to hear any less difficult.

She pressed play.

There was the soft clang of silverware hitting plates, a low murmur of conversation. Then some muffled clicks as Will placed his phone on the table. His voice came out of her laptop speaker like a whisper—

I was in Texas. What a hellhole. One day you don't have power, the next day they're telling you to boil your water. The whole country's going to shit.

Faith cringed at his tone. Will was alarmingly good at sounding like a guy who belonged in a country club. She closed her eyes, trying to imagine the setting, but all she could conjure was the dinner scene in *Titanic* when Jack got to breathe the rarefied air of first class.

She shook her head to clear it, concentrating on the men's voices. They made more small talk; Will's injured hand, Chaz needing to lose some weight, the tits on the waitress. Faith's head went into her hands as she tried to pin down who was who. Richie Dougal, Chaz Penley, Mac McAllister. Their photos were on her kitchen cabinet, but none of them sounded how she had imagined. Richie's voice was kind of nasally. Chaz's was high-pitched. Mac's was soft, but clearly he was the kind of man who was used to other people hanging on his every word. He rarely spoke, but when he did, it was with surgical precision—

What happened to your hand? What happened in Texas? Cam brought you in? I didn't remember that detail.

Faith had quickly picked up on the fact that Mac liked it when Will pushed the other men around. If she had been advising one of her children about dealing with a bully, she'd tell them to turn the other cheek. With Will, she was glad to hear him punching back. He'd managed to bring up Cam early on, to act as if he was in on what had happened with the Merit Barrowe investigation. He even took credit for getting Cam out of Atlanta. And then he slipped in a line that Faith had fed him from the Rape Club chat transcripts. He was talking about his aunt. Or John Trethewey's aunt—

You ask me, somebody needs to gag her mouth shut with his cock.

The explosion of laughter made Faith's stomach sour. She looked at the men's photographs again as they continued to laugh. A hospitalist, a cardiothoracic surgeon, a nephrologist. They all looked so normal, like the sort of people you would trust.

She made herself look away.

The lunch recording played on. Faith could sense a change in tone. They were more comfortable with John Trethewey now. More openly showing who they were. The crass joke about gagging his aunt had bought Will entrée into the club. She listened to the men toast Cam Carmichael as if he was some kind of Viking heading to Valhalla.

Richie: To Cam.

Chaz: Cam.

Mac: One of the great Masters.

Richie: Before the fucker lost his nerve.

"Shit." Faith stopped the recording.

She searched the pages of Rape Club chat transcripts until she found what she was looking for. 007, 004, 003 and 002 were talking about a remark that Prudence Stanley had made at one of their many dinners.

007: She needs a stiff fuck to loosen her up. 002:
Are we seriously doing this again? 004: Not with
me. Tapping out. 007: Would love to smash her vag
to pieces. Part her like the Red Sea. 003: Blood is a
lubricant, Master.

Faith had seen too many vampire movies. She'd
blanked on the *Master* because of its proximity to
blood, not realizing that there might be something
more to the word. It was capitalized, which meant it
was being used as a title. To have it come up twice, to
have it used in reference to Cam, was a giant red flag.

She checked over her shoulder for Jeremy before
she pressed play again. Despite the earlier ease among
the four men, the conversation turned slightly tense.
Faith's anxiety cranked up as Will started answering
more questions, specifically about his wife and kid. She
didn't know which was more jarring, hearing Will talk
like an asshole or listening to him substitute Jeremy's
résumé for a phantom son named Eddie.

The sound of a dog whimpering made her stomach
tighten into a fist.

Will had warned her about Mac's electronic torture of Britt, but hearing it play out in real time was
horrifying. Faith had read about this form of domestic
abuse before. Living with an abuser was excruciating,

but Mac exploiting the tools to monitor and control Britt through the Internet of Things was next-level sadism. The death metal music had Nazi overtones. Faith pressed the volume as low as possible to dampen the sound of Britt's terrified screeching. Faith didn't want to imagine the woman curled up on the floor. She didn't want to think about Britt McAllister as a victim, particularly since she had a habit of victimizing other women.

Faith had broken out into a sweat by the time it was over. She remembered a detail from Dani Cooper's civil case: the server that recorded the McAllisters' security system had crapped out the night that Dani had died. There were no videos to show her arriving at the house or leaving in Tommy's Mercedes. Faith wondered if there were recordings from inside the house.

She made a note in her long list of things to follow up on if this not-a-case became a case. Then she tapped up the volume and listened as the conversation rocked on. The dollar amount these men threw around like Tic Tacs was staggering. Faith had always thought rich people didn't talk about money, but she guessed that was only around poor people. She was almost to the end of the recording when she heard a weird click in the sound. She turned up the volume a few more ticks, then skipped back ten seconds to listen again—

Chaz: I parked my mother-in-law in one of those places.

Will: I would've paid to see the look on Linton's face when she heard about Tommy's settlement.

Faith skipped back again. There was a definite click, a subtle change in the background noise, between Chaz and Will speaking. She felt her brow furrow. Why would he edit the recording? He had never done that before.

Sara.

Chaz must've said something about Sara that Will didn't want Faith to know.

She struggled against her natural nosiness. Aiden wasn't the only annoying beagle ready to bark his head off for a clue. Faith hated it when people tried to hide things. It was one of the characteristics that made her both a good cop and a busy-body mother. She had to make a choice now to let this go. If Will was hiding something private about Sara, then it had to be for a good reason. Besides, Faith had already betrayed Sara by going after Jack Allen Wright.

Still, the decision left a bad taste in her mouth.

Faith listened to the rest of the recording, but there was nothing more about Sara or Cam or anything outside of their purpose for inviting John Trethewey to lunch. She endured the hard sell asking him to be a spy in one of their practices. She was impressed by the cunning way Will managed to turn it all around. He was shockingly good at slipping into other skins. Faith had no idea how he did it. As masterful as she was at lying, she couldn't sustain it for longer than short bursts.

The recording stopped after they'd relayed details about where to meet for the Friday mixer. *Business casual. Drinks on us. Some of the hangers-on will be there. Davie, Mark, Jackson, Benjamin, Layla, Kevin, even crazy Blythe might show her face. Be sure to bring Eddie. We'd love for him to meet the boys.*

Faith looked at her notes.

Master.

She flipped back through the pages, searching for the profiles she'd generated for the anonymous chat members. 001: Royce? 002: Mac? 003: Richie? 004: Mason. 005: Chaz? 006: Cam. 007: Bing?

Faith tried to wrap her head around the question marks. She had been fairly certain of her guesses this morning, but listening to Will's recording had made her rethink the list. Now, Mac definitely struck her more as the 007 type. Then again, he didn't seem to want to get his hands dirty. He had pulled his own son into the stalking and harassment of Britt. The fact that Mac had called setting up the surveillance a father–son project was sickening.

Of all the things that bothered her, the dog whimper really stood out.

There was a part of Faith that wondered why Britt didn't leave, even though she knew it was never that simple. Domestic violence was one of the most complicated crimes—part assault, part coercive control, part brainwashing, part false imprisonment. Whether the victim was living in a mansion or a tract home, there were all different kinds of reasons for staying. Isolation, shame, embarrassment, denial, fear of losing their children, of becoming homeless, and the very real fear of violence because the most dangerous time for a victim was when they tried to leave their abuser. Telling somebody to walk out the door was easy when you'd never had a door slammed into your head so many times that you'd ended up with a skull fracture.

This was one of the many reasons why Faith would never, ever let a man control her money.

"Mom!" Jeremy called. "Will's here!"

Faith turned around as Will entered the kitchen. He was alone.

She asked, "Where's Sara?"

"Still in the air. She had to wait for Sloan's husband to come into the city." Will looked more wound up than usual. "Cam raped Sloan in medical school."

"Fuck," Faith whispered. She stood up to check on

Jeremy again. He was back in The Position, headphones on. She asked Will, "How? I mean, what happened?"

"Date rape. Cam tried to gaslight her, make out like it was a misunderstanding. Wrecked her life. Went on with his." Will sat down at the table, which was strange. He was usually a lurker and leaner. He only sat when Amanda was in the room. "Right before Cam shot himself, he mailed Sloan a box with a thumb drive, a letter, and Merit Barrowe's underwear from the night she died."

Faith sank down into her chair. "Fuck."

"The thumb drive and the letter are gone. Sloan tossed them." Will shrugged, but he knew how valuable the items would've been. "Sara has the underwear. The chain of custody is shit. They've been in a Ziploc bag in a filing cabinet in Sloan's basement for eight years."

Faith tried to wrap her brain around this sudden stream of information. "But if the underwear has DNA on it, we could match it to Merit and somebody in the Rape Club."

"The Rape Club."

Faith winced as he enunciated each word in the phrase. Hearing it said back to her sounded incredibly glib. She stood up, going to the wall to take down the header, thanking the sweet baby Jesus that Sara hadn't seen RAPE CLUB written in all caps. "We need to sequence any DNA on the underwear. Then we need to find a way to get DNA samples from everybody else. None of them are in our system. That's how they've gotten away with it for so many years."

"We can collect DNA tomorrow, during the mixer," Will said. "Bring in our own people to pose as waiters, take away their drinking glasses."

"That's going to cost a lot of money. Amanda won't be happy."

Will shrugged. None of this would make Amanda happy.

He said, "Sloan didn't know about the chat website. She hasn't been back to Atlanta in fifteen years. She cut off ties with Mason a few months after Sara was attacked."

"A few months?"

"Trauma hits everybody differently."

"Which brings us to Britt," Faith said. "I was just reminding myself that leaving an abusive situation is never easy."

"Fear of the unknown is a powerful motivator," Will said. "You get beaten down enough, you don't know how to live without somebody beating you down."

Faith knew he was speaking from experience. His ex-wife had been the kind of woman who'd been shit on so many times that she didn't know how to be with a good man.

"You didn't put up the string?" He was looking at the photos of the three different women's shoes on the table. "We've got two connections, the shoes and 'that's me.'"

"I thought you'd want to string it all together."

Will held up his injured hand to show he could not. "Did you pick up anything from the lunch recording?"

"Mac called Cam one of the best Masters."

"'Before the fucker lost his nerve,'" Will was quoting Richie. "What else?"

Faith thought about the section of the recording that Will had edited out, but said, "They sound like monsters. All of them."

"Because they are." He rested his injured hand on the only part of the table that wasn't covered in paperwork. Blood had seeped through the bandage. His fingers were swollen. Faith knew better than to offer Advil because Will's default response to pain was stoic acceptance.

He asked, "You've got this ready to present to Amanda?"

"Yeah." Faith felt queasy every time she thought about Amanda's reaction. "I've already scanned in everything. I'll upload it to the server if we're still alive after tomorrow morning."

"Let's go over it. Big picture. What do we have?"

"Merit Barrowe, Dani Cooper, Leighann Park." Faith crossed her arms as she leaned back in the chair. "APD won't touch Merit or Dani, but they're investigating Leighann's attack. They're not holding back. The press is all over it. The brass is watching. I talked to the sex crimes investigator. Guy by the name of Adam Humphrey. He's kind of a ferret-face, but he takes this shit seriously. He's not going to blow it like Donnelly. He's got a lot he wants to prove about the right way to do an assault investigation."

"Does Leighann trust him?"

"Adam's working on it, but he'll get her there. Height's not an issue, at least. He's shorter than me." Faith couldn't sit any longer. She gathered the shoe photos together and started taping them to the cabinets. "How's Sara?"

"Not great," Will said, but he didn't look so great himself. Faith had heard him talking about his aunt Eliza on the recording. She had no idea what kind of relationship they had, but the fact of her dying couldn't be an easy thing to deal with.

What Faith was going to say next would not make his life any easier.

She told him, "I was looking at all four cases, trying to find consistencies. Merit, Dani, Leighann, Sara."

Will started nodding. "Sara's case doesn't fit with the other three. The MO is different. The janitor was caught. He wasn't careful. He was acting on his own."

Faith spooled out three lengths of red yarn from her mother's skein. Obviously, she agreed with him, but she had to test the theory. "Britt said there was a connection."

"Edgerton is the connection."

Faith turned around. He sounded very sure of himself.

"Look at the timeline," he said, because Will always wanted to look at the timeline. "Go back fifteen years. Merit Barrowe is abducted, drugged and raped. She manages to get to Grady, but she dies. Some kind of overdose that triggers a seizure. Nobody but her family seems to care. Edgerton doesn't investigate. Cam is poking around, doing his side-investigation, but Edgerton knows how to back him off. The upshot is that it's all going to fade away."

Faith nodded for him to keep going.

"Two weeks later, Sara gets raped. There's a lot of attention around her case. It's not like Merit's. It's in the newspapers. There's a lot of noise. Grady's involved because Sara works there. Emory is involved because she matched from their program. APD brass is watching. There's no way to make Sara's case fade away."

Faith picked up on the narrative. "Edgerton went to Cam the day after Sara was raped. He bribed Cam into dropping his side-investigation."

"Okay, but take Eugene Edgerton completely out of it," Will said. "This is the scenario: You're the zone five detective on call. You get Merit's case. Then, two weeks later, you catch Sara's case. You're good police. You want to do your job. What do you do?"

"Work both cases," Faith said. "Two rapes within two weeks, both near and/or in Grady Hospital. One of them is a student. The other is a doctor. That's task-force-level shit. I've got patrol helping me with knock and talks. Other detectives getting CCTV, pulling previous cases, tracking down field cards. I'm interviewing Merit's girlfriend, her professors, the Morehouse intern. I'm looking for overlap with Sara—witnesses, bystanders, colleagues, locations, events, schedules. I'm trying to figure out if any names show up in both cases."

"Right," Will said. "Now pretend you're Eugene Edgerton and you've been paid to sweep Merit Barrowe's assault and death under the rug. Which you do. Then Sara gets raped."

"And I panic," Faith said. "All the attention around Sara is going to draw attention to Merit. I have to get Merit's case categorized as an overdose so she doesn't come up when they search for similar assaults in the area. I force Cam to change the death certificate. I make sure the medical examiner doesn't ask questions. I let the brass know that the two aren't related—Merit was an overdose; it's a tragedy, but she was a student, shit happens. Meanwhile, I work the hell out of Sara's case. I lock up the janitor within four hours. I feed the prosecutor all the pieces for an air-tight case. Wright goes to prison. Sara goes back home. I look like a fucking hero."

"So?" Will said.

Faith was quiet, working it out in her head. She still wasn't seeing it.

"The connection is that there's no connection," Will said. "Eugene Edgerton made sure of that. He kept Merit's case siloed. He lied about the circumstances surrounding her death so that a larger investigation didn't get triggered. He protected the man who raped Merit and caused her death."

"Fuck," Faith said, which was apparently her go-to response for the evening. "If Sara hadn't been raped, we wouldn't even know Merit Barrowe's name."

"If Britt McAllister had kept her mouth shut, we wouldn't know Merit's name, either. Whoever paid off Edgerton got their money's worth." Will's voice sounded rough. He looked at his watch. He was thinking about Sara. "For what it's worth, Sloan didn't think she was Cam's first victim. She seemed pretty sure that Cam had raped before."

"They generally do." Faith gave up on the red yarn. She sat back down at the table. "We're assuming that Merit was attacked by someone from the Rape Club, right?"

Will nodded. "The texts that Merit got fifteen years ago were similar to the ones Dani and Leighann were sent. We know Dani and Leighann are connected because of the 'that's me.'"

"Okay, so fifteen years ago, did Cam know that Merit was a victim of the Rape Club?" Faith rubbed her face with her hands. "Let's just call it the Club, all right?"

Will nodded again. "Sara thinks Cam knew that someone from the Club was responsible for what happened to Merit. Rape and assault aren't uncommon in the Grady ED. Merit wasn't the first victim that Cam treated, but she was the only one that he was really upset about. Something clicked for him. He saw what the Club was doing, what he was doing, was wrong."

Faith was hard-pressed to give the man any credit. "Cam had to know that pointing Edgerton toward the Club would lead to his own arrest. There's no way they'd all go down without dragging Cam with them."

"Drunks aren't known for their strategic planning," Will said. "And think about it. The guy was still in his twenties and he'd already bagged a DUI. He was a full-on alcoholic. He was tortured about something. He knew what he was doing was wrong. He was looking for absolution in a bottle. He saw Merit as his one chance at redemption and Edgerton wouldn't bite. I'm not one of those 'criminals want to get caught' guys, but Cam Carmichael wanted to get caught."

"Yeah, well, thoughts and prayers." Faith knew that Will's ex had also struggled with drug and alcohol addiction, but she still wasn't going to give Cam a pass. "He could've done us all a favor and put that gun to his head sooner."

"That's basically what Britt told Sara."

"Jesus." Faith blanched at the comparison. "Let's talk about what happened to Leighann Park."

Will waited.

"Somebody drew a circle on the back of her left knee," Faith said. "She's left-handed, but I tried to do it with my right hand on my right knee. God knows I'm not as flexible as a twenty-year-old, but my circle was for shit. And forget about coloring within the lines. Leighann told me it was in the exact center of the back of her knee and almost perfectly round. There's no way she did it to herself."

"Did the friend see it? Jake Calley?"

"Yes. He wanted to take a photo, but she wouldn't let him. She was understandably freaked out."

Will started rubbing his jaw. "Somebody drew the circle. Somebody knew that Leighann was looking for a book at the library. Somebody texted her. Somebody searched her apartment. Somebody knew there was a mirror in her drawer."

"'That's me,'" Faith quoted.

"What about Dani Cooper?"

Faith went down the list. "Somebody knew that she wanted to volunteer for a political campaign. Somebody knew she had a mole on her upper thigh. Somebody knew that she kept a pen and paper in her bedside drawer."

"What would you do if some stranger started texting you like that?"

"Reverse trace and—" Faith realized he meant if she was a normal person. "I don't know. It would definitely freak me out. There are personal, intimate details. Where are you going with this?"

"Would you engage with them, though? Because that's the thing. The women wrote back. They could've blocked him but they didn't. So, is it like spam, where the rapist is sending out a lot of texts hoping one person will bite? Or is it more targeted, as in the rapist does his due diligence? He spends time choosing the women he thinks will be most likely to respond to him."

Faith shook her head. "If the rapist knows the victims, then the victim knows the rapist. Leighann didn't recognize the guy at the club. As far as we know, Merit didn't name the man who abducted her. Dani didn't give Sara a name, either."

Will said, "You listened to the recording of Richie, Mac and Chaz. They sounded like a team, right? The way they each had a role, whether it was pitching me on their corporate spy crap or trying to figure out how much I knew about Cam. They volleyed back and forth."

Faith started nodding, because suddenly, thankfully, things were starting to make sense. "They're working as a team. One of them sends the texts. One of them searches the apartment. One of them listens in on conversations. One of them does surveillance."

"One of them rapes her."

Faith picked up the stack of transcripts from the chat group. "007 brags about all the women he's having sex with. The other guys egg him on. Maybe he wasn't describing conquests. Maybe he was describing rapes."

Will waited for her to continue.

Faith read, "007: Let me tell you boys, the lady from last night had a tight little snatch. Had to pry her open like a can of sardines. 003: Did you have to use your pocketknife? 002: Did she fall asleep?"

Will was silent as Faith searched for another entry.

"This is four months later," she told him. "007: Why do blondes make so much noise? 004: I love a good shout. 003: Maybe she was screaming because your cock is the size of a Pontiac. 002: Matchbox or Hot Wheels? 007: She definitely liked it high and hard. 004: Gents I feel like this isn't for me."

"Mason." Will's jaw was clenched. "They're putting time between the rapes. You said last night that there's usually a four-month gap between posts, right? So that's at least three women a year over sixteen years."

"Forty-eight victims. Jesus." Faith silently scanned more passages. Given their theory about how the Club worked, she was seeing everything in a completely different light.

She read, "007: Could not get away from that screaming bitch fast enough. 002: Are we seriously doing this again? 003: Love them big tittied gals. 007: They were saline. 003: Like squeezing a balloon or squeezing a bean bag? 007: Like squeezing a bike horn judging by the honks she made."

Will asked, "If 007 is the rapist, how would 003 know about the size of the woman's breasts?"

Faith looked at Cam's laptop. "The corrupted files on the site were videos."

"Video surveillance?"

"That would make sense if they're tag-teaming. It's also fucking clever, because if one guy gets caught, he's separated from the others. The charges would be nothing. With a good lawyer, you could get them dropped."

"They can afford good lawyers," Will said. "They're used to buying themselves out of trouble. Look at Tommy's trial. The Coopers settled because Mac's investigators dug up those old photos that Dani sent to her boyfriend. Knocking on doors like that costs money."

Faith rummaged around for the screenshots of the texts that were sent to Dani before she died.

Faith read, "'I know you love taking in the view of the park from your corner bedroom.'"

"He knows because he's been watching her," Will said. "What about Leighann?"

Faith found Leighann's witness statement. She read, "'In one of the texts the Creeper said that he saw me walking around my bedroom in a white T-shirt and pink underwear, and I was freaked out because that's what I was wearing the night before, and I was walking around my bedroom talking on the phone, so he must have seen me through the windows because I forgot to close the blinds.'"

Faith put down the statement. She looked at the piles of documents, her almost-full spiral notebook, the laptop, the phone, the mountains of data. "What's the one question that Amanda is going to ask that we're not going to know the answer to?"

"Where's the case?" Will asked. "APD is handling Leighann. No one has asked us to investigate anything. Where does the GBI come in?"

"She's going to have to shoehorn us into Leighann's case," Faith said. "Amanda's bound to have some favors she can call in. She's really good at making people do what she wants."

Will looked at his watch again. He was probably going to keep looking until Sara landed. He told Faith, "They're bringing their sons into the Club, right? Tommy and Chuck. And now I guess they want John Trethewey to audition Eddie."

Faith had thought the same thing. "Leighann said the guy who drugged her at the club was attractive. There's no way Chaz, Mac or Richie fits that description. They're all a bunch of tubby, gross, fifty-year-old pervs. And you think about what they're doing—surveilling, searching, eavesdropping. They would have to look the part to get that close to these young girls. An old dude would stick out."

"That's another good question. How are they choosing the victims?"

"I mean—" Faith shrugged. "These kids put every second of their lives online. Then there's dating apps, DMs, Snap. Subpoena, subpoena, subpoena."

Will silently studied the wall. "Mac seems to be the guy in charge, right?"

"Right."

"So, it would make sense that he's the one who chooses the victims."

"If Dani had any connection to Mac, it would've come out in Tommy's trial."

"She was friends with his son," Will said. "They wouldn't have looked any further than that."

Faith thought of something else. "The company they're running. CMM&A. The C probably stands for Chaz. The M is Mac. We're assuming mergers and acquisitions is the M and A, but what if M is Mason and the A is someone we don't know about?"

Will stared at her. She'd clearly faceplanted into his dyslexia, but he wasn't going to tell her that.

Faith rephrased, "These guys put their initials on everything—the chat website address, the business name. There's one initial that doesn't have a name to match up to it. The name would start with an A."

He asked, "Could it be a middle name?"

"Maybe?" Faith started to make a note on her list of things to officially follow up on. A family pet, a long-lost relative, a high school girlfriend. The GBI's data-processing team was incredibly good at finding weird bits of personal information. "We can ask Sara when she lands."

"Let's give her the night to sleep," Will said. "She wants to take the lead on talking to Amanda tomorrow morning. She's going to try to take the blame."

"Has she met Amanda?" Faith asked. "She's like a blame camel. She never runs out."

"You're the one she's going to punish. My time will come later. I have to go to the mixer. You're expendable."

Faith felt the return of her sour stomach. Amanda wasn't just Faith's boss. She was her mother's best friend. She was Jeremy and Emma's godmother. They called her Aunt Mandy the same way that Faith and her older brother always had, because she was part of their family.

None of which would prevent Amanda from sticking Faith on running background checks for lottery and liquor licenses for the remainder of her inauspicious law enforcement career.

Will said, "We're going to need heavy surveillance at the mixer. Waitstaff to collect DNA. Some of our people to fill out the background. Maybe that FBI guy I was loaned out to on the Mississippi militia thing can throw in. He owes us a favor."

Faith felt a sudden rush of heat. "Who's that?"

"Van," Will said. "You worked with him on that thing last year."

Aiden Van Zandt.

She asked, "The asshole with the glasses?"

He gave her a curious look.

"You know I don't trust men who wear glasses. Why can't they see?" Faith tapped her laptop to wake it up. She had to move him off of Aiden. "What's the name of the place you're supposed to meet?"

"Andalusia. It's a restaurant off Pharr Road. There's a bar on one side. Looks like an after-work kind of place."

She started to type in the search. Her fingers were sweaty. Will was still watching her closely.

He said, "Hipsters, bankers, lawyers. Buckhead types. We might need to tap APD to find a kid who can pretend to be my son."

Faith licked her lips. She was blinking too much.

Her skin felt itchy. She was a textbook case on deceptive tells. "Good luck finding a cop who doesn't look like a cop."

"I can do it."

Faith swiveled around. Jeremy was standing in the kitchen doorway. Her headphones were dangling around his neck because he'd been listening this entire time.

He said, "I can pretend to be Eddie."

Faith would lecture him about eavesdropping later. "You were supposed to meet up with your friends twenty minutes ago."

"I told them I couldn't make it." Jeremy placed the headphones on the counter. "I can do it. I can pretend to be Will's son."

Faith suppressed an eye roll. "Absolutely not."

"Mom, think about it. No cop is gonna be able to talk like a Tech student. Or look like one. Tommy and Chuck will spot them from a mile away."

Will stood up. "I should walk the dogs before Sara gets home."

Jeremy said, "Mom, I—"

Faith cut him off with a glare of silence. She waited until she heard Will close the front door behind him.

She told Jeremy, "Okay, first, don't say Tommy and Chuck like you're part of this, because you're not, and second, your skinny flat ass is going to be at the 3M dinner tomorrow night so case closed, Inspector Gadget."

Jeremy had a troubling look on his face. He wasn't laughing or teasing her back. He was being very serious. "I canceled on 3M."

Faith was almost too shocked to respond. "You what?"

"I canceled. I don't want to work at 3M."

She needed her own pause to catch her breath.

Faith had a horrific, multiple rape investigation on her hands and her son had decided that now was a good time to throw a grenade in the middle of his perfectly planned life. There was not enough air in the room to supply her lungs. She stood up from the table so she could look him in the eye.

She said, "Okay. You have other opportunities. Dupont is good. Or Dow."

"I know I have other opportunities."

"Good." She tried to keep the anxiety out of her voice. Faith had been terrified of unemployment from the second she had held him in her arms. "You're graduating from Georgia Tech in two months. You can write your own ticket."

"Yeah, writing tickets." Jeremy's face would not let go of that troubling look. "I was thinking maybe that's what I wanted to do. Be in the writing tickets business. Maybe join the APD like you and Grandma did."

Faith started laughing. And laughing. She laughed so hard that she had to bend over at the waist. The sound was like a seal barking. Then choking on an octopus. Then barking again. She wiped tears from her eyes as she stood back up. "Oh, bub, please do that to your grandmother when she gets home from Vegas. She will piss herself."

Jeremy was stone-faced. "I just told you I want to join the Atlanta Police Department. Why are you laughing?"

"Because it's a joke." Faith laughed again. He was taking it too far. "You've got a degree in chemical engineering from one of the most elite public institutions in the country. You're going to work in an office and wear a suit and tie."

"Uncle Will wears a three-piece suit to work."

"Because Uncle Will is a dork," Faith said. "Why are you using him as an example? Your real uncle might be an asshole, but at least he's a doctor."

"Who else am I gonna use?" Jeremy demanded. "Victor was the only dude I knew, but you had to go and have a baby with him."

"Whoa, that was not on purpose," Faith said. "And are you really telling me that your grandfather wasn't there for you every afternoon when you came home from school? He took you to science camp and band camp and—"

"Okay, Mom, I get it. Yes, Grandpa was there for me. I miss him every day. But you need to hear me." Jeremy looked her directly in the eye, which was the most terrifying part of this entire conversation. "I'm not saying this out of the blue, okay? I've given it a lot of thought."

Faith felt like she had taken a sledgehammer to the stomach. He was serious. He could not be fucking serious. "You are *not* going to be a cop."

"You're a cop. Grandma was a cop. Aunt Mandy's a cop." Jeremy was angrily jabbing his finger in her direction. "What are you really trying to say, Mom? Do you think I'm not tough enough? That I can't hack it?"

"I'm saying you're my child!" Faith yelled. Of course he couldn't hack it. He still had his baby fat. His cheeks were like a chipmunk's. "You can do anything with your life, Jeremy—anything. Your whole, beautiful life is laid out in front of you. You have opportunities I could only dream about."

"I'm supposed to give up my dreams so I can live out yours?"

"Dreams?" The word twisted through her brain. Faith needed another moment to catch her breath again. Her body had started to shake. She felt like she was going to have a heart attack. She had to work to keep her voice even.

"Listen to me." She grabbed his arms, longing to shake some sense into him. "You want to write tickets? This is what it's like: you roll up on somebody for speeding, and you don't know if they're gonna shoot you or stab you or—"

"I know what the job is."

"You don't, baby. It's—it's dangerous. It's too dangerous."

"You and Grandma always told me that it wasn't."

"We lied!" she yelled. "We both lie to you all the time!"

"That's great, Mom. Thanks a lot." He started to walk away, but turned back around. "I'm a grown man. I don't need my mother's permission."

"You are not a grown man!" Faith was incredulous. "Do you really wanna know what the job is like? Do you?"

"Do you think you can tell me the truth?"

"Hell yes I can. It fucking sucks," she told him. "It's hard, and you work all hours for shit pay and you see people on their worst possible days. They shoot each other over a pair of socks, or they beat their wives to death or they choke out their children, and you come home and all you can think about is that you'd better put your fucking gun in the safe because you don't want to be tempted to use it."

Jeremy looked stunned. She saw his throat work.

She had said too much. It was all too much.

His throat worked again. "Is that really how you feel?"

Faith could not let herself back down. "Sometimes."

He held her gaze for a few seconds before he had to look down at the floor.

She said, "Baby, I'm sorry, I—"

"You get to help people, too. I know you do. You've told me about them."

"You help maybe one person, but the rest of them fucking hate you." Faith had never spoken so honestly to him before. "I put up with so much shit just to do my job. Do you know how many assholes have grabbed my ass or tried to cop a feel or spit on me—actually spit in my face—or made lewd comments or threatened to rape me if I don't shut the fuck up? And some of that's from the guys in uniform, Jer. The brotherhood doesn't include sisters."

He shook his head, obstinate. "That's not the kind of officer I'm going to be."

She wanted to laugh in his face again. He was so

fucking naive. "No one ever thinks they'll be that kind of officer."

"Do you see the news, Mom? People hate cops for a reason."

"Have I seen the news? Of course I've seen the news. Every person I talk to has seen the news. Why do you think they hate me so much? Why do you think they don't trust me? Why do you think I have to beg them to see that I'm trying to help?"

"That's why I want to do the job." Jeremy had turned even more strident. "You can't change the system from the outside. I don't want to sit in a lab all day. I want to make a difference."

"That's what you want to do—make a difference?" She felt the tiniest hint of relief. "That's great, bub. Get a nice corporate job that pays a lot of money and donate all you can to whatever cause—"

"I'm not going to pay other people to do the work for me."

"Oh for fucksakes. Listen to me. You don't change the job. The job changes you."

"You don't know that."

"I'm living that!" Faith screamed. "Do you know why I have desk duty? It's not because Will was on assignment. It's because this man—this disgusting, sadistic man—mutilated women and raped and tortured them and I can't even close my eyes at night without seeing what he did to their bodies. His teeth marks were on their breasts. He skinned them. He left things inside of them. He didn't even have the decency to kill them. He left them alone to die. No one could save them. I couldn't save them!"

Faith's voice had boomed through the house. She was shaking so hard that she swayed as she stood in front of him.

Jeremy was looking down at the floor again. He was biting his lip to stop the tremble. He had tears in his eyes.

She had said too much again, but he had to know the truth. "I couldn't take it anymore. Amanda put me on desk duty because I was about to lose my shit, okay? Will keeps talking about how I have PTSD because I clearly have PTSD. I'm angry and volatile. I'm not sleeping. The only thing I want to do is work on this stupid case that's gonna end up getting me fired. That's what the job does to you. It takes everything. Everything but *you*, my baby. I won't allow it. I can't allow it. You will not do this."

Jeremy kept looking down at the floor.

Without Faith's shouting, the house felt deadly quiet. She heard the dryer running upstairs, the sound of the bathroom sink dripping because she put her life on the line every day to help people who hated her, but she still couldn't afford a damn plumber.

"Mom." Jeremy's voice was strained. "Why didn't you tell me?"

"Because it's my job to protect you." She put her hand to her heart to keep it from thumping out of her chest. "Please, baby. Please let me protect you."

He was silent for so long. Too long. He was deliberative, her son. Thoughtful, considerate, scientific. He weighed everything so methodically, from which shoes to buy to which movie to see to what he would order for dinner. Nothing with Jeremy was ever spontaneous. Not canceling the 3M dinner. Not telling her that he wanted to become a police officer. Not saying that it was his dream to be in uniform like his mom, his grandmother, his aunt.

And still, Faith had a moment of hope before he started to slowly shake his head.

He looked at her again. Right in the eye. "You can't tell me what to do with my life."

Tears streamed down her face. She was losing him. "I absolutely can. I gave birth to you."

"Once," he said. "Twenty-two years ago."

Faith wanted to laugh but she was too scared. "Jeremy, please."

His slouch disappeared. He had straightened his spine, steeling himself as he looked down at her. He was so tall. When had he gotten so tall?

He asked, "Why don't you quit?"

The question didn't have an answer.

"If you hate your job so much, why don't you quit?"

"Jeremy." Faith put her hands on his arms again. She felt desperate for a way out of this. She had never wanted her mother so much as she did right now. "This is a big decision. Let's talk this through with Grandma when she gets home."

"She won't be home until Sunday," he said. "Will needs someone to go undercover tomorrow night."

Faith dropped away her hands. He certainly had a cop's arrogance. "Do you know how long they train officers before they're allowed to go undercover? The psych evals, the field operations, the legal courses, the years and years of putting in the hard work?"

"I'm a Tech student, just like Eddie. I've known Will for five years. I'm the same age as Tommy and Chuck. I've been to Andalusia before. I know how to look like a student in a bar."

She could only shake her head. "You think it's that easy?"

"I heard the recording, Mom. Will doesn't get along with his son. I know how to sulk in a corner. According to you, that's one of my specialties." Jeremy crossed his arms. "Tell me I'm wrong."

"You're wrong because it's police work. Nothing goes the way you plan it. People are crazy. They are motivated by things you cannot comprehend."

"You always tell me that you learn how to do stuff by doing it."

"I was talking about your fucking laundry, not risking your life."

"Okay," he said. "What if I hate it?"

For once, Faith didn't have an immediate answer.

"I could go undercover and end up hating it and decide to reach out to 3M. Or Dupont. Or Dow. They'll return my calls. I've got a degree in chemical engineering from one of the most elite public institutions in the country."

He was too goddamn smart for his own good.

Thankfully, Faith was smarter. "It's not up to me, bub. It's up to Amanda. You wanna do this? You're gonna have to put on your big boy pants and ask Aunt Mandy for permission."

He grinned, because she had walked right into his trap. "Deal."

16

Will stood outside Amanda's closed office door watching Faith pace toward the end of the hallway. She turned on her heel and headed back his way. She was mumbling to herself. Her eyes were red and swollen. Her clothes were wrinkled. Even Will could tell that her hair was not the way it normally looked.

The thing with Jeremy was killing her. Faith didn't want her son to be a cop, but she didn't have the power to stop him. Either she could get behind Jeremy's decision or make him resent her for the rest of his life. Neither choice seemed like something she could live with. She'd told Will that last night she had spent three hours sobbing hysterically to her mother in Las Vegas, then finally cried herself to sleep on Jeremy's bunk bed.

Will's evening with Sara had been less dramatic, but still painful. As promised, Will had emailed her both the Leighann Park recording and the unedited audio file of his lunch conversation with Mac, Chaz, and Richie. Sara had listened to all of it on the plane, but she hadn't wanted to talk about it when she got home. She had barely made it to the shower. She had collapsed into bed. She'd been exhausted from the flights, wrecked by the conversation with Sloan, deeply upset about Leighann Park, and wildly hung over from her day-drinking. The last part was something Will was going to have to let go of. He'd played it cool, but it bothered him.

It really bothered him.

"Fuck," Faith mumbled, stopping in front of Will. "How long is this going to take?"

"Sara's telling her everything." Will looked at his watch. Sara had been in Amanda's office for almost half an hour. Her attention to detail had its drawbacks. "Do you want to wait in the breakroom?"

"No, I don't want to watch you inhale twelve Snickers bars while I drink chamomile tea that squirted out of a plastic bag." Faith ran her fingers through her messy hair. "He's downstairs, Will. He's waiting in the lobby. He wore a fucking suit."

She meant Jeremy. Will had seen him when he'd

walked into the building. The kid had combed his hair into a neat part. He looked like he was waiting in line for his school pictures.

Faith said, "He doesn't have it, right? He doesn't have what it takes."

Will shrugged, because you didn't know what you had until your ass was on the line. "They don't toss them into a cruiser. He'll go through training. He could wash out."

"My son will not wash out of the police academy," Faith said. "He has a college degree. He's Evelyn Mitchell's grandson. They'll drag him through by his collar if they have to."

Will couldn't argue against that. Faith might have Will's stink, but her mother was still considered APD royalty.

Faith said, "I can't do this. You're going to have to actually talk."

Will wasn't usually the talker. He mentally searched for a safe topic. "It was cold this morning. Betty was shivering when I took the dogs out. Sara's greyhounds have sweaters. Maybe I should . . ."

Faith was looking at him like he was crazy. "No, dummy. In there. With Amanda. You're going to have to actually talk. I can't do it."

Will smoothed down his vest. Faith was usually the one who got pepper-sprayed with Amanda's questions, but he said, "No problem."

The door opened. Sara looked surprised to find them waiting like bad kids outside the principal's office. She said, "I caught her up to speed. I have no idea how it went. She didn't have a lot to say."

"Fuck," Faith whispered. "My son's trying to get himself killed. My daughter will be home in two days. My house is a mess. My life is falling apart. I look like I've been hit in the face with a shovel. I'm about to lose my job."

Sara told her, "I'll come by tomorrow to help you take down the crazy wall."

"Thanks. We'll see if I'm still alive after this." Faith grabbed her briefcase off the floor. She shot Will a desperate look before she walked into Amanda's office.

Will stayed back, asking Sara, "How's your headache?"

Sara didn't answer. She gently held his injured hand. She hadn't stitched it back up because of the timing. "Did you take your antibiotic?"

He nodded.

"I've got to catch up on work. It's going to be a late night." She cupped her hand to his face. "I promised

Faith I would review the chat transcripts to see if I can match names to the numbers. Other than Mason's."

Will felt his teeth grinding. He hated the sound of Mason's name in her mouth. "There's gonna be audio from the bar tonight. Listening to it could help refresh your memory."

"No," she said. "I really don't want to hear Jeremy calling you dad."

Sara touched her hand to his cheek before walking away. She left a sense of sadness in her wake. Will knew better than to go after her. Not everything could be fixed.

"Wilbur," Amanda bellowed. "This doesn't start without you."

He waited until Sara had disappeared around the corner, then braced himself for the hell that he was walking into.

Amanda was perched like a hyena behind her desk. Her claws rested on the leather blotter. Her spine was straight. She tracked Will across the room with something like bloodlust in her eyes.

Faith was slouched across from her like a teenager, briefcase spilling onto the floor.

Will took the other seat. He did not slouch.

Amanda asked, "Why do I feel like the only human in a Muppet movie?"

Will always got a little unsettled when she made pop culture references. "Ma'am, I—"

"Why is Dr. Linton, who is not an investigator, relaying to me the investigative steps that she has taken over the last few days in an attempt to solve three unsolved crimes, none of which fall under the purview of this office?"

Will opened his mouth, but Amanda held up a finger.

"I've got my medical examiner flying off to New York, one of my agents hanging out at a country club, another agent shirking her duties, and now I'm expected to coordinate a sting operation on a moment's notice that will require me to bring in APD, not to mention blow what's left of my budget on a case that isn't even officially a GBI investigation?"

Will said, "It's my fault."

Amanda arched an eyebrow at him.

Will said, "Sara brought this to me, but I made the decision to pursue it. I roped in Faith. I got her to cover for me when I should've been working with the fraud team. This is all on me."

Amanda hadn't blinked since he'd walked in. "Dr. Linton left me with the impression that she was solely to blame."

"Dr. Linton was wrong."

"Is that so?" Amanda asked. "Did you pull strings with Dekalb County to get Jack Allen Wright caught with a copy of *Busty Babes* under his mattress?"

Will felt his mouth go dry. Sara didn't know about Wright, which meant that Amanda had found out on her own. Which meant that, as usual, she was already two steps ahead of them.

She wasn't finished. "Did you tap your contacts at APD so that you could speak on the record with a twenty-year-old woman who was abducted and raped for thirty-six hours?"

Will said, "I spoke to Donnelly about the possibility that there were ongoing cases he might want to investigate. This started with the Dani Cooper trial. There were similarities between—"

Faith groaned. "For fucksakes, Amanda. You know we're both up to our necks in this. What do you want us to say?"

Amanda homed in on her like a laser beam. "You're on very thin ice."

"Break it," Faith said. "Drop me in the freezing water. I don't care. Just do it fast."

Amanda looked prepared to take her up on the request. Will opened his mouth to intercede, but Amanda did something that he very rarely saw her do.

She retreated.

"All right." She sat back in her chair. "What do we think? What do we know? What can we prove?"

Will rubbed his jaw. He looked at Faith. She was equally perplexed. Amanda was asking them to run down the case. Will wasn't going to give her time to reconsider. He started talking.

"What we think: Mac McAllister, Chaz Penley, Richie Dougal, and maybe two or three others have spent the last sixteen years targeting women to rape. They split up the work so that no single person connects to a particular victim. One guy stalks her. One guy sends threatening text messages. Maybe a different guy drugs her. A different guy transports her. A different guy—we think they call him the Master—rapes her. They rotate the tasks so no one person is more exposed than the others. It's like a splinter cell. That's how they've gotten away with it for so long. You have to put them all together in order to trace the crime."

Faith jumped in, "What we know: Merit Barrowe, Dani Cooper and Leighann Park were all victims who fit the MO of the group. The similarities between their cases are too close to be coincidental, even though they're fifteen years apart. They all got threatening texts. They were all drugged, abducted, and raped. They were all missing a left shoe after the attack happened. Air Jordan. Stella McCartney. Marc Jacobs.

Dani was sent a text with the words 'that's me.' When Leighann woke up after the assault, she had the words 'that's me' written on her left breast in black permanent marker."

Will finished. "What we can prove: the left shoes are being taken as trophies. That's the only thing that links all three women together. We haven't found anything else."

Amanda steepled together her fingers as she thought it through. "Dr. Linton's assault is connected how?"

"It's not," Will said. "Britt McAllister's desperate. She wants Sara to stop Mac and the gang. She knows what's happening. She thinks she can protect her son from it."

"A bit late for that," Amanda said. "I told Dr. Linton to leave Merit Barrowe's underwear with forensics. Georgia's statute of limitations on rape is fifteen years, but that resets when there's DNA to test. Not that the DNA will be anything other than fact-finding. With no witnesses, the argument could easily be made that the sex was consensual. Which brings us to Merit's death. Even with the toxicology report, there's no way to prove that she didn't overdose on her own. Ipso facto, no case."

"The Leighann Park investigation isn't a slam dunk, either," Faith said. "She has no memory of what happened. We might get DNA off her dress or her shoe, but even then, it's a rape charge, not murder. She's not a great witness. Which isn't her fault. But jurors can be judgmental assholes. If she's too pretty, that means she led him on. If she's not pretty enough, then she's lying about it for attention. If the rapist is good-looking, then no way he would have to force women for sex. All this points to the guy walking. Best case, he pleads down, maybe registers as a sex offender, then goes on with his life."

Will picked up from there. "We've got even less with Dani Cooper. And we're pretty sure there are other victims, but we don't know who they are."

Amanda asked, "How many victims? How many years?"

Faith provided, "At least three a year going back sixteen years."

"So," Amanda said. "We're not dealing with individual crimes. This is a conspiracy case."

"RICO?" Will hated to admit that this was why they had needed Amanda all along.

She was referring to Georgia's Racketeer Influenced and Corrupt Organizations law. RICO at the federal level had originally been designed to take down the mob. Georgia had expanded the definitions and, most importantly, didn't require the existence of an enterprise to constitute racketeering. You just had to prove a pattern of unlawful conduct. The state had used it to go after anybody from accountant firms to rap artists with varying levels of success.

Amanda told them, "Run it down for me."

Will said, "With RICO, the five-year statute of limitations can extend back to the date of discovery or the last act. The minimum sentence is five years. The max is twenty."

Faith continued, "The predicate crimes include any act or threat involving murder, kidnapping, false imprisonment, assault and battery, bribery, obstruction of justice, dealing in dangerous drugs."

"That brings in Merit Barrowe, Dani Cooper and Leighann Park," Amanda said. "Keep going."

"In 2019, the state added pimping and pandering by compulsion," Faith said. "The chat transcripts could support the argument. Plus, if we can break into those corrupted videos on the website, that's distributing obscene materials through digital means."

"I need to get legal on this, but I like what I'm hearing," Amanda made a note on her blotter. "Do either of you have a theory on how the victims are being selected?"

The same question had come up last night. Will answered, "We think Mac McAllister chooses them, but that's a gut feeling. We don't know that for a fact. We don't have any proof."

Faith said, "And we don't know how he selects them."

Amanda suggested, "Social media? Through his son? What's his name?"

"Tommy," Will supplied. "Tommy grew up with Dani Cooper, so that's how she was chosen. Chaz Penley has a son named Chuck who's around Tommy's age. Maybe one of them spotted Leighann at a bar or a cross-campus thing."

"And Merit Barrowe?"

"No idea," Faith said. "The case wasn't investigated because the detective, Eugene Edgerton—"

"Was a dirty cop," Amanda finished. "Did you ask your mother about him last night?"

Faith's expression turned surly. "How do you know I talked to my mother last night?"

Amanda was done retreating. "Evelyn has been my best friend for forty years. Who do you think she called after speaking with you? You're lucky she didn't send me to your house with a tranquilizer gun."

Faith's nostrils flared, but she didn't say anything.

"Evelyn knew Eugene back in the day," Amanda said. "He took early retirement. Bought a house on Lake Lanier."

"On the lake?" Will knew the area. Current real estate prices on the lake were north of two million. "So he really was dirty."

"He was indeed."

"Before." Faith was talking to Amanda. "Why were you asking about how the victims were selected?"

"That's the weak point in the chain. If we figure out how the girls are being selected, that will lead us back to the man in charge. Once we get the man in charge, he'll turn on the others." Amanda held out her arms in an open shrug. "Trust me. I've dealt with powerful men my entire life. They never throw themselves on their own swords. They try to cut down everyone else around them. What else?"

Faith said, "I've got Cam Carmichael's laptop and Merit Barrowe's phone. We need digital services to break seven password-protected files. There's also some corrupted videos that are on the website. I'm not sure whether they can be repaired, but I'm not a computer specialist."

Amanda rolled her hand for Faith to keep going.

Faith opened her spiral notebook on the desk. "I made a list of subpoenas we need to file."

Amanda traced her finger down the page. "Go-Daddy will take at least two weeks to turn over any website ownership information. Grady will take seven days, tops. The banking information on Edgerton will be a month or longer. Same with the medical examiner. The files are so old they might not even have them any-more. Why isn't Cam Carmichael on here? We need to see his bank statements, too. Making a DUI disappear is nothing. New York is an expensive city. He moved up there at the last minute. Deposits, utilities, moving services across state lines, breaking his lease in At-lanta. I doubt a rapist alcoholic was good at saving for a rainy day."

Faith started writing a new entry on the list.

Amanda asked, "What's this about security camera recordings?"

"From inside the house," Faith said. "Mac wired some of the interior rooms for audio and video. He's electronically abusing his wife."

Will provided, "A bedroom, a bathroom, a living room and the kitchen."

"Keep that on the list, but we'll need more than we have right now if we're going to raid the house. APD isn't the only organization in this state that doesn't want to come up against the wall of McAllister money." Amanda pushed the notebook back toward Faith. "Where are the victims being held?"

Will looked at Faith.

Faith looked at Will.

Another reason to bring in Amanda. They had totally blanked on the question, but the women had been abducted. That meant they'd been held somewhere. Leighann couldn't account for thirty-six hours. Merit Barrowe had at least a two-hour gap in her timeline. No one knew how Dani Cooper had ended up at Grady. The GPS in Tommy's Mercedes wasn't online. The CCTV cameras the city had on almost every corner were either pointed in the wrong direction or broken.

Faith said, "There's something that came up when— when I was looking into the company that Richie Dougal works for. CMM&A."

Amanda asked, "You were looking into it?"

"Yep, all me," Faith said. "The company has a storefront in a building called the Triple Nickel off Buford Highway. I had it checked out. There's a desk with a phone, some chairs, and a door to the back. The nail salon next door says they've never seen anybody use it, but Leighann was drugged. It's not like she'd be screaming. There's an entrance at the back. Somebody could easily sneak in and out without being seen."

"You had it checked out?" Amanda let the question hang for a few seconds before continuing. "Put it on your list, but we can't surveille it. There's no money, no manpower and currently, no legal justification."

Faith was nodding as she added to the list.

"Let's go back to the threatening texts," Amanda said. "How did he get their phone numbers?"

Will looked at Faith again. She was already looking at him. Another thing they hadn't considered. The man who sent the creepy texts would need a way to get the women's phone numbers.

Amanda said, "Go back to Merit Barrowe. Fifteen years ago, most cell phone plans still charged by the minute. iPhones were a very expensive novelty. We were still on BlackBerrys. If you gave out your number, you provided your landline."

Faith asked, "Were people still writing checks? If you were at a store, you had to give your phone number if you paid by check. If someone was behind you, they could hear it."

"Something to consider," Amanda said. "Dr. Linton told me Leighann Park remembered a sheepskin rug."

Will told her, "It didn't come up with Dani or Merit, but one of them died before she could say anything and the other one was never investigated."

"What about the noise Leighann heard? The mechanical sound?"

Faith supplied, "You can listen for yourself. I've got all of the audio files on a thumb drive—Leighann's interview, Will's lunch at the country club. I also scanned in the autopsies, witness statements, investigation notes.

Everything's ready to go. All I need is a case number and I can upload it to the server."

"Let's hope I can give you one," Amanda said. "I'm going to have to call in a very big favor with APD to make tonight happen. Leighann Park's case is high profile. The media is all over it. We'll have to step very carefully."

Will had seen Faith's hand clench. She didn't care about the politics. She was thinking about her son.

Amanda had seen it too. "What do you want me to do about Jeremy?"

Faith put down her pen. She slouched back in her chair. Tears welled in her eyes.

Will figured now was a good time to leave.

Amanda stopped him. "Sit."

Will sat back down. Faith sniffed, wiping her nose with the back of her hand. The room suddenly felt very small.

"Evelyn and I used to take you on stakeouts," Amanda told Faith. "Two women in a station wagon with a baby in the backseat. No one even looked at us. We were invisible."

Will heard Faith sniff again. He longed to be invisible.

"One time we were set up outside a pawnshop," Amanda said. "Perp was paying cash under the table for stolen Rolexes. We go in, catch the bad guy. We're dragging him out in cuffs when we see somebody's in the back part of Ev's station wagon. One of the corner girls needed to get off her feet, took a john into Evelyn's ride. The whole car was shaking. You slept through the entire thing."

"The entire thing?" Faith said. "You let him finish?"

"It didn't take long," Amanda said. "Faith, you were born into this life. Do you remember how Ev and I used to pin up photos and clues on your bedroom wall?"

Faith gave Will a look of warning, as if he would bring up the crazy wall in her kitchen.

"Evelyn was always trying to protect you, but you were such a nosy child. I remember one time she found you on the kitchen floor in the middle of the night reading her case files and looking at autopsy photos." Amanda paused. "Does that remind you of Jeremy?"

"I never looked at the photos."

"Only because you're squeamish," Amanda said. "But you read the reports. You wanted to be involved. And when you told Evelyn you were joining APD, it broke her heart."

"She was proud of me."

"She was terrified," Amanda said. "We went through nearly half a case of tequila that weekend."

Faith used her fist to wipe away tears. Will thought of the handkerchief in his back pocket. There were tissues on Amanda's desk. He could move the box closer to Faith. He could offer her a handkerchief. He could sit in silence and try to blend into the fake leather upholstery.

Amanda said, "Your father offered you five thousand dollars to finish college instead of joining the APD. Do you remember that?"

Faith threw her hand in Will's direction. "Does he really need to be here for this?"

Will did not. He started to leave again, but Amanda pointed for him to sit back down.

She asked him, "Wilbur, have you ever told Faith how you ended up at the GBI?"

Will rubbed his jaw. Now he saw why she was making him stay.

"Will tried the Army. He tried McDonald's. He tried shoplifting. He tried the Atlanta jail."

Will could feel Faith staring at him because he had never told her any of this because it was none of her business.

Amanda said, "I pulled every string I could to make sure he ended up at the GBI. Cops, judges, parole officers—anybody I could squeeze, I squeezed hard. I was not going to let him take the wrong path. And

I sure as hell wasn't going to let him work in a place where I couldn't look out for him."

Will looked down at his injured hand. His fingers were throbbing. He wondered how long he was going to have to take the antibiotics.

"Let me ask you this," Amanda said. "Who do you trust to have Jeremy's back? Leo Donnelly? Or the man sitting next to you?"

Will could see Faith wanting to argue, but Amanda was right. Faith couldn't make Jeremy's choices for him, but she could steer him in a better direction.

"Tonight at the bar," Faith said. "How would it work?"

"We'll treat Jeremy as an informant, that way we're covered for liability."

"Great."

"It's paperwork, Faith. He's old enough to sign on the dotted line."

"He won't hate it." Faith wiped her eyes again. "Jeremy said he might hate it, but he won't. It's exciting. It's dangerous. He's twenty-two years old. He's not thinking about what it's going to be like in ten years."

"He's waiting downstairs." Amanda glanced at her cell phone before turning it over on her desk. She asked Faith, "Tell me what you're feeling. Bring him into the fold or push him out?"

"My feeling is that I have so many feelings that I'm drowning in them." She threw up her hands. "He's legally an adult. I can't lock him in his room. And I'm a shitty judge of whether or not this is a bad idea because he's my baby and I'm terrified of losing him."

"Squirrels lose seventy-five percent of the nuts they bury. That's how we get trees."

"Does now seem like an appropriate time for a nut metaphor?"

Amanda sighed. "Take the laptop and phone down to digital services. Tell Liz to get started immediately. I'll call her with a case number later. Tell Caroline to send up Jeremy."

Faith shoved everything back into her briefcase. She took the box of Kleenex off Amanda's desk and tucked it under her arm before walking out.

Will started to follow her, but he caught a look from Amanda and sat back down. He guessed he was going to end up being a life lesson for Jeremy, too. He gripped the arms of the chair. A sharp pain zig-zagged through his hand.

Amanda said, "Sara told me how you hurt your finger."

Will laughed. Sara hadn't told her anything.

Amanda's sigh conceded the loss. "How is Eliza?"

"Dying."

"It's about time," Amanda said. "How do you see tonight playing out? Mac, Chaz and Richie will be there. Who else?"

"Mason James." Will hated Mason's name being in his mouth almost as much as he hated it in Sara's. "Royce Ellison and Bing Forster. Blythe Creedy might come. There's also a group they call the hangers-on, so a total of ten, maybe fifteen. Richie only gave me first names when he invited me. I figure they'll pretend they know me because Mac's accepted me into the group."

"How many bodies do we need on our side?"

"I found the building layout online. They rent the place for parties," Will said. "The bar area is big, maybe thirty-by-sixty with around twenty high-top tables and eight booths along the wall that separates it from the dining area. I'm thinking we'll need at least three waitstaff to collect the DNA. I'd like two people by the front door, two by the back, one outside the entrance. We need someone in the dining room in case they spill over from the bar. There's a covered smoking area behind the building. Ideally, we'd have someone there, too."

"Ten people," Amanda said. "I can set up inside the restaurant. I'm at that age where I'm invisible again. The detective working Leighann Park's case, Adam Humphrey. We'll need him on side. Faith can't be in the building. She's too close. I'll put her in the mobile command center with Charlie Reed on the monitors. He'll keep her calm. I can pull some women from the fraud team. Who else?"

"Aiden Van Zandt owes us a favor. He's a solid guy. It'd be good to have him there." Will said this last part for Faith's benefit. Sara had seen the FBI agent leaving her house a few nights ago. "We don't have enough time to wire the place. Are we talking body cameras, earbuds, mics?"

"All of the above." Amanda had started making a list. "Considering you're the lead on this, I'm hesitant to rely on APD for our manpower. If you need help, they won't come running. I'm going to have to pull some of my old gals out of retirement. That okay with you?"

Will nodded. He knew that Amanda's gals were hardcore. "What about Jeremy?"

"We need a warm body for John Trethewey to introduce as his son," she said. "If he's nervous or volatile or sullen or does something stupid, you can roll with it. This isn't a guns and knives operation. No one is going to bat an eye at a twenty-two-year-old boy having a hissy fit around his father. Or sitting like a lump on a log. All we need is for him to say his name is Eddie."

Will wasn't so sure about that. "On a professional level, it's a bad idea. He's Faith's kid. My focus will be pulled toward protecting him instead of getting information. He doesn't know what he's doing. Worse, he sees this as a game."

"I'll disabuse him of that notion," Amanda said. "You should know this isn't a lark for Jeremy. He's not trying to dodge his responsibilities or rebelling against his mother. He told Evelyn last year that he wanted to join APD."

Will gathered this wasn't information that Evelyn had shared with Faith. "And?"

"Ev made him promise to wait until he graduated. She thought he'd lose interest."

"Faith didn't lose interest."

"Faith was a nineteen-year-old single mother with a boy to provide for and a burning desire to move out from under her parents' roof. Her priorities were different."

"What are Jeremy's priorities?" Will asked.

"The same as yours were. He wants to do the right thing. He wants to help people. He wants to prove himself as a man."

Will rubbed his jaw. He had only ever been able to read two expressions on Amanda's face: condescension and irritation. He didn't know what she was thinking now. "Do you really believe you can push Jeremy into the GBI?"

"I pushed you, didn't I?" Amanda clearly did not expect a response. "I forgot to show Sara the pearls. Her neck is on the long side. She'll need something to break the line of the princess scoop. But as I said, no pressure. Her mother might have something she likes more."

Will felt caught in a time warp. She was speaking in a made-up language again.

"I suppose with your extracurricular activities, you haven't had time to look into dance lessons."

Will had looked up wedding dances on YouTube. Father/daughter, mother/son, groom/sister, bride/brother, flash mob, striptease. Everybody had a thing. "Sara nixed the father-daughter dance. Slow dancing is just swaying, so I think I'm good."

"Ah." Amanda picked an imaginary speck of dirt off her desk.

Will stared at the top of her salt-and-pepper swirl of hair. His body was telling him that he was missing something. His collar felt tight. He had started to sweat.

"Hey Aunt Mandy." Jeremy walked into the office with a big, goofy grin on his face that Amanda managed to wipe away with a sharp look. "I mean Chief—Deputy Chief—uh—Ms. Wagner."

Amanda let him fester in the silence.

Jeremy looked to Will for help, but Will wasn't here to help. He figured the least he could do for Faith was try to scare the shit out of her son.

"Ma'am," Jeremy told Amanda. "Thank you for your time. I wanted to request—to formally request—that you allow me to work on the sting operation tonight at Andalusia."

Amanda drew out the silence for a beat longer. "Explain your reasoning."

Jeremy started to sit down, then thought better of it. "I fit the profile of Will's son. I'm the right age. I've sort of got his coloring. I'm a Tech student. I've grown up watching my mom and my grandma. I know that police work is hard. I know that there's no such thing as a typical operation. Stuff can go wrong. You have to be ready for that. I'm ready for that."

Amanda asked, "Are you ready to speak with Tommy McAllister and Chuck Penley?"

Jeremy's confidence weakened, but he put on a good front.

"They'll want to talk to you," Amanda said. "That would be the sole reason for your being there. It's a father–son get-together. The sons cannot sit like lumps on a log."

Jeremy nodded so hard that his hair fell into his eyes.

"We're going to role-play this," Amanda said. "Will is Tommy McAllister. Jeremy, you pretend to be Eddie Trethewey."

Will took his time standing up. He was half a foot taller than Jeremy and had an extra forty pounds of muscle. Will had worked undercover in prisons. When you were on the inside, you learned the art of violence. If you were really good at it, you didn't have to use your fists. You looked at a guy a certain way. You cowed him into submission because your posture, your obvious strength, your callous disregard for life, conveyed to them the fact that you would take a knife to the eye before you let them win.

Jeremy's Adam's apple bobbed like a fishing line as he looked up at Will.

Will asked, "Ready?"

Jeremy nodded.

"Hey, man." Will punched him lightly on the shoulder. He borrowed one of Chaz's lines. "Nice tits on that waitress."

Jeremy failed to keep the smirk off his face.

Will had to remind himself that this was Faith's kid,

otherwise he would've given his shoulder a significantly harder punch. "Is this situation funny?"

Jeremy glanced at Amanda.

"Don't look at her. Look at me." Will loomed over Jeremy. "Tommy McAllister raped a woman. She died. Is that funny? Are you going to laugh at him?"

"I wasn't—"

"You read the files on your mom's table. You read the descriptions of what happened to those girls. You heard some of the recordings. This isn't a game. There are three women who were abducted and raped. Two of them died. Is that funny?"

Jeremy's face had gone whiter than white. "No, sir."

"I know what you're thinking," Will told him. "You're saying to yourself, 'I'll be good when it's the real thing. This is just practice.' But that's not how it works. You do the practice so you don't have to think about it in the field."

Jeremy nodded again.

"Tommy McAllister and Chuck Penley are not gonna try to buddy up to Eddie Trethewey because they're lonely. They're trying to see whether or not you've got it in you to rape a woman."

"Okay. Yeah." Jeremy took a quick breath. "What're they gonna say?"

"They're going to test you, push you, try to find your limits. Tits won't be the worst of it."

Jeremy didn't smirk this time.

"They'll start out small. They'll harass the waitress. If you're good with that, they'll pick out a woman at the bar. They'll talk shit about her—nasty shit. Fucking, sucking, cucking. They're going to be listening to how you respond. How you look at them. You're not going to be able to project confidence. You need to work on your anger."

"Anger at them?"

"At me," Will said. "Your dad is an asshole. He doesn't respect you. He thinks you're a fuck-up. You hate him for it, but you want to prove him wrong, too."

"You did something bad in Texas," Jeremy said. "You were accused of sexual assault. All my friends back home found out. Everybody knows you're guilty. My girlfriend's parents made us break up. You moved to Atlanta without talking to me first. Mom cries all the time. I know she won't leave you because of the money, and I hate her for that, but I don't want to be poor, either. I'll lose my car, my allowance. I'll probably have to drop out. My life will be over. All because you couldn't keep your dick in your pants."

Will looked down. Jeremy had jabbed his finger into Will's chest. The kid had the sense to stop.

Will asked, "Did you google 'how to write an origin story' last night?"

Jeremy blanched the same way Faith did when she was caught out. Still, he asked, "Does it matter? I don't even have to talk to them. I'll make it clear I'm not into it."

Amanda asked, "Meaning?"

"When they try to feel me out, I can tell them to shut up." Jeremy shrugged. The gesture was all Faith. So was the logic. "I'm not gonna be there so I can turn myself into Tommy and Chaz's best friend. I'm not a cop or an investigator. I'm not going to find the clue that'll break open this case and put everybody behind bars. That's Will's job. All you need me to do is show up. Right, Dad?"

The last question had been directed at Will. It was unsettling to hear. He could understand now why the thought of it had bothered Sara.

Amanda said, "Jeremy, step outside and close the door."

Will sat back down in the chair as the door closed. He wasn't going to tell Amanda that the kid had just played them because it was obvious the kid had just played them. "Do you want me to tell Faith he's doing it?"

"Evelyn will." Amanda turned her phone back over

and started typing. "She took the red eye last night from Vegas to LA, then turned around and flew to Atlanta. She drove here straight from the airport. She's already in the building."

"That's a hell of a long night."

Amanda looked up from her phone. "That's what mothers do."

17

Will stood outside the mobile command center as he waited for Sara to call him back. Richie Dougal had told him that the mixer started at seven. Will planned on showing up with Jeremy twenty minutes late. Amanda had been slowly feeding in her people over the last hour. Some of the old gals she'd pulled out of retirement. Some of the agents from Bernice's fraud squad. Adam Humphrey, the APD detective who was working Leighann Park's case. They had all studied the layout of the building, marked up all the entrances and exits, noted the chokepoints, gone over best escape routes, and still, Will could not shake the feeling that something bad was going to happen.

This was why Jeremy was a distraction. Will needed to focus on the job. All he could think about right now was that he had to make sure Faith's kid was safe.

He leaned back against the bus. The soft purr of the MCC's generator was muffled by the noise coming from an active loading dock. They had parked behind a big box store two streets away from Andalusia. The spot was secluded but not quiet. Tractor trailers were offloading their goods. Some of the warehouse workers were openly staring at Will. He couldn't blame them. To the outside world, he probably looked like a pimp waiting to hustle some of his girls to a party.

The MCC had once served that purpose. It was a converted party bus that the GBI had confiscated from a drug dealer and retrofitted with monitors and computers so they could spy on bad guys in relative comfort. Will was back in his douche-wear, the tight jeans with a blood stain from his injured hand, the Diesel boots and a tight-fitting, button-up shirt that had a weird paisley pattern.

This last item was not another purchase from the mall but courtesy of the GBI's special investigations division. The paisley design hid the fiber optic cables that powered the microphone inside the collar as well as the pin camera built into the button at the center of his chest. The wire snaked down Will's leg to a transmitter strapped to the side of his ankle. Will's jeans bunched up around the slim black box, which was fine, but he would've rather had his ankle holster with the

Sig Sauer Nitron compact that Sara had given him for his birthday.

His phone vibrated with a call. Will checked the light on the ankle receiver to make sure the transmitter was off before he answered. He did not want every word out of his mouth being heard inside the bus.

He asked Sara, "Everything okay?"

"It is now," she said. "Isabelle dropped one of Tessa's earrings down the garbage disposal. I had to find the Allen wrench to move the impeller plate."

Will figured this was one of the biggest pluses to living with a plumber's daughter. He listened to Sara moving around the kitchen. The dogs' collars were jingling because it was their dinner time. Sara clicked her tongue twice. The greyhounds simmered down. Only Betty's collar was still jingling because Will was a pushover and Sara wasn't going to interfere.

She asked, "How's Faith doing?"

"Not great." Will glanced back at the bus. The windows were blacked out, but he assumed Faith was still standing rigid in the corner as she watched Charlie Reed wire up her son. Fortunately, Jeremy was able to wear glasses so there was no need to put a camera in his shirt. The black plastic frames fit with his student vibe. The high-def lens in the bridge was completely obscured. Still, the way he kept nervously touching the frames was a problem. Will's only hope was that it came across as a tic rather than a dead giveaway.

He asked Sara, "How's your headache?"

"Finally gone. Remind me to take it slow the next time."

Will hoped there wasn't a next time.

She easily read into his silence. "Do you have something to say to me?"

Will watched a skid loader move a pallet of boxes. He'd done warehouse work to help pay his way through college. It was a back-breaking job, but eventually, Will had managed to buy a motorcycle, put a roof over his head, and occasionally splurge on a meal that wasn't from his microwave. Then the woman who'd ended up being his first wife had blown into town and stolen everything he owned so that she could feed her addiction.

He said, "I'm worried about Jeremy. I don't like going in with an unknown."

"You've got plenty of people keeping an eye on him."

"Yeah." Even Will could feel the awkward strain in the conversation. He figured that he should man up about it. "I'm not crazy that you got drunk in the middle of the day."

"Really?" Sara laughed. "I'm surprised you could walk last night with that giant stick up your ass."

Will felt himself smiling. "I'm sorry. I know it's my shit to deal with."

"We both have shit to deal with."

Will could hear the edge of sadness in her voice. He knew that she was thinking about what she had lost fifteen years ago. He also knew there was nothing he could say to make it better.

She told him, "I'd better start reading these chat transcripts. Call me when you're on the way home."

"Hey," he said. "I keep forgetting to say, but I really love you."

"What a crazy coincidence. I really love you, too."

Will waited for her to hang up. He kept his phone in his hand as he opened the door to the MCC. He blinked at the sudden burst of bright light. Charlie Reed was seated at the console checking the feed from Jeremy's glasses. As predicted, Faith stood rigid in the corner, clocking his every move. Jeremy wasn't the only reason she was freaked out. Aiden Van Zandt was adjusting the camera inside his cowboy hat. Amanda and Evelyn were talking to Kate Murphy, who'd come up with them at APD. Murphy was currently serving as executive assistant director of intelligence for the FBI. She also happened to be Aiden's mother.

Faith shot Will a look of unbridled panic as he walked up the stairs.

"Jeremy." Will waited for the kid's attention. "Stop touching your glasses. You're giving yourself away."

"Sorry." Jeremy couldn't help himself. He touched the glasses again. "Sorry."

Will stood in front of him. "Are you nervous?"

Jeremy nodded, but asked, "Is that a trick question? Like, if I say no, you'll tell me I should be, but if I say yes, then you'll tell me that I can't do this?"

Will gripped Jeremy's shoulder to steady him. "Stop overthinking. Fall back into your cover. Angry son of an asshole. Not interested in talking shit with the other assholes. Right?"

Jeremy's head started to nod. "Right."

Will picked up an iPhone Charlie had laid on the console. There was no lock on the screen. The GBI's data services division had mocked up a digital profile for Eddie Trethewey.

Will handed the phone to Jeremy. "This is exactly like your iPhone. Contacts are bogus, but every call you dial will go to this console. Either Charlie or your mom will answer, depending on which contact you choose. Emails, texts, they're all bogus, too, but if anybody reads them, they'll make sense. The photos show a bunch of women. Pick out one who's your girlfriend in case it comes up."

Jeremy's finger left a sweat mark as he swiped the screen.

Will told him, "If you need help, rapid-click the side button five times."

"That's how my phone works," Jeremy said. "I mean, all iPhones. You click five times and it asks you if you wanna call the police."

"This doesn't ask. It makes the call, and *the police* is gonna be your mom running across the parking lot with a shotgun. Understood?"

"Yes, sir."

"Will?" Charlie was holding a micro earbud between a pair of tweezers. The device was small enough to fit inside the ear canal without being seen, but not so small that it would slip down onto the eardrum. "Ready?"

Will tried not to shudder when Charlie inserted the device. The plastic buds tended to run hot, but the sound quality was good. He would be able to listen in on any conversation Jeremy was having. Currently, all Will could hear was heavy breathing. Will glanced at Faith. She needed to get the kid under control.

"Bub," she said. "Let's get some air."

"Team one just took position." Charlie rolled his chair over to the bank of monitors. "We should send in

team two within the next ten minutes. The bar's starting to get busy."

Will looked over Charlie's shoulder. Twelve screens
showed twelve different points of view. Half of the surveillance team was already in place.

The three GBI agents posing as waitstaff were in
charge of collecting drinking glasses or discarded nap-
kins or whatever else they could use to run DNA profiles on the Club.

Adam Humphrey was sitting on a bench outside
the front door. The post had a hint of busy work, but
the detective seemed happy to be included.

Team one was at a high-top table at the front of
the bar. Dona Ross and Vickye Porter were two of
Amanda's old gals. Dona had placed her purse on the
table so that the hidden camera captured the long,
wooden bar.

Evelyn and Amanda were team two. Both had
hidden cameras inside their purses. They would take
up positions at the back of the bar, angled so that they
could record both entrances to the bathrooms as well as
the exit door that led to the smoking area behind the
building.

Outside, Aiden would be stationed on one of the two
picnic tables. The camera concealed in his cowboy hat
would point whichever way he turned his head.

Kate Murphy would be seated in a booth inside the restaurant. The camera inside the brooch on her blazer would catch anyone leaving the bar.

They would all be using their phones to record audio, but only Jeremy and Will were wired with microphones and cameras because only Jeremy and Will would be talking to the suspects: Mac and Tommy McAllister, Richie Dougal, Chaz and Chuck Penley, Royce Ellison, and Mason James.

"Baby."

Faith was outside with Jeremy, but her voice was a whisper inside Will's ear. He searched the control panel for a way to turn off the feed. Three of the volume knobs had three different labels, but Charlie's handwriting was beyond Will's abilities.

Faith said, "Take a deep breath."

Will listened to Jeremy huff like a racehorse.

Faith asked, "Would it make you more comfortable if I stay in my car instead of the bus?"

"It's your job to be in the bus," Jeremy said. "Besides, you'll lie and listen anyway."

"Will isn't here to babysit you. Do you understand that?"

"Yes."

Faith sniffed, which meant that she was crying again.

Will stared desperately at the labels. He asked Charlie, "Did a chicken write these?"

"Sorry." Charlie laughed, pointing. "That's you. The one on the left is Jeremy. The one on the right is Amanda."

Will turned down the middle knob. Faith's crying faded away.

"Will?" Charlie had slipped on his earphones. "Is your transmitter on?"

Will leaned down and flipped the switch on the slim box. "Test? Test?"

Charlie adjusted some of the dials. "We're good to go."

Amanda clapped her hands for attention. "Listen up, gang. We need to be very careful tonight."

Evelyn mocked standing to attention. Kate Murphy had a bemused expression on her face. She probably hadn't been on the receiving end of orders in over a few decades.

Amanda said, "Will, your job is to further ingratiate yourself with the group. We're not going to break this open tonight, but you can make incremental progress. If you can get information out of them, all the better, but our focus is collecting DNA samples. The primary target is Mac McAllister, followed by Richie Dougal, then Chaz Penley. Fall-backs are Tommy McAllister and Chuck Penley, through whom we can match familial DNA. Once we get their profiles, we can make a comparison to the DNA on Merit Barrowe's underwear. If we can get a match, then we've got a starting point. Understood?"

Will nodded. "Understood."

"Aiden," Amanda said. "I want you on comms. Charlie, hook him up so he can listen. If anything happens to Jeremy, I want you in that bar with speed. That's your job tonight: cover Jeremy. Is that clear?"

"Yes, ma'am." Aiden offered his ear to Charlie. Will could tell by the wince on the man's face that he'd worn one of the tiny earbuds before. Charlie dropped in the bud, then made a new label for the board. They started testing the volume levels.

Amanda turned to Kate. "You're packing?"

Will felt his jaw clench. So much for this not being a knives and guns situation.

Kate patted her purse. "Locked and loaded."

Evelyn volunteered, "I've got my revolver."

Kate asked, "Do you still keep it in a Crown Royal bag?"

They all laughed at what was clearly an inside joke.

Amanda was the first to stop. She looked at her

watch. "Kate, take your position in the restaurant. Aiden, you, too. Will, Evelyn, stay. Charlie, we need the bus."

"Ladies," Aiden tipped his cowboy hat on his way toward the door.

Charlie offered his hand to Kate as a sort of escort. She practically glided down the stairs. Will wasn't blind to the fact that there was a certain elegance to the woman. She was Amanda's age, but she looked like she was from a different era.

"Faith?" Amanda snapped her fingers, urging her to come back inside. "Huddle up. Let's go."

Faith wearily climbed the stairs. The look she gave her mother was filled with naked longing that Evelyn would somehow make all of this go away.

Will studied the live feeds on the bank of monitors. The entrance from the outside. From the inside. Three different views from three different agents running around with drinks and bar snacks as they pretended to be waitstaff. The room was only half-full. Men and women in business attire stood around drinking and shoveling peanuts into their mouths. Will searched their faces. No sign of the Club, but Will had to think some of the hangers-on had already populated the bar. They would show up at seven, right on time. The popular kids always strolled in late.

Faith told Amanda, "Jeremy needs a minute."

Will turned the volume knob back up so he could listen in. All he heard was Jeremy's heavy breathing. Whatever Faith had told the kid, it hadn't been a pep talk. Jeremy took a big gulp of air, then puked it out. The splatters echoed inside Will's brain. He adjusted the volume down. Amanda stepped in and adjusted her earbud, too.

Evelyn didn't have to hear Jeremy to know what was going on. She told Faith, "You're making him nervous."

Faith wiped her nose. "Did you put me with Leo Donnelly?"

"What's that?"

"When I made homicide, I got assigned to the laziest detective on the force."

Evelyn winked at Amanda, but she told Faith, "That was bad luck."

"Was it?" Faith asked. "Or did you make sure I got stuck with a partner who was never going to be the first team through the door?"

Evelyn feigned confusion. "Why would I do that?"

"Why did I end up at the GBI when you left the force?"

Amanda chimed in, "That was good luck."

"Was it?" Faith repeated. "Or have you two been micromanaging my career all along?"

"Have we?" Evelyn asked, but no one bothered to answer. "Mandy, I'll be in the car when you're ready."

Faith bit her lip like she needed to keep herself from exploding. Will assumed she wasn't thinking about the open tab on her laptop that connected to the GPS tracker she'd planted on her son's car.

"Faith," Amanda said. "You can pull the plug on this. Will can make excuses."

"It's too late." She started shaking her head. "Jeremy will end up at APD. I won't be able to protect him. Mom's juice is going to run out eventually. All of her guys are retiring. The new guys hate me because of Will."

"Have you thought about the FBI?" Amanda asked. "Aiden could look out for him. He's clearly eager to make you happy."

Faith's mouth opened. Then closed. Then opened again. "Is no part of my life beyond your fucking prying?"

"Not really."

Will adjusted the volume on Jeremy's mic again. Thankfully, the kid had stopped puking. He was getting an earful from his grandmother.

"—and that's not counting my silence over the last year."

"Yes, ma'am," Jeremy said.

"All right, that's the end of the lecture. This is your one chance, my boy. Either nut up or shut up."

"Yes, ma'am."

Will heard Jeremy give a sniff that turned into a snort, which was generally what happened after you vomited, which Will could still recall from the first time he'd gone undercover. He had only been a little older than Jeremy. Amanda hadn't told him to nut up, but she'd had no qualms about ordering Will to stop whining and do his damn job.

He caught movement on the monitor. Dona had moved her purse to capture Richie Dougal walking into the bar. Richie had a frown on his face as he glanced around, then headed straight for a drink.

Amanda had seen it, too. "Will, you go first. Ev and I will stand down for five minutes so you and Jeremy have time to settle."

Will traded out his phone for the one Charlie handed him. He told Faith, "Jeremy's got this, all right? Everything's going to work exactly how we planned. I won't let anything bad happen to your son."

Faith looked desperate to believe him, but for once, she could not speak.

Will left her with Amanda. Charlie passed him on the way down the stairs. He gave Will a firm nod to let him know he'd take care of Faith. The operation was about to go live. Will found Jeremy behind the bus. The kid looked like someone had yanked a string out of the top of his head and tightened every joint in his body. Will took out his handkerchief and offered it to Jeremy. The time for scaring him was over. Now he needed Jeremy to do his damn job.

Will asked, "Are you good?"

"Yeah, no problem. I'm good."

Jeremy's voice echoed in Will's ear. Thankfully, Charlie turned down the volume on the earbud.

Will asked, "Can you drive a stick?"

Jeremy nodded.

Will tossed him the keys to his Porsche. They hit Jeremy square in the chest. Then they started to fall. Jeremy barely managed to catch the keys before they hit the ground. He looked mortified, which was not what Will had been going for. All he could do was walk toward his car. He waited for Jeremy to get in. Then he waited for him to figure out how to unlock the door.

They both had a moment with the seats. Jeremy had to pull his forward. Will had to rake his back because the last person who'd been in the passenger's side was Faith, whose legs were the approximate length of a standard poodle's.

Jeremy held up the key like he couldn't figure out where to put it.

Will said, "The ignition's over—"

"On the left." Jeremy slid in the key. "I've got it."

Will listened to the engine roar to life. The seat was vibrating as the exhaust barked. He told Jeremy, "I put in a mini high torque starter last summer. I was getting hot-starts but didn't want to do the remote-mounted solenoid relay."

Jeremy gave him a look identical to the one Faith had given when he'd told her about the new part. "Dude, you lost me."

"Let's go."

Jeremy carefully rolled the car forward. He hadn't lied about knowing how to drive a stick, but the six-cylinder had 180 horses under the bonnet, and none of them liked to go slow. The car jerked as he took the corner around the building. Jeremy tapped the brake, then the gas, which made them both do a tandem dab.

Will said, "Your aunt Amanda taught me how to drive."

Jeremy looked over at him, and Will imagined that Faith was sitting beside Charlie in the bus with the same surprised expression on her face.

Will said, "She had the Audi A8 Quattro with the long wheelbase. Thing was like a tank."

Jeremy stopped at a red light. "I remember that car. It was dark green."

"Tan leather," Will said. "She kept the seat pulled so far forward that the steering wheel practically touched her chest."

Jeremy laughed. "She still does that."

"I ran up on a curb my first time out. Pinched the back tire." Will felt himself sweating at the memory. "Almost had a heart attack. I knew she was gonna kill me."

"Did she?"

"Nah. She made me change the tire. Then she put me on the hook for a new one. Took an entire year for me to pay her back."

Jeremy turned onto the main road when the light changed. "I know the GBI doesn't pay much, but even my mom can afford a new tire."

"I was still in college," Will said. "Amanda was trying to recruit me. All I'd ever been on was a motorcycle. She told me I'd have to pass the driving test before they'd let me into the academy."

Jeremy was paying close attention now. Faith probably was, too. "Amanda doesn't recruit agents. That's never been her job."

Will didn't have a response because he was right.

Jeremy turned into the parking lot. Neon bar signs flashed in the windows. Colorful blue, turquoise and green feathers fanned out around the door. Peacock statues stuck out from the monkey grass lining the sidewalks. They'd reached the Andalusia Bar and Grill, which, according to its website, was named after Flannery O'Connor's farm, not the autonomous community in Peninsular Spain.

Jeremy said, "APD pays more than the GBI."

"If you're in it for the money, I'd stick with 3M."

Jeremy chewed at the inside of his cheek as he coasted through the lot in search of an empty space. "Did Mom put you up to this?"

Will pointed to a vacant spot. "Over there."

Jeremy parked the car. He looked at Will. "I'm cool, okay? You don't have to babysit me."

He was Faith's son. Will had to babysit him. Still, he didn't have to humiliate him. He gave Jeremy a nod. "Good."

Will got out of the car. He scanned the parking lot. He could've been at the country club. All the cars were luxury brands, mostly SUVs. The tags were Fulton and Gwinnett County. He didn't see a Maserati MC20 coupe in Rosso Vincente, but Mason James was probably tired at the end of the day. Getting in and out of the low-slung sportscar would be hard on his back and knees.

The GBI phone came out of Will's back pocket. The bogus data had been tailored to John Trethewey, but the button on the side didn't call for help. Will clicked it three times, and the view from Jeremy's glasses came on screen. He saw the kid looking down as he slid the key into the door to lock the Porsche. Then Will saw himself looking down at his phone as Jeremy walked toward him across the open parking lot.

Will clicked the button once to get rid of the live feed. He slipped the phone back into his pocket as Jeremy joined him. They both walked toward the entrance.

Adam Humphrey had draped his arm over the back of the bench. His eyes skipped over Will as he stared out at the street. Will knew that the camera in his glasses was feeding the images back to the bus. When Adam looked his way again, Will gave a slight nod of his head, hoping Faith would take it as a reassurance.

He let Jeremy open the door. He figured that was the kind of power play John Trethewey would pull. Right now, Will needed to forget about everything else that was going on in his head—worrying about Faith, her son, Amanda, Sara, even Aiden Van Zandt, because he was a nice guy and Faith's dating history pointed to a bad split—and focus his attention on being an asshole orthopedist who'd slinked away from Texas under the cloud of a rape charge.

"Richie!" he boomed his voice across the room.

Richie did a double take, a big smile of recognition showing off his incredibly white veneers. "Christ, we're the only ones here. Not even the hangers-on bothered to show."

"Fuck 'em," Will said. "This is my boy, Eddie."

"Eddie." Richie gave Jeremy the once-over. "Nice to meet you."

"Sure." Jeremy's phone came out. He showed Richie the top of his head. He started to send a text.

Will shook his head at Richie. Richie shook his head back.

"All right, kiddo." Will clamped his hands on Jeremy's shoulders. "Scram. The adults need to talk."

Jeremy loped off toward the third table from the back door, exactly the table he was supposed to go to. Two of Bernice's fraud agents had been taking up the space. They moved away so he could have the spot.

Will slid onto a bar stool beside Richie. He could see Jeremy reflected in the mirror behind the liquor bottles. Another of Bernice's agents was serving as waitstaff. She walked behind him with a loaded tray.

He told Richie, "Sorry about my kid. Gets it from his mother."

"Don't apologize," Richie said. "At least he showed up. My daughter thinks I'm a fascist, sexist pig. She never returns my calls unless she wants something."

Will heard the earbud crackle in his ear. Charlie had turned the sound back up on Jeremy's mic. Will did a quick scan of the room. Ten agents were going to cover this place for one sad alcoholic at the bar. "Where's the rest of the gang, man? Am I too late or too early?"

"You're fine. They're fucking assholes." Richie threw back his drink and signaled for another. "It's harder and harder to get them to turn out. Nobody respects tradition anymore."

"Surely they respect a few?" Will asked.

Richie shook his head, but Will couldn't tell if he meant not now or not ever.

"Sir?"

Will recognized Louisa Jennings from Bernice's squad. The woman carefully took away Richie's glass and replaced it with a fresh one. At least they would get one DNA sample out of this colossal waste of time and resources.

Will ordered, "Old Pappy, neat."

Louisa set a glass on the counter. The Old Pappy under the bar had been replaced with Snapple iced tea instead of bourbon. She poured him a healthy serving.

He told Richie, "I thought Blythe was going to make an appearance."

"You know what a prick-tease she is. Says she's

going to come, then she doesn't. It's no wonder Bryce is so goddamn neurotic."

"Can't help with Mason sniffing around."

"That." Richie waved his hand, dismissing the affair. "Mason's fucked all the wives. Except for Britt. Only Mac can crack that ice."

Will grabbed his glass of tea off the bar and knocked it back. "Who picked out this place anyway? It's full of bankers and ugly old bitches."

"Mac likes it. Close to home." Richie waved his fingers in the air for his third drink at the bar, though it was clearly not his third of the night. "What did you think about our presentation yesterday?"

Will shrugged. "It was interesting."

"But?"

"Not sure I want to be a spy. Or under Mac's thumb."

"My friend, you are not unwise to feel that way." Richie watched as his glass was filled with a triple of Scotch. Will got some more Snapple. "Don't get me wrong, I'm grateful to have a job, but Mac's not easy to work with. And Britt—well, you know how cunty she can be."

"What about Chaz?"

"As long as the checks come in, he's fine." Richie

slowed down this time, taking a sip instead of a gulp. "I'll tell you what, though—and maybe you can relate to this—it's a fucking lonely life after what we've been through. You're lucky you've still got your family."

Will raised an eyebrow.

"The MeToo bullshit." Richie's voice was a hoarse whisper. "I never thought I'd miss my wife, my daughter. I worked my ass off for nearly twenty years to give them a comfortable life, and the second things get dicey, they both abandon me. No birthday parties. No Thanksgiving. Hell, I'm going to end up eating Christmas dinner out of a box. Megan won't even let me attend her graduation. She says it would be too embarrassing."

"It's not that much easier for me," Will said. "The wife is still breaking my balls. I keep saying, 'You made your choice to stay, so either put a fucking smile on your face or find somebody else who can pay for your life.'"

"How'd that go down?"

"Brother," Will said. "Ain't nothin' goin' down in my house."

Richie guffawed. "Christ, there's nothing better than the feel of a warm, wet mouth."

Will raised his glass in the air. He checked on Jeremy again. The kid was still looking at his phone.

Will didn't know if he was trying to be in character or trying to keep his head down, but either way, he was glad that Jeremy was stuck in the corner.

"What say, gents?"

Will could've guessed that Mason James would sound like a guy from a 1930s gangster movie. He slowly turned on the bar stool. Mason was dressed in jeans and a tight button-down shirt, the same as Will. Yet he somehow managed to look like he'd spent thousands of dollars more on the outfit. Even his boots looked sharper.

"Trethewey," Mason said. "Long time."

Will made his handshake a little firmer than necessary. Mason didn't seem to mind. He clapped Will on the shoulder. He was almost as tall as Will, but some of his height came from the way he'd styled his hair in the front to look like the tip of a duck's ass.

"What've you been up to, Johnny-boy? Had some trouble in Texas, I hear."

"I doubt you heard," Will said. "I paid a lot of money so you wouldn't."

"Of course. Nothing unpleasant." Mason clapped him on the shoulder again. "Where did you land? Was it ortho?"

Sara had given Will a few lines to win over Mason. "Pediatric ortho-nephrology."

Mason took a second before he threw back his head in laughter. "Kid-knees. I love it."

Will laughed, too, but it killed him to watch this jackass laugh at Sara's joke, particularly since it was a joke that she'd had to explain to Will.

"Fellas, next round is on me." Mason extricated his black card from a thick leather wallet. "Don't go crazy, though. I've got school fees coming up."

"You can afford it, you asshole." Chaz Penley had joined the group. He gave Will a handshake, slapped him on the arm. "John. Glad you could make it."

Will saw a younger version of Chaz lingering behind him, an actual Rolf before he turned in the Von Trapps. "Jesus, is that Chuck? He's the spitting image."

"Chuck, this is Dr. Trethewey." Chaz pushed his son in Will's direction. "Where's your boy?"

"Over in the corner with his face in his phone." Will pointed to Jeremy. "Go tell Eddie hello, Chuck."

Chuck clearly didn't like being ordered around by a stranger, but just as clearly, he had no interest in getting drunk with his father's obnoxious friends.

"Where are the hangers-on?" Chaz asked. "Who are we going to make fun of?"

"Not Richie," Mason said. "Unless someone wants to talk about that comb-over."

Will tuned out the laughter as the men teased each

other. He looked in the mirror. Chuck had taken the seat opposite Jeremy. Will could hear their voices in his ear.

". . . not sure why he wanted me to come to this stupid place," Chuck said.

"Same," Jeremy said. "I can't stand being around the asshole."

"Is Tommy here?"

"Who's Tommy?"

"Johnny-boy." Mason's hand was gripping Will's shoulder again, which was eventually going to lead to Mason's hand being broken. "How's your wife?"

"Beautiful," Will said, but only to watch the disappointment on Mason's face.

"Bad for my business, but good for you, I suppose." Mason recovered quickly. "Tell us what you've really been up to."

"Feeling out some offers." Will turned his body so that Mason had to let go of his shoulder. "I'm not sure we're going to stay in Atlanta. The wife likes it here, but Eddie's going to graduate in a couple of months. I'd prefer the West Coast."

"Those woke fucks." Richie was slurring his words. "I'd stay away from there, John. Whole state's going down the shitter."

"Rather amazing how they've managed to build the

fourth largest economy in the world." Mason winked at Will. "Good business opportunities for men like us. No insurance. Cash on the table."

Will guessed he was talking about the piles of dough to be made off Baby Boomers.

"John." Richie's hand rested on Will's arm. "Don't listen to him. You need to keep your head down for a while. Trust me."

Will leveled him with a look. "My head is my own business."

"Which head are you talking about?" Mac had finally made his appearance. He didn't bother to introduce Tommy. Mac's son was already walking toward the table in the back. Will recognized Tommy from the photos, but he would've spotted him easily by Sara's description. The arrogant tilt of his chin made his face look almost more punchable than Mason's.

"John." Mac took Mason's place, resting his hand on Will's shoulder. "Nice-looking boy you've got. Does his mother still comb his hair?"

Will gave an annoyed snort. "She still holds his dick when he pisses."

There was more boisterous laughter.

Will turned, forcing Mac's hand to fall away. He motioned for Louisa's attention. His eyes went to the mirror. Tommy had taken the chair beside Chuck. Suzan, another member of the fraud squad, was clearing away the old glasses and putting down new ones. Chuck Penley's DNA was locked in. Now all they needed were samples from Mac and Mason.

"Sorry, dude." Jeremy's voice mumbled through Will's earbud. "I told my dad I'm outta here in half an hour."

"You getting an Uber?" Tommy asked. "I know a house party that's stepping off over in Brookhaven."

"Not interested." Jeremy stared down at his phone.

Chuck and Tommy looked at each other. They weren't used to being turned down.

"Sir?" Louisa stood behind the bar.

"Clear this shit away," Will said. "Refill for my friend. Pappy for me and—"

"Bruichladdich times two," Chaz interrupted. "Mason?"

"Sorry, gents, I've got surgery bright and early."

Mac said, "Same. I can't stay long. I just wanted to make sure I had a word with John."

Will felt his irritation start to flicker. Mac and Mason were not going to skip out on the DNA samples. He told Mac, "I'm not sure I can trust a man who doesn't drink."

Mac seemed distracted, but the comment worked. He told Louisa, "Scotch, but splash some water in it for God's sake."

Louisa started filling the orders. Will glanced at the trio of boys again. Jeremy still had his eyes on his phone. Tommy and Chuck were clearly not happy. As a tactic, rude silence probably felt safe to Jeremy, but Will had seen tempers flare over lesser slights.

He listened as Chuck tried to engage Jeremy, asking, "So, you're at Tech."

"Yep," Jeremy said.

Tommy asked, "Do you know Bradley Walford?"

"Nope," Jeremy said.

"What are you studying?" Chuck tried again.

Jeremy sighed. "It's too complicated to explain."

"John." Mac was at Will's elbow. He gripped the Scotch and water in his hand. "I hope we didn't come across too strong yesterday. Chaz has a tendency to run his mouth."

"He does." Will clicked his glass against Mac's. "To old friends."

"Uh—right." Mac didn't drink. He put the glass back down on the bar. "Do you mind if we take a moment?"

Will used the back of his hand to move the glass toward Mac. "Sure."

Mac frowned. He wasn't the one who usually got pushed around. Still, he picked up the Scotch and motioned for Will to follow him.

Will didn't try to keep his gaze away from Jeremy as he walked toward the back of the room. Trethewey would be monitoring his son, encouraging him to make friends with the sons of the men who wanted to employ him.

Jeremy glanced up from his phone, but he quickly looked away.

In his ear, Will heard Chuck say, "Your dad is kind of a dick."

"He isn't *kind of* a dick," Jeremy said. "He *is* a dick."

"What'd he do?" Tommy asked. "Can't be worse than Richie. Dude drilled a hole in the wall so he could jerk off to his patients changing in the next room. Nurse caught him fapping off."

Chuck started laughing. "Like that *Family Guy* episode where Peter goes to the hardware store for a drill."

Jeremy said nothing. His attention was still on his phone.

Will passed by Amanda and Evelyn. Their purses were pointed at the bathrooms and the door to the smoking area. Neither of them looked at Will.

"John, I'll get to the point." Mac set his glass on the

windowsill. "What you said about Cam yesterday. That you got him out of town. I realized I never properly thanked you for taking care of our friend."

Will could feel his heart starting to pump faster. He'd been looking for an opportunity to bring up Cam. Still, he shrugged like it didn't matter. "I did what I had to do."

"Well, no. The fact is that you didn't have to do anything. You were never involved in our—" Mac seemed to search for the word. "Activities."

"Is that what you called them?" Will asked. "I wouldn't know because you never let me have a taste."

"I don't know what Cam told you, but it was a lot of talk. Mostly talk. He was the one who acted on it, and—" Mac stopped again. For all his power plays, he wasn't very persuasive. "What Cam did was unconscionable. We had no idea he was actually playing out the fantasy."

"The fantasy?" Will asked.

"Obviously, we were all disgusted when we found out." Mac picked up his glass and finally took a drink. "One thinks about things, all right? One gets these ideas in one's head, and one talks about them, but in real life, in actuality, it's never something that one would ever act upon."

"That's a lot of ones."

Mac gave a self-conscious chuckle. "I'm not usually the person having these conversations."

"No shit," Will said. "Who is?"

Mac finished his Scotch. He returned the glass to the windowsill. "About the job offer—"

"I'm not interested."

"Well, that's okay." Mac glanced back at the group.

Will turned, but he couldn't tell who Mac was looking at.

"How much?" Mac asked. "That's what it boils down to. How much are you looking for?"

Will took a moment to figure out what Mac was trying to say. Cam. The fantasy. The job offer. They were trying to buy off John Trethewey. But he needed Mac to say it. "How much for what?"

"Your silence, obviously."

"My silence about what?"

Mac had started to squirm. He glanced back at the bar again, probably looking for the man who usually did this. Will glanced, too. Chaz? Richie? Mason?

"Tell me," Mac said, "what exactly did Cam share?"

"You mean the website?" Will watched the arrogance melt away from Mac's face. "Or the little round robin you pulled on those girls?"

Mac wiped his mouth with his hand. "Okay, so Cam told you quite a bit."

"Just enough to whet my appetite," Will said. "What you had going, that was clever. Have a little fun while your buddies cover your ass. I could've used that in Texas. And I'd like to take advantage of it now."

"Why do you think this is a current thing?"

"I read about Tommy's trial. You're bringing him into the fold, right? I like that. Has a nice symmetry." Will looked at Jeremy. "I wish my kid had the balls to do something like that."

"Confidence had never been Tommy's weakness."

"Too confident, maybe. He almost got caught. Did he follow the plan?"

Mac wiped his mouth again. "I'm not at liberty to discuss anything other than money."

Will could tell that Mac was close to his breaking point. The worst thing that could happen right now was that a more clever man would take Mac's place. The only substitute who came to mind was Chaz Penley. Which explained the nasty looks the man kept throwing their way. Chaz was clearly making Mac get his hands dirty for a change. Maybe the gang wasn't so tightly knit anymore. Tommy's trial would've spooked all of them.

Will asked, "How much do you think my silence is worth?"

"Would it be—I don't know, something in the mid-six figures?"

Will felt his mouth go dry. Mac McAllister was offering him half a million dollars. "What would I do with that kind of cash? Not like I can stick it in the bank."

"Crypto?"

"Go fuck yourself."

Mac caught Will before he could walk off. "We can pay you out of the company."

Will turned back around. "How would that work?"

"A salary," Mac said. "All above-board. We'll take out taxes, social security, all of that."

He was listing federal crimes like a grocery list. "Your solution is to cut the money in half?"

"No, that's not what I meant," Mac said. "Say we go to seven figures. We could have you paid out within a year. Some of it in cash to help with the little things. The majority in salary so it's all cricket on paper. I'm sure you can work something out with the numbers. Accountants can be creative when it comes down to it."

Will had no idea how a million bucks would pay out over the course of twelve months, but it wasn't the kind of money you could hide on a balance sheet.

Mac said, "We should continue this discussion, yes?"

Will recognized a full retreat when he saw one. He needed to talk to the group. "I usually get paid for my time."

Mac's smirk gave himself away. He thought he'd trapped Will. "What's your hourly rate?"

"Let's start with twenty-five grand." Will needed him in felony territory. "Cash."

"I can arrange that."

"What about the paperwork?" Will asked. "How do I get my salary?"

"I can have the documents drawn up at your discretion," Mac said. "Employment contract, W2, etcetera. We'll call you a consultant."

"Like Richie?"

Mac raised his eyebrows, but he wasn't going to give the whole game away. "What say, John? You forget about the ravings of our drunk, depressed, very dead friend, and we give you a little cushion to help you land on your feet. Do we have a deal?"

Will pretended to think about it. The cash was a good starting point, but laundering the money through the corporation opened Mac up to commercial bribery charges. He had a fiduciary duty to the corporation. Right now, Mac could claim he was just talking out of his ass. Will needed to have the cash in hand, the paycheck wired into a bogus bank account, to make this an air-tight case.

"Let's meet at the club tomorrow," Will said. "We can—"

"Asshole!" Tommy's voice was sharp in Will's ear.

He turned around. Tommy was loud enough so that everyone else in the room did, too. His face was contorted with rage. He told Jeremy, "You're a bigger dick than your stupid father."

Jeremy shrugged, but he was clearly nervous. "Whatever."

"Don't whatever me, you stupid dick."

Will started to go to them, but Mac put a hand on his arm. "Let them figure it out."

"Tom," Chuck said. "Chill, dude. He was just—"

"Stay the fuck out of this!" Tommy violently shoved Chuck into the table. Chairs toppled. Glasses broke. Jeremy nearly dropped his phone as he jumped away from the carnage. His mouth hung open. He looked confused, clueless, afraid and worse—completely alone.

"Pissant motherfucker!" Tommy's fist reared back.

He wasn't going after Chuck.

He was threatening Jeremy.

Will crossed the room in four quick strides. He left Tommy alone. Instead, he grabbed Jeremy up by the collar and marched him toward the back door because he wasn't going to let Faith's kid get his ass kicked. The night air bit into his face. Will smelled cigarette smoke and stale beer. Aiden stood up, fists clenched. Will shot him a look to back him off. A couple was sitting at one of the picnic tables. They quickly rushed inside as Will pushed Jeremy hard enough to make him stumble, but not so hard that he hit the ground.

"Jesus!" Jeremy pulled his shirt back into place. "Will—"

Will heard the abrupt stop. He turned around to see why.

Chuck was watching from the open doorway.

"Will you leave me the fuck alone?" Jeremy kept adjusting his shirt. He was clearly shaken. Just as clearly, he was trying to maintain his cover. "Jesus, Dad. What the fuck?"

"You little shit." Will thumped him in the chest. "I told you Tommy is Mac's kid. You wanna keep your allowance? Your car? Your life? Don't screw this up for me."

Chuck had a familiar smirk on his face when Will turned toward the door, but he had the intelligence to step aside so that Will could pass.

Will scanned the bar. Amanda and Evelyn were still seated at the table. They were both looking at Amanda's phone, probably watching the live feed from Jeremy's glasses.

Mac was back with the gang. The men were laughing it up again, joking, clapping each other on the shoulders. Mac shrugged at Will like, *Whatta ya gonna do?* Chaz was grinning when he waved Will over.

Will didn't go over. He turned toward the men's bathroom. He shut the door and leaned against it. He took out his phone. He clicked the button three times. He saw what Jeremy was seeing: Chuck Penley standing in front of him.

"Gotta placate 'til you graduate," Chuck said.

"He's a cocksucker." Jeremy still sounded shaken, but he was trying. "I can handle myself. I don't need him stepping in like my goddam mother."

"Sho nuff," Chuck said, but he didn't sound convinced.

Jeremy looked at the empty doorway back into the building. "He wouldn't risk pissing off Mac. All he cares about is money."

"Mac's not pissed. He loves pitting us against each other. They all do." Chuck pulled a pack of cigarettes out of his jacket pocket. "You want one?"

The image on the screen swiveled back and forth as Jeremy shook his head.

Will spotted Aiden Van Zandt in the shadows. The

FBI agent was still tensed, ready to jump in if Jeremy needed him. There was no telling if Chuck knew he was there. What Will knew for certain was that Faith was probably screaming at the monitors back in the bus. She would be begging Jeremy to shut the fuck up, to walk away, to sit in Will's car and wait until it was time to leave.

Jeremy wasn't leaving.

He asked Chuck, "What's his problem anyway?"

"Tom?" Chuck blew smoke out of the corner of his mouth. "You heard about his trial, right?"

"He raped that girl."

"Bro! Allegedly!" Chuck had a nasty laugh. "Dani was all right. I mean, she could be stuck up, but she was all right."

"She died."

"Tom didn't have anything to do with that." Chaz blew out more smoke. "She crashed his car. That was on her."

Jeremy looked down at the ground. Will could see one of his Nikes was coming untied. The hem of his jeans was torn. Faith was probably running through the parking lot. She wouldn't be mad at Jeremy. She would be mad at Will. He had promised that he would keep her son safe and Will had frogmarched him through a bar and dropped him outside with the son of a sadist.

Jeremy asked, "Did he do it?"

"Rape her?" Chuck took another hit off the cigarette. "Not really. I mean, Dani got railed by half the guys in middle school, so it's not like her vag wasn't open for business. Highest body count in the hood."

"They dated?"

"Nah, dog. She put Tom in the friend zone. Dude blue-balled it for years. I'm surprised he didn't bag her sooner."

"No doubt." Jeremy was looking down at his shoes again. "Was she hot?"

"Smoking hot," Chuck said. "But uptight. Like Britt, I guess. My dad says it'd take the jaws of life to pry open Britt McAllister's knees."

Jeremy's laugh sounded forced to Will, but Chuck didn't seem to notice.

He asked Jeremy, "You wanna see something?"

Jeremy's glasses moved as he shrugged his shoulders. "Sure."

"You can't tell anybody, all right?" Chuck was watching him carefully. "I mean for reals. This shit is nasty."

Another shrug. "Sure."

Chuck took a last drag on the cigarette before flicking it into the grass. His phone came out. His fingers worked the screen. He held up the phone for Jeremy to see.

The image was paused.

Dani Cooper.

Completely naked. Eyes closed. Head back.

She was lying on a white sheepskin rug.

Jeremy asked, "Who's that?"

"Tom sent it to me." Chuck was grinning. "Hit play."

Jeremy's finger tapped the screen.

Will cupped his hand to his ear to listen, but the bathroom was quiet enough to hear everything that Jeremy was hearing. The muffled sound of skin moving against skin. The soft groans. The rhythmic slaps. The chilling sound of laughter. Will felt like his blood was turning into ground-up glass. He looked up at the ceiling. There was nothing he could do.

Faith's son was watching a video of Dani Cooper being raped.

18

Faith moved around the kitchen like she was sinking through quicksand. She closed the blinds against the mid-morning sun. She'd spent another night tossing, turning, worrying, crying. She hadn't felt this sleep-deprived since Emma had caught RSV during Spring Break.

She stopped, listening for Jeremy upstairs. He was still asleep. All she could hear was the faucet dripping in the hall bathroom. Faith was always happy to have her son stay over, but this was different. She couldn't remember the last time her son had laid down on the couch and put his head in her lap. Jeremy hadn't cried, exactly, but the fact that he'd clearly wanted to was enough to make her feel like she was going to shatter into a million pieces.

The video.

Chuck had only played three minutes of what was clearly a longer recording. Faith had watched it from the mobile command center, her eyes seeing everything through her son's eyes—

Dani Cooper with her head back, her lips parted, eyes closed, not in ecstasy but because she was drugged out of her mind. Her naked body was the only color in the room. The walls had been painted black. The concrete floor was black. The sheepskin rug was bright white, but there were stains on it. Some of the strands had dried into clumps.

The sound of the young woman's moaning still haunted Faith. Dani had been caught somewhere between wakefulness and sleep. If she was aware of what was going on, the one kindness of the drug was that she couldn't remember it by the time she had made it to Grady.

The man who'd abducted her couldn't be seen in the video, but his hands came into view as he manipulated her limp body. No rings on his fingers. No watch. No identifying marks, but they were a young man's hands, the skin smooth, a sprinkling of dark hair on the knuckles, so Faith had to assume they belonged to Tommy McAllister.

The coldblooded sound of his laughter could be heard on the video as he posed Dani for the camera, flipping her on her side, her back, her stomach, as he zoomed in and out. He didn't handle her like a doll because you would be more gentle with a doll. He flopped her around. He pushed and prodded, stuck his fingers in her mouth, between her legs. The camera closed in on her breasts, her intimate places. Then he'd placed it on a small tripod and captured the act of him raping her.

Faith sat down at the kitchen table. She rubbed her eyes. In her law enforcement career, she had seen her share of depravity. The video easily made it into the top five horrible things she had witnessed. Then to layer on the fact that her son had seen it—there were no words to describe her anguish.

The worst part, the most unacceptable part, was that Jeremy still wanted to join the force.

Faith pressed her forehead to the table. She opened her mouth. She took several breaths. The only thing that kept her from screaming was knowing that by the end of the day, someone was going to be paying the price for what her son had been forced to watch.

Amanda's plan required two different teams to strike from two different directions. She was calling it Operation Domino, because one piece would topple the other and hopefully, the rest of the pieces would fall down after.

Will was leading the first team. He was meeting Mac

McAllister for lunch at the country club this afternoon. Mac was supposed to bring $25,000 in cash along with employment paperwork for an additional one million dollars.

The GBI already had Mac on tape admitting that the bribe was in exchange for John Trethewey's silence. The cash being handed over was good, but the paycheck would be the final nail in Mac McAllister's coffin. Once the money was in John Trethewey's account, Mac would be arrested for wire fraud, tax evasion, commercial bribery, and money laundering. He would be looking at five to twenty years. He would also be looking for a deal to keep his ass out of prison.

Which was where the second team came in.

Amanda had easily found a judge to sign off on a search warrant for Chuck Penley's iPhone. Jeremy's glasses had recorded the Dani Cooper video. They had also recorded Chuck telling him that Tommy McAllister had sent him the file. These two bits of information provided more than enough legal justification to search Chuck's phone.

Once the warrant was served, it wouldn't take a genius to figure out that John Trethewey's boy had gone to the police. Chaz Penley would be terrified that the video wasn't the only thing the Trethewey boys were discussing. He would be desperate to save his own ass as well as his son's.

The only question was which man was going to turn first. There was only one bargaining chip they had in their back pockets. Would Mac offer up the Club to get a reduced sentence? Would Chaz offer up the same? Or would they both gut it out at trial, blowing through piles of cash, destroying their reputations, losing their careers, their families, in hopes that a jury would find them innocent?

No matter what they decided, there was no way the Club would survive the bomb that was about to go off in their lives. If Amanda played it right, the dominoes would all start crashing down by the end of the week.

Faith had been sidelined for both operations, but she was determined to do her part. She made herself sit up. She grabbed the stack of pages from the printer. The digital services team hadn't been able to recover the corrupted video files on the chat website. Fortunately, they'd had better luck with the password-protected files on Cam Carmichael's computer.

They were all PDFs. Cam had taken screenshots of chat transcripts that had been erased from the Club website the day after Sara Linton had been raped. The posts created a sort of origin story for the members.

The first entry was from sixteen years ago. Unlike the later entries that were primarily posted by 002, 003, 004, and 007, the entire group seemed to be engaged.

002: You idiots need to be more careful. 005: Who put you in charge? 001: Well said. 003: Why would we listen to you? 002: You almost got caught, you stupid fuckers. 004: Sorry gents, this doesn't involve me. 006: Fucking coward. 002: And you're not? 007: What would you have us do? 003: I'm all for fun but I'm not going to prison for this FYI. 005: Neither am I, so you assholes need to figure this out.

Faith made a note of the date. She would need to reach out to Adam Humphrey to see if he was willing to access the APD database. This was proof that Merit Barrowe had not been the Club's first victim. From what Faith was reading, the woman's rapist had almost been caught. Victim Zero had probably been close to someone in the group. The sophisticated way they covered their tracks with Dani Cooper and Leighann Park pointed to deliberate planning. The transcripts revealed how they'd arrived at the solution.

006: We should split up the tasks. 002: Exactly. 001: Explain? 006: Work it like a case in the ER. Put in specialists. 002: Oh the mighty trauma surgeon speaks. Seriously, here we are doing this again. 007: Stop being a fucking bitch. 006: I'm trying to find a solution. 003: OK you're not far off base. 002: This needs to be compartmentalized. 006: That's what I have been trying to say.

Faith had her spiral notebook open. She found her list of profiles for the chat group. She had assumed that 006 was Cam Carmichael. He was the only trauma surgeon in the Club. She put a check by his name before she continued reading.

005: Did you ever think some of us would like a turn? 001: When did you get the balls for Master? 003: No Master here I like to watch. 005: We all like to watch but some of us want to get our dicks wet. 006: Rotate out like an ER consult. Everyone can take turns. 002: Fuck can you stop with the ER? We all know how to hold a scalpel. 007: He's right. 006: Then this is what we are going to do. 002: Who's going to generate a roster? 007: Who do you think? 002: Why does all the scheduling always fall on me?

Faith ran her finger down the profiles. She had guessed that 002 was Mac McAllister, but 002 had a certain level of bitchiness that Faith had not heard in

Mac's voice last night. She looked up at the crazy wall. Chaz Penley was a strong contender. Nasty, bitchy, organized. At the country club lunch, he'd been the numbers guy, doing the hard sell to bring John Trethewey into the fold.

Which meant that 007 could be Mac. In later posts, he was talking about his conquests, which Faith now understood were acts of rape. She would've bet her next paycheck that the corrupted video files on the website were similar to the one Tommy had filmed of Dani Cooper. Britt had said that Tommy was turning into his father. Did he learn from the man who was called the Master?

Faith tried to push the video out of her mind. She went back to her profiles.

By process of elimination, Richie Dougal had to be 003. He'd said that he liked to watch. Last night, Tommy had revealed that Richie's MeToo moment came about because Richie had drilled a hole in the wall so that he could watch his patients undress.

She made another check on the list.

Royce Ellison or Bing Forster could be either 001 or 005. Or Faith could be going completely down the wrong path because all of these sadists were starting to sound like mid-level management.

002: Positions to fill? 005: Master. Enslaver. 006: Fucksakes do we have to sound like a bunch of racists, too? 002: It's important to maintain political correctness when we're talking about stalking, harassing, abducting, drugging, and raping young women. 007: So those are the positions? 002: Rotate in and out, the bench can watch. 005: I'm good with that. 006: Yes. 001: Yes. 003: Sure. 007: I'll send out next quarter's target when I have details.

Faith had to take a moment. It had been that easy. One to stalk. One to harass. One to abduct. One to drug. One to rape. Five different men. Seven members of the Club. Mason had taken himself out early, Cam had shot himself in the head. Royce and Bing hadn't been at the mixer last night, but Chuck and Tommy had. They were clearly being brought into the Club.

Which brought it all back to what Britt had told Sara four days ago—

I can't stop the rest of them, but I can save my boy.

Faith didn't think that was possible. Last night, Tommy had been ready to punch Jeremy over a disagreement about a targeting foul called in a football game from two years ago. He was volatile, angry, prone to violence. He'd filmed himself raping Dani Cooper. He had been credibly accused of raping a girl in middle school. He'd brought the police to their door in elementary school for harming a neighbor's dog.

It wasn't a matter of saving Tommy. It was a matter of saving everyone around him.

Faith forced herself to read the remaining screenshots. The roster had been posted by 002. Each man was assigned a job. Each man took a turn. No substitutions allowed. Clearly 007 was choosing the victims. Faith's eyes skimmed the lines for his number.

007: Sent you a text with target photo. 007: Target address sent. 007: Phone number for target incoming.

Each man wrote back the same response.

001: Confirmed. 002: Confirmed. 003: Confirmed. 005: Confirmed. 006: Confirmed.

Mason James was noticeably absent from the machinations, but Faith assumed he had read the chats. 004 had still been checking into the site eight years ago when they all found out that Cam had permanently removed himself from the Club.

Faith heard a car pulling into her driveway. Sara had offered to help her take down the crazy wall so that Emma would not see that her Hello Kitty tape was gone and start spinning around the kitchen floor like a screeching starfish.

"Hello?" Sara's voice was soft as she walked down the hallway. Faith had told her to let herself in so that she didn't wake up Jeremy.

"Kitchen." Faith stacked together the seven pages. She placed them on top of the other chat transcripts. She would need a couple of file boxes. Hopefully, digital services would be able to do something with the mountains of paperwork.

"Good morning." Sara put her purse on the counter. She was drawn to the crazy wall again. The red, purple, pink, and yellow strips of construction paper looked like a failed student art project. "I talked to Will on the way over. He's scheduled to meet Mac at the country club at one o'clock."

Faith wasn't going to feel relieved until it was over. "Anything on Merit Barrowe's underwear?"

"The lab found two different strands of DNA. We'll need a sample from Martin Barrowe for a familial comparison on the female profile. The second profile is male, unknown." Sara was looking at the yellow strips of construction paper. "It'll take the weekend to run everybody's DNA from last night. Except for Mason. He never touched a glass."

"Is that unusual?"

"I wouldn't know," Sara admitted. "It's been a long time since we socialized together."

Faith noted Sara's reluctance as she dragged her attention away from the wall. She looked like her night had been as restful as Faith's.

Sara said, "Will is torn up about Jeremy."

"Will did exactly what he should've done." Faith had already talked to him twice this morning. "I could almost live with Jeremy getting punched, but his glasses could've broken. Tommy and Chuck would've seen the electronics for the camera. All of this would've been for nothing."

"Is that how Jeremy sees it?"

"Yes. Unfortunately." Faith bit her lip. She wasn't going to cry again. "He still wants to join the force."

"I could talk to him," Sara offered. "There are other ways to serve. I took a forensics course at Quantico last fall. They've got all the cool toys. I'm sure you know someone who could get him in."

Faith wanted to laugh. Quantico meant the FBI. "Does everybody know I've been seeing Aiden?"

Sara didn't have to answer. "Kate Murphy is amazing."

"She's terrifying." Faith didn't know how to act around Aiden's mother. The woman was too accomplished, too beautiful, too unlike anything Faith would ever be. "This is me changing the subject. Did you get any sense of voice from the chat transcripts? I'm pretty sure Cam is 006. Mason is 004. Mac could be 007."

"That's what I got, too." Sara leaned against the counter. "002 has a tell. He keeps repeating some version of the sentence 'Are we seriously doing this again?'"

So much for Faith's investigative skills. She shuffled back through the pages. Her eyes caught the words—

007: She needs a stiff fuck to loosen her up. 002: Are we seriously doing this again?

007: Could not get away from that screechy bitch fast enough. 002: Are we seriously doing this again?

002: Oh the mighty trauma surgeon speaks. Seriously, here we are doing this again. 007: Stop being a fucking bitch.

Faith picked up on something else. "002 is constantly trash-talking 007. Who would have the balls to trash-talk Mac Fucking McAllister?"

"No one. So, either Mac isn't 007 or—" Sara shrugged. She had hit the same dead ends as Faith. "I got a bit further with the text that was sent to Merit Barrowe. That sounds like Cam to me."

Faith found the screenshot from Merit's phone. She read, "'Who wants to brighten your day by telling you how beautiful you are? Who dreams about you a lot more than he should? Who is slightly more damaged than all the others? Who is someone who doesn't deserve the pleasure of your company? Who is the person who will disappoint you when you find out who I am?'"

"It's kind of pathetic," Sara said. "I'm damaged. I don't deserve your company. You'll be disappointed when you find out who I am."

Faith started nodding, because it seemed obvious now. "He probably romanticized it, made himself believe he was writing a love letter instead of straight-up stalking her. Then Merit comes into Grady and he gets a close-up look at the damage they've done."

"Sloan Bauer told me Cam acted horrified when she called him out for raping her. Apparently, he didn't bother to learn the difference between sex and assault." Sara crossed her arms. She didn't sound sympathetic. "Cam tried to stop the gang by pushing back on Merit's death certificate, collecting the autopsy report, saving her underwear. Then Edgerton gave him an easy way out."

"The Glock gave Cam an easy way out." Faith let out a long sigh. She had to find a way to stop these animals. "The company name—CMM&A. Does the initial A mean anything to you?"

Sara shook her head. "Everything about this is so frustrating. We've learned so much, but we're still back at the same place we were the first night."

Faith knew what she meant. "We can't prove anything. The Club has been active for sixteen years and right now, Tommy's the only one who'll get charged with rape. And who knows whether that will hold up in court? His face isn't on the video."

"Let's talk it through," Sara said. "What other questions do you have?"

"The *zzt-zzt* sound that Leighann Park described has no explanation. We don't know how they're getting the victims' phone numbers. Or how they're being selected in the first place. Amanda thinks that's the key to finding out who's in charge. Make a connection between the Master and the victims, you unlock the case. Then there's the shoes." Faith pointed to the photos she'd taped on the cabinets by the sink. "Merit's Air Jordan Flight 23. Dani's Stella McCartney platform sandal. Leighann's Marc Jacobs velvet lace-up. Somebody's taking trophies. That's the kind of shit a jury eats up. If the shoe fits, you can't acquits."

Sara studied the photos. "I love that chunky heel."

"Right?" Faith hadn't worn heels since Emma had turned her lower back into a trampoline. "The only other thing is the sheepskin rug. Leighann described it in her interview. It also shows up in the Dani video. Looked to me like there was a significant amount of DNA on that rug. What do you think?"

Sara pressed her lips together.

"Didn't you watch it? It's on the server."

Sara shook her head. "I didn't want to put Will through that again. And with all that's been going on, I've had enough trouble sleeping lately."

"No kidding," Faith said. "Until this week, I thought the worst news Jeremy could spring on me was telling me I'm going to be a grandmother before I turned forty."

"I'm so sorry. I can't imagine how scary last night was for you."

"I'm really glad that Will was there." Faith wiped her eyes. She didn't mention that she had been glad that Aiden was there, too. "Nobody warns you that ninety-nine percent of being a mother is walking around in a daze asking yourself what the fuck just happened."

Sara looked down at her hands. She had started twisting her ring. Faith didn't ask her what she was thinking about because they both knew what she was thinking about. Sara would love to be walking around in a daze.

Faith stacked together some of the papers. She neatened the piles. The sound of water dripping upstairs added to the discomfort.

Sara told her, "Send me a photo of your faucet. I can order a washer online."

"You can do that?"

"I'm a plumber's daughter." Sara had put a smile on her face. "Tessa can fix it for you. You could turn it into a playdate with Emma and Isabelle."

This was magic happening right before Faith's eyes. "She would love that. I would love that."

"Then it's settled."

Faith couldn't let go of the forced cheer in Sara's voice. She had to ask, "Do you ever get tired of smoothing things over for other people?"

Sara shook her head, but she wasn't saying no. She was saying that she couldn't talk about it. She waved her hand around the kitchen. "Where do you want to start?"

Faith groaned like an old woman as she stood up. "Let's do the crazy wall. Don't worry about being careful. I already know the tape is going to rip off the paint."

Sara was taller. She started on the cabinets, picking at the multiple strips of adhesive that Mr. McTapey Pants had framed around the Connection.

What happened to you. What happened to Dani. It's all connected.

"I can't believe I sacrificed my cabinets to a stoned rich lady who couldn't keep her fucking mouth shut in a bathroom." Faith slipped the red strips of Britt's toilet missives out from under the magnets. "I keep wondering if Britt was really that stoned. I know she was crying, but maybe it was from relief. She could've been fucking with you from the beginning. We're giving her exactly what she wanted. Tommy's protected. The Club will probably stop once Mac is gone."

"I don't know. Part of me thinks she slipped up. Then part of me remembers that she was one of the most technically skilled surgeons I've ever seen. She certainly cut into me with precision." Sara carefully picked at another corner of tape. "Britt's one of those women who says she gets along better with men when the fact is that other women hate her bullshit and men like her because she shits on other women."

Faith had been coming up against that type of woman her entire law enforcement career. "Will said

Britt's a victim as well as an abuser. I guess he's speaking from experience."

Sara winced as a large gash of paint tore off. She never talked about Will's personal life and Faith knew she wasn't going to start now. "Let's go back through your list of questions. What about the noise Leighann heard?"

Faith clipped up a drawing Emma had made of either a panda bear or a can of black beans. "The only *zzt-zzt* that comes to mind is a bug zapper."

Sara stopped peeling tape. She looked at Faith. "Was it a *zzt*, or was it more like a mechanical whir?"

"What do you mean?"

"When I was little, my dad bought an RCA Camcorder from Radio Shack. There are still hundreds of VHS tapes in our basement."

Faith smiled despite the circumstances. "My dad had one of those, too."

"Do you remember the sound it made when you zoomed in and out?"

Faith remembered now. It sounded exactly like the noise that Leighann had described—a mechanical *zzt-zzt* as the optical stabilization worked in tandem with the auto-focus.

Faith said, "The video was high-def, so they're not using VHS."

"Digital is even better. The metadata will show a location, date, time, maybe even who owns the camera."

"If we can get that sheepskin rug, there's going to be DNA from everybody who's ever been on it."

"If," Sara repeated, because this case was full of ifs and no action. "Did you hear anything like a zooming noise on the video of Dani?"

Faith shook her head. All she could remember was the awful moaning. "I was too busy losing my shit to listen for anything specifically."

"You said the video is on the server, right?" Sara reached into her purse. She pulled out a pair of AirPods.

"My headphones are in the living room." Faith took her seat at the table. She opened her laptop. She paired Sara's AirPods with her Mac. Sara was back with her Beats by the time Faith was logging into the GBI's server.

Sara offered, "I could watch it on my own. You don't have to see it again."

Faith waited for Sara to sit down. She clicked open the file. She turned up the volume. She put on her earphones, then waited until Sara had the AirPods in to press *play*.

The video was just as horrifying the second time around. Dani's arms and legs being manipulated. Her body being violated. Her face slack because she had no idea where she was or what was happening.

Faith closed her eyes, concentrating on the sound. Heavy breathing. A man chuckling. Movement. Lips smacking. Dani's shallow breaths.

Zzt-zzt.

Faith's eyes opened. She looked at Sara. They both recognized the sound. The optical stabilization. The auto-focus.

Faith took off her headphones. She didn't need to hear any more. She tapped the spacebar to stop the video.

"Faith." Sara pressed her hand to her heart. "The nude pictures of Dani. The ones that were shown to her parents. Britt told me one of Dani's ex-boyfriends found them on an old phone. She said they were bad. Bad enough to make the Coopers settle."

"Okay."

"When we were in the locker room," Sara said. "Britt described the photos to me. She said Dani's eyes were closed, but you could see her face. She was squeezing her breasts. Spreading open her labia. That's exactly how Dani is being posed. The photos weren't from a high school boyfriend. They took stills from the video. Look."

Faith watched Sara rewind and fast forward to the

different shots. Dani had no motor control. She left her hands where they were placed. On her breasts. Between her legs. Someone with even a passing knowledge of photo editing could make the poses look voluntary.

Faith said, "Do you think Britt knows about the video?"

"I can ask her. Mac is going to be at the club with Will in two hours. I can go to her house. She might be ready to talk."

"What if Mac sees you on the cameras?"

"Will can keep him from looking at his phone."

Faith didn't doubt that, but there was one problem. "We need to run this by Amanda. I'm done going rogue."

"Agreed," Sara said. "But this could be another domino. I have no doubt that Britt will stand by Mac on the bribery charges, but she won't stand by him if Tommy's life is on the line. She'll throw Mac to the wolves."

"Would you be okay with that deal?" Faith asked. "Letting Tommy walk so that Mac goes to prison?"

"No, Tommy would have to get prison time, too. That's non-negotiable."

Faith couldn't let her believe it would be that simple. "There's the way you want the system to work and the way the system actually works."

"So, Britt wins again?"

Faith didn't have an answer. It wasn't just Britt. Tommy McAllister was going to keep hurting women until someone found a way to stop him. Unfortunately, a lot more women would probably suffer before that happened.

Sara was clearly thinking the same thing. She let out a slow breath as she slumped back in the chair. She stared at the paused image of Dani on the laptop. She was probably thinking of the promise she had made to Dani three years ago.

Or maybe she wasn't.

Sara sat up, pointing at the screen. "Can you enlarge and enhance this area of the video?"

"The area around the mole?"

Sara nodded.

Faith took a screenshot, then opened it in J-Pixia, a free photo-editing app. She adjusted the filters until the mole darkened and Dani's skin lightened. She realized Sara wasn't asking about the mole. She wanted to see the scar that was roughly an inch down and over. The skin was slightly dimpled, almost like a puncture. The blue lines of Dani's veins parted like the flow of a river around a rock. Faith adjusted the color wheel until the scar grew pink.

Then she remembered a detail from the first night

they had put up the crazy wall. "You said the scar was old, probably from Dani's childhood?"

Sara didn't answer. Her head was shaking. She looked confused. "Did Leighann have any visible scars?"

"Uh—" Faith pushed around the piles of documents until she found the three photos she had taken of Leighann's breast: Close-up, distance, from the side.

Sara chose the side view.

Leighann had lifted her arm over her head, making the breast more prominent so that Faith could document the words written around her nipple. At the time, Faith had paid no attention to the faded scar on Leighann's left side. Now she saw that the thin, pink line was a few inches below her armpit, pointing like an arrow toward her breast.

That's me.

Sara asked, "Where's Merit's autopsy report?"

Faith easily found the faxed pages.

Sara pointed to the three X's on the body diagram. They were in the same location as the scar on Leighann Park. "The ME called out a tattoo, but what if it was a scar? What if Edgerton made him change the designation to a tattoo? That would explain why he didn't identify what it said."

"Why would Edgerton want the scar changed to a tattoo?"

Sara placed the report back on the table. The look of confusion had left her face. "This can't be what I think it is."

"What do you think it is?"

Sara looked at Faith. "After open heart surgery, you have a median sternotomy scar, right? The surgeon cracks open your sternum. She wires it back together. Closes the incision. You have a significant scar down the center of your chest, sometimes eight to eleven inches long."

Faith had no idea where this was going. "None of the victims have a scar down the center of their chests."

"Right." Sara held up the photo of Leighann's breast. "This scar is from a left anterolateral minithoracotomy. You'd use that type of incision to repair an ASD or VSD—atrial or ventricular septal defect, a hole between either the two upper or two lower chambers of the heart."

Faith watched as Sara held up the body diagram from Merit Barrowe's autopsy.

She pointed to the three Xs. "Same location: a left anterolateral minithoracotomy scar. Probably the same procedure."

Sara turned the laptop toward Faith.

She pointed at the scar below Dani Cooper's mole. "Transfemoral access for a left cardiac catheterization. If the ASD is small enough, you can feed a special implant through the catheter. The pressure inside the heart holds it in place until the tissue grows over it."

Faith was clueless. "I recognize a lot of those words, but none of them make sense together."

"When I was at Grady, Dr. Nygaard was part of an NIH trial to test minimally invasive cardiac surgery using minithoracotomy with peripheral cannulation. Patients were randomly given the opportunity to enroll. Most of the parents of female children said yes. The outcomes are similar. It's a cosmetic choice. They would rather their daughter grow up with a minimal scar on the side of her chest instead of an eleven-inch scar between her cleavage."

Faith was catching on now. She waited for Sara to continue.

"Dr. Nygaard is left-handed, like me, so her preference was to go in through the left side. All of her surgical residents and fellows were trained on the left approach unless the right was more advantageous. When they weren't in surgery, the fellows shadowed Dr. Nygaard during clinic. They saw follow-up patients, helped evaluate potential surgical candidates, handled anxious parents, walked them through the procedures."

Now Faith understood. "All of Dr. Nygaard's surgical residents and fellows."

"Where do you always have to give a current address and phone number?"

"A doctor's office."

"Merit, Dani, Leighann. That's how the victims are selected. Mac McAllister worked on their hearts."

19

Sara sat alone in the passenger seat of Amanda's Lexus. The engine was running so that the heater stayed on. Frank Sinatra played softly through the speakers. Amanda was leaning against Sara's BMW, which was parked opposite the Lexus. Her head was bent down as she talked on the phone.

The conversation looked tense.

She was on a conference call with the senior assistant district attorney for Fulton County and the state attorney general's office. They were coordinating a kind of sting operation. Sara was about to knock on Britt McAllister's door. This time, there was no relying on Sara's memory or her ability to scribble her recollections on an index card. She was wearing a hunter green corduroy jacket with a camera built into the button on the left breast pocket and a microphone inside the right lapel. The transmitter was in her side pocket. Amanda was strategizing with the lawyers because she wanted to make sure they did everything exactly by the book so that the recording wasn't thrown out in court.

They didn't know if Mac was keeping the videos from the cameras inside the house. They didn't know where the server was. They had no idea whether or not he could remotely wipe the drives the same way the exterior cameras on the house had been wiped the night that Dani Cooper had died.

Amanda had started pacing between the cars. Her hand went out in a broad gesture of frustration, but if there was one thing Sara knew about the deputy director it was that she always managed to find a way.

But for what?

Part of Sara couldn't help but think that this was a lot of trouble to go through considering Britt's long, tedious history of parceling out dead ends. She had cried about *them* but wouldn't provide *their* names. She had brought up Cam, but Cam was dead. She had pointed them toward Merit Barrowe, but there was nothing they could do about it. She had said there was a connection between Sara and Dani Cooper, but the most obvious connection seemed to be that both of them had been raped. Which also connected them to nearly half a million American women every year.

Mac was the real connection.

Britt had never meant to point Sara toward Mac. Her sloppy, drug-induced burst of honesty in the courthouse bathroom had been a mistake. Britt had been forced to play clean-up ever since. She had dropped Merit Barrowe's name in the locker room. She had offered up Cam as a suspect. She had trashed his name and reputation. Blaming everything on a dead man was not a bad strategy, but Britt didn't know that Sara had seen the video of Dani, that she had read the chat transcripts, the autopsy reports, Cam's witness statement. Most importantly, Britt had somehow forgotten that Sara was a damn good doctor.

Residency training programs were designed to give a well-rounded education in multiple disciplines, but in practical terms, they felt engineered to crush your spirit. Long hours. Low pay. No respect. Very few rewards. During your first year, you were basically flailing around, trying not to kill somebody. You didn't earn the title of resident unless you made it to the second year. Each residency is different, but all residents generally go through blocks of clinical rotations within their specialty of either emergency medicine, internal medicine, pediatrics, psychology, neurology, and surgery. Each block can last from four to nine weeks, and while you are working that block, you perform every task from filling out paperwork to screening patients to assisting in open heart surgery.

Sara had fallen in love with pediatric cardiothoracic surgery during her first rotation with Dr. Nygaard. So had Mac, but for different reasons. Anytime you were dealing with operating on an infant's heart, the stakes were higher. So was the prestige. They had each jockeyed to rotate onto Dr. Nygaard's team as often as possible. They had each vied for the fellowship. Both of them had gotten the offer. Only one of them had been in a position to accept it.

And then he had exploited it for his own sick impulses.

Sara looked down at her phone. She had spoken with Dani Cooper's parents. Dani had been born with a secundum atrial septal defect, the most common type of ASD. Her medical team had taken a wait-and-see approach in case the five-millimeter hole spontaneously closed. At the age of six, Dani had reported fatigue and arrythmia, so a catheter had been inserted into her femoral artery to patch the hole.

Dr. Nygaard had been the surgeon.

Mac McAllister had been her fellow.

Faith had called Leighann Park's mother. The young woman had also been treated at Grady. She'd been born with an ASD that was repaired when she started exhibiting symptoms at the age of seven.

Dr. Nygaard had been the surgeon.

Mac McAllister had been her fellow.

Faith had also spoken to Martin Barrowe. He'd been a teenager when his sister had died, so he'd had to make some phone calls to family members to find out the truth. Merit had been born with a mitral valve anomaly. An artificial ring had been implanted to reinforce the valve. The surgery had taken place at Grady. No one in the family could remember who had performed the procedure, but they knew that Merit had to do follow-up visits every year to ensure the ring was properly functioning.

That kind of routine follow-up was usually handled by a surgical resident.

Mac McAllister had been Dr. Nygaard's surgical resident around the time that Merit had died.

Mac was the key Amanda was looking for to unlock the case. He had chosen the victims. He had either facilitated or participated in the rape of Merit Barrowe. He had played the long game with Leighann, waiting until she hit her twenties to attack her. Dani had probably been marked, too, but Tommy had somehow messed that up. There was no telling how many former patients Mac the Master had on his list of targets. In the last sixteen years, he had probably seen thousands of infants and children at their most vulnerable moments. Then he had watched and waited through until they were old enough to fulfill his sick fantasies.

As a medical examiner, Sara had seen horrific examples of cruelty, but as a doctor, as a surgeon, as a woman who had once had the honor of repairing the hearts of so many children, she could not help but think that Mac McAllister was one of the most depraved human beings walking the face of the earth. The violation of the doctor–patient relationship was unspeakable.

The door opened. Amanda had finished her call. She got back into the car. Instead of speaking, she reached into Sara's jacket pocket and took out the slim black box that was connected to the microphone and camera wires that snaked into the lining. The transmitter's light was off, but she still unplugged the leads.

She said, "This is what we need from Britt: How much does she know about the Club? Who are the members? How long has it been operating? How was Tommy brought into the Club?"

"She won't give up Tommy."

"Make it clear that Tommy is already caught dead to rights. We have the video of Dani. No jury will look at that recording and deliver an innocent verdict. The only thing Britt can do now is negotiate terms she can live with. Give us the information on Mac and the Club and we will ensure that her son does not die in prison."

Sara felt her stomach twist into a knot. As far as she was concerned, Tommy deserved to die in prison. "Britt knows I don't have the ability to offer a legally binding deal."

"You're not there to deal. You're there to help," Amanda said. "Make her believe that you're approaching her as a friend. Persuade her that you're looking out for Tommy. You are on her side. Hold her hand, be attentive, appear sympathetic, even understanding, so that she trusts you enough to open up."

Sara didn't know if she was capable of that level of duplicity. "How much can I tell her?"

"As much or as little as it takes to get her to talk," Amanda said. "All the other pieces are in place. The dominoes will fall. It's just a matter of who manages to get out of the way."

"What if Tommy is at the house?"

"He's at the country club playing golf with friends. The mobile command center is already set up on the street for Will's operation. Tommy won't exit the property without us knowing."

"Britt will have staff in the house. On the grounds."

"On a Saturday?" Amanda asked. "I've had someone watching the place since eight this morning. No one has gone in. Tommy left at noon. Mac pulled out of the driveway five minutes ago."

"Okay." Sara didn't add that she'd heard on Will's recording that Britt only had staff in twice a week. "What about the cameras inside the house? Mac gets an alert when Britt goes into one of the rooms that has a camera."

"I've instructed Will to make sure Mac turns off his phone. That won't be a difficult ask considering both of them are ostensibly engaging in a crime."

Sara saw another problem. "These people live on gossip. Someone will call Britt as soon as the warrant is served on Chuck Penley's phone."

"The warrant won't be served until you leave, and the first person Chaz Penley will call is his lawyer, who will tell them both to keep their lips tightly zipped." Amanda turned in her seat to face Sara. "May I offer you some advice?"

Sara nodded. She really needed it.

"When Wilbur was a boy, I arranged for my precinct to do Secret Santa for the children's home. Obviously, I drew his name. He was very artistic. I bought him one of those mechanical drawing toys that you shake to erase—the kind with the red frame and white knobs."

"An Etch-A-Sketch."

"Yes, that's it," Amanda said. "I told him that while he was making a drawing, he should think about all the things that were bothering him. The bad foster parents, the kids who bullied him, his despicable aunt and uncle, anything and anyone who'd ever hurt him. And then when he finished the drawing, all he had to do was shake it away. Just make it disappear. Forget about it."

Sara chewed her lip. This story explained a lot about Will.

"My advice for you now is to do the same," Amanda said. "Forget about what this means to you personally. Stop worrying about Faith and Jeremy and Will and what you experienced fifteen years ago. Block out Britt's pettiness and spite. Shake it all away and focus on turning Britt McAllister to our side. She represents our best chance of stopping these men. We need her to tell the truth. Understood?"

Sara nodded. "Understood."

"Open the glove box."

Sara did as she was told. There was only one item inside, a purple velvet Crown Royal bag, but the distinctively shaped bottle of Canadian whiskey was not inside. Sara could tell the moment she picked it up that she was holding a gun. She pulled apart the gold tasseled drawstring and took out a snub-nosed revolver. The weapon was small, a little longer than a dollar bill, and fit perfectly in her hand. Will was the gun expert, but even Sara knew that the revolver was old. It looked like something Columbo would keep in the pocket of his raincoat.

"That was my first backup piece. Smith and Wesson .38 single action Chief's Special," Amanda said. "It's the same model Angie Dickinson carried when she played Pepper Anderson in *Police Woman*."

Sara was learning all kinds of things about Amanda today. She released the cylinder. The gun was loaded. There was no safety. All you had to do was cock back the hammer and pull the trigger.

Sara asked, "Why is it in a Crown Royal bag?"

"Keeps purse lint off the firing pin. When I was coming up, it was considered unladylike for a woman to wear a holster," Amanda said. "Don't take the gun unless you're comfortable using it."

Sara knew how to use it, but she was undecided on the comfortable part. Still, she stuck the revolver back in the drawstring bag and tucked it into her purse. She looked at the clock on Amanda's dashboard.

12:52.

Will was supposed to meet Mac in eight minutes.

She asked, "What do you think the chances are that Mac will actually go to prison?"

"I think they're good. And even if they were not, fighting the state and the federal government is very expensive. He'll lose his reputation, eventually his practice will fold. The house will be gone. The cars. The country club. The best way to hurt rich people is to make them poor."

Sara knew there were far worse things. "Those are white-collar crimes. He'll end up basket weaving at Club Fed."

Amanda said, "Dr. Linton, if you're going to do this, you have to be all in."

Sara looked down at her hands. She had started twisting her ring again. She turned up her palms. She would never forget what it felt like to hold Dani's heart in her hand. The roadmap of arteries had reminded her of a topographical drawing. Right coronary artery. Posterior descending artery. Right marginal artery. Left anterior descending artery. Circumflex artery.

Leighann Park. Merit Barrowe. Dani Cooper.

Mac had in some way been responsible for the beating of their hearts, but instead of feeling awe of his ability to heal them, he had singled them out for destruction.

She told Amanda, "I'm all in."

"Good girl." Amanda started to plug the wires back into the transmitter. "One more thing. Don't tell Will that you're doing this. He needs to focus on Mac Mc-Allister, not you."

"I can't—"

"Let me disabuse you of the notion that your moral compass directs me," Amanda said. "This is my circus. Will is my monkey. Understood?"

Sara didn't know which was more annoying—what Amanda had said or how she'd said it. Still, she managed a pert, "Yes ma'am."

Amanda turned on the switch to activate the transmitter. She checked that the green light was on, then shoved it back into Sara's jacket pocket. They didn't need a command center for one person. The receiver was in the cup holder. It was the size of an old-fashioned walkie-talkie. A cable connected it to a tablet computer. Amanda held a pair of headphones to her ear to make sure everything was working. Sara looked at the tablet screen. The button camera on her jacket showed Amanda's hands holding the tablet. The resolution was sharp, but she would have to keep some distance from Britt in order to capture the woman's face.

"Be careful of the mic," Amanda said. "It's very sensitive, so if you scratch your neck or move the jacket too much, or God forbid you touch it, the audio won't pick up."

Sara put her fingers to her lapel. She could feel the tiny microphone at the end of the wire.

"Yes, that's what you should not do." Amanda put down the headphones. "The transmitter has a range of half a mile. I'll be set up one street over. The park across from the McAllisters' is heavily trafficked. I don't want to risk anyone phoning APD or Britt about a suspicious car. We need a safe word in case you find yourself in trouble."

Sara had looked up the street view of the McAllister estate. If she was in trouble, Amanda would have to maneuver through a major intersection, drive down a winding road, break through the front gate, and traverse the football-field-length driveway. Then she would have to find Sara inside the house, which was probably north of ten thousand square feet.

Sara suggested, "Luck be a Lady? Strangers in the Night? New York, New York?"

"If you're asking for wedding song suggestions, 'Fly Me to the Moon' is the obvious choice." Amanda had easily recognized the Frank Sinatra classics. "The point of a safe word is that it's easily incorporated into conversation so that you don't tip off the person who is causing you to feel unsafe."

"Etch-A-Sketch," Sara said.

Amanda nodded. "Ready when you are."

Sara got out of the car. The cold air made her skin tingle. She'd started to sweat as soon as Amanda had told her to open the glove box. Was Sara really going into Britt McAllister's house with a loaded weapon? She was a doctor. She wasn't an investigator.

She was also the only person who Britt might actually talk to.

Sara got into her BMW and turned on the engine. The clock read 12:56. She kept the button camera pointing away from her phone as she texted Will a thumbs up because of course she had told him she was doing this. They were going to be married next month. She was not going to be the type of wife who lied to her husband.

Will quickly sent back his own thumbs up. She watched the tiny dots dance, then he sent a stopwatch. The countdown had started. He'd gotten Mac to turn off his phone.

Sara let out a slow breath before putting the gear in drive.

Amanda's Lexus followed at a distance as Sara drove deep into Buckhead. The first time Sara had visited Atlanta, there had been a porn theater in the commercial district, but now the Village was covered up with high-end shops and restaurants that charged $20 for a hamburger. She turned onto a side street, and concrete quickly gave way to lush parks, old-growth trees, and sprawling estate lots. Andrews Drive. Habersham. Argonne. Many of the houses dated back to the

First World War. The lavish building hadn't stopped during the Great Depression. The area had spread exponentially over the years and, like every city everywhere, the Black and poor population had been displaced by wealthy, white elites.

Mac and Britt McAllister were certainly all three of those things. Their Georgian Revival brick home was located on several rolling, beautifully landscaped acres. Sara had looked at the satellite images and seen a swimming pool, pool house, tennis court, soccer pitch, guest house, parking for around twenty cars and at least five garage spaces.

She glanced into the rearview mirror again. Amanda was pulling her Lexus to the side of the road. Sara kept driving. She took a left turn on to the McAllisters' street. There were no other cars in sight. A woman and man were pushing a stroller. Another couple walked with a tween toward the park. Sara thought about her conversation with Sloan Bauer in New York. They had joked about people framing rape as a character-building exercise. Sloan had said that she wouldn't have met her husband but for being assaulted. Sara most certainly would not have ended up living on a spectacular estate in Buckhead if she had never been raped, but she was equally certain that she would've experienced the joy of a child growing inside her body.

A text came through to her phone.

Amanda: *Test?*

She wanted to make sure the microphone was trans-mitting.

Sara said, "Scaphoid, lunate, triquetrum, pisiform, trapezium—"

Another text flashed on the screen.

Amanda: *Good.*

Sara guessed she didn't want to hear the rest of the carpal bones. She also guessed that she should stop fucking around and accept that she was about to do this.

She tried not to watch the clock as she continued up the street, but there was no stopping the counting going on in her head. It wouldn't take Amanda seconds to reach her, but minutes. Very long minutes. Then there would be the wrought iron gates. Then the airbag going off in Amanda's Lexus if she managed to bust through.

Then . . . then . . . then . . .

Sara pulled into the mouth of the driveway and stopped beside the intercom. The imposing gates had a cursive M on either side. Sara wouldn't bet against them versus Amanda's Lexus, but hopefully, that battle would never take place. She rolled down her window. She pressed the button to call up to the house. She looked directly at the camera above the intercom. Sara could imagine Britt inside the house staring at Sara's face on the screen and debating whether or not to answer.

Britt finally made her decision. There was a staticky blast of white noise, then she said, "What are you doing here?"

"I need to talk to you."

"Fuck off."

The static was gone. Britt had ended the call.

Sara pressed the button again. Nothing. When she pressed it a third time, she kept her finger on it long enough to make a point.

The static came back. "What?"

"Do you want to keep Tommy out of prison?"

Britt was silent. Sara could hear upbeat music in the background. A few more seconds passed. Then a few more. Britt ended the call again.

Sara gripped the steering wheel. She looked at the gates. She wasn't going to give up. She would climb them if she had to.

Fortunately, she didn't have to. The gates started to swing open.

Sara took another deep breath before pulling forward. She coasted along the meandering driveway. There was a pond. A bridge spanned a white-water creek. Finally, the house came into view. Sara had to admit it was spectacular. The elaborate entry portico was supported by marble Ionic columns that seemed to be holding up the gorgeous tri-partite window on the second floor. The lavish modillions were carved from the same buttery marble. The driveway turned circular at the top of the hill. A fountain with water bubbling out of an urn served as a centerpiece. Box hedges trimmed the crushed stone drive. Sara could hear a leaf blower in the distance, the unofficial bird of Atlanta.

Britt was standing at the open front door when Sara got out of the car. She was dressed in workout clothes, a pair of lilac joggers and a matching tank top accessorized with a thick gold necklace, tennis bracelet, and her rock of an engagement ring. Her arms were crossed. A fine sheen of sweat was on her tanned skin. That explained the upbeat music. There had to be a full gym in the house. Britt was apparently focusing on her body with the same drive she had exhibited when she'd focused on medicine. Her biceps were well-defined. The muscles along her shoulders were honed from hours on the tennis court.

"What do you mean about Tommy going to prison?" Britt demanded. "Is this some kind of sick joke?"

Sara decided to come out swinging. "Did you think

I wouldn't figure out that the photos you showed Dani Cooper's parents came from the video Tommy made?"

Britt put her hands on her hips. "I don't know what you're talking about."

Sara started to climb the stairs.

"What are you doing?"

"I'm not having this discussion on your front porch."

"Does this look like a fucking *porch* to you?" Britt indicated the columns. "Philip Trammel Shutze hand-selected this marble at a quarry in Italy."

"Golly, how impressive." Sara looked up at her, waiting.

Britt turned on her heel and stomped into the house.

Sara brushed her fingers along one of the marble columns as she walked inside. The foyer wasn't as impressive as the exterior would suggest. Two separate hallways led to the left and right wings. A modest staircase curved up to the second floor. The chandelier was modern, too small for the space. The rug was white. The walls were white. The hardwood floors were stained white. The art on the walls showed charcoal sketches of women's bodies on bright white paper. It was like being trapped in a 1920s sanatorium.

Sara asked, "Did you decorate the place yourself?"

"This isn't a social visit," Britt said. "What video are you talking about?"

"The one Tommy filmed while he was raping Dani Cooper."

Britt's expression gave away nothing. "Can you see Tommy's face? Any identifying marks?"

Sara knew better than to lie. Britt had seen at least parts of the video. "The metadata will show where it was filmed, who took it, what date, the time—everything."

Britt's shoulder jerked up in a shrug. "Metadata can be faked. Any computer expert will testify to that."

Sara could tell Britt was only mildly worried. She had too much money to be truly afraid.

Sara asked, "Why did you start this? In the bathroom at the courthouse. Why?"

"I didn't start anything." Britt had lowered her voice. "What are you trying to accomplish, Sara? You can't have children of your own so you're trying to take away my son?"

The accusation wasn't as hurtful as it had been the first time. What Sara noticed was the fact that Britt kept saying the same thing. Maybe she had lost her edge. Fifteen years ago, her cruelty tended more toward death by a thousand insults.

"Well?" Britt demanded.

Sara duplicated her shrug. "You're right. I can't have children. But I'm not the one who's taking Tommy away from you. Mac's doing that right under your nose."

"Bullshit," Britt said. "You've always been jealous of Mac. You can't stand the fact that he lives his life on his own terms."

"When someone says they're living their life on their own terms, someone else is always paying the price for it."

Britt huffed a laugh. "Saint Sara and her country-girl homilies."

"Here's one from the GBI," Sara told her. "What do we think? What do we know? What can we prove?"

"And?"

Sara laid it out for her. "We know that Mac is part of a group of men who are raping women. We know it's decentralized—every person has their own assignment. We know the victims are stalked. They're sent increasingly threatening texts. They're filmed. Their homes are searched. Then, when the time is right, they're drugged. Abducted. Raped."

Britt's face had turned ashen, but she had trained as an obstetrician. She still had a coolness under pressure. "Where does this theory fall? Think? Know? Prove?"

"We know it. We need help proving it. And you need help saving Tommy from prison."

"He's not in the Dani video."

"How much of it did you watch?"

Britt looked away. "Tommy is innocent. You can't prove anything."

"The thing I've learned about juries in criminal trials is that a lot of times, they don't give a shit about proof. They don't care about the science or the experts. They care about gut feeling and watching that video will make them sick."

"The judge won't allow it into evidence."

"The judge will allow it because the video is the entire case." Sara didn't give her time to regroup. "How do you think the GBI knows about the video in the first place?"

Britt's surprised expression said that she hadn't considered the question until now.

"Tommy sent it to someone. That someone turned on Tommy. Even having the video in their possession is a crime." Sara figured now was the time to lie. "The GBI offered them a deal to testify against Tommy. The paperwork was signed this morning. Tommy will be in jail by the end of the day."

Britt's hand went to her neck. The skin had flushed. "Who?"

"You'll find out when the indictment is unsealed."

Britt stroked her neck. She was thinking, trying to see all the angles. Mac was the one who usually took care of things. She was out of her depth.

Still, she told Sara, "This way."

Sara followed her down the long hallway leading to the right side of the house. There was a closet, a powder room, a spacious library with a white leather chesterfield and recliner. Nothing personal was to be seen. No family photos or knickknacks. No diplomas or awards. The extreme level of tidiness was unsettling. There wasn't a speck of dirt or dust to be seen.

Britt walked through the living room with its giant TV and overstuffed couches and chairs. The kitchen had white cabinets and Calacatta gold marble countertops. The faucets were gold. So was the cabinet hardware. A white leather banquette was built into a nook. A back hallway led to what looked like the wing that held the primary suite. Sara could see a white bench at the end of the bed. The linens were white. The walls were white. The carpet was white.

In fact, everything she had seen of the house was either white or gold except the books in the library, the bowl of fruit on the kitchen island and the green box of Puffs tissues beside it. Even the pool decking was white, which Sara could see through the large windows that overlooked the backyard. Sunlight poured in, making everything seem antiseptically clean. The bright light was probably very useful for the hidden cameras that captured the open concept living space.

Will had described the rooms he'd seen on Mac's phone. The spacious kitchen. The monochromatic living room. The primary bedroom with its four-poster bed. The bathroom with two water closets and a giant walk-in shower.

As far as Sara knew, there was no camera in the foyer. No cameras in the long hallways off the foyer. Britt had led her back to two of the four rooms that Mac could monitor.

Was she putting on a show? Calling for help? Did she expect an alert on Mac's phone would send him rushing home to save her?

"We can sit here." Britt moved her leather tennis bag out of one of the eight captain's chairs at the sprawling center island. She tossed the bag onto the floor. The racket stuck out like the rudder on a ship. "I'm too sweaty for the couch."

Sara took the chair at the opposite end of the island so that the button camera would capture Britt's face. She dropped her purse on the counter. The heavy thud reminded her that Amanda's revolver was inside. She glanced down the back hallway to the bedroom. The light was on in the closet, casting a triangle of white across the end of the hall. Sara felt an overwhelming sense of unease. She hoped Amanda was right that Britt was the only person in the house.

Britt asked, "How can I help Tommy? What would that look like?"

Sara remembered what Amanda had told her about appearing to be on Britt's side. She also remembered something Faith had told her: the best way to keep a suspect from calling a lawyer was to tell them to call a lawyer.

She told Britt, "First, you should talk to a lawyer. Do you have your own money? Your own checking account?"

"Why?"

"Because you want the lawyer to work for you. Not for Mac."

"Okay." Britt nodded. "Then what?"

"The lawyer will reach out to the GBI to make a deal. You can trade Tommy's life for Mac's." Sara added, "But you have to be honest. And it has to be the kind of information that will send Mac to prison."

"What if Mac doesn't have anything to do with it?"

Sara would've laughed under any other circumstance. After everything that had happened, Britt was still trying to protect him. "The GBI knows that Mac is involved."

"How do they know that?"

Sara had nothing to lose. "All the women who were raped were Mac's patients."

"That's ludicrous. He operates on children."

"What I'm about to tell you falls under things the GBI can prove," Sara said. "All of the victims were verified as Mac's patients. He treated them. He helped save their lives. Then he waited for them to grow up and he raped them."

Britt looked away. Finally, something had broken through her hard exterior. There was a sound from her throat as she tried to swallow. Tears wept from her eyes. She reached for a tissue from the box. Her head was shaking. She didn't want to believe it.

Sara told her, "Merit Barrowe saw Mac during his residency. Mac was doing his fellowship when he assisted on surgeries performed on Leighann Park and Dani Cooper. The GBI will get the names of every patient he ever touched and cross-reference them with reported assaults. It's just a matter of time before that list grows."

Britt took another tissue out of the box. "What if Mac agrees to testify?"

"That's not how it works," Sara said. "You don't trade down. You always trade up. Mac is the ringleader."

"You're wrong," she said. "Mac isn't at the top. It's Mason. Mason is in charge."

Sara was almost too surprised to respond. If not for

the chat transcripts, she might've actually believed what Britt was saying. "How do you know it's Mason?"

"I had a fling with him a few years ago. You know how he likes to brag. He told me everything. How it started. What they were doing. I can testify against him. I'll provide dates, names, details."

Sara didn't doubt the affair, but the man in charge was tight-lipped and cunning. Mason was neither of those things. And she had not forgotten where they were sitting. Britt had brought Sara into the kitchen because she had wanted Mac to hear what she was saying. That way, they could keep their stories straight.

Sara played along, asking, "When did it start?"

Britt didn't answer. She reached into the fruit bowl and pulled out an Albuterol inhaler. Mac had developed adult-onset asthma during his residency. Sara had watched him take a puff off his inhaler countless times. Now she watched Britt turn it end over end on the counter the same way Sara twisted her ring when she needed to feel a connection to Will.

Britt had been tortured by Mac. Cowed by him. Watched him poison her own son. But unbelievably, she was still searching for ways to protect him.

Sara gave her another moment before repeating, "When did it start?"

"With Merit Barrowe." Britt sniffed. Her tears were

gone. "That's why I gave you her name in the steam room. I knew you'd look into her case. I had hoped that it would lead you to Mason."

Merit Barrowe had not been the first victim. Sara knew from the chat transcripts that there had been at least one previous assault. They had all panicked because they'd almost been caught.

"Okay," Sara said. "How did it start?"

Britt held the inhaler in her hand. "At first, they all thought it was a game. Following girls, scaring them. Mason wanted to take it to the next level. He raped one of the targets. The others found out, but they didn't do anything about it. They were angry that they didn't get to see it."

Sara noted her use of the word target. That's what 007 had called the victims in the chat group. "What happened next?"

"Mason decided that they needed to share the risk." Britt held tight to the inhaler. "He said they should rotate in like specialists in the ER. Each man would work a different specialty. The system provided them with deniability. If one got caught texting a girl, he couldn't be connected to the one who was following her. That kind of thing."

Sara chewed her lip. Another giant lie. In the chats, 006 had made the suggestion that they should rotate like specialists in the ER. 002 had taunted him—*the mighty trauma surgeon speaks*. Cam Carmichael had been the only trauma surgeon in the group.

She asked Britt, "What about Cam?"

"Cam was pathetic. He drank too much. He talked too much." Britt started turning the inhaler again. The ball bearing inside raked against the metal. "Cam liked texting the girls. He thought he was writing them love letters. He called himself a romantic. The idiot truly believed that he was going to marry Sloan Bauer some day when it was clear to everyone that she couldn't stand to be in the same room with him."

That part at least sounded like the truth. "Then Cam saw Merit at Grady and realized what they were doing was wrong?"

"If you believe his story," Britt said. "Mason had to pay off Cam so that he would leave town. He worked through an intermediary, one of the hangers-on. A man called John Trethewey."

Another demonstrable lie. Also proof that Britt knew a hell of a lot more than they'd initially thought. "John, the orthopod?"

"Cam blabbed to him about what was going on. The only thing that could shut his mouth was a Glock."

"That's all it took to make Cam go away—money?"

"He'd gotten a DUI," Britt said. "There was a detective Mason knew from the ER who would take care of that kind of thing. They all used him at some point. Except for Mac. He wasn't involved in anything to do with the police."

Sara tried to bend her more toward the truth. "So Mason raped the women, but Chaz, Richie, Royce, Bing, Cam and Mac did all of the footwork? Following the girls. Texting them. Breaking into their houses. Stalking them. Recording them."

"At first, they all took turns at the different tasks, but they found their niches. The way it ended up was, Mason primarily did the deed," Britt said, which was a coward's way of saying rape. "Mac never rotated. He never broke into a house or recorded anyone. He followed them sometimes. As a joke. He was having fun. That was all it was for him, a little fun."

Sara doubted any of the women who were being followed thought it was fun. "And?"

"Richie liked recording them. Through their windows or in their cars or at a coffee shop." Britt didn't seem to realize she was offering extensive knowledge of the content of the videos. "I'm sure you know why Richie was fired from the hospital. He's a disgusting pervert."

They were all disgusting. "What about Bing and Royce?"

"Bing was never involved. Royce dropped out early on. He never forgave Mason for screwing Blythe behind his back, so he disappeared from the gang." Britt shrugged, like she was talking about losing someone from her tennis team. "But Chaz—Chaz loved it. He was always egging Ma-Mason on. You know how Mason loves attention. He bragged about it all the time. It was sickening to hear him."

Sara ignored the slip. Britt had almost said Mac instead of Mason because that was who she was talking about. Her husband was the Master. He was the one who chose the targets. He was the one who had raped dozens of women.

She asked, "Who tried to bring in Tommy?"

Britt placed the inhaler upright on the counter. She looked at Sara. "Mason."

"What about Chuck?"

"Penley?" Britt was caught off guard. Her eyes scanned Sara's face. She was thinking back through the conversation, trying to see where the question had come from.

Sara told her, "There's a lot that the GBI knows, Britt. That's how they trick you. They ask questions that they already know the answer to."

"Are you trying to trick me up?"

"I'm trying to help you."

Britt gave a short, sharp laugh. She picked up the inhaler again. "What else do you want to know? Or confirm?"

Sara asked, "What happened to Dani?"

Britt looked up at the ceiling. She had kept it together up until now. She took a deep breath, then slowly let it go. Then she repeated the process.

Sara recognized the coping mechanism. Talking about Dani could mean possibly implicating Tommy. Britt was going to be even more careful going forward.

"The drugs regimen is complicated and—" Britt caught herself. "You have to administer it at the proper times."

Sara felt like she should be making a list of all the ways Britt kept implicating herself. She asked, "Rohypnol and Ketamine?"

Britt gave her a wary look of respect. "Mason was called in to fix it."

Sara noted she hadn't said who had called for help. "Fix what?"

"There was an under correction. The concern was depressed respiration. She woke up. There was a struggle. Things turned physical. They attempted to subdue her. Dani managed to slip away. She got into the car."

"Tommy's car."

Britt didn't acknowledge the clarification. "She

drove to the hospital. She broadsided the ambulance. And then, Saint Sara to the rescue."

Sara ignored the dig, concentrating instead on the careful language Britt was using—*under correction, concern, subdue.* There was an easier way to describe what had happened. "Tommy got worried when Dani's breathing turned shallow. He backed off the drug cocktail. Dani woke up. Tommy called for help. Dani managed to fight them off. Someone beat her with a blunt object. She still managed to get away."

Britt pursed her lips. "I don't know the details. I only heard after the fact."

"Where was Dani being held?"

Britt shook her head. "I have no idea."

Sara knew exactly where Tommy had taken Dani. This mausoleum with its white walls and white furniture. There would be a stained sheepskin rug somewhere. A digital camera. A tripod. Professional lighting. This was where Mac had brought his victims. This was where Tommy had learned to be the man he was today.

And Britt had lived under this same roof while it was happening.

"Is this enough for the GBI to make a deal?" Britt asked. "I've told you everything I know about Mason.

Everything they were doing. Tommy and Mac were on the periphery at best. Mason is the leader. He's the one who should go to prison."

Sara had worried from the beginning that trying to get the truth out of Britt McAllister would be a waste of time. Britt had been given so many opportunities to extricate herself from this madness. Each time, she had retreated back into the safety of her toxic life. She was as addicted to Mac's sadism as she was addicted to her little blue pills.

Sara said, "You were such a good doctor."

Britt looked taken aback by the compliment.

"I know we never got along, but I never doubted that you cared for your patients. You were so kind to them. It's the one thing that kept me from hating you."

Britt huffed a laugh. "Thanks a lot."

"It's not too late," Sara said. "It would be hard, but you could go back into medicine. You could volunteer, or travel, or work with children, or get your PhD, or help other women. You could show Tommy that his mother deserves to be respected."

Britt looked perplexed. "What the hell are you going on about?"

"Why do you always protect him?" Sara asked. "Even when Mac was a lowly intern, you treated him like a god. Is his ego really that fragile? Would his dick fall off if he had to admit that he was wrong?"

"You don't understand," Britt said. "Your life is so small compared to mine."

Sara knew where this was going. "Because I'm not a mother?"

"Yes." Britt's answer was that simple. "Only a mother would understand."

"Try me."

"I can't abandon my child. Mac already has too much influence over his life. Tommy worships him." Her voice was growing harder. "If I left Mac, Tommy would be lost forever. And Mac would find a newer, younger model to replace me. All of our friends would choose Mac and his plaything. I would end up being a dried-up old bitch living alone, and Mac would still be on top of the fucking world."

"That doesn't sound like love. That sounds like you can't let Mac win."

"There's no difference," Britt said. "We've been together twenty-two years. All we have left is competition. How can I hurt him? How can he hurt me?"

Sara knew how Mac hurt Britt. "He abuses you."

Britt looked stunned. She'd thought it was a secret.

"People saw the bruises even as far back as Grady," Sara told her. "You've got a GPS tracker on your keys, on your car. Mac follows your every move. You can't breathe without him knowing."

"He doesn't know everything." Britt's eyebrow was raised. She was talking about what she'd told Sara over the last few days, but she was still so afraid of Mac that she couldn't say the words in view of his cameras. "You are uniquely qualified to understand how delicate Mac's work is. Children and their parents are relying on him. No one else can do what Mac does. The stress can be unbearable. If he distracts himself with a game or two, then that's nothing compared to what he gives the world. I'll gladly sacrifice myself for him."

"A lot of people can do what Mac does," Sara told her. "And even if that wasn't true, that doesn't give him a right to abuse you."

"It's not abuse. It's a compulsion," Britt said. "Everything Mac does, every time he hurts me, I know what he's really saying is that he still sees me. Do you know how many forty-seven-year-old women can say that about their husbands? Mac has always seen me. He loves me."

Sara shook her head. She had no words for this kind of thinking.

"Here." Britt indicated her leather tennis bag. "This set him back ten grand."

Sara watched her pull out the racket and casually

throw it onto the counter. The Chanel logo was prominent on the grip.

"Six grand, and I use it for warm-ups." Britt pointed out her jewelry. "This necklace cost eighteen grand. The bracelet was twenty. I bought myself a new engagement ring. Four carats. Ninety grand. The band cost thirty."

"So Mac tortures you, but that's all right because you buy yourself expensive shit that no one cares about?"

"Everyone cares about it, Sara. That's what you've never understood. You've got that cheap ring on your finger and you think it makes you special, but you'll find out soon enough. You're not getting any younger. You can't reel him back in with a tight snatch and high tits." Britt leaned across the counter. "How you get their attention, how you keep it, that's the game. Marriage is a blood sport. Anyone who claims otherwise is lying."

Sara knew that she was wrong. Her first marriage hadn't been that way. Her relationship with Will was not that way. "You're choosing to make it a blood sport."

"Do you know how many twenty-year-old sluts are out there waiting to replace me? All they have to do is bat their eyelashes and I'm gone. No matter how many meals I skip, or how much I work out, or how many fucking needles are stuck in my face, I can't compete with youth. It's not a level playing field."

"Then don't compete."

Britt's laugh was as hard as her face. "You stupid bitch. You really think it's that easy? Men can do whatever they want. They treat women like tampons. We soak up their rage and abuse, and when we get too soiled by their slime, they change us out for a brand-new one."

"You're only talking about a certain type of man."

"It's all of them. They take and take and give you nothing." Britt held up the inhaler. "Do you know how many goddamn times I've told Mac to stop leaving his stupid fucking Albuterol lying around? It's the one thing I've asked him to do—the one thing—and he can't fucking do it."

Sara watched Britt yank open one of the drawers. She threw the inhaler in with the junk. Pens, loose change, packs of chewing gum and hard candies.

Britt said, "If there's such a thing as a God, he'll have an asthma attack in his car and drive head-first into a fucking bus."

Sara looked at the closed drawer. Another piece of the puzzle had slipped into place. As a pediatrician, she had written her share of Albuterol scripts. The medication caused a dry mouth and left a chalky aftertaste. She always told her patients to chew sugarless gum or suck on hard candies. Because of this, their breath tended to have a cloyingly sweet smell.

Merit Barrowe had told Cam that the man who'd raped her had breath that smelled sweet, like cough medicine.

Leighann Park had told Faith that the man who'd raped her had breath that smelled sweet, like cherry Mountain Dew.

And yet, like everything else Britt had given away, there was nothing they could do with the information. Thinking and knowing were very different from proving.

"This conversation has been a waste of my time," Britt said. "Tommy had nothing to do with that video. It's obviously a Deep Fake. Someone is trying to frame him. For all I know, it could be you. I'd be happy to swear out a statement about how you've always resented Mac."

Sara gave a surprised laugh. "You spent the last twenty minutes implicating yourself in all kinds of criminal activity. You knew when the gang started. You knew the drug regimen, the content of the stalking videos. You knew how they operated. You knew about Dani. You knew she was drugged and beaten. You knew about—"

"Good luck on the witness stand. Our lawyer won't go so easy on you the next time." Britt yanked her tennis bag off the floor. "You're just a jealous, barren cunt."

Sara felt the sudden threat of tears. She hated that Britt could still hurt her.

"You can leave now." Britt started unzipping pockets on the bag. She pulled out a tennis schedule. "I've got to generate the roster for next month. Scheduling always falls to me."

Sara felt the hairs on the back of her neck stand up. The words sounded eerily familiar.

Britt noticed the change. "What?"

Sara was speechless. Something was wrong. She felt shaky and sick.

"For fucksakes." Britt slapped the schedule down on the counter. "Are we seriously doing this again?"

Sara's breath caught. She had to force herself to exhale. The same phrase had appeared so many times in the chat transcripts. 007 would make a snide or sexist comment, then 002 would respond—*are we seriously doing this again?*

Sara pushed out another breath so that she could speak. "You told me that Bing wasn't involved in the group."

Britt looked up from the schedule. "And?"

Seven members of the group. Seven numbers in the chat transcripts. Faith had posed the question earlier: Who would have the balls to trash-talk Mac Fucking McAllister?

His wife.

"It was you," Sara said. "You're 002 in the chat group."

Britt's nostrils flared. She adjusted the schedule on the counter. "You're not making any sense."

"We found the chat website. You helped work out the rules to keep them all safe," Sara said. "That's how you keep Mac's attention. You've spent the last sixteen years helping him rape other women."

The muscles in Britt's throat were strained. "I don't know anything about a website."

"Yes, you do," Sara said. "You posted as 002. Cam posted as 006. Mason was 004. He knew what was happening, but he didn't care. Mac was 007. He's the Master. He picks the targets. You make the roster. You hand out the assignments. You make the rules. And this house, this lunatic asylum, is where Mac films himself raping his former patients."

Britt stood perfectly still. The only thing that gave her away was the red flush working its way up from her chest. "I told you to leave."

"Or what?" Sara asked. "You'll call the police?"

Britt's hand rested on the counter. "You don't—you don't understand."

"Because I'm not a mother?" Sara asked. "You keep using that word like I don't know exactly who you are. Mac isn't the only sadist in this house. You just as good as raped those women. Tommy wouldn't be the way he is if you weren't such a shitty mother."

Britt's icy exterior started to crack. Tears flooded her eyes. Her lips were trembling.

Then she grabbed the tennis racket and swung around.

"Jesus!" Sara threw up her hands to block the blow. The edge of the racket sliced into her left wrist. She heard a bone crack, but she was too stunned to feel the pain.

Britt started to backhand the racket.

Sara scrambled for her purse, fumbling with her right hand. She didn't have time to find the purple velvet bag. She used the purse as a shield. The racket glanced off the bottom. Sara's head whipped back. Her nose splintered. The strap was wrenched from her hand. The contents dumped out. The gun fell from the drawstring bag, clanging against the hardwood floor.

The world stopped.

Neither one of them moved.

Except Britt wasn't looking at the revolver. Her attention was firmly on the slim black box that had fallen out of Sara's jacket pocket. The wires were still connected to the jacks. The green light was on.

"What—" Britt was panting so hard she could barely speak. "What is that?"

Sara was panting, too. Her wrist was throbbing. She couldn't move her fingers. There was no way she could make it to the gun. In the distance, she heard the wail of a police siren. Amanda was one street over. Then an intersection. Then another road. Then a gate. Then the driveway. Then the house.

Sara said, "It's a transmitter. The police have been watching you the whole time. The wire goes to the camera inside this button."

Britt's eyes followed Sara's finger to the button.

"Do you hear the siren?" Air wheezed through Sara's broken nose. She cradled her broken wrist. Distal radial fracture. The initial shock had given way to almost incapacitating pain. "They'll be here soon."

Britt slowly lowered the tennis racket. She didn't look at Sara. She looked directly into the button camera. "It was me. I'm the one who beat Dani. She was trying to get away. I chased her into the garage, and I beat her. I assumed she was dead. I left her there."

Sara's heart shuddered at the confession.

"The tennis racket is still in the garage. The Babolat

Pure Aero Plus in lime green. I tried to clean it, but her blood is caked into the grooves. My DNA is on the wrap. It was me."

Sara only cared about the tennis racket that Britt was still holding. The woman was volatile, out of options. The siren on Amanda's car was too far away. So was the gun on the floor.

"Mac didn't hurt any of them," Britt told the camera. "They were just a little fun, something to burn off stress. The girls didn't even know what was happening. Most of them never complained, or if they did, they took the money. It was good money. They didn't go to the police. They were fine afterward. They were all fine."

Sara bit her tongue. None of them had been fine.

"I didn't just set the rules," Britt said. "I started the website. I assigned the jobs. I knew what they liked, what they were best suited for. They brought the girls here because I told them to. I filmed them. I made all the videos. They're stored on the server in the basement. Everything was orchestrated by me. I'm to blame. I accept full responsibility."

The siren was drawing closer.

Britt heard it too. She looked down at the tennis racket. She didn't swing it again. She placed it back on the counter.

Then she leaned down and picked up the gun.

"Britt!" Sara pushed herself out of the chair.

The effort was unnecessary. Britt didn't aim the gun at Sara.

She pressed the muzzle to the side of her own head.

"This confession is my dying declaration. I swear it's true." Britt was still speaking to the camera. "Tommy, Mac, I love you."

"Put down the gun," Sara said. "Please."

"I don't want my boys to see this." Britt took a step back. Then another. She was going into the bedroom hallway. Away from Sara's camera. Away from Mac's. "Just let me go, Sara. Let me go."

Sara wasn't going to let her go. Britt was going to be held responsible for her crimes. Sara had made a promise to Dani. She had sworn on the girl's heart. The Coopers deserved justice. Leighann Park. Merit Barrowe's family. They all deserved some kind of justice. Sara stumbled into the hallway. Nausea washed over her from the pain. Her nose pulsed. Her left hand was completely numb. She clutched her wrist close to her body.

Britt disappeared into the closet.

Sara went after her. She found Britt standing in the center of the room. The gun was still jammed against the side of her head. The closet was painted bright pink, like a teenage girl's. A crystal chandelier hung from the ceiling. The cabinetry was custom-built. Hundreds of thousands of dollars' worth of shoes and clothes filled every nook and cubby.

Except for one area.

There was an anteroom off the closet. The pocket doors were open. Black walls. Black floors. A filthy sheepskin rug. A digital camera. A tripod. Professional lighting.

"This is where it happens." Britt stood in front of a three-paneled mirror. Her hand started to shake. The muzzle tapped against her skull. "Mac likes for me to watch. He wants me to feel included."

A loud boom shook the air. Amanda had broken through the front gate. The siren wailed as she raced up the driveway.

"We share—" Britt gulped. "We share this. It's something he only does with me."

Sara did not look at Britt, or the black room, or the stained rug. She was looking at the rows of shoes. None of them were Louboutins or Jimmy Choos. There were sneakers, loafers, flip-flops. No pairs, just the left shoe. The lights in the ceiling were trained down like a store display. Almost fifty in all. Sara recognized three from the photos on Faith's crazy wall.

One Air Jordan Flight 23.

One Stella McCartney platform sandal.

One Marc Jacobs velvet lace-up.

"My trophies." Britt sounded proud, happy to finally have everything out in the open. "I took them. I did this. All of this. He may have other women, but I'm the one Mac brings them home to. He knows that I'll protect him. I have always protected him."

Sara couldn't process what she was hearing. Her only goal was to keep Britt from pulling the trigger. "Britt, put down the gun. Tommy still needs you."

"Don't try to save me, Saint Sara. Not after everything I've done to you."

"It doesn't matter. We'll work it out."

"But you haven't worked it out, have you?"

"No." Sara ignored the teasing lilt in her voice. "I haven't worked it out. Why don't you tell me?"

"I'm the reason Jack Allen Wright raped you."

The siren disappeared.

Sara's vision telescoped.

A kind of numbness washed through her body. Her senses started to dull. All she could hear was the soft sound of Britt's voice.

"I knew you were getting the fellowship. I couldn't let you take it from Mac."

Sara felt blood sliding down her throat.

"Jack was obsessed with you. I saw him taking pictures, following you around, stealing things from your purse, collecting strands of your hair. It's so easy to talk a man into doing the violent things he wants to do."

Sara swallowed down the blood.

"I told Jack that you thought you were better than him. That you were fucking every man in the hospital except for him. It didn't take much to push him that night. I left the handcuffs in his locker. I put the Ipecac in your soda to make you sick. I closed off the staff bathroom. I taped off the other stalls. I told Jack exactly where you would be, down to the window of time. It was like winding up a toy and pushing it in the right direction. He took care of the rest."

Sara blinked, and she was back in the bathroom. Wrists cuffed to the rails. Mouth taped. The sharp tinge of cleaning products. The smell of her own urine. Blood dripping from her side, life threatening to slip away, yet all she could think about was the lingering taste from his filthy mouth when he had forced open her jaw to kiss her.

"It was brilliant." Britt's smile didn't falter. "More than I could've ever imagined. I mean, he stabbed you. He actually stabbed you."

Tears blurred Sara's vision.

"You think I'm some pathetic housewife?" Britt let the gun rest on her shoulder. "I got Jack to rape you. I got Edgerton to make the Barrowe case go away. I made the medical examiner change his report. I let Mac have his fun. I protected him. I made sure he got the fellowship. I built us this life—this magnificent life. I raised our beautiful boy. I am incredible."

Sara felt her knees wanting to give. The weight was too much to bear.

"You almost stayed after it happened," Britt said. "But then you had your ectopic pregnancy, and I thought, what a gift. What a fucking gift. She'll never come back from that. Never. And I was right."

Sara's teeth had started to chatter. The pain was crushing. Everything she had lost. The fellowship. Her carefully planned future. Her sense of safety. Her ability to completely trust, to unreservedly love. Her children—two girls. Tessa would have three. They would raise their kids together and live close by and none of that had happened because of Britt McAllister.

"How—" Sara's throat threatened to close. "How could you be so cruel?"

Britt shrugged. "That's me."

She pressed the revolver to her head. Her finger pulled on the trigger.

Nothing happened.

Not even a click.

"Sara!" Amanda was inside the house. She was running down the hall. Her footsteps echoed like drumbeats. She had gone in the wrong direction. "Sara!"

Britt was looking down at the revolver, trying to figure out why it hadn't fired.

Sara reached up to the microphone in her lapel. She pinched the wire to mute the sound. "Pull back the hammer with your thumb."

Britt pulled back the hammer.

She put the gun to her head.

This time, it worked.

One Week Later

Will stood at his kitchen sink drying dishes while Faith washed. The weather had turned warm. The barbecue grill was smoking off the last bits of mesquite. He stared out the window at Sara and her sister. They were sitting at the outdoor table, each with a child in her lap. Tessa was holding Isabelle. Sara held onto Emma. Her nose had been broken and her arm was in a cast, but Sara was somehow managing to blow bubbles through a wand. The girls kept reaching out their tiny hands to pop them. Betty caught the ones they missed. Sara's greyhounds were splayed out in the grass, but they were too lazy to do anything but watch.

He had never held a cookout at his house before. Actually, he had never had this many people over. Jeremy, Aiden, Sara's mother and father, her extremely eccentric aunt, had all come and gone. Faith, Tessa, and their kids were the only stragglers. Which was nice, but also a reminder of why Will had never had this many people over. He didn't need a doctor to tell him he was an introvert. Though a doctor seemed delighted to keep pointing it out.

"Hey," Faith said. "Pay attention. I'm running out of space."

Will picked up a stack of forks and placed them on a paper towel. Before Sara had come into his life, he'd only had two bowls, two plates, two forks, two knives, and two spoons. She had sneaked in more items over the last year. The Lintons had a lot of thoughts about how to properly dine. Her father used a couple of forks at every meal. Her sister rolled through paper towels like a baller. Her mother had expressed a moral offense to disposable cutlery and plates.

Not that Will was complaining. They were all rallying around Sara while she healed. For the first couple of days, none of them would leave her side. It wasn't the first time he'd noticed that a lot of Sara's strength came from her family.

Faith bumped his shoulder. "How's Sara doing?"

He bumped her back. "Ask her."

"I did." Faith bumped him again. "She told me she was trying to deal with it. I can't imagine how. That video of Britt was brutal. What she told Sara about Jack

Allen Wright—I'm not sure I could ever come back from that."

Will started drying another plate.

"It's weird how the sound cut out at the end."

He handed back the plate. "You missed a spot."

Faith used her thumbnail to scrape away a streak of ketchup. "Are you mad at Amanda for letting Sara go to Britt's in the first place?"

"It was Sara's decision," Will said. "You can't Monday-morning quarterback what happened. Amanda would've never let Sara near that house if she'd known what Britt was capable of. I'm just glad it worked out the way it did."

"You're annoyingly diplomatic today." Faith started on another plate. "I'm not glad about how part of it worked out. I'm sick and tired of seeing pictures of Britt's Botoxed face every-fucking-where. You'd think she was a dead celebrity."

Will shared the sentiment. For the first time in his adult life, he had stopped turning on the TV in the morning. He wasn't going online unless he absolutely had to.

"All that anybody cares about is Britt-the-crazy-bitch," Faith said. "They don't care that almost fifty women were raped over sixteen years."

"What about the list?" Will asked. APD had found

a spreadsheet on Britt's laptop that listed all of the targets, but she had only used initials. "Have they tracked down any of the victims?"

"It's tricky because of patient privacy. The doctors' offices and hospitals are resisting the subpoenas. Some of the women have come forward on their own, but they don't want to go on record. They're terrified of their names leaking out, getting death threats, being hounded by reporters. Meanwhile, the press doesn't give a shit about Dani Cooper's parents or Leighann Park. Martin Barrowe might as well not exist. It's all Britt, all the time. No woman ever gets celebrated like a bad woman."

Will had seen this for himself. Britt McAllister was on the front page of every website and newspaper. She'd been turned into several memes, mostly with a tennis racket. Her former friends at the country club were giving exclusive interviews. *Dateline* and *48 Hours* had both rushed out episodes. Hulu was filming a documentary. Some other streamer was working on a biopic. So was HBO.

Britt had finally found a way to overshadow the men in her life.

Fortunately, the legal system didn't run on clickbait and views. The recording Sara had made put everything in context, but the final nail in the coffin was the science.

Dani and Leighann's DNA on the sheepskin rug matched back to Mac and Tommy McAllister. Chaz Penley's DNA was on the walls of the black room. Richie Dougal's DNA was on the floor of the closet. As if that wasn't enough, there was a server in the basement that contained over thirty videos. It was jacked into the home theater system. The Club hadn't been content to leave it at terrorizing women. They had critiqued their methods afterward. Sara had compared it to the morbidity and mortality reviews they'd sat through during their residencies.

"You know what I'm also pissed off about?" Faith had washed all the plates. She started on the ice cream bowls. "APD is getting all the credit for breaking the case. The chief's up at the podium like a rock star. Leo Donnelly's standing behind him at every press conference. We worked our asses off. We could've been fired. Half the paint got stripped off my kitchen cabinets. Jeremy risked his neck at the bar. Sara was attacked by a maniac. The GBI should be taking the victory lap."

Will was pissed, too, but that was the deal Amanda had made with the state attorney general's office and the Fulton County district attorney. "At least Sara's name is being kept out of it."

"We're all being kept out of it."

Will glanced down at her. "What have you found out?"

"You think APD tells me anything?" Even Faith couldn't lie that well. She still had her sources. "They've got nothing on Royce Ellison. He was smart to back out when he did. Chuck Penley spilled his guts in return for probation. He claims he had nothing to do with Dani. He found out after the fact, couldn't believe what he was seeing in the video, there was nothing he could do, bullshit-bullshit-bullshit."

"Did Chuck say what happened to Dani?"

"Tommy got drunk, argued with Dani, and decided that he was going to choose his own target from the list. Mac and Britt were out for the night. Tommy botched up the drugs. He called them in a panic. His parents came home and fixed his problem. Sort of." Faith shrugged. "Britt wasn't lying about the DNA on the tennis racket. She's the one who beat Dani. But felony murder makes them all culpable. Mac and Tommy are trying to cut a deal to avoid the death penalty. Either way, they'll probably both die in prison."

Will started to put up the bowls. Sara was right. He

really needed more counter space. "Was it Mac who recruited Tommy into the Club?"

"Chuck's real hazy on the particulars. He says Tommy discovered the rape videos by accident when he was in middle school." Faith shrugged again. "Who knows what happened next, but Tommy obviously liked what he saw. Maybe Chuck, too. I'd bet you real money this won't be the last time that jerkwad will be talking to the cops."

Will wasn't going to take that bet. "What about Richie Dougal?"

"You won't be surprised to learn that Dr. I-Like-to-Watch developed a case of mouth diarrhea. Traded info on what happened to Leighann so he gets out in ten years. Richie was the one who filmed her. Britt texted her. Tommy abducted her at the Downlow. Mac raped her. Chaz dumped her outside of her apartment building." Faith rinsed a bowl. "That was Richie's bargaining chip. He gave them Chaz. Chaz gets two dimes."

Twenty years in prison would be an eternity for a man like Chaz Penley. "Kind of risky to target Leighann Park during Tommy's trial."

"Yeah, it's like these really rich, really successful dudes get off on taking enormous risks just to fuck with people."

She had earned the sarcastic tone. He asked, "Who drew the circle on the back of Leighann's knee?"

"The same psycho who wrote *that's me* on her breast." Faith drained the sink. "Britt was shadowing Leighann to pick up details about her life. Leighann got sloppy at a party. Passed out poolside on a lounger. Britt swooped in like a White Walker."

"She was more like the Night King. He controlled the—"

"Anyway," she said. "They're all taking deals, which means no trials, which means Sara won't have to testify about the video. Which means nobody will pick it apart. Which is probably a good thing, right?"

Will stacked together the bowls. His pinky finger was still sore from the fight he'd lost with the wall in Sara's condo. "And Mason?"

"No DNA. No evidence. No charges." Faith's hand went to her hip. "Mason's name was registered as the owner of the chat website, but he said that was a clerical error. He has dozens of other sites for services and products that automatically renew. APD is leaving him alone. I'll tell you what, if you want to float through life on a fluffy cloud, it pays to have a white penis."

Will's white penis was content to have Sara. "Did they look into that company he owns with Mac and Chaz?"

"It's totally legit. The back office at the Triple Nickel was used for medical records storage. That's why there was so much security. They were raking in money. And the A in the name—that was Britt. Her maiden name was Anslinger." Faith handed him some bowls to put away. "The business was her idea. She's the one who wrote the pitches to the doctor's offices to help package them for hospitals and investors. She handled the numbers. She chose which practices to approach. She assigned them their tasks. Jesus, can you imagine if Britt had used her brain to do something good instead of evil?"

Britt's name had replaced Mason's in the pantheon of names that Will never wanted to hear again. "APD searched the McAllister house on the Dani Cooper investigation. Why didn't they find the servers in the basement?"

"The warrant specified they could only look for the security camera DVRs, which were kept in a room off the garage. The McAllisters' lawyer made sure they didn't poke around. The cops weren't allowed anywhere near Britt's Rape Closet." Faith used the paper towel to wipe the counter. "I've seen mobile homes taken back to the studs for a warrant on a dime bag of pot. The Constitution is great if you can afford it."

Will opened the silverware drawer. "I can put up the rest of this stuff."

"No fork left behind." Faith dropped some forks into the slot. She glanced up at Will. "Are you sure that Sara will be okay?"

He adjusted the forks so they were all facing in the same direction. "What about you? Are you doin' all right?"

Faith would normally toss the question back to him, but she leaned against the counter. "I'm raising a daughter in a world where people will either blame her or ignore her if she's drugged and raped, in a state that would let her die of a placental abruption, and my son wants to work in a field where a shocking number of his potential co-workers have been accused of domestic violence and still manage to stay on the job. So, yeah. I'm terrific."

"Isn't Jeremy touring Quantico next week?"

Faith rolled her eyes. "He told me he was having dinner with 3M last week."

Will aligned the spoons. He remembered something Jeremy had said in Amanda's office, that he wasn't going to find the clue that would break open this case and put everybody behind bars. Will figured the kid had done exactly that, but he wasn't going to share that with Faith.

Instead, he told her, "Emma seems happy to be back home."

She snorted. "You should've seen her yesterday. The cheese on her sandwich touched her plate, which apparently opened a portal into the gateways of hell."

"I know the last case is still bothering you."

Faith wadded up the paper towel in her hand.

"Shake it away," Will said. "Think of it like an Etch-A-Sketch drawing. Clear it from your mind."

"Where did you get that sage advice?"

He had only recently learned that he'd gotten it from Amanda. "I'm just saying maybe it's better sometimes to let things go."

"Which things specifically?"

"We shut down the Club. Martin Barrowe and Dani's parents got some closure. Leighann is going to see the men who hurt her go to prison. Britt wiped herself off the gameboard." He made it more personal. "If you take the losses, you have to take the wins. Jeremy's a good kid. Emma's smart and funny. Aiden is a solid guy. Sara's going to be okay. Amanda's putting us back in the field. Those are good things."

"Whoa." She held up her hands like she had to stop him. "What's this touchy feely shit? Are you gonna show me on the doll where the bad man hurt you?"

"You're always telling me to talk more."

"Not like Oprah Winfrey." She tossed the paper

towel onto the counter. "Jesus Christ. I'm going to start lactating."

The back door opened, saving him from further lactation references. Emma and Isabelle skipped into the room. They were not screaming, which was a welcome development. The dogs were clearly tired from all of the day's activity. Tessa straggled in next, then Sara. She looked for Will as she took off her sneakers. The bruises under her eyes had started to green. The blue fiberglass cast would be on her arm for at least another six weeks. Her fingers were still swollen. The doctors had been forced to cut off her engagement ring.

"All right, sweetie pie, time to toddle." Faith lifted Emma onto her hip. For all of her complaints, Faith practically glowed with love around her kids. "Give Uncle Will a kiss."

Will offered his cheek for a wet smack. Then Isabelle had to have her turn. He tuned out the other goodbyes as he watched Sara. She was moving around more easily now. The worst of the pain had finally subsided. She had started to wean herself off the opioids they'd prescribed at the hospital because that was what people did when they were not struggling with addiction.

Sara rested her good hand on his shoulder. "Tess and Isabelle are going to adopt a kitten."

Tessa added, "Mom and Dad are helping me buy the condo. We thought we'd round out the family."

Faith said, "You can't spell homeowner without meow."

For some reason, they all started laughing.

Sara smiled at Will.

Will smiled at Sara.

"Okay," Faith told Emma. "Thanks for the food. Let's cheese it."

There were more hugs and goodbyes because, apparently, nobody respected a firm handshake anymore. Sara followed them all to the door for another round of farewells. Will stayed in the kitchen. He straightened the wet paper towel and hung it over the faucet to dry.

"Thank you, my love." Sara was standing in the kitchen doorway. "Thank you for the wonderful day. Thank you for laughing at my father's silly jokes. Thank you for cleaning up."

"Too bad about the cast. I know how much you like washing dishes."

She couldn't hide her grin. "And I know you much you like being surrounded by people who expect you to speak to them."

He grinned too. "I think I'm gonna end up painting Faith's kitchen cabinets."

"I think you're right." She nodded toward the living

room. "Let's sit on the sofa. I'm tired of having conversations in kitchens."

Will wiped his hands on his jeans. She had said conversations like she wanted an actual conversation. He walked into the living room. Sara was already on the couch. The greyhounds were piled on their bed. Betty was still in the kitchen drinking water. He could hear her collar clinking against the metal bowl. They were going to remodel the house after the wedding, but right now, it felt exactly the right size.

He asked Sara, "Do you want a cat?"

"I would love several, but greyhounds are trained to chase fluffy animals." She laid back against the cushions, propping up her arm. "Is Faith still asking questions about what really happened in Britt's closet?"

"I think she knows the sound didn't cut out by itself." Will lifted Sara's feet into his lap as he sat down. "She's asking because she's nosy. Not because she's going to do anything about it. The video tells a believable story. Britt couldn't get the gun to work. She looked at it. She figured it out. She shot herself in the head. No one is worried about how the mic got muted. And it won't come up anyway. They're all taking plea deals. Your part of the narrative won't be told."

Sara nodded, but she didn't look relieved. "Assisted suicide is illegal in Georgia."

"You gave Britt information about how a revolver works. She didn't have to kill herself. She could've just as easily turned the gun on you." He looked at her. Still no relief on her face. This wasn't the conversation, either. They'd been talking about it off and on all week. "What else is bothering you?"

"I hate that I feel better because of what Britt told me." Sara looked up at the ceiling. Her chest rose as she took a deep breath. "After I was raped, I was so worried that I'd done something wrong. Did I accidentally lead him on? Or flirt with him? Or send him the wrong message? And I know that doesn't make sense. Rape isn't sex. It's not an intimate relationship. But knowing that Britt pushed the janitor, that she manipulated him into attacking me, takes away some of that guilt."

Will felt better knowing that Britt would've been really pissed off to hear Sara say this.

She poked him with her foot. "Does it bother you that I can't give you children?"

"No." He liked Emma and Isabelle, but he liked it when they left, too. "Does it bother you that my brain isn't wired for puns?"

"I adore the way your brain is wired." She reached out her good hand so that he could help her sit up.

"If Britt McAllister proved anything, it's that being a mother doesn't make you a better person."

Will had grown up surrounded by abandoned kids. Poverty had put a lot of them in state care. Very few of their mothers had been as bad as Britt. "Are you going to tell Tessa what really happened in the closet?"

"It was hard enough explaining all the other stuff. I never want my family to have to rush to the hospital for me again. Mom and Dad will probably never go home." Tears had flooded her eyes. She hated upsetting her family. "I can't tell Tess the truth. It's not fair to make her carry that secret. I'm not sure it's fair to you."

"We agreed that we were always going to be honest with each other."

"Did you read Eliza's trust documents?"

Will knew that this was the conversation. He wasn't sure he was ready to have it yet. "I scanned it into my speech app. It was weird hearing the name Sara Trent."

"Do you want me to take your last name?"

He shook his head, because his last name had never meant anything to him. "You read the documents, too. What did you think?"

"That she's a bit fucking late to start helping orphaned children."

Will could hear the anger in her voice. "But?"

"There's a lot of good that could be done with that kind of money."

"Like what?"

"Well, first, it wouldn't actually have to be you making the decisions." Sara laced her fingers through his. They both had one pair of uninjured hands between them. "You could appoint someone to oversee a board. They could make decisions about how to help kids as they age out of the system. Rent assistance, college or vocational tuition, healthcare costs, job training, financial instruction. The money could be life changing. It could break the cycle of poverty, keep them out of jail and prison. Help their own children thrive."

Will knew that Sara had been raised to understand money. There was a reason her sister was volunteering for midwife training while buying a $300,000 condo. "Who would I appoint?"

Sara shrugged, but she clearly had a name in mind. "Amanda helped you navigate the system. You didn't realize it at the time, but she was there from the beginning. If single women had been allowed to adopt, she would've taken you home."

Betty's nails clicked across the floor as she walked over to her satin pillow. Will watched her do her routine, taking a few turns before she settled in, then resting her snout on her paws.

He told Sara, "I locked my gun in the safe before the kids came over. I saw Amanda's pearls."

"Aren't they beautiful?" Sara's voice held a hint of reverence. "I've never held real pearls before. They're exquisite."

Will had noticed they weren't perfectly round, and that was about it. "How are they different from fake pearls?"

"I'm glad you asked because I looked it up." She was smiling again. "They're heavier. They're organic, so they feel cold at first, but they warm against your skin. They have a gritty texture. When they're naturally formed, the mollusk secretes tiny concentric layers of nacre in a matrix. You can see the imperfections. Every one is unique."

He loved that she wanted to learn about everything. "Are you going to wear them to the wedding?"

"I want to. They'll look great with my dress. And Amanda is important to you, so she's important to me." Sara gripped his hand. "I think she knows that I muted the sound on purpose. I practically did a test run in her car before it happened."

"Did she bring it up again?"

"No, but she scolded me about not using our safe

word, because a tennis racket swinging at my head apparently wasn't enough of a clue that something was wrong. Then she gave me that look where you don't know if she's going to kill you or pat you on the back."

Will was intimately familiar with that look. "I was wondering about the wedding. I know you've got things planned out, but I wanted to do something."

"It's *our* wedding. You can do whatever you like."

Will didn't know about that. He wasn't crazy about the Chiavaris costing twice as much as the classic folding chair. "You said you don't want to do a first dance with your dad, but maybe you could dance with your sister, and I could ask Amanda to dance with me."

Sara didn't look as surprised as he'd thought she would. It was more like something was finally making sense. "She keeps asking about the wedding because she wants to be part of the wedding."

"I figure she's earned her place."

"I figure you're right." The smile was back. "We can play Sinatra. 'Fly Me to the Moon.'"

"Springsteen does a cover of—"

"Nope," Sara said, which apparently settled it. "I need to tell you something else."

Will hoped it was not about the wedding.

"Last week, you told Eliza that you don't have a family. But Amanda has always been your family. And now Tessa, Isabelle, my mom and dad, and more importantly me—we're all your family, too."

The information hit him in a weird way. He looked at Betty again. She had started scratching her ear. The metal tag sounded like a clapper in a bell.

He told Sara, "I took your engagement ring to the jeweler. She says it'll be about a week."

Sara held up her swollen hand. "I'm more worried about the wedding band that's supposed to go with it. We might need to substitute a donut for the ceremony."

"I asked about getting the scratch out of the glass." Will turned his gaze back toward Betty, though he could feel Sara looking at him. "I know Eliza is full of shit, but it makes sense that my mom would've wanted the scratch fixed. She was a teenager. They don't like when things aren't perfect."

"What did the jeweler say?"

"That I could probably fix it on my own. You make a paste with baking soda and water. Then you get a microfiber cloth and rub in a firm circular motion until the scratch buffs out."

"You're very good at making a firm circular motion with your fingers."

Will realized he was too nervous for teasing. Maybe he wanted to have a conversation, too. "She also told me that some women don't wear their engagement rings after they're married. They just wear the wedding band. Especially if they work with their hands a lot."

Sara reached over and turned his head so that he had to look at her. "Are you trying to tell me something?"

Will didn't know what he was trying to say. "Your shoes are really expensive. And you wear nice things. Which is great. You work hard. You deserve to spend your money how you want. But I don't want people to look at your engagement ring and wonder why I didn't buy you something that you would be proud to wear."

"I've never been more proud than when you put your mother's ring on my finger. Your heart is in that glass. Your history. It pains me to be without it." She sounded so damn earnest. "Will, I don't want to wear a ring for other people. I want to wear your ring for you."

He looked into her eyes. Her tears were really falling now.

She said, "My mother told me something fifteen years ago. It was the night of the mixer. I'd just been offered the fellowship. Everything was falling into place. I had every aspect of my life mapped out. Mama said that I couldn't plan everything. That for good or bad, something was going to change."

Will held on tightly to her hand.

"She called it a profound opportunity, because change tells you who you really are. And she was right.

After that night, my entire life changed. The person I was going to be was gone. I had two choices. I could disappear along with her, or I could fight to get back the parts of her that mattered. I'm not saying that I'm grateful for that lesson. I'm really not. But I'm grateful that it made me the kind of woman who knows how to love you."

Will felt a lump in his throat. He watched Betty settle back on her pillow. His eyes had started to water. "You know this is gonna be forever, right?"

"I do."

Acknowledgments

First thanks as always goes to Kate Elton and Victoria Sanders. Emily Krump provided valuable guidance on children and liquor (among other topics). Thanks to the VSA team, including Diane Dickensheid and my confrere, Bernadette Baker-Baughman. At WME, Hilary Zaitz Michael is doing amazing things, for which I am eternally grateful. Heidi Richter-Ginger and Liz Dawson continue to be expert kitten herders. I would be remiss to not thank my GPP peeps around the world who always take such good care of me, especially when I said that I wanted to ride a bike in Amsterdam because what the hell was I thinking, Miranda?

Shanda London's husband, Shane McRoberts, made a very generous contribution to Writer's Police Academy so that her name would appear in this novel. Daniel Starer at Research for Writers diligently tried to track down the attribution for "Speak from the scar, not the wound." Greg Guthrie and Patricia Friedman answered some legal-ish questions. I am grateful for Dona Robertson and the many current and retired agents with the GBI who are always kind about answering my tedious questions.

For twenty years, Dr. David Harper has been extraordinarily patient in helping me make Sara sound like a doctor. I would be remiss in not making it clear that I truncated some timelines in the steps toward cardiothoracic surgery, probably annoying a lot of cardiothoracic surgeons in the process, but please know that this wasn't David—it was all me writing fiction and moving the story along. Speaking of medical experts, I want to give a shout-out to all healthcare workers, who've been Through It over the last few years: you are valued, you are appreciated and you are amazing. Oh, and it should go without saying, but you are also better than Google.

The statistics on rape and assault cited in this book come from several sources, including the Archives of Sexual Behavior, RAINN, the National Intimate Partner and Sexual Violence Survey, the US Centers for Disease Control, and the US Department of Justice. Where statistics range, I've stated a middle figure. Over 40% of American women and 20% of men have experienced some sort of sexual violence in their lifetimes. Fewer than 20% of these instances were reported to police and fewer still have been prosecuted. RAINN .org is a good resource for victims and survivors seeking support. If you are uncomfortable or feel unsafe accessing the site from home, local libraries generally provide untraceable access. Whatever you decide, know that you are not alone.

Last thanks goes to my dad, the most stubborn person I know, and to D.A. who puts up with the second most stubborn person in my family. As always, you are my heart.

About the Author

Karin Slaughter is one of the world's most popular storytellers. She is the author of more than twenty instant *New York Times* bestselling novels, including the Edgar-nominated *Cop Town* and standalone novels *The Good Daughter* and *Pretty Girls*. An international bestseller, Slaughter is published in 120 countries with more than 40 million copies sold across the globe. *Pieces of Her* is now a #1 Netflix original series starring Toni Collette, *Will Trent* is now a television series starring Ramón Rodríguez on ABC, and further projects are in development for television. Karin Slaughter is the founder of the Save the Libraries project—a nonprofit organization established to support libraries and library programming. A native of Georgia, she lives in Atlanta.

For more information visit KarinSlaughter.com
 AuthorKarinSlaughter
 SlaughterKarin
 karinslaughterauthor

HARPER LARGE PRINT

We hope you enjoyed reading
our new, comfortable print size and found it
an experience you would like to repeat.

Well – you're in luck!

Harper Large Print offers the finest in
fiction and nonfiction books in this same larger
print size and paperback format. Light and easy to read,
Harper Large Print paperbacks are for the book lovers
who want to see what they are reading without strain.

For a full listing of titles and
new releases to come, please visit our website:
www.hc.com

HARPER LARGE PRINT